HE'S COME UNDONE

A ROMANCE ANTHOLOGY

EMMA BARRY OLIVIA DADE ADRIANA HERRERA
RUBY LANG CAT SEBASTIAN

APPASSIONATA

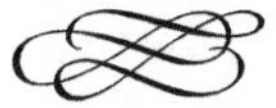

EMMA BARRY

To Miss Mac, who taught me music should feed your soul and an on-pitch ooooo will be cool.

Piano technician Brennan Connelly lives to control details: the tension on a piano string or the compression of hammer felt. But he's never faced demands like those heaped on him by Kristy Kwong, the diva who's haunted his dreams for two decades. Kristy's got her own secrets—the debilitating stage fright that's kept her from performing publicly for years to start—and this concert is the last chance to save her career. But can he locate her lost passion without losing his precious control?

* * *

Content Warnings: on-page sex and alcohol use; profanity; on-page anxiety, depression, and stage fright.

CHAPTER 1

Staccato

As Kristy Kwong flew through her favorite warm up—Hanon's exercise no. 50—she wasn't thinking about the fingering, the dynamics, or the decision she had to make between the three pianos on the stage of Boston Symphony Hall.

Her only goal was not to vomit.

It was the whole touching an instrument thing, to start. Piano keyboards had once been a checkerboard path down which she'd tripped fearlessly. Now, they were a field of scree without safe passage. Every note, every step, felt wrong. Not just wrong, *dangerous*. Kristy was going to play this concert in a few weeks, she had to, but her career was as likely to tumble into a ravine as to reach the summit.

That was the second problem: She sounded like shit.

Two years ago, the force of her trills would've marshaled the audience's heartbeats to an identical driving rhythm. Or, if Kristy preferred, the tone might've been delicately plaintive, a filigree of notes and emotion that had made presidents and kings weep.

Then, Kristy's ability to weave sound had been absolute. She could make it cloying, boisterous, sensual, brooding, magisterial. The score itself wouldn't have mattered; the color she'd brought had been everything. At least until it went to grayscale.

Okay, she might actually puke.

She struck the final chord and then wiped her mouth with the back of her hand.

"What do you think?" a voice called from out in the auditorium. That would be Brennan Connelly, the orchestra's resident piano technician.

Because Kristy was still jumpy about playing in front of, you know, *people*, she'd specified he be the only person in the room until she'd chosen an instrument and he'd adjusted it for her. She'd known Brennan casually for twenty years. He was amazing at what he did, and he was as steady as bedrock. That had been enough for her to capriciously accept this gig.

But even though Brennan and Kristy were the only people in the hall, Kristy's agent and her assistant were waiting in the symphony director's office because Kristy did have appearances to keep up. Divas couldn't go anywhere unaccompanied. They were like Regency debutantes in that regard.

"Not sure yet." Kristy's voice sounded even, a minor miracle. She picked up a bottle of water and took a sip, but it couldn't erase the taste of bile from her mouth.

"I could have them bring up the other Steinway," Brennan said.

"No." She didn't need any grips to witness this, and she definitely didn't need another piano. Lack of selection wasn't her problem. "I'm going to..." She had no idea how to finish that sentence.

She had to play the symphony's gala, and not merely because she'd signed a contract to do so. She'd broken those like she'd broken hearts back before she'd learned to be scared. No, she had to do this now because people had stopped mentioning Kristy in those "whatever happened to so-and-so" articles. It turned out there was something worse than how disappointing people had found her recording of Ernst von Dohnanyi's first piano concerto: people not talking about her at all.

Silence was death. If Kristy didn't find her voice again, she was going to disappear under the sands of time. No resurrection. No redemption.

Bitterness rose in her throat, and she took another hasty sip of water. Kristy's therapist would tell her she had to find something positive with which to replace this spiral of negative thoughts, except she didn't have anything positive.

Mozart. She still had Mozart.

She set the bottle down and started in on his variations on a French folk song. Whatever, it was "Twinkle, Twinkle, Little Star." This had been the first serious piece she'd learned as a child, the piece that had made her want to be a concert pianist. Cascading arpeggios dissolving into a series of triplets. Wolfgang never used a single note when he could use three. He was gold and ivory, brocade and frescos.

But at the end of every turn in the music, sneering doubt lurked.

You can't do this.

You only managed to string together a career because you're pretty.

You ought to quit for good now before you embarrass yourself, spectacularly and publicly.

Her inner asshole had always been there, just below the surface. Was *anyone* absolutely sure of themselves? Maybe Emanuel Ax, but he was it. Everyone else was a hair's breadth away from losing their confidence. In Kristy's case, all it had taken was a few squidgy performances and some bad reviews, and suddenly the asshole in her brain wouldn't stop caterwauling.

Kristy should've been more resilient. Of all the things she'd learned to hate about herself, how thin-skinned she'd turned out to be topped the list. She simply hadn't been able to shake off those mistakes. How could she now that she knew the exact taste of failure?

Even Mozart couldn't help. Midmeasure, Kristy lifted her hands from the keys and pressed them to her eyelids.

Out in the theater, Brennan cleared his throat. "Do you want me to—"

"*No.*" She hadn't intended to snap at him. Nor did she apologize.

She'd learned long ago not to. If people called her difficult, well, that was just a sign of respect. She'd rather be known as prickly than a doormat.

She gave her hands a well-practiced shake and tried to play off her abrupt stop as intentional. "I'm done warming up. I'm going to try the real piece now."

After all, she wasn't going to be crisp and light and Classical in this performance. No, she needed a cleaver of sound: overheated and Bavarian and Romantic. She needed to rip off the bandage and see if this instrument was the one. If it had enough color for the Schubert and the Brahms—if *she* had enough color for them.

Her heart walloped against her ribs, her breath was a scythe in her throat, then...

She tore into the hardest section of the Schubert: a hailstorm of notes immediately before the third movement. She should've been pushing the instrument to its limit. The vibration from the piano's harp should've been resonating up the strings, into the hammers, through the keys, and into her body.

And it wasn't. There wasn't a single pulse-altering tremor. She was playing the Wanderer Fantasy, but she wasn't performing it.

See, her doubts said. *You're an absolute fraud.*

She lifted her hands from the keyboard, but that wasn't enough. She stumbled up, needing the weight of her feet on the ground. *Those are all lies. You've worked toward this for thirty years. You just need to get through this performance, and you'll see everything is fine. You can do this. You were born to do this.*

But while she might repeat those words over and over, they were a staged home; she couldn't live there. Besides, when you suspected deep down that you were a worthless hack, calculating the hours of effort you'd put in was actually the opposite of comforting.

Out in the seating area, Brennan cleared his throat again. Because she was freaking out in front of him.

Terrific. Just what she needed on top of the massive crisis of confidence and identity.

She flipped her hair over her shoulder, thanked God for her resting bitch face, and tried to make this seem like part of her plan. Her plan to suck, apparently.

"Well, we have some work to do, don't we?"

That, she directed at both of them.

* * *

Penseroso

Kristy Kwong was still beautiful.

Two decades after they'd been aspiring teenage pianists, she could make Brennan Connelly breathless with a single shake of her pretty head or a roll of her expressive eyes.

She'd made it, he hadn't, but he'd always followed her career. That had made it easier to study for this moment. To spend considerable time with her catalog, which held a place of honor in his alphabetized CD collection—the sound quality was so much better than digital—in order to inoculate himself.

As he'd flipped from one album to the next, he'd paid particular attention to the lush photo spreads of her that would often gratuitously appear in the album notes. Kristy in some ridiculous getup, Wellingtons and a satin ball gown, outside a studio looking pensive. Kristy reclining next to a soundboard, listening to master tapes with a Mona Lisa smile on her face. And always, always Kristy's hands: stretched across the keyboard, holding a rolled up sheaf of music, twisted in her glossy hair, or clutching a bouquet of scarlet roses.

A steady regime of still photographs, however, hadn't prepared him for the real thing. He walked down the aisle of the symphony hall and climbed the steps to join the flesh and blood woman who was insulting his pianos.

Brennan prided himself on his reserve. He was an instrument, not an artist. Long ago he'd made peace with that. And instruments didn't get to feel. He voiced the piano to someone else's specifications, someone who didn't need to know that middle C should resonate at

261.6 Hz. That part, the mere calibration, was his job. *Feeling* was someone else's.

Except Kristy simply shooting him a cocky grin had him trembling so hard, he wasn't certain he would be able to do what he needed to.

"What's the matter?" Kristy tipped her head to the side, and that glorious hair of hers rippled like a cascade in the Berkshires. "Cat got your tongue?"

No, you do. But he couldn't, wouldn't, say that to her. When #MeToo had thrown open the doors to the concert hall and taken down some of the conductors, soloists, and donors Brennan had known his entire career, he hadn't been in the least surprised. So many men in classical music were arrogant asses.

Brennan's entire goal had been to make himself in their mirror image. When they moved right, he jerked hard to the left. He'd always behaved scrupulously, both because it was correct and also because it was professional. Without decency, a code of conduct, civilization would crumble.

He couldn't imagine how much sexism Kristy had probably put up with in her career. She was female, she was talented, she was successful, and she was beautiful: Most men couldn't handle that combination. Exactly as he'd kept his distance from her when they were fifteen, he'd never do anything now that might make her uncomfortable.

But even if they'd met as old friends—setting aside that they hadn't truly been friends—and she'd... flirted with him, he still wouldn't have said it.

He couldn't banter. Couldn't match wits. Couldn't parley. It was simply beyond him.

So he gave a tight shake of his head and asked instead, "What are you looking for?" Giving her the tone she sought was as much as he might offer her.

When she'd been giving the pianos a try a few minutes prior, the sound had been incongruous. It wasn't what you expected to hear coming out of an instrument Kristy Kwong was playing. It hadn't sounded *bad* as much as constrained. It was not the almost wild display for which she was famous.

He'd heard the rumors about why she'd taken time off, everyone had: She'd had a nervous breakdown and flamed out, and she was never coming back. But Brennan hadn't believed the whispers. Maybe because it was too depressing to imagine someone with as much talent as she had unable to perform.

Now that he'd seen and heard her, he was, frankly, worried.

Even the symphony director, Bernadette Wolcott, had asked him to make a report. "You know, just let me know if you think she's up to it."

"What?" he'd asked. "If you don't think Ms. Kwong is prepared for this concert, shouldn't *you* assess her?" That was Bernadette's job, after all. He just took care of the pianos.

Bernadette had waved this suggestion off. "I know she's *prepared.* I mean...I want to know if you think she's emotionally ready. Stable. You're the only one she wants in the room."

He'd been so shocked, he hadn't given his assent or refusal. Evaluate Kristy Kwong's *emotions*? He could never.

Across the stage, Kristy appeared to be perfectly in control of her humor, and that was good enough for him. Whatever stiffness he'd heard in her playing this morning was doubtless because she'd been warming up.

With regard to his question, Kristy took a deep breath, opened her mouth, and...closed it again.

Pianists weren't always able to clearly explain their goals, he knew. Their relationship with the instrument was different from his, so he was used to coaxing, cajoling, and reading between the lines. He didn't like doing it, but he often had to in order to get them the sound they wanted.

"Was the tone too bright?" he prompted. "Too mellow? Bell-like? Growly?" It couldn't be all of those things as they were contradictory, but he hoped one of those suggestions could be a springboard for Kristy.

A long pause ensued, and then at last Kristy said, "More color. It needs more color."

Her voice was almost as small as her playing had been. The Kristy he'd known was never, ever tentative, and something inside his chest splintered at hearing it from her now.

What had happened?

Rather than ask, he only nodded, trying to encourage her. Needing, frankly, to do so. Needing her to be as he remembered.

She gave a sad shrug. "The sound needs to be big enough, loose enough, to seem reckless but not so much so that I spin out."

The sound needed to be, or *she* needed to be? Because none of the passion he associated with her playing had been in her performances today.

"Right now, it's too..." She gestured, sketching something in the air that doubtless was exactly what she wanted but that he couldn't decipher. "Do you see?"

He didn't. Not at all. But he wanted to.

His envy of virtuosity—it made him feel like an ass. He clung to rules, to politeness, partially because he didn't want his jealousy to show. Brennan had mostly left the pain over not being among such a group in the past, but when Kristy gave him the smallest glimpse into the ineffable cave of her artistry, he *burned* that he couldn't follow her there. He was forever the kid with his nose pressed up against the candy shop window.

Knowing none of this, she tried to explain again. "The tone, it's like a stick pin right now."

"A pin?" he echoed. There was nothing pin-like about any of these pianos, which were all extraordinary instruments that had been played by the world's top talents with one of the most accomplished symphony orchestras in the country—and he shouldn't be taking this so personally. He was going to make a few changes and she'd relax and then, then she'd play how she needed to.

He tried another tack. "Can you...that is, will you, show me?"

"Show you?"

"At the bench. Play something that manifests the sound you want." Because clearly they both agreed her earlier efforts hadn't.

She sat and glared at the keyboard. She set her hands on it—and then moved them back to her lap. Her breaths were coming fast now, her chest bobbing with them. She glanced at him and then back at the instrument.

She was terrified, and her fear was an icy blow to his stomach.

How? What? Was it his proximity? "Do you want me to sit in the house?" Maybe if he went out into the audience she'd feel better. "Or I could stand in the wings?" He sounded as desperate as he felt.

If he had to, he couldn't have explained why—not even hand gestures would help him—but he wanted her to be as remarkable as he knew she could be.

"*No*, I can do it," she ground out.

He wasn't certain she could, however, and a soup of feelings stewed in his gut. Sadness that something had shaken Kristy, since she should never be anything less than a tower of strength. Frustration that anything or anyone might've hurt her. Grief for the music she might not play. Fear because what on earth was he going to tell Bernadette? Hell, *was* Kristy capable of doing the gala?

He simply didn't know.

And even worse, he suspected Kristy didn't either.

He shouldn't feel this much about this situation. He'd known her a long time, and he was a…a fan. But this was his profession. This situation was precisely why he was devoted to his ethos. Could he help her? That was all that mattered.

Then softly, hesitantly, Kristy began to play. Not the devilishly hard Schubert or Brahms pieces she'd scheduled for the gala, but an elegy by Rachmaninov.

The first twelve or so measures were forced, but chord by chord, Kristy gathered herself. The looseness started in her right foot, where her pedaling grew more fluid. Then it spread to her shoulders and down into her fingers. The sick flush left her cheeks, her eyelids fluttered closed, and the piano began to sing.

Her playing wasn't wild; no, it was deeply, deeply sad. The melody drifted over the storm of emotion in him...and pacified it. A balm of notes.

That was the Kristy Kwong he wanted to hear—the one that everyone wanted to hear.

Brennan took a step back and just let it all, the lovely woman, the ceaseless melancholy of the descant, sweep through him.

Her performance wasn't showy. No, he'd bet all the money in his wallet that this was how she played for herself. Seeing it felt illicit, like stumbling on her in the bath. He wouldn't have been more flustered if she'd been nude because this already felt that exposed. His cheeks were burning, but he couldn't look away.

Then a voice came from the darkness of the wings and ruined everything.

"Brennan? Do you have a second?" Quincy, the facilities manager, stepped onstage and held up a stack of work orders.

The effect was instantaneous.

Kristy's hands leapt from the piano. The joy that had been in her face shuttered, replaced by hard rage, and her body went rigid.

"Excuse me? This is supposed to be a closed rehearsal." She was up off the bench, grabbing her water bottle, and flying down the stairs into the house before Brennan had processed what she'd said.

The spell of that moment and the strange embarrassment he felt at having witnessed something so intimate, broke apart into ten thousand irreparable pieces.

Brennan could have slugged Quincy, if he were the sort of person who slugged anyone.

All he could do was to call after her, "Ms. Kwong, I'm sorry. It was a mistake. I'll send him away."

"Don't bother." She didn't even slow her progress. She was every inch the icy diva of legend now. "We'll try again tomorrow—and the stage had better be sealed."

The door slammed shut behind her as he called back, "Of course."

"Well, she seems nice," Quincy deadpanned.

Brennan swung around to glare at him. "You startled her. You know you aren't supposed to be in here."

"I don't see what the big deal is."

Which wasn't the point. "Closed means closed. Even to you."

At least this had given him something to tell Bernadette. Kristy cutting the rehearsal short was the perfect excuse for not having a report—and so he had another day to evaluate, and be stunned by, Kristy Kwong.

CHAPTER 2

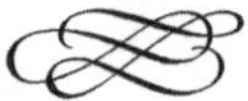

Più vivo

Kristy felt almost embarrassed—almost—about the scene she'd made when she trudged across the stage the next day and found Brennan waiting for her. He sat at one of the pianos with discomfort on his face and his legs crossed in front of him.

He was probably thinking she was a temperamental witch. Everyone did. General disapproval didn't bother her, however; only Brennan's specific disapproval did. But she couldn't correct his assumptions without explaining why she'd flown off the handle or telling him that she'd been so overset by the surprise interruption that she'd thrown up in the lobby bathroom.

The other thing that had surprised her? Meeting Brennan. The years had been kind to him. He was still slim and wearing honest to gosh suspenders, as he had back when they'd been kids, but the rise of hipster fashion had put a slightly different, slightly more attractive, spin on his preferred look. If she remembered how he dressed, though, she'd forgotten his dark brown hair, which he now wore longer on the top than the sides, and the chasms-deep brown eyes behind his wire-rimmed glasses.

He'd turned into quite a hottie, but that didn't mean she wasn't going to give him her fullest diva performance. She made a sweeping stop and gave Brennan what she hoped was an imperious stare.

He acknowledged it with a grave nod. "Good morning. I'd like to apologize for yesterday." Always formal, that was Brennan.

When had Kristy first run into him? Two decades ago, maybe, at Tanglewood back when they'd both been teenagers. If it was in New England and it involved pianos, he'd be there, tuning lever in hand. Knowing he was here had made the Boston Symphony seem as good a place as any to jump back in the water.

But while she liked his dark brown eyes, she didn't like the pity in his expression. For half a minute yesterday, she'd felt like herself, had played like herself. But then she realized someone else had been listening, and her serenity had popped like a bubble. Which Brennan had seen. He had seen, she suspected, far more than she'd meant for him to.

"I don't want to talk about it." Not the moment when her performance had been going well, but especially not the moment when it had crumbled.

"I'd prefer not to—" Of course he would. "—but we need to."

"We really don't."

"Believe me, all I want to discuss are the pianos, but—"

"No buts. Just pianos. Now let's see." She'd had trouble yesterday explaining what she'd wanted, but she'd spent all night in her Airbnb apartment with nothing to do but process and reprocess every moment, and she had her words gathered. She knew that once they started on her selection, he'd get distracted. "Door number one won't work at all." She pointed at the one farthest from where he was sitting. "It has such a *sweet* sound."

From anyone else, this might be a compliment, but Kristy knew she wasn't, could never be, sweet. She'd play the part audiences expected from today's female pianists: She'd grow out her hair, do modelesque photo shoots, and post lots of selfies on Insta, but she couldn't be sweet. It wasn't in her. That hadn't changed even as she had.

"This is less a concert grand than a parlor grand," she told him. If not in size, then in tone. "It just needs a lace doily and a fern. Hell, the action's even stiff—which surprises me in one of yours."

He scoffed. She'd struck a blow, which of course she'd meant to do.

"The action is *not* stiff," he said.

Well, well, well: He wasn't trying to get her to talk about her meltdown now. She walked to the keyboard of the piano in question and hammered out a few measures of the second Brahms rhapsody. The tension in her arms limited the dynamics, but that just proved her point.

"Johannes would retch."

"It sounds perfect."

"Pshaw," she responded, because she was a very serious musician.

Brennan grabbed a beat-up leather bag resting at his feet and carried it to the second piano. "Is this where you'd like to start, then?"

"Aren't you going to defend piano one's honor?"

"I've already said the action is fine."

"What happened to the customer always being right?" Not that she was a customer.

"The touchweight on that piano is fifty-five grams. The other two are closer to fifty."

"You measured?"

He adjusted his glasses with a practiced finger. "Of course."

Point to Brennan.

"So no, the action isn't stiff," he went on. "But if that feel isn't what you want, I certainly won't try to convince you that it is." He wasn't smiling, and there was no amusement in his eyes.

She'd probably annoyed him. She'd been enjoying this, but he'd gotten his nose out of joint. Everyone was always saying she made too many demands, was too caustic. She doubted they'd thought that about Horowitz.

"Do you have a preference between the other two?" Brennan opened his bag and unrolled what appeared to be a plaid picnic blanket before arranging his tools on it. Some she knew the names of: a hammer, a screwdriver, a chromatic tuner, several mutes, a roll of red felt. But there were several sharp instruments she couldn't name and a hair dryer she couldn't begin to guess how he used.

"Or should I voice them both before you decide?" he asked.

"That." It would give her more time.

He didn't complain. Technicians at this level never did—not to her face—but they would roll their eyes and, afterward, they'd whisper and post about her on the classical music forums. Maybe it was the boobs and the long shiny hair—they expected her to be an airhead and were disappointed when she wasn't. Maybe they hoped she would be a docile China doll, which, ha. But she'd seen the comments over the years: She was a ball-buster. A diva. Overrated.

Well, yes, at least to the first two. The jury was still out on the third.

Brennan didn't cop any attitude, though. He simply lifted the key slip off piano number two and laid it down almost reverentially on the bed he'd prepared for it. Off came the blocks and the fall board, revealing the action cavity. He slid the key frame forward, and both she and Brennan canted forward to look down the length of the piano.

If the outside of a grand was an impenetrable lacquer shell, the interior was claustrophobic and cram jam. With the action pulled forward, the piano gaped, a toothless skull. On the action itself, the hammer shanks and pins were squeezed one beside the next like the legs of some giant centipede.

Kristy's nausea was definitely back.

Next to her, Brennan made an appreciative grunt. To him, this was probably some toy-land fantasy park. She gave him a sidelong look. Technicians all seemed to have backed into the gig down idiosyncratic paths. But if she opened her mouth to ask about his, she might be sick again.

So she merely watched him remove the action completely and carry it to a table on the side of the stage. Intense focus had come over his features. Sparring with her didn't get him going, but this did. Kristy doubted Brennan was aware she was even there. He lifted and dropped several of the hammers, then repeated the gesture, seemingly judging their response times. His nod was approving, and his touch almost indecent.

The expression of blissed out concentration on his face: Damn, but she envied that. She could still recall how she used to hide in practicing. How playing had once put her into a state somewhere between meditation and hyperfocus. Every shade and emotion amplified by the audience. Every breath and note flowing from the previous one.

Doubt had corroded any beatified feelings she'd once had. She'd get around to being angry about what she'd lost once she got over being so scared.

He stooped to pick up a tool with a fat handle and three sharp points protruding from the head like some sort of torture device. "Once we agree on a direction, you can step out if you like. It will take me a bit to get this one done."

"I don't mind waiting." She would've once. Heck, at one point she would've thrown a fit if anyone had made her wait for any reason. But walking out of the concert hall would necessitate walking back in and then getting back on stage, and those acts hadn't come easy lately. It would be better to remain and try to master her anxiety. She couldn't very well get ill midgala.

He didn't acknowledge what she'd said; he only had eyes for the mechanism. He pushed the tool into the felt of the first hammer, withdrew it, and considered.

"What tone do you want?" he asked, still examining the action.

He'd asked it the day before too. *Who are you*—that was what he really wanted to know. Her sound was, or at least had been, romantic without being weedy. Emotional enough to sweep someone rational off their feet. Intimate enough to make the concertgoer forget there were two thousand other people in the room.

But all the certainty she'd once had in the glorious contradiction of her had collapsed, leaving a black hole where a star had once been. There were no words to articulate that. Even just saying it out loud might make it permanent. Thinking about it, having it ricochet off her insides, was bad enough.

Brennan finally, finally looked up, and even in her agitation, she could appreciate those eyes of his.

"It needs to sound like the Rachmaninov yesterday felt." Had felt for thirty seconds before the asshole had burst in, anyhow, and wrecked her best performance in recent memory.

"Aren't these pieces…larger?" he asked.

"Yes." In length, in scope, but that wasn't what she meant.

"So shouldn't the sound be—"

"Are you always so literal?"

"Yes."

His answer was so matter-of-fact, it diffused her annoyance—and raised an interesting hypothesis. She'd managed to play yesterday knowing he was watching. Knowing he might be judging her.

Could she do it again?

"What about this?" She walked to piano number three and played the section of the second Brahms rhapsody where the melody fragmented. The logic of the piece dissolved into chords that wouldn't line up, never resolved. It was a moody stew of notes. Romantic, yes, but arching toward Modernism.

She needed to play it faster, and she wasn't quite wringing the emotion out of it like she wanted, but her playing was tolerable. That was a relief.

"Do you see—" she began, but the rest of the sentence wouldn't come.

Brennan had followed her and was leaning over the piano's harp, one ear cocked to hear what she was trying to say to him. She was suddenly, intensely aware of his aftershave. Of a faint scar along the index finger resting on the music shelf. Of the bones of his wrist peeking from beneath his sleeve cuff.

Sure, one moment of sheer terror pinged through her—*he's listening to you*—but she grabbed at the bodily details of him to blot it out. He needed to hear. He needed to hear. He was an Aeolian harp, and she was going to set him humming.

She started to play again, shoving all her focus into him and into the music. A descending chromatic scale, and the freckle below his left ear. A voice shift from one hand to the other, and the way he inhaled sharply when he heard something notable. A sweeping crescendo, and the way he rubbed his fingertips together.

His body swayed—no, not swayed, *shivered* with the music. Caught in it like a leaf in an autumn breeze. If Brahms spoke to him, then there was something unsatisfied lurking underneath that man's windowpane shirt.

Why, Brennan Connelly, what a revelation.

She sounded the last chord feeling giddy and, okay, smug too. That had been at least as good as yesterday. She hadn't played that physically close to another human being in years, since before her breakdown. She'd refused to play for her agent, and she'd kept the symphony director across the studio when they'd selected pieces a few months prior.

Moreover, she hadn't noticed someone, really noticed the color and texture of him, in...years. At least since she'd stopped performing. The knowledge pealed through her.

Oh. She was supposed to be talking to Brennan and not ogling him.

"The sound isn't perfect because this piano's not voiced correctly. I mean correctly for me." She didn't want to insult him, at least not when she'd only just decided there was a sensual creature lurking under those suspenders. "I need it to be able to do *that* but better."

"Right."

Because his nearness still had her flushed, she didn't hear the skepticism in his answer.

* * *

Impetuoso

A headache was brewing behind Brennan's eyes. He and Kristy had worked for eight hours, right through lunch and now into dinnertime. He'd tuned and voiced the pianos she was deciding between. He'd listened to her play both, and then he'd revoiced them to her additional specifications.

At her command, he'd made the tones rounder and then made them flatter. He'd adjusted the touchweight for various keys, replaced felt, applied lubricant to several mechanisms she'd insisted were stuck, and heated a section of the action she thought might be slow.

"So that's what you use a hair dryer for," she'd drawled.

Throughout this process, she'd been charming and dedicated, but her playing was still hesitant. They were rapidly approaching the limit of what Brennan could do to adjust the pianos; she still wasn't satisfied because she didn't know what she was searching for.

Brennan had more than a hunch.

"It doesn't sound right," she said after finishing a rendition of a Tchaikovsky mazurka, which had been somewhat bland.

You. You are the problem. The words were on the tip of Brennan's tongue, but his rules kept them inside. He was a master piano technician, not a therapist. This wasn't remotely his area of expertise. Saying something to her would be cruel and unprofessional, and he tried so hard to be neither.

But they couldn't go on like this. It wasn't good for either of them. "I suggest we break."

She'd been glaring at the piano cabinet, as if the fault were somewhere inside it, but she looked up at him, her brow creased. "For dinner?"

"No, for the night. We're not making progress."

She wrinkled her nose. "I can't believe you're giving up this easily."

Nothing about this had been easy. From the expertise required to the physicality of the work to his growing desire for this maddening, brilliant woman he didn't know how to help. No, this hadn't been an easy day.

If Kristy didn't know she was a genius, if she couldn't sit at the bench and let go of whatever held her in check, what could he say? He wished he had half the talent with human beings he had with pianos, but this wasn't his area.

Not wanting to argue with her, he began to pack his bag.

But she wouldn't let it go. "I would've thought you were a fighter."

"Discretion, I'm told, is the better part of valor."

That earned him the smaller but warmer smile he'd started to recognize as her truest expression of amusement. He wished he were the kind of man who could put that smile on her lips every day. That man would likely know how to heal what ailed her.

"See, you're witty." Kristy's voice was pitched low and coy, and it brushed up his spine. "I could tell that about you."

"Have you decided which piano to use?"

She grimaced. "Number…three."

"Ah, excellent. I'll let the grips know." At least they'd accomplished something.

"But first—"

"No, we're going to let those poor hammers be. We've tortured them enough."

"How can you have enough of something so fun?"

She was putting him on, trying to get him to stay and fight this battle with her. But even as he recognized the play, it began to work. He was going pliable, wanting to give her anything, everything. The effect was so acute, he didn't trust his voice to contradict her. He simply shook his head.

"You might be witty, but you're also a quitter. Everyone says *I'm* the quitter, but—"

"No one says you're a quitter," he ground out.

"—because they're not talking about me at all." She raised her brows to punctuate this statement.

Brennan's pulse kicked up. This was the closest they'd come to acknowledging her—break. And this, this was the crux of why she wasn't satisfied with her playing. This was the part she needed to face.

"Is that something you'd like to discuss?" he asked.

He honestly didn't know what he'd do if she said yes. How could he respond? What comfort might he offer? He really should call Caroline. His sister was a professional musician, so she understood the artist side in ways Brennan didn't, and she was also good with feelings. Caroline might have some useful advice here.

For a moment, he thought Kristy might start talking. She canted toward him, wetted her lips—and then she laughed. "Ha! No. You almost had me."

He wasn't surprised, but he also wasn't relieved. She needed to get to the bottom of this.

"Then we should adjourn." He finished putting his things in his bag and started toward his office.

Kristy remained at the bench.

"Is your agent waiting?" Or maybe her parents, a friend, or a romantic partner. For all that he'd been trying not to slobber over her, he hoped she wouldn't say there was a boyfriend out in the lobby.

"No, Patrice is probably long gone." Kristy's expression was genuinely forlorn.

"Do you want me to…to call a cab?"

"Nooo." She paused. Then, "But maybe we could try to brighten the top two octaves here."

That was when he detonated. "No, we can't. We really can't. Or I should say *I* can't. We've been working all day, and if I knew what you wanted, if I felt as if I were helping, I'd work all night, but I don't. The problem isn't the pianos: It's you. You aren't happy with the sound because it's not your sound. That isn't because of the instrument, but because of your performance. You're too reserved when you play. Too in control. In two days, I've heard you peel your mask away only once. When you did, you were extraordinary. You took my breath away. But for the life of me, I can't help you do that all the time. And that, *that* is what you need to work on."

She'd ripped the words from him, and his throat burned with their poison.

Her mouth didn't drop open. There was no comic display of shock. Instead her spine straightened vertebrae by vertebrae. Her mouth fell into a fixed line. Her shoulders pushed back. Hardness entered her eyes.

His own body responded in kind. Adrenaline pumped through him, made his mouth bitter, his hands swell. He couldn't catch his breath and the ache in his head was now an erratic throb. He'd broken every one of his rules—and it felt even more awful than he could have imagined. He had to explain what he'd really meant.

But before he could, she said, "I see."

She didn't shout it or grit it out; that would've been better. Would've shown that she still intended to prove him wrong, which he knew that she could. Wanted her to do, in fact.

No, her tone was resigned, and there was nothing he could say to soothe her. That was the worst part.

Feeling endlessly, endlessly wretched, he watched her leave the auditorium for the second time in as many days.

CHAPTER 3

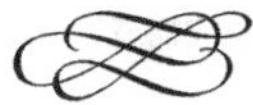

Agitato

"I can't."

The proclamation brought Brennan to a halt. Was Kristy talking to *him*? Telling him that she couldn't play with more abandon?

No. She was fifteen feet away, addressing her agent. Both women were silhouetted against the light spilling into the wings, but he had no trouble reading the emotion in the set of Kristy's body, the armor of her arms wrapped around herself.

She was supposed to be rehearsing right about—he checked his watch—now. The piano she'd finally chosen was on stage; a few of the symphony bigwigs were too. But there was no absurdly difficult Schubert, no gloriously tempestuous pianist.

He'd screwed up utterly last night. There was no moment in his professional life he'd take back before that one. He'd never been more foolish, bumbling, and callous than he had been in those moments, and he loathed himself.

On the edge of the stage, Kristy's agent, a wire-thin woman with a coiled blond bun, tossed her hand the way she might dismiss a gnat. "We're not doing this again."

"You're right, we're not. I'm not going out there."

He recognized that tone: Kristy Kwong setting her feet grave-deep. Refusing to budge. Issuing an ultimatum.

That had been what he'd clung to when he'd emailed Bernadette after Kristy had stormed out last night: *Ms. Kwong is too stubborn and too talented not to play the gala.* He'd omitted any reference to her emotions, because he didn't understand those at all. He assumed Kristy was livid, but he'd prefer not to tell his boss that he'd infuriated one of the world's most important pianists. That wasn't exactly a feather in his cap.

Still recalcitrant, Kristy changed tack with her agent. "It's too soon."

"It's been more than two years."

"Time's relative."

For all that had been written and whispered about her, few people mentioned Kristy's impish sense of humor, probably because that wouldn't fit with the notion that she was a cold-hearted bitch. She'd been funny as a teenager, but it surprised him that she'd been able to maintain it given her stage fright.

"You're the one who said you wanted to do this," her agent said. "You pushed for this contract."

"That was a mistake."

"Stop being dramatic. Get out there."

Until then, the exchange could've been playful. Two friends lightly teasing, maybe hinting at something painful that was true but making a joke out of it. However, her agent spat that out like a slap. This wasn't affable bickering. Not at all.

Several seconds of stunned silence passed.

When Kristy answered, it was softer than he'd ever heard her.

"I'm not ready." Her voice had gone thready, and something desperate simmered beneath her resolve.

He shouldn't be watching this. It wasn't part of his job, he wasn't going to pass any more information on to Bernadette, and Kristy would hate him listening in. He knew that the same way he knew how to brighten the voice of a Viennese baby grand: half training, half instinct. She was too proud to want him to see how bad her anxiety was.

He'd gotten a taste of it when she'd bolted after Quincy had barged in, but this was so much worse because there was no surprise or reversal here. One of the most talented concert pianists under forty in the world was too petrified to perform.

"You *are* ready," her agent insisted. "You are going to do this now."

"I...I don't think I can."

The words sent an icy wave of anguish through him. He wanted to march across the wings and present Kristy with ninety-five theses about her talent. Her technical prowess. Her expressiveness. Her musicianship.

But no doubt many, many people had tried to do precisely that. The problem wasn't coming from outside, but from within. What an infinitely more terrible betrayal.

"I'll walk if you can't." Her agent's words were every bit as implacable as Kristy's.

"Patrice, I—"

"No, listen to me. You will play right now, or we're done. I've indulged this long enough. You've worked too hard to get to where you are, and if you don't want it any longer, that's up to you. But I won't waste any more time on this."

This being Kristy.

Had Brennan sounded like that last night when he'd lost it? Probably. How could he ever apologize to her enough? How could he make this right?

Patrice obviously wasn't worried about any of that, which made this conversation even worse.

Kristy threaded her hands into that absolutely beautiful hair of hers. Beneath her thin black dress, her rib cage expanded and contracted rapidly. "Can I just have a moment?"

"No. Get out there."

For a sickening few seconds, Brennan wasn't certain what Kristy would do. Was he spying on the last beat of her career?

Then she dropped her hands rigidly to her sides and propelled herself forward. The instant she moved from the darkness of backstage into the light, she shuddered briefly, but she kept moving. She didn't acknowledge Bernadette's greeting; she only pushed steadily forward toward the piano.

Her agent followed and made some apology for the delay. Brennan ignored that; it didn't matter. He merely moved to the edge of the proscenium arch, all his attention welded to Kristy.

Other than the transcendent Brahms, everything she'd played had been hesitating and self-conscious, with only flashes of her raw power.

The first time he'd heard her at Tanglewood, he'd thought she was talented, but he'd wrongly labeled her a lightweight. Her style could be so aggressive that it lacked finesse, and he hadn't appreciated what she got in exchange. By the time she was at Juilliard, it was clear that his assessment had been sour grapes. Kristy had a unique voice as well as the technical virtuosity and interpretive perspective to have a real career. He was the lightweight.

Postbreak, her voice had changed. In the few moments when she'd let herself go, it was clear she'd acquired new poignancy. He wanted her to find a way to work through this so other people could hear what he had. So *she* could hear it.

Now, Kristy set her hands on the keys, and he took a deep breath exactly as she did. He assumed they both sent up identical pleas: that she would be confident enough for her voice to come through.

She started playing the Brahms rhapsodies. They weren't nearly as hairy as the Schubert, but she wasn't performing as well as she had for him the day before. Her movements were guarded, her shoulders set.

She was still the loveliest thing he'd ever seen.

Brennan didn't want to be like those other men, the ones who saw her as a gorgeous woman and not a musician. Or who saw her as both and somehow, therefore, lesser. He didn't get addled over women; that wasn't *him*. But he couldn't deny how Kristy made him feel.

When she finished a solid if unexceptional performance, she stood. "I'm not going to do the Schubert. I'm still not happy with the instrument. But you got what you were looking for, I assume." She meant she'd proved she was up to the concert.

Her agent was gushing and so was Bernadette, and thus Brennan had no more excuse to playing the Peeping Tom. She'd bought herself more time, and he ought to feel relieved.

Somehow he didn't, but he also knew it wasn't his problem. It shouldn't occupy him in this way.

Thirty minutes later, he'd dropped some paperwork in the front office and was crossing through backstage again when curiosity made him do something stupid. He walked down the row of greenrooms until he came to the one with a sliver of light under the doorway.

Kristy was still there. He could apologize for what he'd said.

He knocked once, softly. She ought to have a fair chance to ignore him. Honestly, he wouldn't blame her if she slammed a door in his face. He deserved it.

But her voice came from inside. "Yes?"

"It's Brennan Connelly."

A few seconds later, she swung the door open. She'd taken off the cardigan she'd been wearing earlier, and there were her bare shoulders and arms, the long sweep of her collarbones, all those lovely inches of skin...he bit the inside of his mouth, hard. He wasn't so much blushing as incinerating.

For her part, Kristy was as much the cold tower of steel as she had been the previous evening, exactly as she ought to be. "I didn't realize you were around."

"I—I'm supposed to be here whenever you are. Every walk-through and rehearsal, and the night of the gala. In case you need anything."

"Well, I don't."

He'd earned that. "I didn't come by for that. I'm here because I want to tell you I'm sorry."

"For?"

"What I said. There was absolutely no excuse for it, and I regret it. Your requests were completely reasonable, and I never should've given you the feedback I did. It was inappropriate and wrong—very wrong. You played well today, and I was out of line. I wanted to tell you I can find another technician if you'd prefer to work with someone else."

Maybe he could drag his mentor, Phil, out of retirement.

She watched his groveling in equivocal silence. Finally, she said, "So you're trying to quit again?"

"No! But I want you to be comfortable. After what I said, Ms. Kwong, I wouldn't blame you if you aren't comfortable with me." He wasn't feeling terribly comfortable with himself at the moment.

"For the love of Czerny, we're the same age. We've known each other forever. Call me Kristy."

This wasn't the response he'd been expecting. At all.

"Kristy, please forgive me."

She leaned up against the doorway. "Before I do, tell me this: Did you mean it?"

"Which part? Because it was mostly exhaustion, hunger, and headache." He didn't offer those as excuses, but he knew that was why his rules had crumbled.

"A potent combination," she agreed. "But I meant the part about how I'm the problem not the piano. Did you say it because you needed a Snickers?"

He swallowed. He didn't want to compound his transgression by lying to her.

Which somehow she knew and found a little funny. She snorted. "There's my answer then."

"No, it's…" He had to tell her the truth even if it was going to make things worse. "Your playing is going to change over two years, all right? If you'd been doing concerts and dazzling the world the entire time, you still would've changed. We don't, none of us, stay the same. The way you play now is more mature in some ways. There are shadows, I guess, that wouldn't have been there before. That development is beautiful. But it's also…it's just more restrained. That doesn't fit with the style of Brahms and Schubert."

This was what he ought to have said to her last night. Too bad there weren't time machines.

A beat passed, and then Kristy's posture softened. She'd forgiven him, and he exhaled in relief.

"I know, I know," she said. "I'm sorry I was blaming your pianos. It's just so disappointing."

"You don't need to apologize. In fact, please don't. I feel awful."

"That makes two of us."

"I heard your rehearsal just now—" He tensed, preparing himself for the onslaught this would probably set off. "—but I was also backstage before. Before you played." *And I heard your conversation with your agent,* he wanted to add, but Kristy would understand from what he'd said.

And of course she did. "Ah."

"I asked yesterday if you wanted to talk about it," he tacked on hastily. "And again I—"

"You're charming when you're apologizing, Brennan, and I'm not mad at you. I'm sort of like the queen of boiling over. Or at least the duchess. No, can I be the marchioness? That's a wonderful title." She made her tone faux-sweet, but her voice sped up as if she couldn't get the words out of her mouth fast enough. "Anyhow, clearly it would be ridiculous for me to hold that against you since it's sort of my signature move. It doesn't hurt that you're probably right. But that doesn't mean I want to talk to you about how I feel like a no-talent hack and I'm scared witless at the thought of people watching me play and so I can't do the thing I've worked my entire life for."

She blinked in seeming shock at what she'd admitted.

He couldn't blame her. Her confession tasted foul to him too, and if that was how she saw herself, he knew why she would want to cower in the wings.

"Absolutely none of those things are true." He hoped his tone conveyed half the empathy he felt. "But I'm sorry if you've felt that way for a single moment."

"I..." She closed her eyes before taking and releasing a long breath. "Thank you. Except I don't really want to talk about it. I've seen every single expert on stage fright, and I've—yeah. I can't yammer about it anymore. I'm tired of hearing myself whine."

While he wanted her to make an exception for him, he also didn't blame her in the least. He preferred to keep his feelings locked away in the damp cellar of his heart. That was why his own career playing the piano had ended before it began: He would never be able to display his heart on his sleeve the way Kristy or Caroline did. He truly was better suited to the cold, rational, technical side of music where emotions didn't rate.

"I understand. I merely wanted to apologize for what I said and for eavesdropping."

"That's courtly of you."

"Not really." None of his feelings about her were remotely gentlemanly, but saying so would truly be beyond him. "I should let you get home."

She shrugged. "Eh, it's not like I have any grand plans."

Kristy and her agent clearly weren't friendly, and if she had other people around her while she prepared for this concert, he hadn't heard about them. In fact, Kristy had actually spelled out in the contract that no one could be there except for him.

She seemed singularly alone.

Brennan's family was, in a word, chaotic. The silence and the order he found in his work were a refuge in many ways. If he were trying to come back from something like she was, though, they'd be there. With all their noise and their mess, sure, but they'd surround him. Comfort him. Distract him.

Knowing he was taking a risk, he asked, "What are you going to do for dinner?"

"Not sure. Go back to my Airbnb, stare at the wall, and order some takeout."

She was truly by herself. Should he…apologize? Congratulate her? Confess that only a microwavable Trader Joe's meal and an empty apartment waited for him?

Before he could decide, she went on. "You guys don't even have the decency to have baseball on."

He hadn't realized the Red Sox season had ended. "I'm, uh, sorry. You're a fan?"

"It passes the time."

She turned those eyes of hers to him, all stormy and vulnerable, and his knees went watery. He was no good at not giving this woman what she wanted—if only he knew what that was.

He set a hand on the wall to steady himself. "What would you rather do?"

"Not think about it for a night. Not think about music or this place or my career or anything."

There was some part of this conversation he didn't understand, the bulk of the iceberg lurking beneath the surface. Was it possible that Kristy wanted to see him…socially?

His blood started fizzling and popping at the possibility.

"We could have a drink." He sounded hesitant and highly speculative.

"We could." An equally measured response.

"Does that mean you want to?"

She half laughed. "Won't we just talk about work?"

There was that risk. Beyond music, they couldn't have much in common. She was so lovely, so cultured, so famous. And he was… himself. An instrument, in his own way, contrasted with her genius. But he could buy her a drink, be her distraction for an evening. He could do that much.

"Is music work?"

"Once, I would've said music was life." She didn't seem to know what she thought music was these days.

"Well, as long as you don't mind if I drone on about, I don't know, Japanese versus American actions or which decade produced the best Steinways." The answer to the latter was clearly the 1920s.

"I'd love it."

His heart sounded a triplet. He shouldn't enmesh himself in this; it wasn't his business. But he couldn't leave her alone when she was in pain. He just couldn't.

"Let me lock my office."

When he got back, she'd put her sweater back on—thank God—and he led her out the back of the theater and down to the reflecting pool. There was a slight breeze, so the gleaming stone edifices of the buildings were fractured in the pool's surface like a print by Escher. It was a glorious October day, all sunshine and crispness. The kind of day that made July and February in Boston worth it.

Walking next to her was the sharpest pleasure. He'd seen pianists show up for rehearsal in all kinds of outfits, ranging from formal attire to jeans. Kristy had on canvas sneakers, a long black cotton dress, and a ratty black cardigan, nothing like the ballgowns they loved to put her in on album covers. But despite her informality, something about her demanded your attention and held it. She oozed charisma.

"Where'd you grow up?" she asked him after they'd walked for a few minutes.

He couldn't remember the last time a soloist had asked about him, or the last time he'd had this kind of "getting to know you" conversation with someone. He generally abhorred small talk, but, well, Kristy was Kristy.

"Here, actually."

"And you never wanted to leave?"

"My parents are still here, and my brothers and sister. It would be...I just can't imagine living anywhere else." He knew that his baby sister longed to get away, but all he could feel was what he'd lose if he did. Generations of Connellys had passed their lives in Boston. These streets and squares were in their stories, in their blood. He'd be extirpated anywhere else.

"I can't imagine *that*," she responded. "The big family, the deep roots somewhere."

He realized, suddenly, that he didn't know a thing about her private life. It had never come up when they were kids, and she never talked about it in interviews. Kristy could even be married or involved with someone—but of course even if she were, this wasn't a date. They were merely having a drink.

"Did your family move around a lot?" he asked.

"A bit. But it's more that I built my home, so to speak, in a certain instrument, the one that we're *not* talking about." Her grin was puckish, and his insides went sloshy again.

Except this was the opening for him to ask what he cared about: whether she might want to unburden herself to him. "If you did want to talk about it—"

"I don't."

"—fair enough. But I'm here." To offer absolutely nothing helpful, he was sure, but he meant it. If she needed something, he'd provide it. She made him want to play the white knight.

Needing to change the subject, he asked, "So what's the last book you read?"

She told him about some thrillers she'd loved, and he talked about a history of Venice he'd been slowly working through, and then they arrived at an Italian wine bar he'd been to before. They were lucky enough to snag a table, and they ordered.

"How did you get into the piano tech gig?" she asked.

"Isn't that about work?"

"I have no objection to talking about your work, only mine." Her eyes flashed, and his cheeks went febrile. Again.

The real story had a painful beginning, and so Brennan picked up the thread at the more cheerful part. "Uh, well, a neighbor of ours was in the business. Phil." He loved that man like a second father.

Back then, Brennan had still been playing seriously. His interest in the technical side came from wanting to perfect his abilities—so when he'd diagnosed Kristy's problems as originating with her and not the instrument, he was confident he was right.

Seeing her brought his history back. Kristy's story wasn't going to end as his had, of that he was certain, but he knew how it felt to be betrayed by something you loved.

"Anyhow, Phil knew I had an interest in…*that instrument*."

She giggled, and he wanted to preen.

"I started watching him tune and voice pianos. There's no formal schooling to be a technician. I took a course from the guild and became Phil's assistant. He was good about making sure I was exposed to different styles, different approaches. He was the one who arranged for my internship with the concert tech at Tanglewood."

What he omitted: He'd auditioned for the piano program first and not been admitted. Just before he'd met her, he'd given up the very dream she'd achieved.

Even across the decades, the rejection stung.

But soothing the ache was Kristy. She took a sip of her wine and watched him over the rim of the glass. Her expression was smoldering, and he would've given up on any number of dreams to know what she was thinking.

"You were so serious, even then," she finally said.

Her words didn't make any sense. They had, both of them, been ridiculously devoted to their respective crafts.

"Because you were such a wild child." He hadn't meant to accuse her, but it wasn't fair to suggest he'd been any more serious than she was. It was just that she hadn't *only* been serious. At least from the outside, she'd seemed to be able to balance musicianship with...with normalcy.

He didn't know how to follow his rules and still be normal. He'd never been able to affect the ease others could, let alone the effortless coolness that Kristy radiated. At some level, he was the stuffed shirt Caroline often accused him of being. Restraint was professional. Restraint was safe. He'd shattered his restraint the previous night, and look where that had gotten him.

Across the table, Kristy's lips twitched. "Were you there the night we snuck beer into the dorms?"

"No, but I heard about it." They hadn't exactly run with the same crowd, and not just because he'd been no more successful socially at fifteen than he was at thirty-five. No, he knew that he'd kept his distance from her and the other pianists in part because they'd gotten in and he hadn't. He'd mostly socialized with the technicians and the strings players instead. He hadn't resented them irrationally.

"So you wouldn't have drunk pilfered beer with me?"

"I wouldn't have drunk pilfered beer with anyone."

"Oh, poor baby." She gave him a wry grin. "So I was a 'wild

child'—" She added exaggerated air quotes to that. "—but no one ever seemed to know what to make of me."

"Pardon? We all knew exactly what to make of you." She'd been the prettiest and most talented woman there; everyone had been more than half in love with her.

"Well, they settled for calling me a diva."

He grunted. She was quite correct—that had been something they'd called her. One of the less colorful things.

"Did you think I was a diva?" she demanded.

"I'd be mortified to tell you what I thought."

"Is that so?" she purred. "Now you have to spill."

"Hey, if there are things you refuse to talk about it, I get to set some limits too. You encouraged—I mean, you *seemed* to encourage the diva label." He didn't want to admit he'd had a riotous crush on her, and he was also trying to get around to what he really wanted to know: how and why she'd shaped her public brand and where it had all gone wrong.

"Sure. It was easier, sometimes. At least a diva has a role, has respect. So what happened next?"

She was bringing the conversation back to him because she didn't want to talk about herself, which he accepted. This kind of disclosure wasn't terribly comfortable for him, but he'd give it to her.

"Eventually, I'd learned what I needed to from Phil, so I went into business for myself. But this is a tough market." There were scarcely more high-end piano techs than there were concert pianists. "Eventually I started working on the pianos at Berklee, and that turned into the gig with the symphony."

"You're young for it."

He shrugged. "Maybe."

"It suits you." Her gaze was appreciative—and unmistakable.

He tried to swallow, but something about his physiology had changed and the process didn't work any longer. Kristy was flirting with him. She was. Really.

"Thanks." He managed to quaff most of his glass of wine. His throat burned, but it was a welcome distraction. Holy hell. This just couldn't be real.

He shot her a glance. She was still watching him.

He'd backed into relationships almost by accident in the past. Mostly with women he thought were kind and funny and who felt safe. Together, they'd been more lukewarm than scalding.

Kristy was vulnerable and hurting, and he'd never been racked with this kind of volcanic sexual longing before. This was a terrible idea for both of them—even if he could set aside his ethical qualms about intimacy with coworkers, and he'd never set ethical qualms aside in his life.

The air was humid with possibility. He suspected he could close the last inches between them and kiss her. He was almost certain she wanted him to. As a distraction. To gratify them both.

It hurt, how much he wanted to do exactly that. To be as selfish and shortsighted as everyone else seemed to be just this once.

But the fear he'd seen in her eyes, the vulnerability in her voice when she told her agent she couldn't play, rose in his mind and doused him with ice water.

In taking her out, he'd meant to ease her loneliness, but he'd smacked into his own instead. He was susceptible to Kristy because she was brilliant in every way, but also because he'd been by himself for too long.

He wasn't going to let mere desire for human contact pull him under and shatter his rules, however. He'd broken them because of her once already, and it had felt dreadful. He wasn't going to do it again. No, he was going to take care of them both and put an end to this flirtation.

He leaned back in his chair, trying to put as much space between them as possible, and then he gestured broadly. Oh God, that felt unnatural.

"So, that's my story." He tried to make his voice jovial. All he managed was anemic. "Now let me give you a complete rundown of the features of various Steinways before comparing them to golden age Mason & Hamlins. *Very* interesting stuff."

A long break followed this. He hadn't managed the shift deftly being too agitated to be subtle. Hopefully his rejection wouldn't sting.

When the moment passed and Kristy laughed, it was false and muted. She knew he'd turned her down, but perhaps she also understood why he'd done it.

"Bore me with technicalities, then," she said.

Those, at least, were safe.

CHAPTER 4

Furioso

Kristy wanted to play.

She couldn't remember the last time she'd felt like this, as if she needed to whale on something and the most obvious choice was a keyboard. She needed to be able to control every aspect: the pacing, the color, the phrasing. Because she sure as hell couldn't make people do what she wanted.

Take yesterday. During the semipublic rehearsal when she'd basically auditioned for the symphony leaders, she hadn't known if she could do it. But she'd believed Patrice when her agent had threatened to quit and that icy fear—*oh my God, I can't look for another agent, not now, and without an agent, I'm not a professional anymore*—had been enough to compel her to play.

Fear wasn't the ideal motivation, but it had served. Kristy had given a perfectly adequate performance.

Now she wanted to try rage as the seed. Because she was damn pissed at how she'd thrown herself at Brennan the night before, and how he'd gently, gently communicated his disinterest before putting her into an Uber an hour later.

So she'd shown up at the symphony hall early and without her normal entourage. When the panicked stage manager had told Kristy that Brennan wasn't around yet, she'd said, "Whatever. Have someone turn on the lights, and I'll get to work."

She didn't need Brennan. He'd said the problem was with her, and he'd probably been right. If she was the weakest link, then she fucking well ought to fix herself.

The facilities manager had set up "her" piano in a rehearsal space. The acoustics weren't the same but that didn't matter. She needed to ensure that she could play with abandon. She certainly felt reckless enough right now.

"Anything else?" The grip was the same one who had interrupted her the first day. He was scruffily good-looking and carried himself with that uniquely Boston brand of arrogance, a smug turn of the lip that assured you you weren't worth crap.

Don't worry, buddy. I think that all by myself.

"Just leave me alone." She said it as coldly as possible. If bitch was what people expected from her, that was what she'd give them.

She skipped her warm-up; she didn't have the restraint for Hanon today. She blasted straight into the opening of the Wanderer Fantasy.

Brennan had told her to play fearlessly, to take off the chains, and so she did. She slammed her fingers into the keys, compressed the pedal as hard as it would go. She didn't know if it sounded good, but it certainly sounded loud.

When she got into the second section, it was clear she didn't have it in her today to play quietly. Pianissimo wasn't her thing right now, but she could ignore the dynamics. They didn't matter.

After a little stumble here and a discordant note there, it was clear the dynamics were the least of her problem. Because when she got to the fugue, well, things began to fall apart.

She removed her left hand from the keyboard—it wasn't helping matters—and played through the section with only her right hand, like a child at her earliest lessons. For a dozen measures it was okay, and then Kristy fucked up a key change.

Again, she stopped. Reminded herself that her screw-ups didn't have any larger import. She was just in a foul mood, and besides, she was only getting started. This was what she got for being impatient and not going through her process.

She got up and made herself take a few steps away from the bench. The rehearsal room was silent, safe. No one had heard her. She hadn't done her reputation any harm.

For once, she did the wrist stretches her physical therapist recommended. Then she sat again and played a four-octave scale in C major. It was the key of Waldstein, the Beethoven sonata she'd played on her first major recording. Then she did A flat major, the first Chopin prelude she'd memorized had been in that. Followed by E major, a Haydn trio she'd absolutely nailed at Tanglewood once. And B flat major, her favorite of the Songs Without Words.

There was nothing she could play or listen to that wouldn't be haunted with memories. Success, failure, fear; two dozen dresses she'd worn and hotel rooms she'd occupied and reviews she'd read between her fingers. The memories assaulted her with every note. The ascending and descending runs were crusted over, and to play, she had to prick the scabs. There was no way out except through.

She finished and nodded slowly. The scales were fine. So she was fine.

Here goes nothing.

She jumped to the adagio of the Schubert, the easiest section of the piece, but her body still felt...not right. She was playing better technically, but the tone, while loud, was monotonous. Just a hulking monolith of sound without variety. She was, again, playing not performing.

Kristy stopped and tried to empty her mind. To quiet the voices and the doubts before they started screaming. She rubbed her temples and whispered, "You're just warming up. Everything you need is in you."

It was, but it didn't matter. The epochs of rehearsal time she'd put in, even when she wanted to do nothing more the entire time than quit, hadn't gotten the job done. She'd logged the hours, and it wasn't enough. Perhaps nothing she did would ever be enough.

You could quit now.

The words beckoned to her like they always did.

She gave them the middle finger and ran at the piece again and again. Sometimes for ten or twenty measures at a time, she managed to put together a decent run. But then the spark would cool, and all the urgency would drain out. Flat. She sounded flat. When she tried to fix that, the tone went brutal. Hard.

Again and again, she hammered into the piece. And again and again, it felt wrong.

If she played like this in ten days, it'd be a snuff film. She didn't need to play decently: She needed to play astonishingly. Anything less would kill her career for good. Maybe that was what she needed. An utter disaster to end this charade once and for all. It might even come as a relief.

Almost three hours later, she finished a run-through of the Schubert without an interruption. Lurching between too mild and too shrill, it hadn't been good. But it had been complete.

She fisted her hands in her lap, too enervated to puke or cry. She had poured out every bit of herself, and the ground around her remained bone dry. All she could do was hope the drought wasn't permanent.

Kristy clambered to her feet. Where had she left her bag? Here or—

And that was when she spied Brennan sitting in the small bank of chairs, his expression carefully neutral. But while he might be able to set his jaw and smooth his brow, he couldn't do anything about his eyes, which were brimming with concern.

That at least smashed through her numbness. She wanted to tongue-lash the sympathy right out of him.

"You're late," she said.

He hadn't been, he couldn't know what time she'd planned to arrive, but she wanted to be every inch the witch everyone always accused her of being.

"I'm sorry for that. What adjustments do you want me to make?"

Had he heard her? The issue hadn't been related to the instrument.

"Don't bother. You were right. I'm the problem."

"Kristy, *no*." He put up his hands in apology, and somehow his contentiousness about her feelings made her feel worse. He had on a cozy-looking maroon sweater, and between the warmth of the color and the depth of his eyes, she wanted to fall into him—but he didn't want that, and so she was doubly the fool.

"Sorry, Quincy told me you were in here. I only meant to stick my head in, but your playing is so compelling that I had to stay."

"Well, I'm sorry to have disappointed you. That wasn't my finest hour." But it seemed to be all she was capable of these days.

"Kristy—"

She started toward the door. "I need to, to go." She had to run, to explode, to purge her embarrassment somehow. If she could find the parts of herself that had rotted, she could carve them out of her. Get back, somehow, to good.

"Stop. Please."

He set his hands on her shoulders, and that brought her up short. His touch was featherlight, but it still echoed through her, a hammer on an anvil. Everything she'd wanted last night, he could have provided. They had that kind of spark between them.

Brennan wasn't anchoring her, wasn't forcing himself on her, wasn't touching her as pruriently as she wanted—damn him. So for that reason, the second she drained a little of his warmth for herself, she was going break free from him.

"Let's talk about this," he said.

After her performance at the restaurant yesterday, she was done talking. "You heard that. It sort of spoke for itself."

"I heard a virtuoso performer have an off day."

There was a time when she would have been able to believe him. Back when she'd known she was a golden girl, one bad day or rehearsal could be explained. Once your confidence fell to the table like a house of cards, the illusion could only be seen for what it was: a goddamn lie.

She'd never been a golden girl. She'd never earned or been owed success. All she'd had was luck, and now it had run out.

She pulled away from him and rushed out into the hallway. Her bag must be in the green room, where at least she could slam a door in Brennan's stupidly kind face.

He dogged her steps. "I realize this must feel like a 'one step forward, two steps back' thing—"

"It doesn't feel like I'm making any progress at all."

"—but you were playing with so much energy. That alone is already such an improvement."

"Failing. I was failing with so much energy."

She opened a door and stepped through it into the darkness of the stage wings. At least she couldn't see him any longer.

"Why are you doing this?" she asked. "You prepared the piano for me; your job is over. So what's up with all the rest of it? Buying me wine, trying to get me to open up. Are you making a play for employee of the month here?"

"This isn't about work at all."

"Are you sure? Because I've already decided to fill out the positive comment card for you and everything."

She was being as deliberately insulting as she knew how to be, and it wasn't working. The man wouldn't take the hint.

"How can I convince you?" he asked gently.

"You can't. You look at me, and you see one of your pianos. Something to be tuned and twisted and voiced. But I'm not an instrument." At the moment, she couldn't even play an instrument.

"That's *not* what I think when I look at you."

"Really?" She opened the door to her greenroom. Her purse and cup were there, though her coffee had probably gone lukewarm. Whatever, they made her feel more like herself. More in control.

They gave her the confidence to twist in the doorway, face Brennan, and demand, "What do you see?"

She was sincerely curious, although she didn't trust him to tell her the truth. He pitied her, but he didn't want her. How could he after what he'd just heard? He couldn't respect her.

"So?" she prompted again.

For a few long minutes, she wasn't certain if he was going to answer her at all. He stood in the half shadows of the hallway, his hands at his sides twitching slightly. He was probably weighing how much of the truth to tell her. What lie could he offer now to placate her without undermining her fragile confidence?

There wasn't one.

The day before, for a single second, she'd thought maybe he could understand, maybe she could trust him with parts of herself she'd guarded jealously. But in the end, he was every bit as disappointing as everyone else.

She hated how much that pissed her off.

"I see someone with incredible talent," he finally ground out.

"Ha." Maybe once but not any longer.

"I see someone with stunning courage."

"More like stunning stupidity." Because if she got up and played in ten days, there was little chance she'd achieve the comeback she needed. It wasn't brave to fight a battle you knew you were going to lose. It was poor planning and heedlessness. She'd been rash in the past, but she'd also never taken this big a risk.

"I see someone doing all of this by herself."

"I'm a soloist. I can't depend on anyone else." At the end of the day, she'd live or die in the spotlight—all by herself.

He drew a deep breath, and, with his eyes closed, he said, "I see a beautiful woman."

Those words were soft, confessional, and she almost laughed at them.

"I was literally one of *People*'s most beautiful people three years ago."

He wasn't exactly revealing anything shocking and she wasn't being vain; her good looks were carefully cultivated and just a fact.

He gave his head a slight shake. "But when other people look at you, they see the façade. You...dazzle them."

"Damn right I do." The façade was all she had left.

"When *I* say you're beautiful, I don't mean the obvious things."

A long pause, in which her heart, her stupid heart, *yearned.*

Then, "I mean the way you brazen through a music world that doesn't know what to do with you, throwing it in the faces of those condescending assholes. You give them exactly what they want, but then you play ten times better then they expect and so they worship you. And I mean the plaintive twist you've made on the motif in the Schubert now—no, don't argue with me."

She'd been about to, partially because she needed to hide behind something, anything. She didn't ever want him to stop talking, but she couldn't stop from wringing her hands while he did it. It was too much. It was everything.

"There are ways in which you play better today than you did two years ago," he went on. "I can see the moments when your doubt flares back up, but in the last four days, I've seen you wrestle it down over and over again. You screwed up today, I get that. But the way you did it? So much grit. Nothing held back. It slayed me. You slay me. I wouldn't blame you a bit if you wanted to walk away from this entire thing. You don't have to do this. You could be anything. But your determination, it's beautiful. You're beautiful."

He opened his eyes then, and the truth of what he'd said was written there. He believed those words. He did see her, all of the broken bits of her, and he still thought she was beautiful.

Fucking Paganini on a pogo stick.

Maybe the problem with spending your career trying to convince other people you're fabulous is that when you hoodwink them, you don't trust the resulting adulation. Audiences were marks, and she'd fleeced them all.

But with Brennan, she'd been too focused on her task to try to astonish him. Too low to even try. Which meant that this was real.

A new kind of awareness shimmered in her body.

As if he felt it too, he rubbed his fingers together. "My God, Kristy, say something."

"You really believe all that?" She'd already decided he did, but her brain was still churning like the sea before a hurricane.

"How many times do you need to hear me say it?"

"A few more."

They shared…not a smile. Something too secret, too complex for that. But the space around them tightened.

"You're beautiful," he repeated.

She shoved her hair out of her face, touched her mouth, shifted her weight. This was stupid. It was madness. Why was this making her squirm? How could she feel good after how she'd just played?

But she did. He took all of that away.

"You're beautiful. So damn beautiful."

"You probably try that line on everyone."

"I try it on no one."

It was probably naïve of her, but she believed that too.

Which was why she motioned to him with one finger. "Come here."

He stammered, "I shouldn't, I—"

"You really should."

After an elegant moment of hesitation, he curved into the room, closed and locked the door, and pinned her against the wall.

CHAPTER 5

Passionato

Brennan couldn't stop trembling. Even once his fists were pressed into the wall, his elbows too, and Kristy was watching him through those perceptive eyes of hers, he kept quaking inside. Little aftershocks from the seismic blow she'd delivered: In this moment, she needed him.

Damn the rules. Burn them. Abolish them. They had no place in this greenroom.

He'd wanted to be of service to her, and he'd wanted her. God, how he'd wanted her. For now, just for today, he could touch her. He could chase away the chill of her imperfect rehearsal. Banish her fears, at least for a few minutes. Make real what he saw in her.

"I can kiss you? That is, you're sure?" He had a trillion billion other questions for her—*why?* chief among them—but they could wait. As long as she wanted him, the rest didn't matter. He was going to make her feel good, whatever the cost to himself.

"Yes."

Kristy might struggle to have confidence in herself, but there was no hesitation in her assent. The word reverberated in him.

Because this would never happen again, he didn't rush. Slowly,

slowly he dipped his forehead until it rested against hers. She shifted against him, and he shivered from the profound intimacy of belly brushing belly. Thigh snaking between thigh.

When he trailed two fingers across one of her cheeks, he knew her skin wasn't the softest thing he'd ever touched. When he came to her mouth and traced its bow, they weren't the lushest lips on earth. When he fitted his hand into her hair, the strands weren't pure silk. But somehow, he couldn't believe any of that. She was the softest, the lushest, the most lovely.

Her breathing was shallow, her exhales impatient. So he caught her lower lip in his mouth for the barest instant. Just one moment of contact, and he had to catch his breath. He was dizzy enough that his next kiss caught the corner of her mouth, where her almost smile originated.

She giggled, quietly but with pleasure.

"That's what I want to hear," he whispered.

"*I* want more kissing."

Feeling foolish, he pressed his lips into her hair—he'd been wrong, it *was* the silkiest thing on earth—and then to the hinge of her jaw, and, at last, he fused his mouth to hers. This was temporary. It was discrete. But his hunger for her was so acute, that kissing her felt like taking. As if he could consume these sensations and possess them forever. He couldn't be gentle when her tongue stroked his, or when he realized she tasted like coffee and mint. There wasn't restraint when she made a noise like he'd only begun to satisfy her and her hips rocked into his. What was control when her fingernails were scoring his neck and back?

The kiss was frantic, and growing more so by the minute. Now that the rules had been rescinded, all pretense had evaporated. They'd gone feral.

He dragged his hands over her sides, cataloguing the places he wanted to linger later. Her breasts, which were small and firm and made him salivate. Her nipples, which were already reaching for him through her bra and dress. Her waist, and the swell of her stomach, and her ass, oh sweet Lord, her ass.

He palmed it, feeling filthy, but when she shivered and rasped herself against him, against where his cock was aching for her—well, he did it again. Brought their hips level. Mimed what he wanted to do to her: against the wall, over that ratty couch, on top of the makeup table.

Tonguing her neck, he groaned, "I wish I were the kind of man who carries condoms."

"We'll be creative."

Where she was concerned, that wasn't a problem. His desire for her was a mania, overwhelming even his own reticence. As long as she kept gasping for air every time their mouths broke apart, he wasn't worried whether he was being too forward. Too hungry. Too needy.

He didn't feel self-conscious as he dropped open-mouthed kisses over her collarbone. As he bent and bit her breasts, actually bit them, through her dress. As he put a hand over her mouth to muffle her cries as he did it again. As he knelt and kissed down her stomach. As he rubbed his knuckles against her mons.

Her back bowed and her chin instantly tipped up at that. "Oh God, please. Please, please, please."

He might be worshipping at her feet, but she'd given him the control. He stroked his hand against her again, finding the spot she needed and setting the pace. Anchoring her with the clenched fingers of his free hand and his face, the dimple of her belly button against his nose with only some cotton in between, as he worked her flesh. The intimacy of groping toward her pleasure like this bewildered him.

When she came with one stunned whimper, it rang through him. Set all of his nerves alight. But he wasn't satisfied. Not half so.

When her breathing had leveled out, he dropped his hand to the floor, then yanked the hem of her dress up and began to rain kisses on her legs. Blunt, strong calves—that didn't surprise him. Even the woman's gosh darn knees were sexy. When he reached her waist and discovered that her panties were lacy, black, and damp, he had to take a minute to catch his breath at the sight. But then he began working them down her hips and over her Chuck Taylors.

"Brennan, I..." Her fingers knitted in his hair, and she tugged gently, trying to get him to look up. "I don't think I can again."

"You can."

He knew it the same way the taste of her arousal on her thighs, when he put his mouth there a moment later, was familiar. This might be the first and only time for them, but it had the tang of rightness.

He gently coaxed one of her legs over his shoulder, opening her up. Bringing his mouth precisely where he wanted it to be, and, based on the breathy noises she was making, where she wanted it too.

Her hips jerked, and for an instant she ground herself against him. Then she recoiled, pushing her spine flat against the wall. That was *not* what he wanted. He wanted her to work out every single greedy, selfish impulse she had with him. He wanted to tick off every one of her boxes.

He hummed against her, urged her on with his fingers on her hips, lured her with the stroke of his tongue. *Come on, honey. Let loose with me.*

At last, tentatively, she rolled her body. He groaned. And then her next efforts weren't shy in the least.

This wasn't him performing anything on her; this was a thing they did together. Her clit, his tongue, her rhythm, their desire. And in the end, he was right. She could come again.

Finally, reluctantly, he sat back on his heels.

She had her hands glued against the wall, as if the ridges on her fingers had found microscopic purchase. Her hair was tousled, her eyes closed, her lips twisted in a crooked smile—and there wasn't a hint of tension in her body.

When she turned her eyes to him, her expression was halfway between sleepy and drunk. "*That* was something."

"Do you believe me now? That I think you're beautiful?"

She shook her head, but the shape of her smile was a bit smug. "I think you're far, far more wild than you let on, Brennan Connelly." She pushed off of the wall. "Come 'ere."

Good things, delicious things, came after that prompt.

He clambered to his feet, and she pulled him across the room and gently shoved him down onto the couch. She rucked her long dress up to her waist before straddling his lap.

"That was amazing," she said, setting one hand on his shoulders.

"Thank you, I—"

She gave him a squeeze, and he closed his mouth. He hadn't been certain what he had been about to say anyhow, and Kristy looked like a woman with a plan.

She pulled the tongue of his belt free from its buckle. "That second day, when you were voicing the piano, I was fantasizing about you."

His brain short circuited. "I, you, what?"

"Yup. I was nervous, playing in front of someone. And some like, I don't know, electric awareness of you crackled through me. So I just… went with it. I played better than I have in months."

She pulled down the zipper on his jeans, and then her cool, powerful fingers slipped inside his boxer-briefs.

"This isn't a quid pro quo thing," he managed through gritted teeth.

"Shut up and let me stroke your cock."

He wasn't going to argue with that.

Her grip allowed him no quarter. It was so firm that it could've felt punishing, but with her gaze on his, he simply felt achingly exposed. He couldn't have looked away from her, and he didn't even want to, but he knew he was slack-jawed. Panting. Absolutely desperate to come and in complete awe of her.

Kristy was biting her lip and moving with his thrusts. She looked as if she wanted his release every bit as much as he did. With her that intent on him, that invested in him, he couldn't last long. He also couldn't keep from mumbling her name when he did it. It felt as if she'd wrung his soul from his body.

She pressed her mouth to his temple, and he tapped on the side table for a tissue and cleaned them both up.

But then she surprised him when she slumped in his arms and asked, "Do you think we're the first people who've fucked in this greenroom?"

He managed a breathless laugh. "I don't want to consider it." All he could think about was what they'd just done together—and how much it was going to hurt when she left after a triumphant performance in ten days.

"I'm serious. How much action do you think this couch has seen?"

"I hope very little."

"You see, I hope a lot. Maybe then it would be lucky. The lucky banging couch."

Brennan had done his level best, but it didn't seem to be enough: she was still thinking. He tightened his arms around her, prepared to hold her still if need be until she talked to him about what was wrong. Why did she think she couldn't do this when he knew she could?

"I think it's a talking couch."

As always, she saw through him immediately. "Hmm."

"Kristy, if we can do…that." He'd wanted to say *make love,* but he didn't know how that would go over with her, and so he went with a pronoun instead. "Then you can trust me. I'm not pushing, but I'm here. And I care about you." He wouldn't pretend that wasn't true.

For a long, long time, she was silent, and he enjoyed the feel of her against him. He could wait forever like this.

"When I do talk to people about it, they don't understand," she whispered at last.

Thank God she was considering telling him. "I won't pretend I can." *But tell me anyway.*

"Which I appreciate."

"But—"

"No, don't ruin it by adding a but! You were doing so well."

"I'll take my chances. I don't understand what you feel, but I know what it's like to…to lose confidence in yourself." She wasn't going to believe him unless he got her to trust him. If him licking her to ecstasy hadn't gotten it done, then he'd need to try something else. Maybe giving her a confession in fair exchange? "The story I told you last night, about how I got into this—I might have left out some salient details."

She pushed up from his chest and gave him an evil look. "Such as?"

"I used to play."

She blinked and some of the anger in her eyes paled. "I didn't know that."

"It was a long time ago. I auditioned for BUTI that summer, but I —I didn't get in. What I do, piano technician work, wasn't what I wanted to do. It started in a last-ditch effort to salvage that other career. I thought maybe if I understood the mechanism better, I could elevate my playing. It didn't work."

He wished he could tell her that his own sturm und drang had been short and painless, but he couldn't. Still, she was worth exhuming his pain. His own origin story, such as it was, might convince her to open up to him.

Her expression had gone fully empathetic. "You really must've hated all the kids in the piano program that summer."

"Hate is a strong word."

"Ah." She didn't believe him. "But that's why you were a bit…chilly?"

"I don't think I was." Okay, that was a lie.

"You were always so formal. So—distanced. So correct."

She had him there. "There are more things I could tell you. My family is…messy." That was a polite way of putting it. "Music is where I went to hide because I liked the rules and the logic of it. If anything, moving from performing into being a technician suited that part of myself. So if I was cold, I didn't mean to be. I was hurt because I was coming to terms with the fact I wasn't good enough, and I was clinging to the rules because they made sense to me. Kept me safe."

And he'd just shattered them for her. He probably ought to be afraid, but instead, what they'd done together had felt inevitable. He'd trade anything if it would help her find her voice and confidence again, but it would sound silly to say that out loud.

"I'm just surprised you let one rejection do that to you—and no, don't even think of saying I'm being a hypocrite. It's just…we were, what, fifteen?" she demanded.

"What else were you up to that year? I mean, in terms of your music?"

"Um, I had my Carnegie Hall debut then."

"This is my point. And my little sister, Caroline, she's a violinist now with the symphony—"

"Really?"

"—she was having those kinds of successes too. And I...wasn't. At first, I didn't react well. I threw myself into practicing. Four hours of scales and technique exercises every day, that sort of thing. And it did help. I became better technically."

"But?"

"Now who's throwing around but." That he could joke about this showed how long ago it was. It certainly hadn't felt manageable at the time. "*But*...technical skills hadn't been my problem. It was something more indescribable. A lack of a voice. Charisma, maybe. I played pretty well, but I didn't have It, whatever It is."

He fixed his gaze on her, trying to put into his expression all the conviction he felt in his heart. "This is important, Kristy, listen to me: you do. You have It in spades. You're fecund with It."

After twenty years of trying to hide what he felt, he was sure it was a poor show, but he wanted her to see his certainty and believe too.

"Hmm."

He hadn't managed to convince her, but of course it wasn't going to be as easy as giving her a few orgasms and offering a handful of supportive words. He was willing to keep searching for the right spell if she was willing to let him keep trying, though.

She snuggled back down into his arms. "Tell me another story."

If it wasn't what he'd asked for, her demand implied an emotional intimacy that had his blood feeling carbonated. "About what?"

"Is it strange working with your sister? Is she one of the messy ones?"

"No, Caroline's wonderful. She's the one who understands me. But it's not as if we interact much." For weeks at a time, he wouldn't see her at work. Sometimes he even forgot they technically shared a place of employment.

"Are your parents proud?"

"Yes."

His answer came out vacillating, and of course she picked up on it. "There's a story there."

"Not really. They're not classical music people. They know it's a big deal, but they can't really get it in the way a symphony subscriber could. My dad's an electrician, and so are my brothers. This world won't ever be as clear to him as that one."

She tipped her head back. Finally she asked, "Is that hard?"

The question was so matter of fact, so free of condemnation of his parents, that he fell for her a little more. "No, it's actually a relief."

She nodded, understanding. "My parents wanted me to play. When they started me on lessons, they'd been thinking piano would look good to Stanford when I applied to be a pre-med, you know? My success sort of surprised them, maybe even scared them. What could be more risky than trying to be a musician? After a while, they got used to it because I was doing too well for them to doubt me, but then these past two years..."

"We don't have to talk about it." He meant that absolutely.

"It seems I can't prevent myself from talking to you about it." She gave him a cheeky grin, but it didn't quite reach her eyes. "When I stopped performing, my parents and I pretty much stopped talking. At first they found all these different experts to refer me to, but when nothing seemed to work, when I just couldn't get it together, they didn't know what to do. They couldn't not talk about it, and I couldn't fix myself, and it was fucking awful. So we stopped calling each other. I just stopped visiting, and so did they. And then it was...radio silence. For months and months."

Fifty questions rushed into his mouth, but he kept himself quiet. So, so quiet. Not pushing. Not judging. Just waiting.

"Aren't you going to tell me that's unhealthy?" she prompted.

"No."

"Do you think they're jerks?"

"I don't even know them." He was annoyed they hadn't found a way to help their daughter—even as he knew he hadn't found a way to help their daughter either—but that wasn't the point.

"Do you think I'm wasting my talent?"

"No, it's not even about that. Kristy." He repeated her name, loving how the two syllables felt on his tongue. "You're one of the most phenomenally talented artists I've ever heard play."

"But?"

He hadn't meant to say it with conditions, but there was an implied one. "That it would be a waste if you stopped is not a good enough reason to do this if you don't want it."

That was the part that made the least sense to him. If she'd lost the fire, she could walk away. Why keep doing it if it was causing her so much angst?

"Believe it or not, I never, ever stopped wanting it." She wasn't watching him anymore. She was staring at the wall, and her expression was almost dreamy. "At times, actually, I felt like the wanting would consume me. It was more I knew, just as intensely, I wasn't good enough to have it. And I—look, let me stop you right here."

He had been raising his hand to interrupt. He set it back on her hip—and it was still shocking to touch her like that. To know she wanted him to. And perhaps equally shocking to have her confess all of this.

"Whatever you were about to say, it would've made me itchy. I have mantras I'm supposed to recite, lists of accomplishments and awards and honors. I'm supposed to focus on my process, my work. Intellectually, it's all there. But it's not—" Her eyes were glossy, almost overfilled with tears, and she slammed her fist against the back of the couch. "*—here*. Once those doubts wriggled in, they spread like ivy. In my studio with no one else, I can shut them out sometimes. But as soon as I know someone is listening, there's too many thoughts pressing in on me. And I just can't do it. When you say I play without passion, you're right. I'm playing out of unadulterated fear."

He wanted to refute the things she thought about herself point by point. He'd have no trouble assembling the evidence. But he knew there was nothing he could say to quiet the doubts in her mind. He couldn't make this go away for her, no matter how much his heart ached.

Even so, he also couldn't let what she'd said go by without

comment. "I meant what I said. Watching you play the last few days has been one of the bravest things I've ever seen."

She scoffed. "Brave?"

"Yes. And that was before I knew what you just told me."

At last she managed to toss her hair and look mostly herself. Poised, if also a bit mussed—and he thrilled at knowing he'd been the one to muss her.

"Well, that's just wrong. There was no courage in it," she said.

"We'll have to disagree about that. But, Kristy?" He waited for her to look at him before he added, "Thank you for sharing your doubts with me."

He'd tried to put some small measure of the things she made him feel into the words, but because he wasn't an artist like she was, he failed.

She finally managed a real smile. "And thank you for making me come. Twice."

He gathered her back against him and kissed the top of her head. "It was an honor."

In that, at least, he'd succeeded.

CHAPTER 6

Intimo

Kristy was as happy as she'd ever been in a place she'd never thought she'd be: naked in Brennan Connelly's bed in his tiny Charlestown apartment.

For nearly a week, he'd been the perfect distraction from her worries, a role he was utterly committed to. He never talked about her upcoming performance unless she brought it up first, and he was endless fun to tease—at least until she pushed him too far, and he shattered. And then he tended to make *her* shatter. She'd never had as much fun with a lover, and it had been good, very good, to pretend she could have warm constancy at the end of the day.

If she wasn't going to resume her concert schedule, she could have this all the time, here with him, or—but that was the conflict. Who did she want to be? And was she brave enough to be whatever she'd decided?

"You're thinking again," he whispered against her shoulder. The last bit of light was disappearing as twilight fell. Out the windows of Brennan's bedroom, the city spread like a child's forest of block towers against the darkening sky.

"Sorry," she whispered back.

"I thought I'd worn you out."

He'd certainly tried. The relentlessness he'd brought to voicing pianos for her had been a preview of coming attractions. The man had the most talented hands...

"Should we go to dinner?" he asked.

That had been the plan when she'd come over. They hadn't made it.

"I'm not really hungry," she said.

"What are you thinking, then?"

She knew he wasn't fishing. He'd accept it if she lied and told him politics or movies or the meaning of life. She also knew now that she could trust him and that, as far as it was possible, he understood the torrent of different emotions she was experiencing.

Four days. She had four days until she had to play the gala in front of a packed house. To conquer her fears and to see if she could still perform with reckless abandon. Could she get onto that stage and show everyone the crinkles and pleats on her soul, knowing that they wouldn't all appreciate the view?

Well, she certainly couldn't if she wouldn't show it to Brennan. The man had been inside her not ten minutes prior.

She swallowed and then said lightly, "I was trying to name my fears."

"Oh." Brennan hadn't been expecting that. He rubbed his hands over his face and sat up a little, pulling away from her in the process. "What are you afraid of?"

He wasn't trying to pretend he wasn't interested. He didn't ever play it cool. That was the extension of his seriousness: Everything he did and said, he meant. He was utterly sincere. Even now, his eyes were riveted to her. He wanted desperately to know, because he thought if she could say it out loud, she'd be able to fix it and he'd able to help. She was less convinced about this, but what could she do at this point but try?

She cleared her throat and began ticking things off on her fingers. "That people will listen. That people won't listen. That they'll think I sound terrible. That they'll think I should have stayed retired.

That I'll play the concert and be adequate. I don't want to be adequate."

For most of her life, she'd taken her talent for granted. She'd been so extraordinary for so long, she'd blindly believed she always would be. But as she'd played for Brennan in the past week, she'd had to face the nasty gnawing possibility that the ember of her genius had gone cold.

He nodded. "Those are all bad things. But...what would happen if they occur? If you play the concert in a few days, and the critics say, 'Eh,' what's the harm?"

Her career would end. But worse than that: "I could believe them."

Her fingers and gut had gone icy. She'd never said the words out loud, and even in her head, she'd tried not to form them all the way into language.

She didn't know who she was if she wasn't Kristy Kwong, concert pianist. While her parents might have had another vision for her life, Kristy never had. It was this, and this to its fullest, highest level, or it was nothing.

Now that she'd admitted it, her eyelids were heavy with the effort not to cry.

"Is that why you can't play like you used to?" Brennan asked.

"Playing like that—" She broke off and wrestled a sob back down. "—it means I have to rip my heart out of my chest. Set it right out there on stage where everyone can see it. I guess I thought my heart was made of iron. Or maybe I just didn't think. I got successful young. There wasn't time to worry, until...until it was all I could do."

Hesitantly, he reached out and ran his fingertips over her cheekbones. "Do you think the audience can't be trusted with your heart?"

She didn't know if he meant his question literally, or if he'd said *the audience* when he meant himself. As intense as the last week had been, they'd never talked about what they were doing together. They'd never discussed their feelings. It had been all chitchat and orgasms. Lots and lots of orgasms.

"Honestly, I don't expect them to care about my heart on its own terms. It doesn't have intrinsic value to them."

Brennan swallowed. It might have intrinsic value to him, but she wasn't going to let herself contemplate that. She couldn't. Not with what she had to do in four days. She only had enough space in her brain for one problem, and it had to be the gala, not what she and Brennan could—no. She wasn't going to go there.

"They only care about my heart if it can do something for theirs," she said. "Make them feel something. Experience something. I think when the album came out and people hated it, the reviews made me go cautious. But that was the beginning of the end. I don't know how to work when I'm wary. Wildness was the secret to my success."

When she was trying to guard herself, she couldn't play. Not like she wanted to. She could be music or she could be safe. Not both.

"Now what?" he asked.

"I guess I have to learn how to be secure and still let go on stage."

"You could try not worrying about how people respond to you."

Ha, as if it were that simple. "I hear what you're saying, but I don't think I can pick and choose like that. How do I experience all the emotions I need to feel to play Brahms but then suddenly not care about reviews? You can't be a sponge for all these feelings and then go, 'but not those ones.' It doesn't work like that."

Or at least that was what she'd been telling herself for years.

She'd also told herself that she didn't need anyone. But looking at Brennan now, at the warmth in his face and the sheet cradling his chest, she knew she could shelter in his arms for as long as she needed to. It made her wonder if those mantras were true.

If she did need someone, could she filter who she listened to? Could she learn to tune out some voices?

They contemplated the heft of what she'd said for a moment.

Finally, Brennan replied, "I avoided feelings for a long time. I kept telling myself I was bad at them."

How stupid. "You really aren't," she insisted. "You don't like emotions because they're disordered. They don't follow rules. But you're great at reading me and giving me what I need."

His brown eyes grew darker, but he dismissed the nascent lust with a shake of his head. "But with you this week, I realize it was something else. Fear."

For an instant, she couldn't breathe. She understood *that* on her deepest cellular level.

"I hated how my…failure had made me feel," he said. "When I accepted I wasn't going to be a concert pianist, it was crushing. I never, ever wanted to experience that kind of pain again. So I buried stuff, clung to what centered me. I told myself there was no art to what I did. That I was a tool. But that's not living, it's existing."

Something in Kristy's chest splintered. She fisted his sheets in one hand and spat out, "You see yourself as a, a screwdriver?"

"Probably a tuning lever."

"That's absurd. You're every bit as much an artist as I am. Do you really think some random piano tuner out of the phone book in Des Moines can do what you do?"

He gave a sheepish shrug. "No."

"Good. Because you're special." She was practically shouting, but that was only because she needed to convince him. She'd worked with lots of technicians—and he was every bit as one in a million as she had been at her peak.

Which must have shown in her expression because Brennan's gaze swept over her face and he gave a grave nod. "It feels really good to hear you say that."

He sounded as breathless as she felt.

"It ought to. I don't give compliments often."

"That you would want to be with me for any length of time, for anything…it means a lot."

That was the most either of them had said explicitly about their relationship.

Because when she'd been shouting at him about how he was special—holy Hanon, she'd really chosen that insipid word—it had become a relationship. They were…together. Not just fucking, but sharing all their deepest secrets and trying to soothe one another's anguish, and it was wonderful. Too much. Not the right time.

She needed to make a joke, to get things back on safe ground. "So what you're saying is *I* changed *you*."

She'd meant it teasingly, but his response was utterly serious: "Yes. You have."

"I, I mean—" she spluttered.

"I had the most absurd crush on you when we met." His words were low and earnest. "Oh, I resented you too. But you were so... unrestricted. And talented. And, of course, gorgeous. Getting to know you now, getting to kiss you now—it's a dream come true. But it's even better because you're an extraordinary woman. And I don't mean Pianist Kristy, I mean Woman Kristy. Beyond the music. Beyond the success. I could talk to you about the paper and the weather forever and be happy."

The gooey ooze in her chest couldn't be stopped now. It was colonizing her limbs. Mucking with her brain. Overriding her good sense. "Stop it! You're making me blush."

No, it was worse than that. She was falling for him, or she had already. If she'd let herself, she could love Brennan Connelly. She already loved how he took care of her, and she wasn't a person who was good at giving up even the tiniest bit of control. But this man was somehow exactly what she needed.

"Tell me what you're thinking." He clearly knew that he'd just said a mouthful, and he wanted to know where she was at.

For once, she couldn't lie or play the bitch or plead confusion. She owed him the truth.

"I'm thinking we wasted a lot of time."

He started to move toward her, predatory intent in his eyes, but then he froze. Something more joyful came into his face. "That's it."

"What's *it*? I liked that look."

"Forget that. Do it. Play now."

Play? He was thinking about the piano? With what she'd just almost admitted?

"*Now* now? I'd rather do the other thing."

But Brennan had already climbed out of bed and pulled on some shorts. He tossed a blanket to her. "Come with me."

Grumbling, she wrapped herself up and followed him into the living room/dining room/kitchen space where Brennan had a Baldwin baby grand that he'd rebuilt. When he flipped on a few lamps, the walnut of the piano's cabinet gleamed. He gestured for her to sit.

He couldn't be serious. "Won't I bother your neighbors?"

"Nah, it's not late. They're always hollering about Patriots games anyhow. This will serve them right. Play. Play for me. Play what you're feeling."

Wasn't that just a sea of choices?

She arranged herself on the bench and ran her fingers over the keyboard. She didn't feel nauseated any longer. That had passed. And she wasn't afraid, not of what Brennan might think. Not of screwing up.

She looked at him, and his eyes were full, so full. All the tenderness, all the liking, all the lust: Everything she felt for him was there, reflected back to her like moonlight.

She could do this now, for them.

"The music for this is Chopin," she told him.

After a brief pause, she started on the final movement of the third piano sonata. The chords in the opening section were huge, and she attacked them. She leaned hard into the dynamics, into the emotions. Some of it sounded...sloppy. It wasn't as if she'd anticipated this or practiced for it. So she forgot some notes and slurred others.

But it didn't matter. Measure by measure, she gave the most reckless, the most jubilant performance she had in years. It came from her entire unshielded heart. It wasn't that she was certain of its reception—though, in this case, she was—it was that she knew it was better to take the risk than to ration her heart and be left wanting.

That she could still do this in spite of everything didn't mean that her performance at the gala would be good. Certainly she didn't believe in anything like guarantees, not anymore and not ever again. But this performance meant that it *might* be good. That Kristy hadn't exhausted her lifetime supply of potential.

When she finished, she looked at her hands. They could still do it. They could. She hadn't lost everything, and Brennan had given her back the map to herself. Whatever came next, however she played in four days, she cared for him now.

The weight of that realization still tumbling through her, Kristy stood and held the knot of the blanket at her chest. "So?"

Brennan's regard was everything. Adoration. Respect. Heat. Smugness. He felt like he was partially responsible for that breakthrough—and she'd allow it. He was.

"You're a goddess," he finally said. "Euterpe made real."

"She was a muse, but close enough." Kristy gave the knot a tug and let the blanket fall to the floor. "Make love to me."

And he did.

CHAPTER 7

Grandioso

Kristy's greenroom was full to bursting with flowers. Gaudy red roses, sprays of pale lilies, and one enormous pot of orange mums. Seriously, who sent an itinerant concert pianist *mums*? What the fucking fuck was she going to do with mums?

But she hadn't opened any of the cards. Until she knew how she was going to perform, she couldn't bring herself to care who was wishing her well. She couldn't think beyond the next hour. That, she was trying not to contemplate at all.

Her pulse was relatively even, her palms sweat-free, but her insides were as twisted and convoluted as the contestant intrigue on a season of *The Bachelor*, which she'd sadly become obsessed with during her break.

Or perhaps the right comparison was to Kristy's own love life. She'd spent as much time as possible with Brennan...and under Brennan and straddling Brennan. Arguing with him over tea and toast, teasing him at the Gardener Museum, and making him teach her the basics of piano tuning. Falling in love with him, though she still hadn't given him those words. And playing for him without any limits.

She hoped that practice and their conversations would be enough for her to play well now in this very different context. In a few minutes, she'd be onstage alone in front of thousands of people. If she imploded, she would do it by herself. Kristy wasn't playing a concerto; the orchestra wouldn't be backing her. Her success or failure would be entirely hers.

Kristy ran her hands down the front of her dress and hissed out a long exhale. She could do this. Maybe. Perhaps.

Patrice knocked and then opened the greenroom door without so much as a pause. Her expression was even more pinched than usual.

"How are you?" Patrice no longer tried to hide the trepidation in her voice. There wasn't the pretense of kindness anymore, only self-interest.

In an odd way, Kristy appreciated the honesty. "I haven't hurled yet." She hadn't since that very first day in Boston, actually.

Kristy offered this fact with jazz hands. They didn't really go with her dress, which was constructed out of black hammered silk panels. While it was gown length and voluminous, it had a dark, edgy vibe as if it had been made for a Disney villain. It fit her present mood.

"I was sort of expecting to find you with your head in a bin," Patrice admitted.

Actually, it would serve Patrice right if one day she walked into a greenroom and found Kristy in flagrante. But the only person Kristy had ever gotten in flagrante with in this setting was Brennan.

They still hadn't talked about the future. In the past few days, Patrice had hinted that there were numerous pseudo-offers percolating, and if this went well, they'd turn into real invitations like reverse Cinderellas at midnight. And then Kristy could be off to Kyoto, Heidelberg, Kyiv, or wherever else. If she chose that path, she'd think of Brennan fondly from afar and that would be that.

If she went down in a blazing streak of ignominy, well, she'd slink home to Los Angeles and become a Realtor or something equally depressing.

"I'm sorry to disappoint you," Kristy said to Patrice drily.

"Just don't screw up tonight."

"I make no promises." But she hoped, fervently, and she knew that she was willing to risk everything for it.

A few tense, silent minutes ticked by, and then at last Kristy was called to the stage. Brennan stood in the wings, conversing in low tones with that arrogant facilities manager, whom he dismissed before coming to stand next to her.

Brennan didn't have an overwhelming physical presence. They were approximately the same height, and he was thin as a birch sapling. But it was different now that she was an expert on the textures of him. The tastes. Now that they knew every secret thing about one another.

"A group of otters is called a raft," he finally said.

"A raft? Did you get that from a Snapple top?"

"You never can tell."

A mere twenty feet away, the audience was applauding and the conductor was bowing. Someone was talking, and Kristy was...numb. She couldn't feel her fingers, wasn't even certain she had fingers. Her guts were a Gordian knot, and her demons in her head were bellowing all sorts of unprintable things.

But then Brennan brushed the back of her hand.

"A group of apes?" he said. "A shrewdness."

"You're making these up."

"I would never."

And that was true. He wouldn't. He was all that was kind and steady and good.

Her, on the other hand? She was flippant and a liar and she couldn't do this. Her head swirled, and her stomach rose in her throat.

She balled her hands and pressed her fists to her eyes. "I don't think I can—"

"You can." Brennan moved his hand to the small of her back and his mouth to her ear. He was so certain. "You will or you won't, and I'll be here no matter what. And when you're playing? I'll be thinking about what we're going to do later tonight."

She swallowed. Took a few breaths.

So he thought they had one more night together, did he? She pulled the warm promise of that into her head, let it fill her.

The pounding of her heart was now for a much more pleasant reason.

"We'll see," she finally managed to whisper, hoping that it sounded seductive and not terrified.

Then someone with a headset and a clipboard was telling her it was time to go on, and for a blood-curdling second, she couldn't.

All she could hear were the goddamn voices of her doubts.

You'll screw up.

You aren't ready.

You were never any good.

There were so many reasons to stay here. To run away. It felt like playing Russian roulette, but instead of an overwhelming likelihood of success tinged by deadly risk, there was an overwhelming likelihood of failure. But in the last two years as she'd hid, what she'd mostly experienced hadn't been relief. It had been dread.

If she went out there and ruined everything, it would be awful. After the awful, however, she wouldn't need to dread performing. She could finally, finally close the door. And if somehow, she managed to pull it off, well, then she'd know that too.

Kristy was so tired of being afraid. She was going to do this—and she *was* going to do this—not because of fear, but because of love. She owed this to herself and to Brennan, who didn't push her. Didn't prod. Just waited. And she knew he'd be there when it was done, regardless of how she finished it.

So she walked onstage and raised a hand to the conductor and the audience. She refused to look at them, but she went through the motions, vaguely aware of when the conductor exited the stage and left her alone to face her fate.

She set her hands on the keys, which somehow felt cold even under the glare of the stage lights.

No limits. All heart.

She struck the opening chords. *Hmm, listen to that.* She hadn't spoiled the first bit of the Schubert.

Then her mind just…smeared.

The performance didn't feel like those that had come before, when at times she would've sworn she could see the molecules in the air vibrating in time with the notes. When she had been painfully, hyper aware of every measure.

Now, she could hear herself playing at a remove, like a soft radio humming in another room. She sounded good. Unselfconscious. Not tight.

She fixed her attention not on that, though, but on a rare grin from Brennan when he'd taken her queen during a game of chess. God, she was crap at chess. On the awe in his face when he'd taken her to see his favorite Sargent painting. On her hand sliding over the cool of his mattress and tucking under the warm pressure of his body. On the way he kissed her as if she were the most precious thing on earth.

Fragments of conversation, shadows of their bodies coming together—she pulled them into her mind for an instant and then let them drop. Shimmering moments of what he'd given her, what she'd taken from him, in order to get to here. To do it, to embody it, but to be removed from it. Separated from her fear.

Oxygen moved in and out of her chest, her fingers danced over the keys, slammed into them at times, and she was safe behind the wall of glass she'd built. *Here is my heart,* she was saying to the audience. *I'm showing it to you, but I'm keeping it for myself.*

She completed the Schubert. The audience was clapping wildly, but she couldn't let herself feel that. She wasn't finished—and their reaction didn't matter. She was performing for herself.

So she moved into the Brahms, into the rhapsodies that weren't rhapsodies. The fervid imaginings of the composer who couldn't seem to let himself have the women he loved. She'd always resented him on behalf of Clara Schumann, but now, maybe, as Kristy climbed the mountain of musical passion he'd built, she had a small measure of sympathy for him.

To perform music was to drag your shame and desire, your naked spirit, into public. To use everything you'd ever felt to color how you played. To stroke and prod and hammer all of it into an instrument. To give away pieces of yourself for the price of a ticket.

No wonder she'd panicked two years ago. No wonder she wasn't sure if she could keep doing this. But she was doing it. By God, was she doing it now.

She hit the final two chords of the second rhapsody, and those, those she felt.

Holy shit, she'd really done it.

Kristy rose from the bench. When she grabbed her skirt to curtsey, she was surprised that her palms were damp, but she managed to keep her expression even. She nodded to the conductor, whose eyes gleamed with reflected satisfaction, and then she swished from the stage.

Patrice was there, clapping her hands and gibbering into her phone and slapping Kristy on the shoulder and saying she'd had no doubts. Oh look, now that Kristy wasn't a complete screwup, her agent was back to lying.

And there were other people, and Kristy knew she was talking and she was posing and someone took a picture.

Against the back wall, smiling faintly, was Brennan.

She wanted to part the crowd and latch onto him like a whelk on a dock pylon, but that would have raised uncomfortable questions for both of them.

The symphony director, one of those exceedingly rich, exceedingly elegant women who would unquestionably win any knife fights in which they became engaged, waved him over, however.

"Ms. Kwong, what a wonderful performance," she gushed.

"Thank you. I'm pleased."

"And Brennan!" she said. "What good work. I didn't know the Steinway could sound like that."

He gave an embarrassed shrug of his shoulders. "I didn't do so much. It was mostly Ms. Kwong."

Sweet shit, Ms. Kwong wished they'd all stop calling her that.

"I don't know," Kristy said a little too innocently. "I found Mr. Connelly to be incredibly helpful. Very hands on." Okay, she couldn't resist adding some innuendo to that. She'd finished her concert; she had to amuse herself somehow.

The symphony director didn't pick up on that. She was still handing out platitudes. "And I'm very grateful for the confidence you gave me, Brennan, to go ahead with the concert."

Silence descended like sudden snow, and Kristy asked, "Pardon?"

"Oh, you know, since it had been so long since you'd played a major concert, I just asked Brennan for a heads up about how the rehearsals were going."

He'd been spying on her. Giving little reports about her.

For the first time in a week, Kristy could've emptied the contents of her stomach onto the floor. She was suddenly and viscerally pissed. Too pissed for her body to contain it all.

"Right," Kristy replied after entirely too much time had passed. As if she were the dupe she so obviously had been played for. Except a dupe probably would be too dense to feel rage—and Kristy could've been made of rage.

Brennan's expression was stricken, and he gave a tight shake of his head. Kristy looked away from him, blinked at the sudden moisture in her eyes, and rubbed her stomach to try to void the tumbling-through-space feeling growing there.

More people were talking, and Kristy said...words. Of some kind. Who knew if they were the right ones? She didn't much care. All she cared about was hollering, and she couldn't do that, not yet.

For his part, Brennan remained as still and soundless as a statue. Which obviously meant that he knew he'd informed on her, because if he could've mounted some defense, where was it? Why wasn't he sharing it?

She wanted to kick him in the shins, but she also knew that wouldn't help a whit. She needed all the details first. He'd shared precisely what about Kristy with precisely whom?

When it seemed that no one was looking at her, Kristy announced, "I just need a moment." She hoped her words weren't too bitchy, but then again, that was sort of her brand.

The route to the greenroom was well worn, familiar. She'd walked this path during the two weeks she'd spent here in fear, rage, and lust. Now she was experiencing some new and livid smoothie of emotion.

She'd thought when she returned here tonight it would either be in triumph or disgrace. Who knew there was some other option? Pyrrhic victory.

Kristy didn't bother closing the door behind her. The man she wanted to talk to would be along in a second, no doubt. She just sat on the couch and contemplated her hands.

They'd performed, all right, but there wasn't anything remarkable there. She'd heard about famous composers having casts made of their hands. Chopin. Rachmaninov. As if their genius had been something about their anatomy. Kristy's hands looked utterly normal. Small even, though she guessed her fingers were long.

But in the muscle, she'd managed to lodge something. If not genius, then at least reflex. And somehow, tonight, the stars had aligned and it had fired and she hadn't blown it.

And it didn't matter because she had fallen in love and gotten kicked in the chest for her trouble.

How—funny. To get what she wanted and to have it be proved insignificant. It was terribly, terribly ironic.

"It isn't what you think." He hadn't stepped into the room. Because he was the most proper human being on the planet, he would remain out there until she asked him in.

"What do I think?" she asked.

"That I betrayed your trust."

"You didn't?" If only those words could hit the floor with the same force as a sledgehammer.

"After the first day, when Quincy showed up and you left, I emailed Bernadette and told her what had happened."

"Okay." Kristy had assumed what she'd done would become part of the lore of the symphony hall, for good or ill, depending on how her performance went. That sort of thing just added to her mystique, she supposed.

But that wasn't the entire story. "Did you tell her anything else?"

"After the second day, I told her I thought you could do it."

Brennan was still unevenly and dimly lit in the hallway. It didn't matter, though. She could've read his emotions in the dark. Over the phone. Because she knew him—or at least she'd thought she did.

He was telling the truth, and he felt terrible.

She took a few breaths, trying to let go of some of the emotions that had built up in her body. Maybe she didn't need them all.

"Were there any other details? Anything beyond that?"

"No, I swear to God. It was two emails. Maybe thirty words. You can read them. There isn't a thing in there that you wouldn't have said to her, I don't think. And I've shared nothing with her at all since... since." Since Kristy and Brennan had become lovers, presumably. Since they'd let each other in.

She let the truth of what had happened filter through her. It wasn't a real betrayal. But it stung like acid all the same, because it revealed how far in she was.

She couldn't fall in love and figure out her life at the same time. She couldn't.

Even as this had been happening, she'd tried to keep one foot on the floor, to resist just enough. She hadn't managed the trick, but she could pull back now. Give herself the space of a postage stamp to figure out her own damn mind.

"Kristy...please talk to me. Or shout at me." He sounded a bit desperate.

"I don't feel like shouting." Not anymore.

"What do you feel like?"

"I'm just numb. Confused." Not only because of him, but because of what she'd done. How she'd performed. She hadn't the slightest idea what she wanted. Whatever else she thought tonight might be, she'd assumed it would be definitive. Now she was confused about him and about the future. She was a tornado, razing everything in her path. What a fucking mess.

"Can I come in?" he asked.

"Oh. Yes." She still couldn't look directly at him, at the contrition and sincerity that was likely in his face. But she didn't want to keep him out in the hallway.

So instead, she looked in the mirror. Her hair was in a perfectly deconstructed bun. Her eyes were unfocused. Her mouth gaped. Her color was off. She had done it, she had, but it hadn't changed anything at all.

"How do you feel about how your performance?" he asked.

"It went well."

"Well?" He was trying to brighten the mood. It wasn't working. "You played with so much passion. You didn't check yourself in the least. That was your heart."

That had been the problem. "I said it went well."

"But how do you *feel*?"

For a man who said he didn't like feelings, he was pretty obsessed with them. "Really fucking confused."

At that, she looked at him. His eyelids were fluttering and his jaw working beneath his cheek. He was as measured as a Swiss watch. She'd learned his small tells in the past two weeks. Had so enjoyed poking at them. Watching what he'd reveal and what he'd keep inside.

"What is there to be confused about?" he finally asked.

"I thought tonight would be..." She lifted her hands and then struck the air with her flattened palms. "Like that. Do you see?"

"No, but I want to."

"I don't know how to explain it. It's not...fixed for me yet." Either in terms of her future or...theirs. If they could have a future together. If she wanted to after what he'd done. "But—"

Kristy rose. It was too hard, sitting where they had been together. She reached for the nearest vase and pulled out the card if only to have something to do with her hands. Her eyes moved over the text again and again, but she couldn't have comprehended the words if she had to.

Space. She just needed a little space.

This was going to sting, but it would be better for him. Better for both of them.

"You've been beyond kind." She said it without looking at him, because she didn't have the nonchalance for this moment. He'd been everything, actually. The first and perhaps only man she'd loved. She never would've gotten through that concert without him. And someday, perhaps she'd be able to express that.

"Kind?"

"Yes. And I'm grateful."

She waited for him to echo grateful, but he didn't. She'd drummed everything right out of him.

"No one could've managed the instruments better." *No one could've managed* me *better*. "I, well, thank you."

She'd become the twisting melody in the second Brahms rhapsody. Aching. Plaintive. Wanting a thing she might not reach for.

Brennan had gone as rigid as she felt. The pain was visible in the crinkles around his eyes, but she had no doubt that underneath his poise, all his gears and wheels were whirling away, trying to figure out what was happening and why.

Kristy offered her coldest smile. "I think Patrice wants me to see a few more people."

No doubt she did, but Kristy had absolutely no desire or intent to see them. However, that would at least end this conversation.

"Right. I just...I'll go."

"Goodbye," she offered his retreating back.

When he didn't reply, it was just one more cut on a night that had brought a surprising number of them.

CHAPTER 8

Teneramente

Brennan was drunk, which was not, all things considered, a place he normally spent much time. But after being dumped—jeez, he thought he'd been dumped, but he wasn't entirely sure what had happened—and wrapping up what he needed to at the symphony, drunk seemed as good a place as any to be.

So, for once, he'd accepted an invitation from his baby sister to go out after a concert. Now, as he stumbled up the stairs to his apartment, his head throbbing and absolutely none of the pain in his heart eased, he regretted each and every one of his life choices.

"Are you going to be okay?" Caroline asked. Her voice was low, earnest, and brimming with concern. Tentative, almost terrified, concern, because no one ever thought to be worried for him. He was the one everyone else took for granted and didn't think of because he didn't demand their attention. It was something of a role reversal.

"Course I am. I just needed to let loose, lil sis."

God, the words might as well have been rocks in his mouth. Big muddy rocks, coating his tongue with grime. They weren't his words. Weren't his ideas.

Caroline just patted his shoulder. "Right, but why?"

"Good intentions gone...rancid." He'd only meant to get Kristy through this performance. He hadn't banked on her finding out that he'd reported to Bernadette. Or on how one thing would lead to another. Or how he'd rationalized everything he'd done as being for her, rather than admitting it had been his own selfishness and desire.

He deserved this pain; he'd earned it. He had been so damn stupid. How could he have reached for her? How could he have fallen for her? How could he have betrayed her trust? He'd known better and he'd done it anyhow, and this was why he only colored inside the lines. Which he was totally going to do from now on. He was back to following all the rules.

They reached his door, and Brennan propped himself against the wall and handed Caroline his keys. He couldn't handle that sort of detailed work, not now.

With a chuckle, Caroline unlocked the door and flicked on a light inside. "Good intentions will do that to you. You want to tell me who the intentions were directed toward?"

"Not especially."

"You skipped two dinners with Mom."

Yup. He had, and that had been unprecedented. Mom was, no doubt, livid.

"Give me a hint. It must've been someone important."

"I'll make it up to Mom. I'll tell her I fell in love."

"You *what*?" Caroline shrieked, an unnecessary reminder that she was Brennan's opposite in every way. Loud where he was quiet. Technicolor where he was sepia. Confident where he was diffident.

"Shh," he hissed and dragged his sister inside his apartment.

She wouldn't be quieted, though. "Are you kidding?"

He didn't even begin to know how to answer that, and that wasn't just because of the bourbon. "No. Maybe. I don't know. It's not..." For a second, he was tempted to answer with an implacable hand gesture like Kristy would. Something dense and idiosyncratic and perfectly adorable.

"Not clear," he finished.

"Who is she? This woman you might kinda love?" Caroline asked, solemn and stunned.

"You don't know her."

Caroline knew *of* Kristy. Had heard her play tonight, in fact. But she didn't know her. No one did. He might have kissed every inch of Kristy's body, but even he didn't know her. Hell, Kristy didn't seem to know Kristy.

His sister's eyes narrowed. "Brennan Connelly, is it someone from work?"

"Why would you say that?"

"Because the only place you ever go is work."

That wasn't true. He saw his closest childhood friend, Ian, at least once a week. But more to the point, he had eaten out more, had visited more museums, had walked through the parks and streets more in the past two weeks than he had in the prior three decades because of Kristy. He had broken out of his shell entirely because of her.

"I do too go out."

"Is it Kristy Kwong?"

His pulse throbbed in his wrists. How had she guessed?

He almost denied it, but, well, Caroline would find out eventually. And if he was back to following the rules, not lying was a major one.

"Yes," he said.

He hated to admit it, because now Caroline was going to take his side and trash Kristy for breaking his heart, and he didn't want to hear Caroline do it. Much as he might be confused about what had happened, much as he might hate it, Kristy didn't deserve anyone's scorn. If he had been more restrained like he always was, like he knew he should've been, he could've skipped this part. The broken heart part.

"Oh," Caroline said.

That was all. *Oh.*

Brennan squeezed his eyes shut tight, as if that would sober him up. Make this conversation comprehensible.

Then Caroline added, "God, she played well tonight."

And she had. Better than he'd ever heard her. Better than anyone had ever heard her. Better than she'd played two years ago. Brennan had checked his phone once—okay, three times—while he and Caroline had been drinking, and the reviews of Kristy's big comeback had been ecstatic. But of course he wasn't surprised, only confused as to why Kristy had been so...what had she been? Even now, he didn't know. Had she rejected him just because of his spying, or was there something else going on? He had no idea.

"She's brilliant," was all he said.

"And gorgeous."

"Yup."

"And you love her."

"That's probably going too far."

No, it wasn't. As soon as he'd said the words, he knew he loved Kristy. Loved her talent. Loved the vulnerabilities that let her play as she did. Loved her body and her mind. Loved the things about her that were strong and the things that needed to be shielded.

He didn't know how and whether they could fit together, but he knew that for a moment at least, he'd been what she'd needed. And he was honored, he'd always be honored, that she'd let him play that part.

Now he just had to adjust to the fact that he wouldn't get to play it anymore.

"Yes, okay, I love her," he said. "I love Kristy Kwong." He shouted that bit because, well, they'd closed the door and his neighbors really did deserve it. If Brennan had to hear about every single thing Tom Whoever did, the rest of building could hear about how Brennan had broken his stupid heart.

Actually, Brennan considered shouting it again, because it was so strange and wonderful and awful. But he stopped himself. He was normally a far more serious person.

"Happy now?" he asked his sister.

"Thrilled," she offered drily. "What are you going to do about it?"

"Do? What can I do? She's leaving, like, soon." He had no idea when she would depart Boston, actually. They'd never talked about it. He'd been too terrified to bring it up.

"And that's it?" Caroline asked.

"Yup. Signed, sealed...and the other thing."

"You're such a dork."

"What's your point?"

"How often do you think this happens?"

"To me? Never. It has never happened."

"Right, so you're a dork."

He was, but he wasn't certain how that was relevant. For the first time in his life, he'd done something reckless. He'd unbent. And it had made him feel like his entire insides had been bruised.

"I love you," he said to Caroline. If he'd learned anything, it was that when you loved someone, you needed to speak up. If he could see Kristy just one more time, that was what he'd say.

"I love you too, bro." She thumped him on the chest twice. "I'm going home."

"How?"

She wiggled her phone at him. "I called a car like five minutes ago."

"Oh. Text me when you get there."

She snorted and kissed his cheek, but when she opened the door her eyes went wide and she immediately slammed it shut.

"Is it a ghost?" he asked, knowing an irate neighbor was more likely.

"Yep." Caroline was even worse at lying than he was. Her cheeks were vermillion and almost matched her hair. "And so I'm out of here."

"What did you see in the hall?"

"Who. The question you should be asking is who. And I hate playing the third wheel." She opened the door again and strode out.

Third...wheel? What?

A knock sounded from the doorjamb. And when he let his head fall to the side so he could see into the hallway, he was stunned. He was shocked. He was dumbfounded to find Kristy Kwong standing there. Every one of his brain cells shrieked in unison.

She gave him a jaunty wave. "Hey."

Back in the greenroom, she'd been a shadow of herself. Pale, wan, indecisive. She was still wearing the gown she'd performed in. Her dress was limp and wrinkled, but her eyes were sparkling.

Beautiful, she was so beautiful.

"How long have you been there?" he asked, which was a redundant question because he knew the answer.

His sister had no idea how big a dork he was. He'd been yelling about being in love with Kristy, and she'd heard him. He squeezed his eyes shut. The shame was tactile. He could feel it moving through is veins. He might not actually survive this.

"A bit," Kristy admitted, trying to maintain some teensy shred of his dignity.

But it was too late for that. He cracked his eyes open. "Did you hear what I said?"

"Shouted. You shouted it." She was enjoying this.

"I was being rhetorical." Or hyperbolic. Maybe both.

"You were being loud."

"I've had a bit to drink."

"Ah." She snickered, but it felt like the best kind of teasing. Like how they'd been together two days ago.

Ears beginning to toast, Brennan asked, "Other than eavesdropping, what are you doing here?"

She tipped her head to the side but didn't answer him. Kristy just stepped out of her shoes and walked farther into his apartment. Framed by the archway into his living room, she just fit. She was a superstar, of course, intended for all the great stages of the world. She'd leave him behind soon. Even so, he'd never wanted to believe in something as much as that she might stay—and he wasn't a man for make-believe.

"I need to say some things to you," she said.

"I'm listening, then."

She entwined her hands together in front of herself. Not as protection this time, but because she seemed...uncertain. Which she shouldn't be, not after what she'd heard him admit. But it made his heart skip some beats all the same.

"I'm not really good at talking," she said at last.

"You actually are."

"I'm good at deflecting, maybe." Her lips twisted, released, and twisted again. She was working around to something.

Now it was his turn to wait—and to try not to hope.

"I panicked earlier. And I'm still sort of panicking. I thought I was going to..." She started to do something with her hands, and then dropped them to her sides. "Fail tonight. And there was some level on which I was relieved about it. I was ready for it to be over, you know? And it's not. Or," she rushed this next bit, "it doesn't have to be. But now I feel like I'm back at the start, facing a decision I can't quite make. And the idea you'd share things about me with anyone...I didn't like that."

"I'm so sorry I didn't tell you."

"I know."

Brennan took and released several breaths. She was decrying her lack of control, her sense of powerlessness—and he knew what that felt like. As a kid, he'd wanted to be an artist, and when he couldn't, he'd mastered the piano in another way. It had always felt like settling, though, until he'd been able to help her. He had made magic; it just hadn't been his.

Suddenly, he was confident. He understood this dynamic, and his purpose in it.

"What do you want, Kristy?"

"I...I don't know. I wanted to play this concert, and I did. I want to stop being afraid. I want you. I want to feel like the person you seem to see when you looked at me."

It was too dark to see her expression clearly, but he could feel her attention on him, more real than the light. More real than anything.

"I told you what I see. Nothing has changed." If anything, he was even more awed by her now.

"I didn't feel like that woman tonight—at least not once I got offstage. I was just discombobulated. I was only certain I wanted to talk to you."

His heart pounded a staccato rhythm against his sternum. "It didn't seem like it earlier."

"I know." Her jawline tensed with her grimace. "I might've mentioned I'm not good with words."

"You did."

"I thought I was doing the right thing, sending you away tonight. I didn't think I could tackle all my problems at once. You're a complication I didn't anticipate, so I pushed you to the backburner, shoved you away, and then I fired my agent."

"You what?" He was all the way sober now.

She smiled. "Yup. One of those things was exactly right, the other was a terrible mistake."

"Which am I?"

There was another pause, but the atmosphere in his living room had somehow become friendly.

At last she said, "I should've explained what I was feeling to you. I was—am—chaos incarnate. In that moment, I didn't know if I could work out myself and us. So I thought I should be a hero and take care of you. Protect you from the black hole I've become. Then I went back to my room, and I was...desolate. I—" Her voice shook, but she squeezed her hands into fists and pressed on. "—I'm not used to feeling like that. Two years on my own, just me and my mind demons, and I felt pissed and scared and confused, but never, ever *lonely*. And, Brennan, someday, when I think about this more, I might be pissed at you for taking that away from me. But tonight I kept seeing you shooting me down when I first tried to hit on you. Trying to keep us both safe."

They were both terrible at caretaking. Their reflex was to self-sacrifice, which made no one happy. No, they needed to be direct instead—if they were going to remain in each other's lives.

Carefully, he said, "You're not a black hole, and you're not chaos. Far from it. But the material point is we have to stop sparing each other's feelings. Being mavericks." Presuming that this wasn't their last conversation. But if they were going to try this, they would have to trust each other enough not to act unilaterally. "We have to make decisions together instead."

"Yes. We do."

Her gaze was steady and her expression was serene. He hadn't been dumped this evening. He wasn't being dumped now. He could have the woman he loved, and maybe, someday, she might love him back.

His head was featherlight, and his pulse a song. He started toward her then, because he couldn't not touch her, not now. "What are you saying?"

"I'm done going it alone. My soloist days are over. I want to be with you—if you'll have me."

His hands shook when he set them on her waist but only a little. It was scary, reaching for her, but it was scarier not to. When he kissed her, it felt like weeks and not hours since he'd done it. It was as bright as a dawn and as soothing as a homecoming.

Finally, after a few minutes of reacquaintance, reassurance, they broke apart.

"I was only able to play tonight because of you." She canted back so he could see the sincerity in her face. The pleading. "You ground me. Distract me. But you also ignite me. Make me secure enough to show other people my passion. I'm still scared, and I don't have all the answers. And I know—" Her grip on him tightened. "—I know I don't deserve your forgiveness. I feel like an idiot even asking for it."

"Not an idiot. Maybe a chump."

There was a beat in which she caught his sarcasm and then offered, "A boob?" Her eyes flashed with banked heat.

"Nah, just a tiny bit the fool." His words were playful, and two weeks ago, he wouldn't have said them. She made him spark.

"I'm a chastened fool, then," she assured him. "Like the most chastened."

He pulled her close. They didn't need to flay themselves. They'd both made missteps, but the past had ceased to matter. This was about what came next. "And I'm a string that's been overwound. You loosen me up just enough."

It wasn't even that, really. It was that when she struck him, he rang true to pitch.

"Everyone else was afraid to pound on you," she teased.

"But not you."

"Not me. I'm going to keep being a mess. And I don't know if I can play again. That won't frustrate you?"

The muscles of her back tensed under his hands, and he tried to stroke her worries away. "Never. Whatever you do, I'll be here…probably still being really uptight."

"I'd be sad if you weren't."

"Which is just one of the things I love about you."

He laughed as he kissed her and as she melted into him. Heat, joy, and trust: They were a prelude, a motif on which he and Kristy would play variations on through the years.

Brennan couldn't wait.

ACKNOWLEDGMENTS

The genesis of "Appassionata" is the voice and piano teachers, choir directors, and piano technicians who've been in my life: Peggy, Miss Mac, Mary, Denise, Su, and Jim. If I can't play Brahms and Schubert, that's my own fault, but you taught me to love music, respect instruments, and value creativity and beauty, and this story wouldn't have been possible without you.

I am deeply grateful to my critique partner Genevieve Turner for reading, oh, six versions of "Appassionata" and never making me feel guilty for vacillating, dithering, and handwringing about it. Brennan and Kristy would not have come into focus without beta reads from Ruby Lang and Olivia Dade. Olivia deserves a double shout out for conceiving of this anthology, inviting me to be part of it, and being the rarest and most wonderful friend. Kristi Yanta's developmental edit of this story improved it immeasurably, and I'm so thankful for her notes and generosity. Finally, Crystalle at Victory Editing did the final proofread of the manuscript, and any remaining errors are mine.

BIOGRAPHY

Emma Barry is a novelist, full-time mama, recovering academic, and former political staffer. When she's not reading or writing, she loves her twins' hugs, her husband's cooking, her cat's whiskers, her dog's tail, and Earl Grey tea.

For more info about the author, visit

Emma's website: https://authoremmabarry.com/

ALSO BY EMMA BARRY

The Easy Part

Special Interests (Book 1)

Private Politics (Book 2)

Party Lines (Book 3)

Fly Me to the Moon with Genevieve Turner

Star Dust (Book 1)

Earth Bound (Book 2)

Round Midnight (Book 3)

A Midnight Feast (Book 4)

Free Fall (Book 5)

Fly Me to the Moon, Volume One, Box Set

Standalones, Anthologies, and Collections

Free

Dispatches

"Kissing and Other Forms of Sedition" in Rogue Desire

"The Fourth Estate" in Rogue Affair

"Run" in Rogue Hearts

UNRAVELED

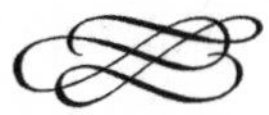

OLIVIA DADE

This story is dedicated to my mom, the sort of elementary school teacher kids hugged around the knees in the grocery store, faces alight with joy at seeing her. I love you.

The more tightly wound the man, the faster he unravels.
Math teacher Simon Burnham—cool, calm, controlled—can't abide problems with no good solution. Which makes his current work assignment, mentoring art teacher Poppy Wick, nothing short of torture. She's warm but sharp. Chaotic but meticulous. Simultaneously the most frustrating and most alluring woman he's ever known. And in her free time, she makes murder dioramas. *Murder dioramas,* for heaven's sake. But the more tightly wound a man is, the faster he unravels—and despite his best efforts, he soon finds himself attempting to solve three separate mysteries: a murder in miniature, the unexplained disappearance of a colleague…and the unexpected theft of his cold, cold heart.

* * *

Content warnings: on-page sex, profanity, brief mentions of witnessed family violence during childhood, and discussion of a fictional diorama murder.

CHAPTER 1

A mere ten minutes after first setting eyes on her, Simon had already drawn his initial conclusion: In terms of professional appearance and deportment, Ms. Poppy Wick was a disgrace.

In defiance of the faculty dress code, she was wearing jeans. Not even dark, trouser-style jeans, which at a casual glance might be mistaken for appropriate work pants. No, hers clung faithfully to her ample hips and bottom. More importantly, they were faded and splotched with…what *was* that? Some sort of floury glue concoction? And now that he was looking more closely, flecks of paint revealed themselves on the denim covering her round thighs. A rainbow of color, and a silent testament to her defiance of necessary rules.

On Fridays, to be fair, teachers could donate money to charity in exchange for wearing jeans. But today was Tuesday, and the entire faculty of Marysburg High was sitting around cafeteria tables listening to the superintendent's latest consultant drone on while wearing a suit more expensive than any teacher could ever afford, and Ms. Wick was *doodling*.

He glanced closer.

A skull, surrounded by ivy. Dear Lord.

At the very least, she might have had the dignity to sketch cubes or other three-dimensional geometric shapes, as he sometimes did. Although not during faculty meetings, and never with his hair in two wispy, drooping little reddish-blond buns, perched high on either side of the head. He kept his own dark hair neatly trimmed every two weeks and in strict order, despite its distressing tendency to wave.

She'd had a free seat beside her for the faculty meeting, and he'd taken it in hopes of observing her at least once before their respective positions became clear. Which was optimal, since knowledge of his scrutiny and its purpose would naturally change her behavior. Heisenberg's Uncertainty Principle: The Teacher Observation Corollary.

He sighed and began making a list of topics he and Ms. Wick would need to address in their initial consultation.

Why their principal, Tess Dunn, had assigned him as the mentor to an art teacher, he hadn't faintest clue. Yes, Ms. Wick had recently joined the faculty, and all first-year teachers at MHS received a mentor, no matter how long they'd taught in other school districts. Yes, mentors were chosen at random. But he was the chair of the math department, unsuited for—

Something was nudging his arm.

When he looked up and to the right, his mentee winked at him, hazel eyes sparkling above rosy cheeks. She nudged him again, and he looked down at her spiral-bound notebook, currently poking against his forearm.

Her looping script wasn't difficult to read. *Want to play Hangman?*

Ms. Wick appeared to be in her mid-forties, perhaps a year or two older than him. Still, she'd passed him a note, invited him to play a juvenile game, as if she were one of their sophomores.

He stared at her, aghast.

Retrieving her notebook, she added more, then slid it back in his direction.

C'mon. You're obviously distracted too.

Well, yes. But that was her fault entirely. Especially since, now that they were face-to-face, he could spot yet more paint flecks dappling her high, broad forehead and rounded chin. There was even a little blue smear just above the bow of her curved lips.

Another quick note. *I'll let you choose the word or phrase.*

Sighing, he turned to a fresh page in his own legal pad, determined to quash her unacceptable behavior.

Ms. Wick, we are in a professional sett—

The legal pad was yanked out from beneath his hand, and she jotted something beneath his half-finished scold. On *his* paper.

How did you know my name? She paused, then huffed out an amused breath. *I'm that memorable, am I?*

Eyes narrowed at her audaciousness, he reclaimed his notebook with a decisive tug.

Not at all. Earlier today, I was assigned to be your first-year mentor.

There. That should put an end to her unprofessionalism.

She tilted her head for a moment, forehead crinkled, before her impish grin flickered back to full brightness. *Damn. I was hoping for Candy Albright.*

Well, she'd at least written it on her own notebook this time. Small victories.

He shouldn't ask. He wouldn't ask.

Yet the word somehow appeared on his paper, in his usual, careful print. *Why?*

She's equally terrifying, but in a FUN way.

Ms. Wick had underlined *FUN* three times.

He paused, unable to understand why that stung. Being fun had never constituted one of his goals, and if he terrified her, wouldn't that better assure her compliance with faculty rules and regulations?

He should be glad he both bored and terrified her, after a mere quarter-hour in her presence. He *was* glad.

Odd, though. She didn't *seem* terrified. In fact, she seemed to be writing him yet another note, despite his scowling disfavor.

Candy cornered me about Oxford commas last week. It was a memorable discussion.

Yes, he imagined so. Candy's opinions on grammar were both numerous and intense, and usually shared at top volume.

Ms. Wick still wasn't done writing. *She left me an informative pamphlet on my desk. Then she told me how glad she was that I'd replaced Mildred, cackled, and shouted DING-DONG, THE WITCH IS DEAD.*

She beamed at him, as if inviting him to share the humor, and for a moment he almost smiled back.

Clearing his throat, he turned away instead, as if preoccupied by the consultant's PowerPoint slides. No, he would not encourage his mentee's behavior. This conversation was done, at least until after the faculty meeting.

But minutes later, when he again glanced at his legal pad, he discovered that she'd managed to write a question there without him noticing, a question so simple he'd be churlish not to answer.

I should know my mentor's name. What is it?

Dammit. He had to respond. The rules of politeness required it, as did a smoothly functioning mentor-mentee relationship.

Simon Burnham, he wrote on his paper. *Chair of the Math Department.*

At some point, she'd returned to her doodling. Now the ivy swept across the page, sliding through openings in the skull, the vines encroaching and ominous, edged and shadowed in black.

She wasn't paying him a bit of attention anymore, and he stared at her profile for a moment, unable to reconcile her blend of cheer and macabre sensibilities, unable to determine why he suddenly wanted her eyes back on him.

His dignity wouldn't allow him to poke her with his notebook, as she'd done to him. Instead, he lightly tapped her bare arm with his fingertips, just below where she'd pushed up the sleeves of her cardigan.

Her skin was warm and giving, even under such a tentative touch. When he withdrew his hand, he clenched it around an unexpected burn.

As she turned those bright eyes back to him, he pointed to his paper. She read his note, then contemplated him for a moment, smile absent, her scrutiny uncomfortably sharp.

Shall I call you Simon or Mr. Burnham? she finally wrote in her notebook.

He knew trouble when it nudged him in the arm.

If first impressions proved accurate, Ms. Wick was a problem with no clear solution, a human version of the Riemann Hypothesis, and he wanted none of it. None of her.

Mr. Burnham, he wrote, and determinedly ignored her for the rest of the faculty meeting.

* * *

When the lengthy meeting ended, Ms. Wick tucked her notebook beneath her arm, slung her purse over her shoulder, and raised a pale eyebrow. "Have I passed initial inspection, Mr. Burnham?"

Her voice was slightly hoarse, low and warm with amusement. It seemed expressly designed for sharing confidences and laughter. But Simon had never indulged in those sorts of dangerous intimacies, and he didn't intend to start now. Especially with someone like her.

"I'll meet you in your room shortly," he said.

At that, she snorted. "I'll take that as a no."

The prospect didn't seem to bother her. She left the table after a saucy salute in his direction, and within a dozen confident strides, she was linking arms with one of the other art teachers and whispering briefly before they both convulsed with mirth as they left the cafeteria.

Maybe she was laughing at him. His rigidity. His coldness.

Fortunately, he didn't care about her good opinion. He cared about professionalism and hard work and creating an orderly, calm environment for himself and his students alike. As long as the personal lives and judgments of his colleagues didn't affect job performance, they were irrelevant. Hell, he didn't even know why Mildred had left, or why Candy was so happy to see the older woman gone. He didn't need to know, and he didn't want to.

Although Mildred, as of last year, hadn't mentioned the prospect of leaving, and the customary ceremonies accompanying the retirement of such a long-time teacher hadn't occurred. No announcement in a faculty meeting or presentation of flowers and a gift. No potluck in the library, which he visited only to offer a handshake before promptly departing once more.

Odd. Very odd.

Considering the matter, he slowly walked to the cafeteria door, only to find himself beside Candy and one of the newer English teachers—Greg? Griff? It didn't matter.

"Ms. Albright." Simon was speaking to her. Why was he speaking to her? "Please pardon the interruption. I was wondering—"

No, he wasn't a gossip, and he didn't care.

Her brows rose behind her horn-rimmed glasses. "Yes, Mr. Burnham?"

He wrestled with himself for a moment.

"Mildred. Mrs. Krackel." There. That wasn't a question. Thus, he wasn't a gossip.

Greg-Griff-Whoever turned away to cough into his fist, shoulders shaking, while a tiny, evil smile curved Ms. Albright's mouth.

"Mildred got what she deserved," she declared. "Mary Shelley would be pleased."

Then she marched down the hall without another word, her English Department colleague at her shoulder.

Terrifying, Ms. Wick had called Ms. Albright.

Mary Shelley had written *Frankenstein,* a story of horror and violence and transgression. And the author would be pleased about what happened to Mrs. Krackel? What precisely had Ms. Albright thought Mildred *deserved?*

The halls of the school seemed to empty with astonishing quickness that evening, and by the time he'd stopped by his room to gather his briefcase and journeyed to the opposite end of the school, where Ms. Wick's classroom was located, shadows were amassing in the corners. His footsteps echoed in an unsettling way as he strode down halls he'd rarely visited.

His pace quickened as he neared her door. It was getting late, and he didn't intend to spend longer with his mentee than absolutely necessary.

She was sitting at her desk, her high forehead crinkled as she typed on her laptop. Another man, one less intent on the business at hand, one interested in such matters, might have called that evidence of her concentration *endearing*.

Her shades were closed against the gathering dusk outside, and the overhead fluorescent lights didn't entirely banish the gloom. To his surprise, however, the expansive room, stuffed with work tables and cabinets, was neater than Ms. Wick herself upon first glance.

He'd have time to inspect her classroom organization later. His first priority: making the rules and expectations regarding their relationship—their mentor-mentee relationship, that is—clear.

When he knocked on her doorframe, she looked up from her laptop placidly, with no sign of startlement.

Even as he approached her desk, he began instructing her. "Per Principal Dunn's request, I will observe your seventh period class for five consecutive days, beginning this upcoming Monday. Since seventh period is one of my planning periods, I will stay the entire length of the class. As I observe, I will evaluate your performance based on criteria outlined in the memo you should have received via e-mail about the mentorship program last month. If you need another copy, I can forward one to you."

"I don't need one." Her lips quivering, she shook her head. "Shockingly, I managed to keep track of the memo."

Ignoring her impertinent choice of adverb, he continued. "After class, assuming you don't have to leave for any necessary meetings, I will share my observations with you, and at the end of the week, I will write my initial evaluation, which, once approved by Principal Dunn, will be sent to you. After next week, we will meet monthly to discuss your progress or lack thereof. Other observations may occur, based on necessity. Any questions?"

If he'd expected her to be cowed by his blunt speech, intimidated into silence by the prospect of his judgment, he would have been disappointed. If anything, those hazel eyes of hers had brightened further, alight with...challenge? Amusement?

"Of course I have questions." She propped her elbows on her desk and rested her chin on her entwined, paint-flecked fingers. "How long have you been teaching, Mr. Burnham?"

His frown pinched his brows. "Twenty years last fall. How is that relevant? Are you concerned I have insufficient expertise in pedagogy to serve as your mentor?"

"No," she said, one of her little buns now sagging only half an inch above her left ear. "I was merely curious."

To return her question in kind would not indicate curiosity of his own, but instead provide necessary context for his mentoring efforts. Professionalism demanded more information, and he was always, always a consummate professional.

"And yourself, Ms. Wick? How many years have you been a teacher?"

"Twenty-four." Her gaze remained solely on him, and he found himself shifting beneath its keen sharpness. "Before this, I taught near D.C., but I wanted to move closer to my parents. I'm an only child, and their health is getting more precarious by the year."

Fortunately, she'd answered the question he wouldn't have allowed himself to ask: *Why did you change schools?*

"Any other concerns or queries?" If not, he intended to perform a preliminary inspection of her room and evaluate her organizational system and abilities.

"Oh, countless. But we have plenty of time for those." She smiled at him, very slowly. One might almost have called the expression *smug*. "That said, I should probably warn you about the unit we're starting next week."

He merely looked at her, waiting for whatever had prompted that mischievous curve of her pink, pink mouth.

Her explanation didn't provide any clarity. "We're tackling three-dimensional representation of objects and scenes and discussing the intersection of art and public service."

That all sounded completely, laudably appropriate and professional to him. So why—

"Specifically," she continued, "we're studying Frances Glessner Lee's mid-century efforts to advance forensic science through her

Nutshell Studies of Unexplained Death. Then the students will create their own educational dioramas, upon topics of their choosing."

Unexplained death? What the hell?

She waved a casual hand. "And, of course, I'll bring in an example of my own work as further inspiration."

He blinked at her, still stuck on the *unexplained death* bit. "Your... own work?"

"During summers and in my spare time, I create and sell my own dioramas." Her smile was no longer merely smug. It was now a wide, gleaming, toothy taunt. "If I didn't enjoy teaching so much, I might consider doing my dioramas full-time, since I've amassed an appreciative audience for my work."

This. This was why she was pleased, why her rosy cheeks glowed so cheerily. He could tell that much, but he still didn't understand *why*.

And she wasn't offering him the necessary context. Not this time. Oh, no, her soft lips were pressed shut as she waited for the question. Waited for him to break.

Ten minutes ago, he'd have sworn he never would. But that stupid, wispy bun was almost touching the flushed tip of her ear, and the blue streak above her mouth was mocking him, and her delighted grin plumped those round cheeks, and he had to ask. He *had* to.

"What—" He cleared his throat, studying her file cabinet as if it held vast importance in his eventual evaluation of her teaching. "What is your work, specifically?"

She didn't answer until he met her gaze again, and he didn't know whether to admire or despise her for it.

"Murder dioramas," she said.

As soon as he noticed he was gaping at her, open-mouthed, he snapped his jaw shut.

Deep breath. Raise an eyebrow. Seem only distantly engaged in the discussion.

"Murder dioramas?" he repeatedly coolly. "I'm afraid I'll require more detail, so as to determine the appropriateness of your work for a classroom setting."

Her grin only widened. "Oh, naturally."

She made him wait again, because of course she did.

"Yes, Ms. Wick?" he eventually prodded.

"Sorry. My mind must have wandered for a moment. It's getting late, isn't it?" She glanced at the clock on the wall, and then gave what seemed to be a genuine gasp. "Oh, damn, I'm going to be late for my oil change."

Jumping to her feet, she began shoving papers into a tote and searching for her keys.

From all appearances, she intended to leave him without further explanation, and that was unacceptable. Completely and utterly unacceptable.

He stepped close enough to interrupt her frantic efforts. "An explanation, Ms. Wick."

"Fine." Apparently lacking the time to taunt him further, she met his eyes and quickly summarized her ghoulish hobby. "My business is called Crafting the Perfect Murder. I imagine and recreate a violent crime in miniature form, complete with subtle clues as to what happened, why, and who was responsible. I also provide witness statements. People buy the dioramas and attempt to unravel the mystery, and I can either send them the solution or not, as they desire."

His mouth temporarily refused to form words.

"My dioramas are art, but people with plenty of spending money also buy them as a party game, especially around Halloween. You know, competing as to who can solve the case first." Glancing down, she finally located her keys and brandished them in triumph. "There they are!"

Finally, his tongue came untethered.

"People *pay* for that?" he asked, incredulous.

Immediately, he wished he'd bitten that tongue instead, because she took a step backward and flinched, her smile vanishing in a microsecond. At the sudden movement, her failing bun unraveled entirely, the spiral of fine hair falling over her ear and against her reddening cheek.

Dammit.

The remark hadn't been intended as a referendum on the quality of her work, as he had no way of judging that. He hadn't even meant it as an insult, although he undoubtedly found such a hobby macabre in the extreme. More, he'd been confused as to why anyone would invite violence and confusion into their home if they had a choice not to, and wondering whether she could possibly get paid enough for her work to defray the costs of her creations.

But she'd clearly taken his thoughtless comment as a slight against her work, and perhaps rightly so. Politeness required that he make amends. Immediately. Before the memory of the hurt in her eyes, however quickly masked, twisted his gut further.

"Ms. Wick, please for—"

But it was too late for apologies. She was already speaking, already headed for the door.

"If you think what I do deserves so little respect, I dare you to solve the mystery in the diorama I'm bringing to class next week. Maybe then you'll have a better idea why people *pay for that*, as you so charmingly put it." When she reached the door, she swiveled to face him. "I have to leave. Are you coming or not?"

He dropped his chin to his chest for a moment. "I, uh—I'd planned to evaluate the layout and organization of your classroom, if that's acceptable."

The inspection could have occurred next week, of course, but he needed to sit and think a minute. Wait until solid ground formed beneath him once more.

She shrugged. "Knock yourself out. Just ask a custodian to lock up behind you, please."

"I will." He didn't offer another apology. Instead, he simply watched her flee from his presence, her rapid footsteps retreating into silence.

Terrifying. Not in a fun way.

That was him.

He sat in her desk chair, and it was still warm from her body.

Math. That would clear his troubled thoughts. Seven squared was forty-nine. Seven cubed was 343. Seven to the fourth power was 2,401. Seven to the fifth power was—

The lights went out. In the evening, the hallway lights were dim, and they barely penetrated the sudden, choking blackness of the classroom.

"Hello?" he called. "I'm still here."

There were footsteps in the distance, shuffling and steady. Coming closer.

"Hello!" he called again.

No one answered, but someone was approaching. Only steps away now.

Mildred got what she deserved.

Involuntarily, he shivered and leapt to his feet. He wasn't staying any longer in a dark room, with mysterious footsteps—

The lights flickered back on, and a moment later, Mrs. Denham, one of the custodians, poked her head in the doorway. "Did you say something?"

His heart was rabbiting, and he gripped the edge of Ms. Wick's desk with both hands. "The lights..." He pointed at them, as if the custodian couldn't locate them for herself. "There's a problem with them. They went out without warning."

Mrs. Denham's smile was kind, if a bit patronizing. "In this wing of the school, the overheads use motion sensors to reduce energy consumption. If you don't move for a while, they'll go out, but as soon as you wave an arm, they'll come right back on. Don't worry."

"Oh." Of course. Of course. "Thank you."

"Next summer, they'll install the sensors on your side of the school," the custodian added. "Why are you here, anyway, instead of your own classroom?"

It was yet another question that didn't have a single, clear answer.

He hated those sorts of questions. Always had, always would.

So before he could make a fool of himself yet again, before he spent another moment contemplating a problem with no solution, he said goodbye to Mrs. Denham and left.

CHAPTER 2

By the following Monday, Simon's mind had settled itself, regaining its accustomed calm clarity.

Or at least it would have, had he not overhead part of a murmured conversation in the faculty lounge, as he was removing his usual healthy-but-filling lunch from the shared refrigerator. Two members of the science department were huddled up close at the round table, brows furrowed in…was that concern? Fear?

When he heard the word *Mildred,* he lingered in front of the refrigerator. Bending at the waist, he extended an arm, as if unable to locate the insulated bag positioned directly in front of him, in its normal spot.

"…such a shame, what happened," one of his colleagues whispered.

The other teacher nodded emphatically. "I feel so much less safe now."

At that moment, he happened to accidentally knock over a can of Diet Coke in the refrigerator, and the noise halted the conversation behind him. When it didn't resume after a moment, he admitted defeat, righted the can of soda, gathered his lunch, and left to eat in his classroom.

If the incident left him rattled, that was only to be expected.

Anyone would be distressed by the possibility that a longtime coworker had mysteriously vanished, or possibly even met a violent end.

And if the memory of how Ms. Wick had cringed and stepped back from him, hurt dousing the sparkle in those hazel eyes, also came to mind uncomfortably often, surely that was natural under the circumstances. For the purposes of a productive mentor-mentee relationship, open lines of communication would prove crucial. Any logical professional would feel compelled to apologize and make necessary amends as soon as possible.

Accordingly, he'd hoped to arrive in her classroom several minutes before the start of seventh period, allowing him enough time to speak privately with Ms. Wick and offer his regrets for his unguarded, hurtful remark. But one of his sixth-period students had appeared distressed at the results of the test he'd handed back earlier in the period, and he needed to talk with her at the end of class to reiterate the various ways she could receive extra help and/or raise her grade. His regular after-school hours for struggling students, for example, or extra credit work—or even the option of retaking the test at a future date, when she felt more confident in the mathematical concepts covered.

"You can rectify the situation," he'd calmly promised, after outlining her various avenues for assistance. "I will help."

By the time the student departed his classroom, no longer near tears, he had no hopes of a private discussion with Ms. Wick. In fact, he arrived at her doorway just as the bell rang for the start of seventh period. Closing the door behind him, he leaned against it and observed.

Her students had already settled at their two-person tables and were beginning to write in notebooks they'd evidently retrieved from the open cabinet near the doorway. On the whiteboard, Ms. Wick had written their initial task for the class, a five-minute writing prompt to settle them down and channel their thoughts toward the day's lesson: *What one topic do you wish people understood more fully? Why? What do you wish they knew about that topic?*

He'd known, of course, what work awaited the students. Ms. Wick had e-mailed him her week's lesson plans on Saturday, attaching the agendas and objectives for each day and listing the state standards her lessons satisfied.

Her thoroughness had surprised him, although perhaps it shouldn't have. Not once he'd seen the orderliness of her classroom, despite all the potential for mess and chaos inherent in art classes.

He blamed those droopy buns for misleading him so badly.

Today, as she set up her laptop and prepared her presentation about Frances Glessner Lee, she looked much more professional in her clothing choices and overall appearance. Her black dress fell softly to her calves, swirling as she bustled around the room. Her chunky amber-colored necklace and dangling earrings framed her round, lively face.

Only one bun today, it seemed. It perched high atop her head, still messy, but in a way that looked somehow deliberate and neat nevertheless. Wavy, fine tendrils caressed her cheeks.

She was the prettiest witch in the forest.

Startled by his uncharacteristic flight of fancy, he jotted a note in his legal pad: *Discuss faculty dress code.*

Speaking of witchy, there was an unusual number of young women clad entirely in black in this class. If he wasn't mistaken, all members of the state-champion girls' softball team.

When Ms. Wick turned away for a minute, producing something large and cloth-covered from behind her desk and setting it on an empty table nearby, he heard one girl whispering to another.

"Freakin' finally," the student with cornrows hissed excitedly. "The murder unit."

The other young woman, her skin powdered pale, extended her fist for bumping. "This is our moment, Tori."

Then Ms. Wick called the class to order, and he watched over twenty years of teaching experience at work. Using a well-organized PowerPoint presentation, she relayed Frances Glessner Lee's story with enthusiasm, covering various objectives while inviting student interaction and gearing it toward their interests whenever possible.

And their interests all appeared to tend toward one topic, and one topic alone: bloodshed.

"Dude," Tori muttered to her friend. "Look at those stab wounds."

In the current slide, projected onto the whiteboard, a male doll lay face-down on the floor of a meticulously crafted and detailed bedroom, red splotches marring his blue-striped pajamas. A female doll lay equally dead and bloody in the bed nearby.

"—included witness statements," Ms. Wick said. "Her attention to detail was remarkable, as you can see. Let's focus on another scene, which includes a calendar with flippable pages. Using a single-hair paintbrush, she would write tiny letters, one by one. And please note those amazing stockings on the victim here, knitted by hand with straight pins, as well as the working locks she created for windows and—"

Given the subject, Ms. Wick's enthusiasm was inappropriate at best.

Nevertheless, her students seemed enthralled. Whenever she paused, various hands waved in the air, while other kids took feverish notes.

"Wasn't it weird for a woman to do things like that, back in the '40s and '50s?" the pale-powdered girl asked.

Ms. Wick considered her answer for a moment. "Although forensic science was a relatively new field then, police work was dominated almost entirely by men. Some bristled at her intrusion into that domain, yes."

A greasy-haired kid, slouched in his chair, raised his hand. "I bet it helped that she was rich."

"You're exactly right, Travis." Ms. Wick smiled at him. "Because of her family's prominence, she had influential supporters. Her money also allowed her to woo students to her week-long courses, complete with a concluding banquet at the Ritz-Carlton."

Several students groaned at that, while one boy in a hoodie muttered, "The Ritz? Sweet."

"But whatever encouraged investigators to take her classes," she continued, "by the end of their week of instruction, after studying her dioramas, those students found themselves much better able to evaluate crime scenes in a systematic way, gather evidence, and draw logical conclusions from what they'd seen. And her work was so brilliant, her Nutshell Studies are used to train investigators to this day. That's why the solutions aren't publicly available."

A girl at the table next to him twitched suddenly. As her hand shot into the air, her face alight, she began to grin.

Revelation. Watching it dawn on a student's face was a privilege, one he didn't take for granted. He'd been chasing that particular expression for over twenty years, day by day.

"Go ahead, Amanda," Ms. Wick said to the young woman.

"If you think about it, what she did was really clever." Amanda waved an impatient, dismissive hand. "I mean, obviously her dioramas were smart, and awesome in an artistic sense and all, but that's not what I'm talking about."

Ms. Wick rested her elbows on her lectern. "Okay."

"If she was going to barge into a male-dominated field, what better way to do it than with dollhouses? Something that was considered girly or whatever." Amanda twisted her mouth, trying to find the right words. "She used the things girls were allowed to do, the things they were taught, to elbow her way into things she wasn't supposed to do."

If he'd been the recipient of such an approving beam from Ms. Wick, he imagined he'd feel exactly as pleased as her student currently looked.

"I think you've touched on a key point there, Amanda," she said. "Let's talk a bit more about that, and then discuss the specific techniques Lee used to recreate her scenes in three dimensions, as well as how art and public service are often intertwined. After that, you'll have some time to consider what you'd like your own educational dioramas to include. I've also brought one of my own dioramas for your inspection. If any of you manage to solve its mystery before the end of the week, I have a reward waiting for you."

Over twenty heads swiveled toward the table near her desk, where her cloth-covered diorama was evidently waiting.

"I Googled her dioramas, and they're extra-gory," Tori whispered to her friend. "This is the best day ever."

"Bring on the carnage," the pale girl declared with unmistakable glee. "Do you think the reward is, like, an invitation to watch an autopsy?"

Pinching the bridge of his nose between thumb and forefinger, Simon sighed.

* * *

As the students spent the end of the class planning their own dioramas, Simon claimed one of the magnifying glasses provided by Ms. Wick and studied her work up close.

The diorama she'd created included three rooms of a small house: a bedroom, a bathroom, and a living room. The living room was charred almost beyond recognition, with a blackened corpse on the floor. The edges of the bedroom also showed evidence of fire, but the room hadn't been incinerated in the same way as the living room. The bathroom, in contrast, appeared entirely undamaged, pristine other than the hair clippings glistening with faux-moisture in the marble sink's drain.

According to the written information provided, two brothers had lived in the house. One, Kaden, lay dead in the living room. The other —Barron—had managed to escape through the bedroom window in a panic, the encroaching flames too intense to attempt to save his sibling.

Outside the dwelling, a police officer stood near her four primary witnesses and suspects. The surviving brother, of course, but also an ex-girlfriend of the victim, who was suspected of having violated the restraining order Kaden had filed against her. Lingering nearby were a neighbor with a grudge—the two brothers had a habit of throwing loud parties late at night, evidently—and a landlord who'd threatened consequences if Kaden didn't stop smoking inside the unit.

Simon had all week to solve the mystery, so he decided to study the witness statements another day and focus on the diorama itself today. Not so much the evidence of murder contained within and outside the miniature home, but rather the evidence of Ms. Wick's labors. The diorama as a piece of art, rather than a crime scene.

Simon could not claim to be an aesthete, by any means.

Still. Her artistry, however macabre its inspiration, was...astonishing. Rigorous precision coupled with unbounded creativity and skill. Some of the furnishings she'd bought as is, perhaps, but no miniature store provided half-burned recliners or stacks of papers on a desk, their written contents just visible with a magnifying glass and the use of tweezers, or the impression of a heeled shoe in the dirt outside the living room window, or a bandage on an elderly landlord's arm.

He would have bet his 401K that the suspects' clothes were hand-stitched. She hadn't missed a detail, not the miniscule lighter just poking out of the neighbor's back pocket, not the way all the men's shoelaces were double-knotted, not the spurned ex-girlfriend's choppy haircut.

To complete her gruesome creation, Ms. Wick had to have mastered an astounding array of mediums and techniques, and her hands must have been steady as a neurosurgeon's.

Everything was exactly in scale, which required mathematical skill too.

The realization pleased him more than it should have.

The final bell rang while he was still lost in contemplation, but he barely noted the buzz of students chatting, packing up their backpacks, and heading out the door, bound toward home or work or extracurricular activities.

"Are you ready to make an arrest?"

Her voice, though mischievous, didn't quite contain the warmth of their previous meeting, and he knew why. But her body next to his, their shoulders almost—almost—touching, radiated heat in a way that made him want to close his eyes and simply breathe in her faint scent of turpentine and soap.

He didn't, of course. Instead, ignoring her question, he turned stiffly and gestured toward the nearest table. "Let's discuss my initial observations."

With a mocking little bow of her head, she sat in a student chair. Tempted to choose the one beside her, he instead selected a seat safely across the table.

They were both professionals. No small talk was necessary.

"If today's lesson is any indication, you're obviously a teacher of great experience and skill, well able to keep the attention of a roomful of students while covering all necessary topics and meeting all required objectives. Your rapport with your students is remarkable, as is your ability to elicit participation from them. Your classroom is impeccably organized." He kept his voice cool, as befitted an objective mentor. "If the rest of this week's lessons prove similar to today's, I can only conclude that Marysburg High is fortunate to have you amongst its faculty."

He flicked a glance up from his notes, meeting her wide eyes.

An unkind observer might have described her mouth as agape, and a more whimsical man might have been tempted to throw a grape in there.

Those soft lips snapped shut quickly enough, however, when he continued.

"That said, the faculty's dress code appears to have escaped you. Today's outfit is appropriate and very, uh, becoming—"

Shit.

"—um, becoming *for a professional teacher*." There. Saved it. No room for misinterpretation. "But your clothing at the faculty meeting did not meet the standards set by school guidelines. No jeans, except on Denim Fridays, and all garments worn by teachers must be clean."

Since her eyes were currently narrowed slits of hazel affront, he was smart enough not to mention the faculty meeting's droopy buns. Those could wait for a debriefing session later in the week.

In the spirit of tearing off a bandage as quickly as possible, he continued hastily, before her glare lasered actual holes through his skull. "The contents of today's lecture, while fascinating and well-presented, also put you at risk for student and parental complaints. The topic was, in short, overly macabre and ghoulish. I would suggest you pick more school-appropriate topics in the future."

One of her pale eyebrows arched high. "Would you?"

She'd settled back in her chair, affront replaced by steely calm.

The expression bolted down his spine in a way he couldn't interpret. Was that electric jolt warning him he'd erred somehow? Was it a visceral response to the challenge betrayed by her pugnacious, upturned chin and haughty stare? Was it because, beneath that witchy, alluring dress, her plump thighs had shifted and rubbed—

No, it wasn't excitement. Professional evaluations did not prompt passion of any sort. Not for him, anyway.

If his tie suddenly constricted his breath, he'd merely fastened it a bit too tightly that morning. The prickling heat spreading lower and lower, making his button-down tease against every nerve ending his skin possessed, was simply the result of the school's inadequate HVAC system. Nothing more.

His throat might be dry, but he would remain entirely businesslike.

"I also believe you left the student diorama assignment too open-ended, given the limited time available for this unit. You might consider providing a handout of preapproved topics in the future." That was the last item on today's list, but he continued looking down at his legal pad. "Finally, I inadvertently insulted both you and your work last week. My remark was rude and uncollegial."

After sketching a tiny, perfect cube on the edge of his paper, he continued. "Furthermore, my study of your work today elucidated my comment's essential injustice. I might consider the subject matter disturbing, but it was quite evident why consumers would pay a great deal of money to possess such a wondrous, meticulous piece of artistry."

Two squared is four. Two cubed is eight. Two to the fourth power is sixteen.

He raised an expressionless face. "Please accept my sincere apologies."

Her face had also turned unreadable, but at least she wasn't openly scowling at him anymore. As always, small victories.

After a lengthy pause, she spoke slowly. "I'll address your feedback one topic at a time, if that's acceptable to you?"

He gave her a jerky nod, and somehow he already knew.

By the end of this conversation, he'd feel like a fool once more.

"Last Tuesday, the day of the faculty meeting, my students were making papier-mâché masks using paper plates, aluminum foil, hot glue guns, newspapers, flour, water, and paint. I defy anyone to oversee the making of those masks without finding their clothing soiled in some fashion, protective apron be damned." Her lips tilted up in a little, satisfied smile, a silent warning that this entire conversation was only going to get worse for him. "More importantly, if you'd consulted with Principal Dunn, you'd have discovered that we already discussed the issue of appropriate clothing and came to a mutual agreement on the matter."

Yes. This was definitely worse.

"On days like today, when I'm lecturing and likely to remain clean, I follow the standard dress code." She swept a hand downward, indicating her current outfit. "On days when my clothing is likely to get stained, I'm allowed to wear jeans and more casual tops. Because, as we both concluded, asking me to replenish my work wardrobe every time an item became slightly soiled was both unreasonable and cost-prohibitive."

No amount of exponential multiplication was going to save him now. "It appears I owe you another ap—"

"If I were you, I'd save further apologies until we're finished," she interrupted, still smiling. "You might as well beg forgiveness for everything at once. For the sake of efficiency, which I know is of the utmost importance to you."

Shit. *Worse* appeared to be an understatement.

"Now onto your next critique, concerning the inappropriateness of today's lesson." She ticked off her multipart response on her fingers. "First, inappropriateness is very much a subjective matter. I'm surprised a man like you, who seems to prize objectivity, would use such a nebulous, essentially undefinable concept as part of your feedback. Second, I ran the unit and its contents by Principal Dunn before the school year even began. She gave her approval. She did so because, third, I sent a letter home to the parents and guardians of my students weeks ago, one that described this week's topic in detail and required their signatures for student participation."

How he'd fucked up so badly, he couldn't even say. All he could do was keep listening, silent, as she enumerated the flaws in his conclusions.

"As far as listing a set of preapproved diorama topics—I agree such a list would contribute to greater efficiency in my classroom." She leaned forward, elbows on the desk. "But it would detract from the actual experience of making art, which is as much about the creative process as it is about the final result. I want my students to find topics that speak to them on an individual level, and I certainly don't know them well enough to be able to predict the contents of their hearts or the subjects that consume their innermost thoughts. I'm happy to guide them if they have difficulty choosing a topic, but I don't want to prematurely limit the expanse of their imaginations."

It all sounded like chaos to him. Total and complete chaos.

She tapped a fingertip on the table. "This isn't a math problem with one right answer, Mr. Burnham. There aren't even ten right answers, or a million right answers. There are *infinite* right answers."

That lack of surety was discomfiting at best. Terrifying at worst.

But it didn't matter how much he feared problems without a clear solution. What mattered: the wrong he'd done his colleague by presuming her less a professional than she actually was.

"I apologize, Ms. Wick. Again." He maintained eye contact as a reassurance of his sincerity, despite his desire to turn away in shame. "I've underestimated you, and I promise to try my best not to do so in the future."

He wouldn't make excuses for himself. He wouldn't. But she needed to understand, if only to comprehend—

Well, not the contents of his heart. But maybe his innermost thoughts. Some of them, anyway.

"I just—" Under her scrutiny, he fumbled for the right words. "As you said, maybe I should have talked to Principal Dunn before offering my critique. But I didn't want to get..."

No, he should just keep his mouth shut. His innermost thoughts were his to keep.

But it was too late. That same glow of revelation he'd seen on her student transfused Ms. Wick's expression, and her mouth pursed in a silent *oh*.

She blinked at him, her throat shifting as she swallowed.

"You didn't want to get me into trouble," she finally finished for him, her voice hoarse and warm and so liquid he could have bathed in it.

Yes. Yes, that was exactly what he'd tried not to say.

After giving herself a little shake, she sat up straighter. "I appreciate your consideration, Mr. Burnham, but you still could have *asked* me if I'd somehow addressed your concerns ahead of time, instead of assuming I hadn't."

He could have. It would, in fact, have been the logical way to handle the situation.

Which was…a disturbing realization.

An outside observer would almost conclude that he was, for some reason, *trying* to think badly of Ms. Wick. *Determined* to see flaws where they didn't necessarily exist.

It was yet another problem whose answer wasn't quite clear to him. Yet another mystery to unravel, when he'd never, ever, been good at interpreting clues.

"You're right." He didn't equivocate. "That's what I should have done."

Her chin dipped in a firm little nod. "Graciously conceded, Mr. Burnham. I forgive you. For everything."

The chunky amber spheres of her necklace glowed against her pale skin, and her eyes were fathomless.

"Please call me Simon," he said.

"Gladly." The curve of her lips was small and sweet. "And I'm Poppy."

She offered her hand, as if they were meeting for the first time, and he shook it. Her fingers were long and blunt, her palm warm and slightly rough, her grip firm.

He couldn't breathe.

As quickly as was polite, he let go and met her gaze. "If you're leaving soon, why don't I walk you to your car? The sun's going down earlier and earlier these days."

Shuffling steps in the darkness.

I feel so much less safe now.

Mildred got what she deserved.

No, Poppy wasn't going to that deserted parking lot alone. Not if he could help it.

"All right," she said after a moment, her gaze tentative, the words halting. "I just need five minutes, if you don't mind waiting."

He shook his head. "I don't."

The rules of gentlemanly behavior were clear under the circumstances, and he followed them. After she'd packed her belongings in her tote, he offered to carry it for her. As she locked her classroom door behind them, he scanned the dim hallway to ensure her safety. Once they reached her car, he made certain she left the lot before driving away himself.

The entire time, he tried to hide the disconcerting truth.

Her touch had incinerated him so thoroughly, he might as well be the house in her diorama. And the burn had left him feeling anything—anything—but gentlemanly and professional.

CHAPTER 3

As the seventh period bell rang on Wednesday, Simon sat at his usual table and congratulated himself on having remained cool, calm, and controlled for almost a full forty-eight hours, despite having spent several of those hours in Poppy's unsettling presence.

Yesterday, the students had begun creating their dioramas. *Controlled chaos* was perhaps the best way to describe her classroom then. Or possibly *paint-bedecked* and *glue-soaked*.

No wonder she'd worn her faded jeans again. That pretty black dress would have been absolutely *ruined*.

At the end of class, he'd asked whether she knew of any reasonable way to limit the mess created by her students during their projects. Not so much because the mess was excessive—which it wasn't, under the circumstances—or because mess bothered him in general—which it did, of course—but rather because cleaning up that mess required a considerable chunk of student time at the end of the period and an even more considerable chunk of Poppy's time after the students left.

"Well, I can't leave everything to the custodial staff. Mildred, the teacher I replaced, apparently used to have poor Mrs. Denham do all the cleanup, but that's just cruel. No wonder they hated her so much." Poppy had patted him on the arm then, the gesture not quite pitying, but not quite *not* pitying either. "Besides, Simon, mess is both inevitable and part of the artistic process for most people. Don't worry."

Yes, the contact burned, but her near-pity had helped temper the worst of it.

He'd helped her clean and made a quick stop back in his own classroom to gather the night's grading. Then once again, he'd walked her to her car, and once again, he'd been forced to recite prime numbers to himself that night before he could fall asleep.

Still, he'd neither insulted her nor pinned her against the classroom wall to claim that wide, impish mouth of hers. He hadn't even buried his fingers in her drooping bun and angled her head to reveal her soft neck, hadn't sucked at her rapid pulse there, hadn't left a mark with his teeth on her pale flesh.

Small victories. Small, small victories.

Today, he hoped, would prove equally satisfying.

Or, rather, *un*satisfying, but predictable. Understandable and under control.

The students were hard at work again this period, their educational dioramas beginning to take shape minute by minute. Occasionally, someone paused a moment to peruse the half-charred diorama perched at his table, but for the most part, no one went near him.

Which, now that he considered the matter, was rather odd.

Two students shared each work station, and space was tight. He'd deliberately placed himself at the very end of his long table, right next to the diorama, to leave Poppy's kids as much room as possible. But no one had moved to claim the open space or even bothered to deposit an overflow of supplies there.

Maybe she'd previously told them not to spread out on his table. It was the closest one to her desk, so maybe she reserved it for her sole use. Or maybe the students were simply too terrified of him, *not in a fun way*, to share the space.

Or maybe—

He could swear some of the Goth softball players kept looking at the table. Not him, not the diorama, the *table*. In fact, Tori was saying something to her pale-powdered friend right now, in between glances at the faux-wood surface. In response, the poor girl blanched even further, her black-lined eyes round with horror.

Casually, Simon got to his feet and wandered closer.

"I mean…" Tori said with a shudder. "Can you believe it?"

"I—" The other young woman clapped a hand to her belly. "I think I'm going to be sick."

Tori corralled a nearby trash can with her boot, nudging it toward their work station. "Here you go. If you have to hork, keep it as clean as possible."

Very practical. Simon was growing fonder of Tori by the minute.

"I'll never be able to use that table again." Nausea apparently conquered for the moment, the pale girl wrinkled her nose. "Not without picturing what happened…there."

He couldn't deny it any longer, even to himself. He really, really wanted a full explanation for Mildred's departure, because some of his imaginings were…

Well, he'd clearly seen one too many blood-soaked dioramas.

Just as Simon was mentally urging the Goth girls to elaborate, *elaborate,* they caught sight of him and hurriedly turned back to their dioramas-in-progress.

"So as I was telling you," Tori said a bit too loudly, "art often serves a crucial societal role when it comes to dissemination of important information."

"Why, yes," her friend affirmed. "I remember you saying that very thing only moments ago, as we discussed our class objectives for the day."

No point in lingering, except for the sheer entertainment value of their faux-conversation. He wasn't going to get any more information out of them.

Accordingly, he returned to the diorama and studied the booklet containing witness statements, looking for information he hadn't properly registered the first time. But no new clues stood out to him. Not a surprise, given his lack of—

Poppy gasped loudly, and his head jerked up.

He knew exactly where she was. Of course he did. If she was within sight, part of his attention never, ever left her.

"Ms. Wick, are you—" a tall young man with thick-framed glasses was asking, but she was already striding toward the classroom sink, her forehead pinched in seeming distress.

Simon intercepted her along the way. "What happened?"

"I'm fine, Demetrius. Don't worry," she called over her shoulder, and then answered Simon. "Hot-glue-gun burn on the back of my hand. I just need to—"

With a flick of his wrist, the water was running and set to a cool temperature. He guided her right hand beneath the spray, pulse hammering in his ears.

A reddening blotch marked the spot of her injury, visible even through the streaming water, and he scowled at it.

"Simon." Her voice was low and gentle. "To an art teacher, hot-glue-gun burns are basically badges of honor. They're inevitable and nothing to be concerned about."

His scowl only deepened. "You're in pain. Do you need to see the nurse?"

"No, Simon." Her hand moved, and suddenly he wasn't supporting it anymore. Instead, she was holding his, as if comforting *him*. "No. It's already feeling better. But I'll cover the spot with a bandage, if that would make you less worried."

If that would make you less worried.

The utter ridiculousness of his reaction—his *over*reaction—struck him in that moment, and he dropped her hand as if he'd been scorched himself.

Despite her minor injury, she was in complete control of herself and the situation, while he—he—

He wasn't. He wasn't in control of himself.

Spinning away from her, he hurried to the classroom door. "I'll get you a bandage from the nurse's office."

"But I—Simon!" She was calling out to him, trying to flag him down, but he pretended not to hear or see. "I already have ban—"

The door shut behind him, and he forced himself to walk, not run, away from her.

* * *

WHEN SIMON RETURNED toward the end of the period, a fresh box of bandages in hand, he found Poppy—no, Ms. Wick—bent over a student project, her burn already covered neatly.

At his arrival, she glanced up at him, but only for a moment before turning back to Amanda's diorama-in-progress. Which appeared, upon first glance, even more grisly than the murder scene on the table beside him. God help them all.

He settled in his usual spot, beside Ms. Wick's diorama. His heartbeat no longer echoed in his skull, and his hands were almost steady enough to create his own miniature crime scene. Not that he ever would ever employ his limited free time in such a disturbing manner.

Yes, fifteen minutes spent locked in his unlit room and mentally multiplying had accomplished wonders, as always. Outside his colleague's orbit, the impetus behind his urgent concern for her well-being had become clear, clear and comforting.

The rules of professional and gentlemanly conduct required him to assist a colleague in distress. Accordingly, he'd done so.

No need for either panic or concern.

In fact, he'd emerged from his classroom certain he could find rational solutions to all the mysteries cluttering his brain. With a little effort, he'd explain Mildred Krackel's disappearance, solve the miniature murder in Ms. Wick's diorama, and pinpoint precisely why the woman herself fascinated him so much. To accomplish the latter, he merely needed to determine the precise equation governing her behavior and the workings of her mind.

Then, solution in hand, he'd relegate her to the appropriate slot in his life.

Wick, Poppy. Talented but impertinent colleague. Best avoided for peace of mind.

Similarly, once he'd solved the other mysteries, he'd dismiss them from his thoughts. Simple as that.

And he could make progress this very moment, with the miniature crime scene. Given ample opportunity to observe the diorama and its clues more closely, surely he could discover the arsonist and murderer. Besides, P—*Ms. Wick* had dared him to solve the case. Doing so would prove his intelligence, and thus his ability to mentor her effectively.

Any professional would do the same.

With the help of a magnifying glass, he studied the blackened living room again. The shriveled corpse. The half-burned recliner. The bar cart, complete with tiny, tiny glass bottles full of amber liquid. The bookshelves. The overturned television. The ashtray. The neat row of shoes just inside the door. The charred jackets on a metal coat rack.

So much detail. She must have set those books on the shelves and positioned those sneakers and shiny Oxford shoes on the floor one by one. A jacket's sleeve was inside out, as if stripped off in a hurry. The laces of the shoes were all untied. The books seemed shoved into place with a careless hand.

Because of her meticulous labor, Simon could picture it clearly. Two young brothers coming home from a jog or a day's work, hanging their coats, unlacing and removing their shoes before relaxing into their shared home. Going about their typical evening.

They'd settled onto the recliner and the couch, drinks in hand. Kaden had lit a cigarette, tapping its burning end into the ashtray. Together, they'd watched their favorite show and read timeworn paperbacks.

Finally, Barron had gone to bed. Kaden had stretched out in the recliner and inadvertently fallen asleep. Then: disaster. Arson.

Murder.

Simon tried not to shudder.

Inside the bedroom, he didn't spy anything remarkable other than Ms. Wick's artistry. Singed walls. Two narrow beds, their covers smoke-darkened. Two nightstands, with more paperbacks set atop them. Two dressers. A desk with scattered papers. The open window, where Barron had escaped in a panic. A closet filled with both professional and casual clothing, only a laundry hamper cluttering its floor.

The brothers had lived neatly, it seemed.

Which made the pile of glistening hair at the bottom of the bathroom sink—the cramped space otherwise spotless—rather odd.

Were they saving money by cutting their hair at home? Had Barron been doing some impromptu manscaping?

Flipping through the witness statements, Simon searched for an explanation.

There wasn't any. Huh.

As he scrutinized the outside of the home—the green bushes, the faux-dirt under the windows, the suspects clustered around the police officer—the bell rang, and students were rushing out of the classroom.

Silently, he helped Poppy sweep the floor and sponge down the work stations, doing his best to stay across the classroom from her whenever possible.

"You don't have to do this, Simon," she said after a minute, her voice cautious.

He didn't look up from an intransigent smear of brown paint. "I understand that, Ms. Wick."

"Ms. Wick," she repeated, so quietly he almost didn't hear her.

After that, she didn't speak either. Instead, brow puckered in apparent thought, she set her classroom in order.

When the room was relatively pristine, he approached her desk. She was shutting down her laptop and gathering papers in preparation to work at home. Because, as she'd told him yesterday, her wing of the school sometimes seemed a bit too empty and quiet for her in the late afternoon. After admitting that, she'd turned her face away and fallen uncharacteristically silent.

She hadn't used the word *lonely*, but he'd heard it anyway.

Her situation was easy enough to understand, even without further explanation. Most of her fellow teachers didn't know her well, not yet. She'd only moved to the area several months ago, leaving her former colleagues and friends behind. Her parents required her support, from what she'd indicated on Monday.

Did she have support of her own? Anyone to help her unpack or offer comfort or—

"I'm ready, Mr. Burnham." The words were a near-sigh, and she slumped in her office chair. "What are today's observations?"

Those dark smudges beneath her eyes weren't paint, and her mouth was pale and pinched at the corners. Her hazel eyes had dulled.

Her wispy little buns were drooping. Not in a fun way.

Right now, as her mentor, he should be offering his thoughts about the lesson, giving guidance wherever necessary. Not that she really required any, from what he could tell.

Instead, he found himself asking, "Did it blister?"

She blinked up at him, confused.

"Your burn." He nodded down at her bandage. "Did it blister?"

"Oh." Her brow furrowed even more. "Uh, no. No blister. It barely even hurts anymore."

Which meant it *was* still hurting. He scowled at the cabinet containing her glue guns.

When he didn't say more, she added, "Thank you for bringing me a new package of bandages, by the way. It's good to have extras."

In the awkward silence that followed, the growl of her stomach was clearly audible.

No wonder she'd collapsed into her chair. She was hungry and hurting and tired and almost as alone as—

"Would you like to have dinner? With me?" He cleared his dry, dry throat. "We can go over my observations while we eat. Make it a working meal."

When she wrinkled her nose in an apologetic wince, he kept his expression blank.

A colleague refusing an invitation to a last-minute meeting did not and could not cause a pinch in his chest, and that twist in his gut indicated nothing but his own hunger.

"I'm sorry." Her round cheeks had pinkened, and she was smiling up at him, eyes alight once more. "I'd love to, but I have dinner with my parents every Wednesday night. They like to eat early, so we wouldn't even have time to grab coffee before I'd need to go."

The painful tension in his shoulders eased. "I understand."

"How about tomorrow night?" Her brows arched in question.

His lungs filled with air, so much air he was suddenly buoyant, and the tips of his ears flushed with heat. The HVAC system in this wing of the building must be malfunctioning.

"Certainly." Working dinners needn't be confined to Wednesdays alone. "I'll make a note of the appointment in my calendar."

Her lips twitched. "Please do."

Another long pause as his entire body seemed to vibrate with every heartbeat.

"I should probably head out." She pushed up the sleeves of her cardigan. "Will you walk me to the parking lot?"

He inclined his head. "Of course."

Earlier, as he'd calmed himself in his classroom, he'd packed everything he needed in his briefcase. After locking her room, then, they said goodbye to Mrs. Denham and walked to her car without any detours.

In the half-empty lot, instead of immediately easing herself inside her bright red car—an electric vehicle, he noted—she turned to him. "Where would you have taken me?"

Where would he have *taken* her?

If he didn't know better? If he weren't a rational man and a professional?

Anywhere. God, anywhere. Anywhere and everywhere.

Last night, he'd dreamed about it. Woken in sweat-soaked sheets, so hard he'd ached and throbbed. Stroked himself in the shower until he'd shuddered and gasped out an obscenity, eyes closed beneath the stinging spray, breath stuttering.

He'd take her in a soft bed, her round thighs spread wide, wide enough for his shoulders, her agile hands clutching his headboard as she moaned and squirmed and came against his tongue. He'd take her over the desk in his home office, her eyes hot and heavy-lidded as she watched him over her pale shoulder, his fingertips firm on her hips while he—

"Simon?" She was squinting at him, head tilted.

He shook his head. Hard. "Excuse me?"

"If I'd been able to go to dinner tonight, where would you have taken me?" she clarified. "Where are you taking me tomorrow, for that matter?"

Oh. Oh, yes. Dinner.

"Um..." The afternoon sunlight was in her eyes, so he moved slightly to the side, until his shadow blocked the blinding rays. "Your choice."

Whatever she wanted, he could accommodate. Normally, he selected restaurants after careful study of both online reviews and sanitation grades, but a polite coworker bowed to the preferences of others.

Mischief sparked in her expression. "Uh-uh. I don't think so. You're not spoiling my fun, Mr. Burnham."

When she said his last name like that, it didn't sound distant or formal at all.

Instead, it was a tease. A dart of affection aimed right between his ribs, where it lodged and stung.

"Your—" He licked his lips. "Your fun?"

She rested that generous, gorgeous butt against the side of her car and tilted her chin in challenge. "I'm curious where you like to eat. More than that, I'm curious where you think *I'd* like to eat."

His mouth opened, then closed.

He didn't go out for dinner much, so his favorite restaurants offered both takeout and faultless inspection records. Which now seemed inadequate, not to mention boring as fuck.

No, he'd do better to focus on where *she* might like to eat. Places that would please *her*.

But how could he possibly predict something like that? How could he solve a problem with so many unknown variables? They'd known each other less than two weeks, so how could he even try to guess what she'd want?

"Let's hear who you are and what you think of me, as expressed in restaurant form." She was grinning at him now, amused by his discomfiture. "C'mon. Out with it."

He couldn't help a tiny snort. "No pressure there."

What did he know about her, really? Other than how velvety her skin looked beneath the fluorescent lights, and how warmly she responded to student questions, and how focused and creative and patient she must be to create those bloody, bloody—

Wait. He had it.

At the sudden epiphany, a smug smile spread across his face.

For once, he'd put together clues and solved a mystery, and it tasted like victory. A small one, as always, but delicious nevertheless.

Delicious and morbid. So very morbid.

"Well..." His chest had puffed out a tad, and he didn't even care. "If you wouldn't mind driving into Richmond, there's a place you'd love."

He'd read about it months ago and cringed at the very thought of eating there. But, if his memory was correct, the review had praised the food and the restaurant's wholehearted commitment to its theme. Its terrible theme.

"Really?" Those reddish-gold brows arched again. "Tell me more."

Oh, this was going to feel *great*. "It's called That Good Night. It's only open for dinner."

"That Good Night." Her lips pressed together as she thought. "As in, *do not go gentle into?*"

He dipped his chin. "Exactly."

"So." She was gazing up at him, hair aglow in the sun, with such rampant curiosity and *warmth*. "The restaurant's name refers to death?"

"It's a former mortuary," he told her. "If I'm remembering correctly, the knives are actually scalpels, the water comes in formaldehyde bottles, and they serve their food in little coffins. The whole restaurant is death-themed."

"That's..." Her whisper was barely audible, and her eyes were wide. "That's the most amazing thing I've ever heard. Yes. Yes, I'd love to go there tomorrow."

He resisted buffing his nails against his cotton button-down, but it was a close call. "Good. I'll make reservations."

"I really need to go, but—" Somehow, she was only inches away now, so close the heat from her body taunted him. "Where would you have picked? For yourself, I mean?"

Since she was still leaning against her car, he must have moved forward without conscious volition. As if he were a compass needle seeking true north, or a man irresistibly drawn to temptation and trouble.

Which he wasn't. He never had been, not once in over four decades.

"When I invite someone for dinner, it's about that person. Not me." It wasn't a real answer, but it wasn't a lie either. "Even in a professional context."

He didn't feel like a professional, though. In such close proximity to her, he felt like nothing more than a mammal in rut.

"Oh, I think your invitation says plenty about you." She wasn't smiling anymore. Instead, her gaze was solemn and fixed on him with such clarity, he had to fight a flinch. "More than you probably realize."

When she got into her car, he stepped safely away and watched her leave. She was long gone before he managed to think of the smartest response to her statement.

And by then, it was much too late to run.

CHAPTER 4

If Simon and Poppy's shared meal at That Good Night were a train, it remained safely on track for a full two courses.

Over their Stopped Hearts of Palm bao bun appetizers and Dismembered Duck Confit entrées—both her picks, both unfamiliar to him, both served in coffins, both utterly delicious—they discussed the ways Marysburg High differed from her previous school. How to operate most efficiently in her new environment. When to visit the copy room, which administrator to see for certain questions and concerns, the most helpful front-desk secretary, and so forth.

As he'd learned through painful experience, she didn't need assistance with teaching. Still, he could offer practical tips about their specific school. And if he found himself admiring how the flicker of candlelight highlighted the curve of her neck, or noting the golden glow it imparted to her strawberry blond hair, well, no one needed to know that but him. It might constitute a weakness, but the chink in his armor wasn't visible to the naked eye.

Then, with almost no warning, and entirely due to his own negligence, their conversational train jumped the professional rails.

The server placed two thick slices of Murder by Chocolate cake in front of them, and Simon had no way to know they were speeding toward disaster with every bite.

"I'm sure you've noticed Amanda's diorama. Did you figure out the topic?" Poppy sipped at her mocktail, The Embalmer, between forkfuls of cake. "I'll give you a hint: Her mom's a nurse in the maternity ward of the local hospital."

With that information, everything he'd seen suddenly slotted into place. "Her diorama is about America's egregious maternal mortality rate."

That explained the stirrups, at least. He'd been concerned about those.

She pointed her fork at him. "Exactly. Nicely done, Mr. Burnham."

If he could, he would bathe in the warm approval of her smile.

Fuck, she was pretty. Her high buns exposed the sweet roundness of her rosy cheeks, the modest plunge of her neckline allowed a stunning, shadowy glimpse of cleavage every time she leaned forward, and her dangling jet earrings tickled the curves of her shoulders. Under the table, her leg brushed his, a moment of glancing, sliding contact that left him as dizzied as a blow to the head.

And somehow, before he thought through what he should say, he was asking her a personal question. "Why murder?"

She swallowed a bite before answering. "I'm not sure what you mean. In my lesson plans? In my dioramas? On a societal level?"

There it was. The smart way forward. He could steer the conversation back toward professionalism, back on track, with two words. *Lesson plans.*

In response, she'd say something about the inherent love of most teenagers for gore and drama, or about her years of gauging student response to different subjects, and he'd nod, and they'd get back to talking about which particular copier most often collated and stapled without overheating.

Instead, he said, "In your dioramas."

Because he was a fucking train wreck in human form, evidently. At least around her.

"Well..." With a muted *clink,* she set her fork down on the edge of her plate. "I'm not sure there's a simple, straightforward answer to that question."

"I don't need simple or straightforward," he told her, and that was news to him. He'd always wanted both. He'd wanted—needed—solvable problems he could comprehend and explain and set aside neatly at the end of the day.

Poppy Wick was many things, but she wasn't neat. Not in the ways that had long mattered to him. And so far, he'd been unable to comprehend her, explain her, or set her aside.

But he still wanted her.

To his horror, even *wanted* might not be a strong enough word for how he felt. Over the last few hours, he'd begun wondering whether—

"My best guess is that I've always been fascinated by things I don't quite understand. I think that's why I was drawn to art in the first place. Great artists..." Resting her elbows on the table, she set her chin on her clasped hands. "I don't understand how they find their inspiration, and I don't understand what allows them to translate that inspiration into art in such disparate, stunning ways."

He dipped his head in understanding. "And you don't understand murder either."

"No, I don't." Her forehead puckered in thought. "I understand motive and means and opportunity, at least enough to create my dioramas. I can even understand hatred and greed and lust. But how those emotions plunge over some invisible ledge and lead someone to shed blood, I don't get. I never will, I don't think. And I can't even *begin* to understand murderers with antisocial personality disorder, although I've read so many books about them."

"Of course you don't understand. You couldn't." Maybe he couldn't grasp Poppy in her complex entirety, but he knew that much. He'd seen her bent low, conferring with her students. He'd seen her in the grips of justified anger, directed his way, and then watched her forgive him minutes later after a single, inadequate apology. He'd seen her clean her classroom without complaint each afternoon, in lieu of unfairly burdening the custodial staff. "You care about other people too much. You'd never hurt someone without a damn good reason."

"Umm..." Her cheeks suddenly seemed pinker, but maybe that was a trick of the candlelight. "Thank you. I hope that's true."

"It is." His tone didn't allow for argument. "Are the dioramas your way of working through how people can do such terrible things to each other?"

The damage humans inflicted on one another didn't need to be physical, of course, much less murderous. But a diorama couldn't capture arguments conducted via shrieks and shouts and obscenities and slamming doors, or the terrible silence that descended on a home in the aftermath of rage.

"Maybe?" Her lips quirked. "But mostly I just think they're interesting, and they sell well. Plus, coming up with the crimes and clues is a good challenge, and so is putting it all together in miniature form. I'm damn good at what I do."

Why had he never realized how seductive confidence could be? "You are. Both in the classroom and as an artist. It's impressive."

No wonder she hadn't let his initial disapproval bow her. She knew her worth, and thank goodness for it.

She flicked a glance down at her plate, carefully portioning another bite. "Thank you, Simon. Not everyone in my life has felt that way."

He frowned. Coworkers? Family? Lovers? Who'd disparaged her talent?

Other than him, of course, at their first meeting in her classroom. But he'd learned better quickly enough, even if the shame of the memory still prickled at the back of his neck.

"Would you..." Her swallow was visible, and she was still staring down at her plate. "Would you maybe like to, um, visit my workshop? Tonight? I could show you my diorama-in-progress."

It wasn't an invitation to bed her. He realized that.

Sadly, his erection didn't.

Before he could manage a coherent answer, she kept speaking, the words breathless and rapid. "Since we left right after work, it's still pretty early, and we could talk more about lesson plans or the school or..." Her pink tongue swiped a crumb from her bottom lip, and he almost choked on his own cake. "Or whatever."

Maybe she rented a studio of some sort? Or…was she inviting him home with her?

After clearing his throat once, then again, he managed to form actual, audible words. "You—you have a workshop in your house?"

She nodded and quickly took another huge bite of her cake, busily chewing while looking anywhere but at him.

Even when he ducked his head a bit, she didn't meet his eyes.

She was nervous?

No. That was unacceptable. She should never feel uncertain around him. Having just admired her pride and confidence, there was no goddamn way he'd let either be stripped from her.

His answer was abrupt, but he couldn't help that. "Yes. Of course. I'd like that."

"You would?" Her hazel eyes peeked at him through a darkened fan of lashes, but they were bright. Mesmerizing, really. "I mean, great. Okay. We can pick up my car in the school lot, and you can follow me home from there."

"That sounds, uh, good." His heart was skittering, and his hands weren't entirely steady. "Very logical."

In that moment, he could have been the same age as their students. A teenager fumbling for words, lost and confused and hopeful. So hopeful.

She tucked a tendril of hair behind the lovely curve of her ear. "Then it's a plan."

In his giddiness, he'd lost all his remaining appetite. He pushed away his plate, then set his napkin beside it.

"I'm almost done," she told him. "I know I'm a slow eater. Sorry."

He shook his head firmly. "Don't be sorry. Take your time."

The answering beam of her smile was so dazzling, so bursting with affection and happiness, he had to blink.

While Poppy finished her dessert, they sat in a silence that wasn't quite awkward. More…expectant. And then she was finally down to her last bite, and he couldn't seem to get enough oxygen to his straining lungs.

"If I'd known embalming fluid tasted like rosemary and ginger and lemon, I'd have been preserving myself decades ago." She tipped back her glass, draining the dregs of her mocktail. "I can only assume the carbonation keeps the skin of the deceased firm and supple."

He couldn't resist playing along. "That's just science."

Her laughter rang through the restaurant, and several nearby diners turned their way. He met their disapproving gazes with a hard stare, because he'd earned that laugh. No humorless assholes with scalpels were going to taint the moment.

"There may be a reason we don't teach biology," she said, still grinning.

With her fork, she scraped up the last crumbs of her cake. While she was distracted, he discreetly took care of the bill.

It's the least a mentor can do for his mentee, he told himself. But even he knew that was complete and utter bullshit.

None of this, not their walks to the parking lot or his panic over her hot-glue-gun burn or the way his gaze was drawn to the pale, plump curve of her earlobe, was entirely professional. Certainly not their dinner tonight, or their imminent trip to her home.

This time, he couldn't even fool himself.

And maybe—maybe—he was getting tired of trying.

CHAPTER 5

"I haven't finished setting up all the rooms." Poppy held the front door open for Simon, waving him ahead of her. "There are still boxes stacked to the ceiling of the guest bedroom. But the crucial spaces are done. The kitchen. The den. The workroom. My, uh, bedroom."

At first glance, the home perfectly reflected the woman who lived there: colorful, crammed full of interesting details, and orderly despite the potential for absolute chaos.

Her entryway and den were the blue of a sunny day on the beach, her kitchen the color of key lime pie. Further down the shadowed hallway, he'd have bet his year's salary that the open doorways to dark rooms promised yet more colors of the rainbow.

Her hands twisting together at her waist, she led him through the public spaces in her home. All the while, she chattered about nothing in particular, her voice breathier than normal. All the while, he observed. Her. Her home. His reaction to both.

Built-in shelves lined almost the entire den. They contained plenty of books, certainly, but also photo frames and sculptures and geological specimens and what definitely appeared to be a rodent of some sort, preserved through taxidermy.

He'd have to ask her about that…creature?…later, because she'd have a good reason for displaying it. He would bet good money on that too.

Other than its cleanliness, her home couldn't have provided a greater contrast to his own house, all of which he'd painted a pale gray. Upon moving in, he'd figured neutrals would prove soothing, so his furniture featured dark wood and forgettable colors, and he kept clutter to a minimum. No unnecessary decorative touches. Nothing breakable.

Years ago, one of the few women he'd ever brought home had deemed the space *monk-like* and *spartan,* and he hadn't disputed the assessment. Even though he'd realized it wasn't a compliment, it wasn't a comment about his home alone, and it also wasn't a good omen for the relationship as a whole.

There was no gray in sight here. Hundreds of objects and colors and textures competed for his attention, and he should have found it all disorienting. Chaotic. Objectionable.

"My workroom is down the hall," she said, shifting her weight from foot to foot. "If you—if you're still interested in seeing it."

His gaze caught on her, because how could it not? How could he *not* look at Poppy Wick, no matter the distractions surrounding them both?

Her hair was red-gold, her knit top the green of a wintry forest, her lips and cheeks pink, her wispy buns inevitably slipping, her jeans and sneakers splattered with paint. He was pretty sure that was chocolate cake smeared on the elbow of her cardigan.

A week ago, he'd have called her a mess.

A week ago, he'd have been a judgmental dick.

Tonight, he saw nothing but beauty, around him and before him. She should know that, so she could stop wringing her hands and frowning at the sight of her own kitchen.

Her nose scrunched up. "I know my home is a lot."

"Your home is…homey," he told her.

She tilted her head, blinking owlishly, and then she was giggling, and he didn't blame her.

"Damned with faint praise!" The words were a gasp, barely intelligible.

"I meant—" He closed his eyes, impatient with himself. "It wasn't intended to—"

She was slightly bent at the waist, bracing herself against her refrigerator with one hand, eyes bright as a torch as she laughed at him.

He couldn't help it. He had to laugh with her, because, yes. *Homey*.

She wiped at her eyes, and he wanted to do it for her.

So he did.

Reaching out slowly, carefully, he cupped her sweet face in his hands. Her breath caught, and her eyes flew to his. He brushed away her tears of hilarity with a light, careful sweep of his thumbs.

Her skin was so fucking soft. So warm under his fingertips. As he stared down at her, those pink lips parted, and she wet them with her tongue.

He wasn't laughing anymore. Neither was she.

But he wasn't entirely certain yet, and he needed to be before this went any further.

When he lowered his hands and stepped back, she drew one shuddering breath. Another. He did the same.

When his control returned, so did his ability to speak. "May I visit your workroom?"

"Y—" Her swallow was audible in the stillness of her home. "Yes."

He followed her down the hall to the room at the very end, forbidding his eyes to wander in search of her bed through the darkened doorways they passed.

When she flicked the light switch, he smiled at the vivid turquoise of her walls, then studied the space itself and how she'd transformed it.

This was her master bedroom. Or, at least, it had been. She'd made it her workspace instead, and no wonder. Given the multitude of windows and the French doors leading outside, the room no doubt received plenty of light. Perfect for an artist's studio. One of the walls was lined, floor to ceiling, with yet more white-painted shelves, each filled neatly with a labeled box.

She gestured to them. "I had a carpenter install the shelves before I moved in. I have so many supplies, it seemed like the best option."

Her work table was huge and solid, the wooden surface scarred, stained, and entirely free from dust. A mesh chair was positioned by its side. On top of the table sat her diorama-in-progress, complete with a male corpse sprawled on a rumpled bed, one who appeared to have been stabbed in his—

Involuntarily, Simon took a step backward.

She snickered. "Yeah, I imagine that will be most men's reaction."

"Did he deserve"—deep breath—"that?"

"Oh, definitely." Her cheeks plumped with her wicked grin. "Making this body anatomically correct was even more fun than usual."

He wanted to ask for more detail, but he also very much didn't.

Instead of contemplating the murder victim's mangled manhood, he studied the tools of her trade. A free-standing magnifier stood next to the miniature crime scene, as did a mug of paint brushes. A handful of other supplies—tweezers, glue, tubes of paint—also sat nearby her work in a tidy pile.

She nudged a single-hair brush with her blunt fingertip. "I try to put away anything I won't be using soon, because otherwise I don't have enough space to work. Or, worse, I'll inadvertently contaminate my scene with something that isn't supposed to be there."

Controlled, meticulous mess, just like her classroom.

There was no television in the room, no computer, no electronics of any sort—with one exception. On the shelf closest to her desk, she'd set up a little speaker for her cell phone.

Her eyes followed his. "I listen to music or podcasts while I work, usually." When he didn't respond, she let out a long breath. "Say something, Simon. Is this too creepy, or too—"

"You should put a comfortable chair in here." Frowning, he considered an unoccupied corner of the large room. "A chaise, perhaps. Near the windows."

With a charming tilt of her head, she studied the space too. "Huh. That's an idea."

He could see her laid full-length on that lounge already. It would be velvet, soft as her skin, and some color he'd never, ever choose. One that would complement both the turquoise and her beautiful, fine, reddish-gold hair. Mustard, maybe, or plum. She'd bask in the sun, eyes closed, a lazy smile indenting the corners of that tempting mouth. Or maybe she'd pluck one of those countless books from the shelves in her den and read while reclining, lips pursed in concentration.

Or maybe she could put a leather club chair in that spot instead. An ottoman too.

Suddenly, the image in his mind shifted.

Suddenly, he was the one in the leather chair. He was the one reading with his feet up, napping, smiling, laughing as Poppy worked on her crime scene at her sunny desk and probably sang along to her music badly and at top volume until, unable to resist any longer, he set aside his book and swiveled her work chair to face him and kissed her and kissed her—

He shook his head near-violently, dismissing the vision.

How he'd even imagined such an unlikely scenario, he had no idea. He'd never witnessed that kind of affection, that kind of peaceful but passionate intimacy, anywhere outside of fiction. Certainly not in his own experience of home and family.

Which reminded him: He owed her an explanation, because he wouldn't let her continue to believe he'd insulted her in her own kitchen.

"When I said your house is homey, I meant it feels like a home." No, that didn't express what he wanted to say. He needed to abandon tautology in favor of specificity, no matter how uncomfortable he found it. "It feels—it feels like you. Warm and bright. Comfortable. Interesting. A place you can relax."

It feels like the home I would have wanted. The home some part of me still wants.

Her fingers curled slightly on her tabletop, but otherwise, she'd gone completely still. "So that *was* praise, after all. Not faint."

"No." He didn't smile, because he wasn't joking. "Not faint."

"Why math?"

It was an abrupt question, an echo of what he'd said at dinner: *Why murder?* It was also something no one had ever asked him before, probably because his interest in numbers had always seemed self-evident. Cold, logical man; cold, logical subject.

But it wasn't that simple. Nothing ever was, no matter what he'd prefer.

He held her gaze, unflinching. Flinty, his expression so blank nothing could grab hold of its pristine surface. "My childhood was...chaotic."

His parents' arguments followed no logic. They happened after stressful days at work, and they happened on vacation weekends, at a peaceful beach. They circled recent offenses, and then addressed affronts from decades before, and then leaped to predictions of enraging future behavior.

The only things Simon himself could predict: He'd hide in his room. Something—a glass, a plate, a table—would end up shattered on the floor. The shouted accusations would hurt his ears. The sobs would hurt his heart. And it would all happen again, the following day or week.

There was no end to their problems, no solution to their conflicts.

Poppy was still waiting, eyes solemn and expectant, so he elaborated. "Math was a comfort for me. It seemed clean. Orderly. Rational."

Safe.

"Okay." Although one droopy bun was unraveling above her ear, she paid it no heed. "But if you wanted rationality and order, why teach high school? Teenagers are chaos incarnate."

She was evaluating him like a crime scene, sharp as a sliver of broken glass on carpet. So sharp, she could make him bleed before he even knew she'd pierced his skin and burrowed beneath.

His shoulders had tightened to the point of pain. "Higher levels of math often involve problems with no clear solutions."

"You could have become an accountant instead."

No, she definitely wasn't accepting half-truths. Not after having let him see her most private space, displaying it for his judgment despite his disdain of less than a week ago.

Maybe he was wrong, but he suspected she'd consider showing him her bedroom, her unclothed body, less intimate than guiding him inside her workroom.

Those hazel eyes flayed him, peeling away layer after layer until he stood shivering and exposed before her. He closed his eyes, because if he couldn't see her, she couldn't see him.

The illogic was galling and humiliating, but he clung to its scant protection.

"As a teacher—" His throat worked. "As a teacher, I can provide an orderly, quiet, safe space for children like me. Like the boy I was."

If he'd had his wish, he'd have slept at school. Camped out in Mrs. Delgado's classroom, which was always neat and clean. Her voice never rose. Her floor never cut his feet. Her hand was warm on his back as he worked on long division. Her questions always had answers, and he could provide them.

"I've seen you teach, you know," she said, her voice slightly muffled, and he blinked his eyes open.

She'd turned away from him, and was pretending to deposit something in one of her labeled boxes, but he knew better. She was giving him time to recover himself.

"When?" His voice was embarrassingly gravelly. "I would have noticed if—"

Wait. He knew.

"You were part of the group that observed me the second week of school." In his files, he still had their feedback forms. Now that he knew Poppy's was among them, he'd search for her comments and reread them. "For ten minutes, while we talked about derivatives."

He'd taken no notice of her, really, or any of the other observers.

His students commanded his undivided attention and efforts between the bells, except in case of emergency.

It seemed impossible now—that he hadn't recognized her presence, hadn't acknowledged it, even without knowing her name or having exchanged a single word.

Somehow, he should have known. Should have seen.

"I stood in a corner and watched you discuss derivatives," she affirmed. "It was the quietest, most structured classroom and lesson I'd ever seen."

Terrifying. Not in a fun way.

But her eyes were soft, her lips curved. "You knew all their names already. You called them Ms. Blackwell and Mr. Jones and so on. Except for Sam, because those sorts of titles cause them gender dysphoria. Which I know, since Sam's in my second period class. Earlier this week, they told me you always used their preferred pronouns and name. From the moment you received their information form."

Her voice lowered almost to a whisper, as if they were sharing secrets, and maybe they were. "During the observation, when one kid didn't understand how you'd solved the problem on the board, you explained everything a second time, clearly and patiently."

Her praise was a warm tide in his chest, soaking into his limbs, spreading through his cold, aching bones. So welcome he had to fight against closing his eyes again.

"I was impressed. Beyond impressed. Those kids already adored you, Simon. After less than two weeks. If you wanted to provide them a peaceful, safe space..." In a graceful gesture, she spread her hands wide. "Mission accomplished."

The question was neither his business nor appropriate to ask. He shouldn't ask. Couldn't.

But *really*. She was standing there, fine wisps of disordered hair haloed around her head, round and kind and so very lovely, smart and funny and accomplished, and—

"How the hell are you single?" *Goddammit, Burnham.* "Not that it's any of my concern, and perhaps you have a partner you haven't mentioned, but—"

"Oh, I'm single." Her smile vanished. "No doubt about that."

Thank fuck.

"I am too," he told her without the slightest intention of doing so. "Never married."

Which was way less surprising than her lack of a partner. A man like him neither experienced nor inspired passion and lust and devotion.

At least, he hadn't. Before now.

Poppy's mouth had tightened into a thin, pale line.

"I listen to podcasts about unsolved murders and serial killers." It was a stark announcement, seemingly disconnected from the topic he'd raised. "I read books about psychopathology and Jack the Ripper and forensics. I watch terrible, hilarious reenactments of crimes late at night on cable. I make some tiny dolls bleed and others kill. And I do all that happily. Enthusiastically."

She spoke slowly, giving each word emphasis.

A warning: *Caveat emptor*.

"The last woman I dated and brought home told me I was creepy as fuck. When she saw the workroom in my old house, she was out the door in less than five minutes. And when I'm not being creepy, I'm grading or planning lessons or going to IEP meetings." Her chin had tipped high, and she didn't break eye contact once. "I'm too wrapped up in my work and my hobbies. Which is why my last ex-boyfriend said I was a terrible partner and broke up with me after two months."

He scoffed in mingled disbelief and disdain. "Because you refused to make yourself *less* for him? What a jackass."

Her amused huff flared her nostrils, and her shoulders dropped a fraction. "Can't disagree with you there."

"And you're not creepy." His tone dared her to argue. "You're curious."

"About murder. Which isn't at all creepy," she said dryly. "But enough about me. Why aren't *you* in a long-term relationship, Simon?"

Another question no one had asked him before now.

His instinctive response, true but incomplete: *I've never been interested in one.*

But unlike last time, he wasn't going to make her work for the full, honest answer. Not after she'd bared at least a corner of her scarred heart to him, despite her obvious wariness.

"If I were going to invite that kind of upheaval into my life..." The words were slippery, but he was trying to grasp them, trying to explain himself in a way he'd never attempted before. "Sometimes, two people come together and become less than what they were separately. They subtract from one another. One and one making zero."

His mother and father. On their own, decent people. Decent parents. Together: nothing he wanted in his life.

When she nodded in understanding, he continued. "Other times, two people in a relationship make nothing more than the sum of their parts. One plus one equals two." He rested his fists on his hips and made himself say it. "But if I'm going to risk a relationship, I want something more. Something transformative. Not just a sum."

She was listening so carefully, with no attempt to fill in words for him or interrupt, and it was just one more reason he needed to kiss her.

"I want a product. An exponent. I want one plus one to equal eighty, or a thousand, or infinity." He shook his head, exasperated with himself. "It isn't logical. I know that. My entire life, I've doubted that kind of partnership, that kind of love, even existed. I've never seen a hint of it. Not on any date I've ever had."

Until now went unspoken.

With Poppy, he could glimpse the possibility of more.

His gaze dropped to her hand, because his reaction to her burn had been the first warning siren he'd actually acknowledged, the first unmistakable sign he could be transformed by her.

He stepped closer than necessary, closer than was wise. Closer, until her back was pressed against her shelves, her lips soft and parted, her breath hitching with each deliberate step he took.

If he gripped the shelves on either side of her, he could cage her with his body. Lower his open mouth to her jaw. Whisper hotly in her ear, then trace its curve with his tongue.

Instead, their only point of contact was comparatively innocent. His hold on her wrist, raising her hand for his inspection. She gasped at the contact, and he swayed even closer, until the brush of his knee against her thigh sent lightning arcing through his veins.

The burn was a faded pink spot now.

"Does this still hurt?" His voice was raspy and quiet, foreign to his ears.

She shook her head, round cheeks flushed with heat.

"Good."

He turned her hand, exposing the cup of her palm and the pale, velvety skin of her forearm. Blue veins traced just beneath the surface of that skin, curving and branching like the ivy she'd doodled in her notebook.

Beneath his thumb, her pulse was rabbiting.

He slowly stroked that tiny, frantic beat. "Do I scare you?"

She shook her head again, then hesitated.

"Not..." When she licked her lips, he wanted to taste that pink tongue. "Not in that way. Not physically."

He met her half-lidded gaze. "You scare me too."

More truth, offered freely in the hush of a quiet, shadowed home, her bedroom barely more than a heartbeat distant.

He had thinking to do, and it wouldn't happen with temptation inches away, all warm skin and lush curves and sharp eyes.

"Tonight's a school night." He inclined his head in a stiff little nod, released her hand, and stepped back. "I should head home."

She paused, opening her mouth as if to say something. Her fingers curled into fists. Then her gaze flicked to the floor, and she silently led the way to her front door.

Out on her small porch, the night's autumnal chill transformed their breath to fog. Turning to him, arms wrapped around herself, she spoke before he could take the two steps down to her driveway.

"Simon." Her brow was puckered. "That first conversation in my classroom."

He waited. Listened.

"You hurt me," she finally said, her voice nearly a whisper. "I barely knew you, and you hurt me."

The rest didn't need to be stated aloud.

Please don't hurt me again.

He wanted to tell her he wouldn't, but he might. He wanted to tell her not to worry, but he was terrified too. He wanted to brush a fingertip over that puckered brow and kiss the telltale sign of anxiety away, but he couldn't. Not yet.

Instead, he bowed his head, then left her in the cold.

CHAPTER 6

Those same two science teachers were whispering to one another in the faculty lounge as Simon gathered his lunch from the refrigerator the next day.

They were veteran educators, near retirement. Respectable enough in reputation, he supposed, although he generally didn't pay attention to such things. One—for reasons he couldn't explain—wore a large brooch in the shape of an arched, hissing cat, its jeweled eyes glinting with malice. The other appeared half-swallowed by her oversized scarf.

And right now, he wanted both of them to eat that fucking scarf and choke on it.

"Can you believe they replaced Mildred with *her*?" Murderous Cat Teacher said. "She's an embarrassment to our school. Have you *seen* what she wears every day?"

Smothering Scarf Teacher shook her head. "Shirts smeared with paint. Jeans. Messy hair. It's a disgrace."

"I can't believe she's gotten away with it." Murderous Cat Teacher sniffed loudly. "I knew Principal Dunn wasn't up to the job. Too soft-hearted, as Mildred and I always said."

"Have you heard about Ms. Wick's little *art* projects?" Smothering Scarf Teacher's lip curled. "They're grotesque and—and *creepy*."

Creepy.

Poppy had described herself that way too, chin high, hurt darkening her clear eyes.

He didn't slam the door of the refrigerator, but he wanted to. Not just because of his rage at Mildred's cruel cronies, but also because he'd thought—he'd *said*—almost the exact same things such a short time ago, and it shamed him. Gutted him.

You hurt me.

After a fraught, sleepless night, he'd finally solved his problems. He'd found his solutions, unnerving though they might be.

He was done hurting Poppy, and he wasn't about to let others do it instead.

"Excuse me." Rising to his full height, he stepped closer to the table, until he was looming over them. Deliberately. "Or, rather, excuse *you*."

They blinked up at him, Murderous Cat Teacher's eyes wide and magnified behind her glasses.

"Ms. Wick, your colleague, received administrative permission to dress in a manner appropriate to her daily tasks, which involve ably shepherding bloodthirsty teens through a sea of paint and glue and other horrible substances." His tone was icy enough to freeze them in place. "Furthermore, when I talked to various students this week, I discovered the reason Mrs. Krackel was able to wear formal clothing when she taught."

He planted both his hands on the table and leaned forward, eyes narrowed. "Because, on a daily basis, *Mildred* didn't do a goddamn thing."

The women gasped, and he was almost certain they'd report him for his word choice. He couldn't have given less of a fuck.

"She didn't help students with projects. She didn't help clean their mess." He spoke slowly, so they had to take in every word. "Ms. Wick's dioramas are stunning examples of meticulous, clever artistry, and they accordingly command a high price. In contrast, from my understanding, Mildred's main talent was collecting a monthly paycheck."

"How—how dare you?" Smothering Scarf Teacher sputtered. "Mildred—"

"—is gone," he finished for her. "I don't know how or why, and for these purposes, it doesn't matter."

He had a theory he intended to run by Poppy later, though. He hoped she'd prove impressed by his reasoning abilities and investigative prowess.

"No matter what happened with Mrs. Krackel, Ms. Wick is an invaluable asset to this school, and she is anything but grotesque. She's kind and warm and talented." Heaving himself upright once more, he stalked to the door, then turned to make one final, chilly statement. "*You*, on the other hand, *are* grotesque."

When he slammed out of the faculty lounge, two of his long-time colleagues staring aghast at him—their cold, controlled colleague, fuming and foul-mouthed—he dimly realized he'd lost his temper. At work. For the first time ever.

But it was for good reason. The best reason.

And quite honestly?

It felt *amazing*.

* * *

Bending over, Simon inspected Tori's diorama-in-progress with a magnifying glass. "It's a coffin. With bloody claw marks and a corpse inside."

Because *of course* it was a coffin with bloody claw marks and a corpse inside. Why had he expected anything else from one of the Goth softball players in Poppy's class?

"It's the first of *two* coffins," Tori corrected with an easy grin. "I'm educating my teachers and classmates about a very special period in our history via my diorama, Mr. Burnham."

He lifted a brow, and she took the gesture as the invitation it was.

"In the nineteenth century, people were very nervous about being buried alive." Turning to her friend, she tucked some of her braids behind her ear. "Do you remember that project we did in Mr. Krause's class, Stacey? About how that one woman in England in the 1600s—"

"Alice Blunden," Stacey provided, face lit with excitement.

"—drank too much poppy tea, which was an opiate, and they thought she was dead, so they buried her, but then kids heard sounds from her grave, so someone exhumed her and saw she'd tried to escape, but they thought she was dead again, so they reburied her, but *then*—

He pinched the bridge of his nose.

"—the next day, she really was dead, but there were signs she'd revived and struggled a second time before finally, totally, dying. For real."

Jesus, he'd be having nightmares about that.

Tori beamed at him. "So people were scared, and they invented special coffins with ladders and air inlets and bells so if supposedly-dead people woke up in the grave, they could save themselves. My other coffin will be a miniature of that invention. It'll show a woman safely climbing out of her grave, only half-dead, instead of all-the-way dead."

Stacey frowned thoughtfully. "Did you consider including zombies in your diorama?"

"Of course I did." Tori tossed her braids over her shoulder. "But Ms. Wick said zombies were insufficiently educational, and thus did not meet class objectives."

There were many, many things he could say in response to Tori's diorama, but Simon confined himself to one. The truth, however inadequate.

"Impressive work, Ms...." He trailed off, uncertain of her last name.

"Walker," she supplied, then shook the hand he offered. "I'll probably be in your calculus class next year."

"Good," he said, again with perfect honesty. "I look forward to it."

Then he fled back to his accustomed table, before either she or Stacey could inspire further nightmares.

A few moments later, Poppy found him taking notes on his legal pad. "You doing okay, Mr. Burnham? You look…I don't know. Kind of pale and nauseated?"

Her usual buns were slipping from the top of her head, but she was wearing a dress today, for some unknown reason. Rust-red and silky-looking, the material suited her coloring, and the hem flirted around her knees in a distracting way. The garment was also stained with fresh smears of paint and glue, which was exactly why she should have been wearing her jeans instead.

Although he'd been studying her almost nonstop, she'd been cautious around him the entire period. Meeting his eyes for fleeting moments before looking quickly away. Keeping her distance, so they never quite found themselves within arm's length of one another. Addressing him with all the formality due a colleague.

He understood why, and if he had anything to say about it, that professional reserve would disappear within the next hour. But it still made him want to snatch her into his lap and thread his fingers through her hair and yank her mouth to his.

"Tori described her diorama," he told Poppy.

She nodded. "Ah. That would explain your expression." After eyeing him carefully, she strode over to one of her cabinets and returned with a handful of blank paper and a freshly sharpened pencil. "I am absolutely certain you've already written your evaluation, so today's observation is simply a formality."

He dipped his chin in acknowledgment.

In fact, he'd drafted the praise-packed evaluation Wednesday evening, and was prepared to send it to Principal Dunn as soon as the school day ended. The notes he'd been taking on his legal pad weren't about Poppy's teaching talents, manifold though they were. They were his thoughts about Mildred's disappearance, and about the murder in miniature currently sitting on his table, approximately eight inches to his left.

He'd solved the mysteries—he hoped—last night, but wanted to order his thoughts before presenting his findings to Poppy.

She set her stack of paper in front of him, then handed him the pencil. "Since you're done with your evaluation, why don't you distract yourself from the prospect of being buried alive by drawing something?"

"I'm—" He winced. "I'm not much of an artist, I'm afraid."

"It's not about the result, Simon." Her voice was gentle. "It's about the process. There's literally no way for you to be wrong, as long as you try. Just…express yourself."

Her warm fingers trailed along his shoulder as she walked away, and he clenched his eyes shut. Thirty more minutes, and they'd be alone. He could keep control that long. He had to.

* * *

By the time the final bell rang, Simon had finished his drawing. Such as it was.

In one of their early conversations, Poppy had said she couldn't predict the contents of her students' hearts or the subjects that consumed their innermost thoughts. That applied to him too, he imagined.

One glance at his paper, which now lay face-down on the table, and she'd know his heart. His innermost thoughts.

He wanted her to know.

As the students filed from the room, he helped her clean up. Then he sat down at the table again and waited for her to venture near.

She fiddled with paperwork on her desk. She typed something into her laptop. She fussed over a splotch of paint on one of the student chairs.

She was nervous.

"Poppy…" At the sight of her right bun, now sagging a millimeter above her ear, he had to smile. "Come here."

Without turning to him, she shook her head. "I just need to…"

She couldn't even finish the breathless sentence, and she still didn't come close. He'd spooked her last night, no doubt. All that heat, all that intimacy, and he'd left her in the cold.

No matter. He knew how to draw her back to him.

"The brother did it. Barron. He set the fire that killed Kaden." He crossed his arms over his chest and leaned back in his chair. "What's my reward?"

At that, she spun around and eyed him suspiciously. "Is that your best guess?"

"It's not a guess. It's a fact." His smile was arrogant, deliberately so. "I solved your murder diorama."

Despite the continued wariness in her expression, she strode to the table and set her fists on her hips. "Explain your reasoning."

This victory didn't feel small. Not in the slightest.

"The brothers came home from work." Simon had pictured the sequence of events over and over last night, until the progression finally made sense. "Barron fixed them drinks from their bar cart. He sat on the couch, while Kaden sat on the recliner and smoked. They watched television. Eventually, Kaden fell asleep. Deeply asleep, because Barron put a few of those sleeping pills from the bathroom medicine cabinet in his drink."

Poppy's lips were pressed together as she tried not to smile. "Go on."

"Then Barron sprayed the recliner and the living room with lighter fluid, set everything ablaze, and retreated to his bedroom to climb out the window and feign panic and grief." He lifted his shoulders. "All the other suspects had reasons to dislike Kaden, but they were red herrings. Distractions from the true criminal."

Her eyes sparkled as she edged closer. "What's your proof?"

"The discarded bottle of lighter fluid hidden under a bush outside their bedroom window, so well placed you couldn't see it without a magnifying glass. The papers I found on the bedroom desk, which showed how quickly Kaden was piling up debt and emptying their joint account." He couldn't even imagine how long writing the papers had taken, given the tiny, tiny print. "Those bank and credit card statements required tweezers *and* a magnifying glass to read. Which I employed Wednesday, while you were consulting with Tori about coffins."

She sank into the seat behind her desk, only a foot away. "Good eye, Sherlock."

"But that was all circumstantial evidence. Someone else could have placed the bottle there, and lots of families have money issues without resorting to arson and murder." Unfolding his arms, he tapped his forefinger on the table. "The clinching detail was something entirely different."

"Really?" She was openly smiling at him now, seemingly delighted by his observations. "Tell me."

"Barron's shoes," he said with satisfaction.

Jesus, she could light the entire fucking school with that beam of hers. "I was wondering if anyone would catch that."

"All the shoes were stored in the living room, just inside the front door, and they were all unlaced. Without exception." He leaned forward to rest his weight on his elbows. "So if Barron woke up to a smoke-filled bedroom, saw the living room entirely aflame and realized he couldn't save his brother, then panicked and fled out the window, how exactly did he manage to retrieve a pair of shoes? Much less have the time and patience to double-knot them once putting them on?"

Instead of answering, she waved him on with a grin.

He stabbed his finger into the table again. "The only possible answer: He *wasn't* in a hurry or panicked, because he set the fire himself. He stayed in pajamas to reinforce his story, but didn't want to go barefoot outside. So before dousing his brother's recliner with lighter fluid and setting it alight, he put on shoes and double-knotted them out of habit."

She applauded. "Bravo, Mr. Burnham. You've solved the case."

He gave a little seated bow, his own grin nearly cracking his cheeks. "There was only one thing I couldn't figure out. Why the hair in the sink? At first, I figured it was another red herring, meant to indicate the ex-girlfriend's involvement, but it didn't match her hair color. It was Barron's, not hers."

"Ah. The wet hair in the sink." She plucked at her cardigan, preening a bit herself. "That clue requires a bit of background knowledge or research."

"Which you've done." All those podcasts and books and television reenactments had taught her well.

"Which I've done," she agreed. "Inexperienced arsonists are often surprised by how quickly accelerants flame up once lit, and they frequently burn themselves. Their fingers, their arms—"

"Or their hair." Oh, that was a nice touch. "In the process of killing his brother, Barron set his own hair on fire. So he ran to the bathroom and doused his head in the sink, then cut off the burned parts so the police wouldn't be suspicious. He probably thought the whole house would burn down, concealing the evidence, but it didn't. The bathroom was almost untouched, so the hair remained."

"Precisely." She swiveled back and forth in her chair, eyeing him with open approval. "You're a quick study. What do you want as your reward?"

"I have some ideas." They involved privacy. A quiet bedroom. A soft mattress. Her plump thighs cradling his hips and his name gasped through her parted, swollen lips. "But first, I want to earn another."

"Another reward?" Her brow crinkled. "I don't understand."

"I think I've explained Mildred Krackel's disappearance as well." He held up two fingers. "Two cases, two rewards."

She only looked more confused. "But that's not a mystery."

"It was to me."

"Simon..." Her snort made her breasts jiggle in an entirely distracting way. "You need to gossip more."

Well, that was somewhat dampening. Still, he persevered. "Okay, so here's what I think happened: Mildred didn't simply retire due to old age. There was foul play involved."

"*Foul play?*" Poppy made a sort of choking sound. "In—in a sense, I suppose that's true."

"Let me explain the likely sequence of events." He glanced at his notes, then nodded to himself. "Mildred made enemies. Lots of them."

"Also true." Fingers interlaced, Poppy rested her chin on her hands. "Go on."

"Students resented her lack of care. Other teachers resented her lack of hard work and lesson plans. Candy Albright, as I discovered after speaking with her yesterday, resented Mrs. Krackel's insistence on having students make a Frankenstein mask every Halloween. Complete with green skin and bolts in the neck."

Poppy cringed. "Mildred specified Frankenstein? Not Frankenstein's monster?"

"Even after the English Department's Frankenstein Is *Not* the Monster puppet show. The assignment was a deliberate taunt, according to Ms. Albright."

After the very strong, very loud case Candy had made in defense of that accusation, Simon had to agree. Mrs. Krackel had been mocking her colleague, which was a dangerous game indeed.

"But Ms. Albright wasn't Mrs. Krackel's most devoted enemy." Leaning forward, he lowered his voice. "No, that would be..."

He paused, because apparently he harbored a heretofore unknown love for the dramatic.

Poppy's eyes glinted with amusement. "Yes?"

"Mrs. Denham," he announced.

Her eyebrows beetled, and her smile faded. "Mrs. Denham? Our custodian? Simon, what in the world—"

"Hear me out." For confidence, he consulted his notes one last time. "Please."

Pinching her mouth shut, Poppy waved him on.

"Mrs. Krackel left a horrible mess for Mrs. Denham and the other custodians to clean every day. From what I understand, Mildred refused to either clean it herself or allot sufficient class time so students could do it instead."

Poppy inclined her head. "I've heard the same."

"The rest is sheer speculation, but it would explain everything." He tapped his forefinger on the table. "I think Mrs. Denham finally decided she'd had enough. So she confronted Mrs. Krackel one afternoon and threatened to stop cleaning the classroom unless Mildred or her students did some of the work themselves."

Poppy's brows were now arching toward her hairline, but she didn't interrupt.

"Mildred refused. Laughed her off, or pulled rank. And then—" He spread his hands. "Mrs. Denham made her stand."

Her lips twitched again, possibly at the portentous note in his voice. "Go on."

This final twist in the story, he'd considered for the first time last night. However improbable, it would explain everything. The whispered comments, the horror-filled half-glances toward the table, the unceremonious nature of Mildred's departure. All of it.

"One evening, after Mildred left for the day, Mrs. Denham left a warning. Right here." He dipped his chin to indicate the table where he'd sat every day, the table all the students seemed to avoid so assiduously. "The custodial equivalent of a horse's head."

"Wow," Poppy murmured. "Hadn't expected a *Godfather* reference."

He barreled on, ignoring her. "Maybe a pool of red paint, splattered to resemble blood. Maybe a clay figure stabbed with a carving tool. Something so egregious, so horrifying, Mrs. Krackel had to take action. So she went to Principal Dunn."

"Who said...what?" Poppy's head was tilted as she considered his theory. "Since Mrs. Denham still works here, and Mildred doesn't, I assume Mildred didn't receive the response she anticipated?"

"Exactly." He smiled at her, pleased by her quick understanding. "Tess backed Mrs. Denham, not Mrs. Krackel. At which point, Mildred quit and left the school in a huff, never to return. Mystery solved."

He sat back in smug satisfaction, waiting for praise of his investigative prowess.

It didn't come.

"Um, Simon." Poppy's voice was cautious, its tone familiar. Not quite pitying, but not quite *not* pitying either. "One small problem with your theory. Well, several rather large problems, actually."

Oh, God. He was going to feel like a fool again. He could already tell. "Yes?"

Poppy held up a finger. "First of all, if Mrs. Denham had made that kind of violent threat with Mildred's art supplies, she would no longer be employed at our school. No matter how much our principal might sympathize with the custodial staff or loathe Mrs. Krackel."

Dammit. He'd hoped she wouldn't pinpoint the weakest link in his chain of events so quickly. But the woman made murder dioramas, for heaven's sake. Of *course* she'd immediately spotted the glaring flaw in his theory.

Another finger. "Second, Mildred did make lots of enemies here. But Mrs. Denham wouldn't have done anything to threaten or sabotage—"

"Mr. Burnham is right. At least to a certain extent." The familiar voice came from the open doorway. "I loathed that woman. So did the rest of the custodial staff."

Mrs. Denham stood by her cart, unbowed and unapologetic.

At the sight of their visitor, Poppy turned a shade of red he'd never witnessed in person before. "Mrs. Denham, I'm so sorry. Simon doesn't know the circumstances of Mildred's departure, so he suspects—"

"Oh, there was definitely foul play involved, just like he said." A slow, evil smile emphasized the wrinkles on the older woman's face. "I know that for a fact."

Poppy stared openmouthed at Mrs. Denham. "But—but she was caught screwing the head of security in her classroom after hours! By the superintendent! Who was leading VIPs on a tour of the school! How can that possibly be the result of anything but her own bad judgment?"

Simon's own eyebrows flew to his hairline.

Oh. Oh, my.

That, he hadn't expected. But now that he considered the matter, it still made sense. Mrs. Denham didn't have to threaten Mildred to get rid of her.

No, she could simply—

Mrs. Denham shook her huge ring of keys. "The classroom was locked. I opened it for the group, knowing exactly what they'd find inside." Her mouth pursed. "For her age, Mildred was surprisingly limber. I'm sorry I didn't ask her about joint supplements before she left."

Simon cringed.

"You mean, before she and Harvey were both forced to retire, due to their indiscretions." Poppy's jaw was still slightly agape, and she was shaking her head in disbelief. "When the tour came to this wing… did you—"

"Oh, I definitely encouraged the group to visit this classroom. I told them to expect an eye-popping display inside." Mrs. Denham's cackle echoed in the room. "And they got one."

So much for his theory. Still, he'd chosen the correct suspect, which had to count for *something*.

"Remind me not to piss you off," Poppy whispered, wide-eyed.

"So far, so good." Mrs. Denham winked at her. "No tours scheduled tonight. Just FYI."

Even after the custodian closed the door, the sound of her whistling floated through the classroom, getting fainter as she pushed her cart down the hallway.

Then it was silent once more, and he and Poppy were staring at one another, and he couldn't seem to breathe properly. His palms grew damp where they rested on the—

Wait.

I'll never be able to use that table again, Stacey had said. *Not without picturing what happened…there.*

He looked down at the wooden surface under his hands, and a few other clues fell into place. With a muttered and heartfelt *fuck,* he leapt to his feet and ran to the sink.

Poppy groaned. "What now?"

"Is that—where I've been sitting—" There wasn't enough soap in the world. "Is that Mrs. Krackel's, uh…"

"Sex table?" Poppy's giggle was infectious, much like the germs he'd probably encountered while using that damn table all week. "Why, yes. Yes, it is."

"Dammit, Poppy." He stopped scrubbing and glared in her direction. "You could have said something."

She appeared blithely unbothered by his disfavor, as usual. "It's been disinfected multiple times since Mildred's adventures there. Trust me. I took care of that personally, once I heard the story."

He supposed that was a reasonable response. Besides, his plans for the afternoon didn't involve scowling at Poppy or reenacting Lady Macbeth's endless, frantic hand-washing.

No, he had other priorities. Business first, and then...

And then.

After rinsing and drying his hands, he crossed the room, bent down to open his briefcase, produced a neatly stapled document, and placed it on her desk. "Here's your evaluation. You can read it later. In case you're worried, it's positive. In fact, it's so glowing, it may give you a sunburn."

Her eyes didn't leave his, not even when the paper hit the desk.

"Why, Mr. Burnham." She was grinning at him again, delighted. "What a poetical turn of phrase. Thank you."

"No need to thank me. You earned every word." Now, onto the scary part of this conversation. "We need to, um..."

He rolled his shoulders. Widened his stance slightly. Closed his eyes and swallowed.

"Simon?"

Decades of avoiding vulnerability and risk ended today. Now.

The possibility of Poppy, of entirely illogical transformation, of *more*—it was worth the risk. He had to trust her, and he had to trust his own heart.

When he blinked his eyes open, she was waiting for him, forehead puckered in that endearing, familiar way. Her hazel eyes were cautious, concerned, but so very soft.

She could wreck him. Maybe she already had.

"You may need to find another mentor." He wanted to draw a soothing rectangular prism on his legal pad, but instead he held her gaze. "I'm not familiar with the rules governing the mentor-mentee relationship, at least not the ones that apply to our particular situation."

Quickly, he corrected himself. "I mean, the ones I *want* to apply."

Her brows drew together in confusion. "I'm sorry?"

However embarrassingly inept, his picture would literally tell her more than a thousand words. With a tremor in his hands, he flipped over his drawing and slid it across the table, until she could see it clearly.

He understood his artistic limits, and he hadn't tried to achieve realism.

The stick figures boasted neat labels above their circular heads: POPPY and SIMON. Her figure stood by a table, whose very straight edges he'd achieved with a ruler. There was a little house atop the table. Another tiny stick figure lay beside the house, each of its eyes indicated with an X. A corpse, as best Simon could indicate one.

His stick figure was sitting—awkwardly, with limbs of an odd length—in a chair. The small table next to the chair had a paper on it, marked with an A+.

Poppy's figure leaned toward his. Simon's figure leaned toward hers. Their eyes were hearts. Between them, he'd drawn more hearts.

In his vision, in his dreams, Poppy worked on her dioramas and sang at her workroom desk while he graded nearby, and they—

Well, he'd known his drawing abilities couldn't convey a passionate kiss.

"Simon." The word was a sigh. A caress. "Dearest."

He dared to look up from the drawing, and she was still studying it. Her finger traced one of the hearts that hung in the air between their stick figures, and she was biting her lower lip, eyes glossy with tears.

Dearest was good. He knew that much. But the tears?

"Poppy, is this..." He gulped a breath. Another. "Is this okay? Is this —is this what you want too?"

She touched her forefinger to her puckered lips, then set it gently on his stick figure. A kiss, offered to his penciled counterpart as she blinked back those gut-wrenching tears.

Before he could reach for her, she was speaking, and he listened with every ounce of his being. Every atom.

"If you left my classroom today without kissing me," she said, "I was going to make a diorama of myself, dead of a broken heart, with you as the culprit. It was going to be overly dramatic and much too blunt, but…"

Her eyes lifted to his, and her smile trembled. "I can't be blamed. I make murder dioramas. *Overly dramatic* is kind of my thing."

On the table, her capable hand was shaking too. He covered it with his own, and she immediately parted her fingers so he could slide his in between, and it felt like a buoy to a man lost at sea for years.

"I understand now." He stepped to her side, so close the scent of turpentine and soap filled his lungs. "The importance of process over result. The relief of expression. If you hadn't already taught me, this drawing would have."

"Good." The corners of her lips indented as her smile turned mischievous. "I only have one complaint about this picture, Mr. Burnham."

"What's that, Ms. Wick?" Fuck, he loved that expression on her.

"Well, unless you count the corpse on the table…" Bending at the waist, she studied his drawing. "There's no crime here."

He bumped into her, hip to hip, and it wasn't an accident.

"On the contrary. A crime has most definitely occurred." Holding out his free arm, he displayed the pencil smudges on his pristine button-down. "Sartorial assault. Attempted murder of my shirt."

Her giggle rang through him, vibrating and joyful as a chime.

"I've changed my mind." She turned to face him. "The crime is that your stick figures aren't kissing, and neither are we."

"That was what I wanted for my reward," he told her. "A kiss from you."

More than his next breath. So much his chest ached.

If they kissed, though, he'd need to keep hold of himself until she was willing to take it further. Until they had privacy and time and a comfortable bed nearby.

"You want a kiss?" She tipped her chin upward, a mute challenge in her bright, sharp eyes. "Take it, then."

So he did.

CHAPTER 7

Poppy's mouth was a revelation beneath his. Soft, warm, eager, sweet with mint.

She must have brushed her teeth between periods, just in case this happened, his rational brain deduced, before his rational brain entirely left the premises.

He took it slow, exploring every corner of those wide, plush lips, her sweet face cupped in his hands as she leaned back against her desk and he stepped into the cradle of her body. The electric charge of the contact dizzied him, buzzing in his ears as she opened her mouth for his tongue.

Her lower lip was trembling between his, its inner surface slick, and suddenly his hand was buried in her hair, twisted below one of those adorable buns, and he inhaled with a gasp before swooping down to kiss her again. Their tongues tangled, and he was sucking on hers, and she was making little sounds in her throat that seared a path straight to his cock.

"Hold on," she panted. "The door—I need to lock it, and maybe wedge a chair—Shit, Simon—"

She tore herself from his arms and half-ran to the door, locking it, before yanking down the shades over her windows.

"Which chair do you think—" she began, and he couldn't stand it any longer.

He caught up with her partway to the door, removed the student chair from her hands, hauled her close, and backed her into the nearby wall, her mouth open under his even before her shoulders hit the shelves.

Her tongue chased his this time, swirling and exploring until he saw nothing but light behind his eyelids. She shoved up his shirt, yanking it free from his pants, and splayed those capable artist's hands on his hot back, and he lurched against her in reaction.

Both his own hands were tangled in her hair now, angling her head so he could drag his open mouth over her jaw and down the pale length of her neck, then back up. Her short nails bit into his back as he licked the curve of her ear.

"You wore a dress today." He bit her lobe, and she moaned. "For me?"

Her frantic little nod, he rewarded with another fevered kiss.

When he raised his head again, she clutched his hips and whispered, "Wanted to look pretty for our last day together."

"You're always pretty. Always." Disentangling his right hand from her hair, he reached for the hem of that flirty, silky dress. "And this isn't our last day, but—"

Oh, a dress was so much easier than jeans, and her thigh was so soft and dimpled and warm under his palm.

With the hand still buried in her hair, he tipped her head to meet his gaze before exploring further. Higher. "Okay?"

"Yes." Her throat worked as she swallowed, and he sucked at the spot. "Yes, please."

Her cheeks were flushed now, her lips as swollen as he'd imagined, and he wanted to watch her come with an agony of desperation he'd never experienced before.

"Look at me," he rasped. "Look at me as I touch you."

She wet her lips and nodded as much as she could with his fist in her hair, and then he was pulling her cotton panties down those lovely thighs, just far enough so he could explore her without any obstructions.

He palmed her sex, and her head thumped against the shelves as she gasped, but she held his stare. Her hair was coarse between her legs, her flesh slick and hot, and he couldn't wait.

He wouldn't.

Her eyes went hazy with the first stroke of his fingertips, her mouth parted for each rapid inhalation. She was so soft, plump and delicate against his hand, and so responsive to each light, exploring pass over her flesh. Her back arched, the breath seemingly punched from her lungs as he brushed his forefinger over her clit, and he watched her pupils expand with each gentle circle, each rub.

Her shaking thighs spread further, and her cheek was hot against his as he whispered in her ear, "Does that feel good, Poppy?"

"Yes." When his finger sank inside her, her breath hitched. "God, yes."

He drew back enough to watch her swallow and half-close her eyes when he fucked her with one finger, then two. And when he used that slickness to circle her clit again, only his hand in her hair kept that heavy-lidded gaze on his.

She was moving against him, grinding, panting, her face flushed.

"Cover my mouth. Your hand." It was a desperate gasp, her brows drawn as if in pain. "Simon, I'm—"

As soon as he freed his hand from her hair and pressed it over her mouth, she moaned against his palm once, then again, and came hard.

Her legs quaked and her flesh pulsed against his fingertips, and he worked her until the very last spasm of pleasure eased, watching her face turn slack, her expression beatific. Sweaty wisps of hair clung to her temples, and her buns had entirely ceased to exist. She was gripping his bare shoulders—had she unbuttoned his shirt at some point, or had he?—so hard she might leave bruises.

At that moment, nothing else existed but her pleasure and his savage satisfaction at having given it to her. Nothing. Not the danger of what they'd just done, not the fierce throb of his cock.

When she was still, he lowered his hand from her mouth so he could kiss her hard, and she returned the embrace with equal heat.

Then, somehow, his pants were down around his thighs, and so were his boxer-briefs, and she was the one pressing him up against the shelves. Before he could muster a single coherent word, her strong, pale hand wrapped around his dick and stroked.

He made a strangled sound deep in his chest and jerked against her.

When her hand stilled in response, he almost wept.

"I'm sorry, Simon. I should have asked." She touched his cheek. "May I?"

His only response was his hand atop hers, setting it back in motion as she grinned up at him. When she paused to slip her hand between her legs, then resumed gripping his cock with slick fingers, he thunked his head against the shelves hard enough to bruise.

Each squeeze of that capable hand raced up his spine like a line of fire. Lighter fluid set aflame, flaring with such immediate heat, he was surprised his hair wasn't singed.

"Look," she murmured, and he set his forehead to hers as she grasped his neck with her free hand. Together, they watched her pump his dick, his panting breaths and low groans gathering in the space between their mouths.

Helplessly, he was fucking her fingers now, the nape of his neck sweaty. She was squeezing there too, holding him steady, making him watch, tugging his hair until he was so overwhelmed by sensation he whimpered.

His hands were on her breasts, on that amazing, generous ass, roaming as if she might leave at any moment, as if he needed to touch all of her at once.

He was making too much noise, he knew it, but he couldn't—he couldn't—

With one final squeeze, one more ounce of pressure against the underside of his cockhead, one more lungful of turpentine and musk and sweat, he bucked his hips and buried his face in the damp crook of her neck and sank his teeth into her flesh and came with a muffled shout, jerking hard with every spasm.

She stroked him through it, her grip gentling, her murmur soothing.

When he could see again, when he could stand without her support, he registered what they'd just done. What he'd just done.

If anyone unlocked her classroom door, there was no mistaking the situation.

They were propped against the shelves along one wall. Her panties were still around her knees, and his pants and boxer-briefs rested just below his ass. His shirt was unbuttoned, gaping open, and it wasn't only paint and glue staining her dress now.

If his expression resembled hers at all, they both looked pink and dazed and well-fucked. Her hair bore the marks of his hands. They smelled distinctly of sex. And the pink imprint of his teeth on her pale skin…

That, honestly, was the only thing he regretted.

"Did I hurt you?" He touched the mark carefully, mouth pinched tight. "I'm sorry."

As always, her smile dazzled him. "I'm not."

"Good." He pressed his lips to that mark, then her temple, her cheek, her nose, her round chin. "After we clean up, may I come home with you?"

"Yes." Her fingertips on his own cheek were tender. "Yes, Simon."

When he kissed her again, her mouth sweet and soft beneath his, he found once more what he'd discovered the previous night. The certainty he'd been seeking. The solution to his final mystery. The answer to a problem that wasn't really a problem—not when her heart ached for him the same way his ached for her.

In her presence, one plus one didn't equal two. The two of them weren't a sum, or a product, or even an exponent. Nothing that mundane. Nothing that obvious or simple or safe.

He wouldn't have unraveled so quickly, so thoroughly, for obvious or simple or safe.

No, he and Poppy together made an entirely irrational number, expansive and infinite.

And for the first time, he was delighted there was no known end.

ACKNOWLEDGMENTS

I am so proud to have worked with my incredibly talented friends for this anthology. I owe a huge debt of gratitude to Emma, Adriana, Ruby, and Cat for agreeing to this idea and ensuring there was nothing but joy in the process of making it reality. Thank you too for reading over my story and providing notes, encouragement, and emoji-laden DMs! You're all the literal best. :-) I am also so grateful to the wonderful Zoe York, who made our sexy AF cover. THANK YOU. Finally, a special shout-out and even more hugs to Adriana, who kindly took on a bunch of extra responsibilities when my mental health wobbled over the course of a long, dark Swedish winter. I adore you, and I owe you big. ♥

BIOGRAPHY

Olivia Dade grew up an undeniable nerd, prone to ignoring the world around her as she read any book she could find. Her favorites, though, were always, always romances. As an adult, she earned an M.A. in American history and worked in a variety of jobs that required the donning of actual pants: Colonial Williamsburg interpreter, high school teacher, academic tutor, and (of course) librarian. Now, however, she has finally achieved her lifelong goal of wearing pajamas all day as a hermit-like writer and enthusiastic hag. She currently lives outside Stockholm with her patient Swedish husband, their whip-smart daughter, and the family's ever-burgeoning collection of books.

For more info about the author, visit

Olivia's Website: https://oliviadade.com

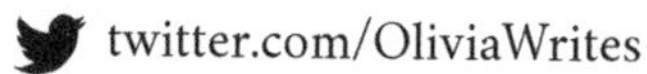

ALSO BY OLIVIA DADE

THERE'S SOMETHING ABOUT MARYSBURG

Teach Me

40-Love

Sweetest in the Gale: A Marysburg Story Collection

LOVE UNSCRIPTED

Desire and the Deep Blue Sea

Tiny House, Big Love

SPOILER ALERT

LOVESTRUCK LIBRARIANS

Broken Resolutions

My Reckless Valentine

Mayday

Ready to Fall

Driven to Distraction

Hidden Hearts

CAUGHT LOOKING

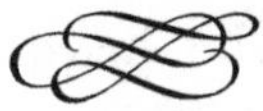

ADRIANA HERRERA

This story is for my Romance Twitter peeps, one of my most cherished Romancelandia communities.

When best friends Yariel and Hatuey's gaming night turns into an unexpected and intense hook up, Hatuey can't wait to do it again. Yariel is less certain--the major leaguer might seem to all the world like he has a heart of stone, but he's been carrying a torch for his friend for years, and worries this will ruin the most important relationship in his life. That means Hatuey has to do all the work, and he's planning to give it all he's got. Yariel may be the one hitting home runs on the field...but Hatuey is playing a game of seduction, and he knows exactly how to make Yariel crumble.

* * *

Content Warnings: on-page sex, references to homophobia

CHAPTER 1

TUESDAY

Yariel

"What the fuck?" I asked into the stillness of my bedroom as I ran a hand over my fade. Even with my eyes closed I could tell I'd forgotten to pull down the black-out shades, which meant my twenty-fifth floor apartment was probably flooded with Brooklyn waterfront sunshine.

I was still half-sleep, but even in my semi-conscious state I knew something was off. For a second I panicked, thinking I'd missed morning PT, but then remembered we were still in the off-season. No, whatever it was had nothing to do with my job as a shortstop for the Brooklyn Bombers. My head wasn't pounding so it wasn't a hangover, although from how fucking dry my mouth felt, drinking had definitely happened.

"Shit," I moaned as I gingerly prodded a sore spot on my collarbone...and that's when it all came back to me.

Hatuey. I'd slept with...Hatuey.

"Coño." I croaked, squeezing my eyes tight for a few seconds, not ready to find my best friend lying naked next to me. Not after what felt like an entire lifetime of restraint and careful control only to blow it all up in one night. I didn't dare turn around, not wanting to see the horror when he opened his eyes and realized what we'd done.

I took a couple of breaths, fighting down the anger at myself for letting this happen. I tried to remember that acting pissed with him would only make things more difficult—and they were bad enough. But when I finally opened one eye and turned around, I realized shit was way worse than I imagined.

He was gone.

"Fuck." I sat up, with a million scary thoughts running through my head as I quickly ran through the events of last night. Hatuey coming over upset about another dating app shit show. The two of us gaming and talking over a couple of beers and then the question, that damn question. The one I knew I should've ignored—that I fucking knew would end in disaster.

My stomach churned as the panic rose in my throat. I squeezed my eyes shut again, and as if my mind were one of those old-school movie reels, I saw Hatuey's wide mouth, his generous lips open just enough to give me a peek of his tongue, as he leaned in to kiss me.

Nope, not going there.

Last night had to go back to where all my thoughts about Hatuey and sex went: to the vault. The vault that kept my ill-advised obsession with my straight friend on lock. The vault that kept me from losing the most important person in my life because I could not keep my dick in order. I squeezed that motherfucker on the head for good measure, because he was not running the show this morning like he had last night.

I wasn't some lovesick teenager—I was a grown fucking man. I would fix this. I would make this all go away like I had for the last ten years.

As soon as I figured out where the hell Hatuey'd gone.

After throwing on some underwear, I ran a hand over my belly and almost threw up when I felt the dry patch right over my groin... come. Come from when I'd fucked my best friend last night. "Mierda. Mierda. *Mierda.*" I breathed out so close to losing it.

He must be freaking out. I had been a fucking monster last night too. My stomach roiled at the memory of the things I'd said. It was a side of me Hatuey had never seen in all the years we'd been friends, one that I'd worked very hard to keep under control. Feeling more worried with every passing second, I hurried to the bathroom hoping and dreading I'd find him there.

Nothing.

"Hat? Donde tu estas?" I called as I walked from room to room, until I'd run out of places to look. And with every step the fear I'd ruined things with the most important person in my life wound me up until I was hardly able to breathe. The skin on my face felt tight, stretched on the bone. My heart raced as I walked back to the bedroom, wondering what could be going through his head. I hated this feeling, and it was all my fault. I let this happen, and I had to be the one to make things go back to how they were.

I glanced around the room, looking for some evidence that he'd really been here, some hysterical, desperate part of me hoping I'd imagined the whole thing. That the moment I'd dreamed about for so long and had told myself a thousand times could be never happen, actually hadn't. Then I spotted the glass on my side of the bed, full of water. Next to it a packet of Vitamin C and two ibuprofen tablets. And right under the pills was a little sheet of paper he'd probably ripped off the magnetized pad stuck to my fridge. He'd left them, because they hadn't been there last night.

Hatuey left those for me. To make sure I didn't feel like shit this morning. And he'd left me a message too. I pressed a fist to my chest as I looked at the scrap of paper that quite possibly held the few words that would upend my life. Where my best friend probably wrote he was never talking to me again, freaked out about what we'd done. After what I'd let happen.

I stumbled back feeling once again out of breath, tightening my fists to keep them from shaking.

None of this was supposed to be happening. Hatuey was my friend, my Day One, my resting place, but not my lover. *Never* my lover. That had always been clear and I had never—but for one foolish second almost ten years ago—crossed that boundary. But last night I'd barreled through all those firmly set barriers and fucked with every one of the rules.

I couldn't even really blame it on alcohol. I'd just wanted him. Like I had since the moment I'd laid eyes on him when we were both fourteen years old and I was the new kid in school. The kid whose parents sent him to Santo Domingo to live with and aunt when our part of the Bronx got so hot they were afraid I'd end up hurt or caught up in the wrong crowd.

I'd been scared shitless walking into that building, a fancy private international high school my parents could've never afforded in the States, but could pay for in the DR. I was paralyzed as I stepped on to gleaming marble floors and watched rows of kids in every shade of brown walking around in pristine uniforms, Ferragamo loafers and Cartier watches. It was like some kind of Dominican version of *Gossip Girl*. They all passed me and whispered when they saw my Air Force 1s or got close enough to look at my cornrows and Yankees hoodie.

"Un Dominican York." That's what they called me. A Dominican from New York.

Someone who didn't belong in DR high society, where blackness was diluted by using words like *canela* to describe brown skin. As if using the word for cinnamon instead of the actual color would somehow bury the African roots deep enough to make them disappear. It was a world I was never meant to fit into...until Hatuey. His was the first real smile I'd seen that morning—it felt to me like it had been the first one I'd seen since I left my family's apartment in Castle Hill— and my body even then didn't know what to do with the full impact of Hatuey Sanchez's smile.

The boy with the dark brown eyes and unruly curls. He was the sun of that school. Every girl wanted to be his. Every boy wanted him as a friend. And from the first moment we met, to the confusion of everyone, we became inseparable. Me from the other side of the bridge, him from the oldest part of Santo Domingo where the families could trace their ancestry back to Madre España. Two different worlds, but it didn't matter, because Hatuey wanted me around, and I couldn't stay away. He was slim and cocky, and even back then, a good six inches shorter than me, but the moment I saw him my entire existence tilted on its axis.

And that had been us for ten years and counting. Because other than a second-long drunken moment the night of our high school graduation, I had never blurred the lines.

I stood there, paralyzed, angry at the fear I felt slithering up my spine. I was certain that note on my dresser had the words that would rip him out my life. The phone skittered on the top of the table, making me jump. As soon as I saw a notification flashing on the screen, I gritted my teeth fighting off a wave of nausea. I ignored it and kept my focus on the note. I fucking hated feeling this rattled. If Hatuey were here he'd say it was because my control freak ways turned me into a monster the moment anything in my life seemed out of order. But he *wasn't* here and *that* was the fucking issue.

Had to go deal with a work thing. One of the rookies needed an interpreter last minute. Take the ibuprofen and go back to bed. Everything's fine.

I read it twice, not sure what to think, fixating on the squiggles at the end of the note that were supposed to be a smiley face. Did he really have to go or was this his way of avoiding having to deal with me this morning?

Hatuey was the interpreter program coordinator for the Brooklyn Bombers but as far as I knew, it wasn't usually the kind of job that involved field emergencies. Him leaving before seven a.m. even on a weekday wasn't the norm, and I had to wonder if this was just an excuse for him to get some space.

I let out a shaky breath as my head swam. Images of last night, of the way he'd responded to me. They way he'd moaned with pleasure as I ran my tongue over every inch of skin I'd spent the last ten years fantasizing about. The way his body felt under my hands. The way they itched to have him there again.

My phone rang this time, which meant it was one of the five people who I was always available for. I walked back to the bed and sat as I looked at the screen and realized Hatuey had left me half a dozen messages and tried to call me about the same amount of times. But he wasn't calling me now. It was Monserrat, one-third of the threesome that had gotten me through high school, college and most of the last few years in the majors.

I accepted the call, bracing for whatever jokes she had, certain Hatuey had already told her what happened. It wasn't like I'd ever told anyone about my crush, but Monsi had made enough comments over the years that I was pretty certain meant she had an inkling about my feelings for my best friend.

But when I accepted the call, the typical half-sneering, half-bored tone Monsi usually used was completely gone. "Are you okay, friend?"

I flopped heavily onto the massive headboard of my gigantic bed, not sure what to make of Monserrat's serious tone.

I closed my eyes, breathing through my nose, all the words on the tip of my tongue. Wanting to tell this to someone. But getting into a decade of my self-made baggage with Hatuey was not going to help. I needed things to go back to normal. Where Hatuey was my friend and I didn't risk destroying our relationship by breaking rules I'd promised to keep ten years ago.

I'd seen plenty of people ruin things by crossing lines. Sex was messy, which was why it was madness to do this with the one person in my life who was always steady. Why would I open us both up to complications that could mess up the one thing I could not lose?

So I did what had always worked before—I shoved my feelings for Hatuey way down and acted like they weren't trying to claw up my throat. "I'm fine."

CHAPTER 2

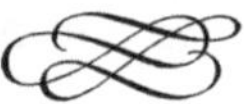

Hatuey

I ran out on him.

I could tell myself a thousand times I'd left Yariel's house at the crack of dawn looking like I'd been ridden hard and put away wet because I was doing my job. And technically I was, but mostly I was being a coward. I'd woken up with my back plastered to my best friend's chest, his skin like a fire iron against mine. His much bigger, much stronger body wrapping mine up. And after a few blissful moments feeling like my entire life finally made sense, I panicked.

It wasn't like I hadn't had the chance to wonder about him that way in the last ten years. Yariel's sexuality was not just incidental—it was a major topic of conversation in the sports world and in our homeland. My best friend was out and proud. The first MLB player ever to come out in his rookie year.

But Yariel and I had never been complicated. Becoming friends wasn't ever a question. It just was. I saw him walk into our school—where sometimes it seemed like I'd drown in the pretentious posing—and felt like he was the only real thing I'd seen in that building since I could remember. His mouth set in a hard line, so clearly trying to look tough, and so obviously terrified. And alone, so alone.

It had always felt like a lot more than friendship between us, but back then in the DR, that had been a dangerous proposition. If we were just best friends, there would never be a reason for my family to oppose our friendship. There would never be a reason for us to ever be split apart. If we were best friends, I'd always have to be there. I could just continue to tell myself every one of the hundreds of dates I went on never worked because I was too picky or too busy—and not because I had met my perfect mate in high school and never had the guts to tell myself, let alone him.

But I had gone and ruined it with that kiss last night, and now I was fucked…literally. And no matter what happened, everything would be different. Because I knew Yariel. I knew his stubborn ass was going to blame it all on himself and use it as a reason to push me away. The thought of it was unbearable. But what we'd done last night had changed things even if we never mentioned it again. My throat constricted at the idea of not being able to see him whenever I wanted.

I looked at myself in the mirror behind the bathroom door of my tiny studio apartment and winced when I noticed the bruises on my hips from where Yariel had grabbed me. He'd been so tentative at first, so careful, and I'd let him think I'd never thought about him touching me like that before. But when I'd begged him for more, when I'd told him that I wanted him, he'd unleashed himself on me. And know I was utterly ruined with the knowledge of how Yariel and I could be together.

I had to talk to Yariel. The longer I waited, the more he would get into his own head.

My phone ringing pulled me out from the chaos in my head. I jumped to get it, hoping it was him. I assumed that, like usual, he had gotten it together first. But it was my father. I couldn't handle a conversation about when I was planning to come home and get into politics like the rest of my siblings. I couldn't bear to lie about what I was doing now, what I'd be doing last night. So I tapped the ignore button on the call and sat down to do what I should've done hours before.

He picked up after two rings. "Hatuey."

My heart pounded when I heard his voice, and it wasn't dread or embarrassment that made my pulse throb between my temples. Breathless. I was breathless from the intensity with which my body responded to his voice. I hated my phone and every decision I'd made in the last few hours. I should've been there with him.

Because Yariel was in a panic. "I will never let this happen again."

My stomach lurched at the agony I heard in his voice. He thought I'd run because I regretted what happened last night.

"Are you okay? Are you in pain?" He sounded frantic and scared, and I should've said then that I'd been wanting this for so long. That even though I was a clueless prick for a good part of that time, I'd always known. I also knew his control-freak ways had to be at an all-time high right now. The first step was to reassure him that our friendship was still solid.

"I'm fine. I'm sorry I ran off this morning." He grunted in response and I sighed, eyes tightly shut as I remembered how we'd been locked together when I woke up. How his massive arm kept me plastered to him all night. How the aches of what we'd done together had brought the memories crashing back as soon as I'd opened my eyes.

"Everything's fine, Yari. You want me to come over?" I offered, thinking if we were in the same room we could at least explore whatever it was that had ignited things. Because my head and my body were caught up in a tidal wave of want, and if I left it up to Yariel he would shut it all down before we got any further.

When he didn't answer, worry started to worm into the desire I was feeling. I had to get over myself and focus on Yariel. I could hear him doing the deep breathing his therapist had taught him to do for the moments when he was overwhelmed. Which, since he started playing in the majors, seemed to happen all the time. No good was coming from him getting more wound up; I had to interrupt whatever was happening.

"Let's switch to video call." I knew that seeing his face would help me, and maybe it could do the same for him.

Without saying a word, he started the video call. His beautiful, familiar face filled the screen. He was still him, but different, and he did not look happy. Smooth brown skin like caramel. Strong jaw clenched, those light gray eyes unhappy. I wanted to reach out and run the pads of my finger over that furrowed brow. Coax him in for a kiss so I could, now in the light of the day, get to taste that mouth. Pull on those lips I'd barely gotten to savor.

Yeah, there was no undoing this. There was no stopping that dark and sharp thing pulsing in my chest with the words mine, mine, *mio*.

My heart lurched when I saw the worry lines around his mouth. "Hablame, Yariel." His eyes were all over the place, as if he was taking inventory that all my parts were still there. I lifted my hand, and then switched so I could show him the other. "All my limbs are still attached. I'd show you my feet, but I know my pinky toe creeps you out."

That got a very tiny lift from the right side of his mouth. "It doesn't have a nail," he explained with a grunt for the seven hundredth time. I smiled, still worried about how serious he looked, as he continued to examine every inch of my face. "We can get past this. This won't hurt us," he assured me as his eyes did another scan of whatever parts of my torso he could see through the screen.

Ah, Dictator Yariel, not my favorite of his moods. There was no talking to Yariel when he was like this. He just passed out edicts and the rest of us had to go with it.

It cut that he didn't seem to even want to discuss what happened last night, but I also knew Yariel couldn't handle feeling like his personal life was in disarray. He always said it came from growing up watching his parents struggle with the pressures of immigrant life in the States. Of feeling like their lives were not in their control for so many years when they were undocumented. So if anything slipped even an inch outside of Yariel's master plan, he forced it back to its place. And it seemed I was currently very much outside the spot where I belonged. That was not the headspace I wanted to work with.

His breathing was still coming fast, and despite the tension of the moment, my eyes roamed hungrily over his bare, smooth chest. He was vain and waxed the little of bit of chest hair he had—all the better for those many candid workout shots he put on social media. Fuck, I wanted to lick him, and he was going to make us struggle to get back to that every step of the way.

"Of course we're fine," I snapped, my own temper rising, as his nostrils flared. I sat there in silence, waiting for it.

"Why did you leave this morning then? Were you hurt and didn't want me to know?" He shook that hard head of his, eyes shut tight. "I should've never let this happen, forced myself on you."

That was enough of that bullshit.

"I literally threw myself at you," I said harshly, as I struggled to find a way to get through to him. I could just say I'd had my own moment of panic this morning. Or I could say the other truth: that I needed my own space to quietly have my entire world rocked by what I was feeling. By the truth he'd given me last night and I now had to finally face up to. That I'd retreated to think on what this meant, if I was ready to say this to myself, or out loud to the world, to my family.

When I looked up, I found Yari's flinty stare, and the set to his jaw promised wrongheaded bullshit coming my way. "No. You were upset about the date. We were drinking—

I put my hand up in protest, because he was not going there. "Yariel, we each had two beers." I raised the phone so he had a very clear view of my face. "*I*," I said, pointing a finger to my chest, "kissed *you*."

He flinched like I'd slapped him, and once again I dearly wished I'd had the guts to stay at his house this morning.

He ran a hand over the top of his fade like he did on those rare occasions he was unsure of himself. Yariel Cabral always knew what to do, and if he didn't, he pretended he did. I was the only person who ever seemed to trip him up.

But when he looked up, I knew he was going to piss me off before he even opened his mouth. "I did it. I'm fully responsible and I will make sure it never happens again."

Not fucking likely, motherfucker.

"No. Asi no, Yariel," I said with a roll of my neck, trying to talk some sense into him. "This is not how any of this works, you asshole." Dammit, cursing him out was not going to help. Fuck.

He shook his head hard, like he wanted to knock whatever was in it right out. "I can't do this with you. This is not how it's supposed to be." He looked pale, like he was about to be sick, and for the first time I wondered if *I'd* pushed *him* too far. Maybe he was trying to let me down easy or not make it more awkward.

Oh god.

"Yari, did I pressure you?" I asked, mortified at the idea of Yariel going along with this, because he didn't want to embarrass me. "Did I make you do something you didn't want?"

He didn't let me continue. "You know you don't ever have to ask me that." Every word was like an ember lighting up in my chest, the need in his eyes turning me inside out. "That's not the issue here, Hatuey, and never will be."

The relief of knowing we'd both been into what had happened was absolute, and so was the frustration of knowing he was just being a stubborn ass.

I turned my head to the side, trying not to speak in the heat of the moment even though I was certainly feeling hot. "So if that's not the issue...if you want me, and I want to try—"

More head shaking. "I'm not trying anything like that. No repeat. We go back to normal. To how we are, Hatuey." He had his hand up in his signature sanctimonious move, and I was starting to think not being close enough to rip it off was probably for the best. "We have a trip this week, and we can't be playing games."

Who was playing games?

I was about to protest, to tell him he was being an asshole, that this was *our* life. That this was our *fucking future*. That nothing had ever been less of a game than the possibility that we could be more to each other.

But the way the he pursed his mouth, the fear in his eyes, gave me pause. Something was way off.

"What is really going on, Yariel? Are you seeing anyone?" I asked, more sharply than I had a right to, as a dark and unfriendly thing unfurled in my gut at the thought of Yariel with someone else. At the very idea that another man would get to have him, like I'd only barely gotten to. The intensity of it shook me to the core. Because until this moment, I would've sworn on my life that I was not the jealous type.

His scoff should've been answer enough, but then it was his turn to look bitter. "No, Hatuey. There's nobody else." He sighed, looking up this time. I noticed this conversation involved a lot of him avoiding eye contact with me. "It's too complicated. I can't do complicated right now."

I wasn't going to yell. I told myself it was foolish to push for something I wasn't even sure I could handle. Yariel was right: taking this further would not be simple. There would be fallout for him and for me, and I almost gave in. But this was Yariel, and it felt like a sin to not try. To not take this chance when it was being handed to us. "Just one last thing. And then we can go on this trip without me bringing it up again."

"Fine." He sucked his teeth and flexed his shoulders, bratty and moody like he got, and I hated the hot pool of want gathering in my gut from watching him.

"I loved it." I said it looking straight at him. My eyes locked with his, holding them so he could see. "How you touched me, how you kissed me." I discreetly let my hand snake down to my dick, which was rock hard by now. "And when you were inside me..." I closed my eyes when he groaned, a deep and needy sound. "Everything made sense. I want to do it again. Don't you?"

He made a strangled noise, but I knew he wouldn't answer. When he looked at me though...*that* was nowhere near a no. I opened my mouth to try and convince him that despite all the perfectly good reasons not to start something between us, last night had been a game changer.

Before I got a chance to, he sat up and pointed to something off where I couldn't see. "Mary's here." His housekeeper. "See you at the airport."

I guessed the conversation was over. "So you're not going to say anything. We fucked and you're unbothered by the whole thing," I said, sounding hurt.

He laughed, and this time the slash of a smile on his face was so sharp it could cut. "If you knew the things I want to do to you. The ways I'd fuck you." He looked down and then up again, as if searching the heavens for answers while his words made every muscle in my body tighten with need.

"Then why are you acting this way, Yariel?"

"Because I can fuck any guy I want, any time. There's only one of you. And I would never do anything to mess with that."

He ended the call, and I sat there staring at the dark screen. We would be in each other's pockets for days. Private plane, luxury villa for just the two of us. I could already see it, him doing his best to act like he was made out of marble and me letting him get away with it. Not wanting to push his buttons. Letting Yariel shut it all down.

Well, fuck that.

If I was going to get four days with the only person in the world I seemed to want, I was going to shoot my shot. It took me all these years to figure out that stubborn bastard was my fucking soulmate, and I'd be damned if I was going to let him get in the way of me making him mine.

CHAPTER 3

THURSDAY

Hatuey

"I'm still gagged about how easy you're taking all of this."

I rolled my eyes at my friend Monserrat's surprised tone as I sat in the back of the Escalade Yariel had sent to bring me to the airport.

"What do you expect me to do, Monsi? A," I said, holding up a finger in the air. "He's been my best friend forever, and he's been out to me most of that time. So why would I be freaking out about having sex with him?"

I cringed when I heard the driver in the front seat make a choking sound. I couldn't even say she was homophobic, because I would probably not be into hearing about a passenger's sex life if I was trying to drive either.

So I lowered my voice as I went back to my rant. "B. I'm a grown man, and—" Monsi interrupted. I loved her, but she was rude as fuck.

"A grown man who as far as I know was straight and who had to be aware—or at least suspect a little bit—that your best friend has had the hots for you since tenth grade." Monsi interrupted. I loved her, but she was rude as fuck.

She was screaming so loud by the last part, I had to hold the phone away. "Chill out, Monsi. Jesus. Does the whole of Santo Domingo need to know my business?"

I looked out the window and saw the exit for JFK, where Yariel was probably already waiting. I wasn't sure, though, since he'd tacitly avoided all communication with me for the last forty-eight hours. The car had been there right on time, but I'd left my apartment later than anticipated. This morning I'd roamed around my place for hours, agonizing over what to pack, what to wear on the plane, and had made a last-minute run to the store to buy condoms and lube. I second-guessed myself on everything because I knew these next few days were my chance to talk some sense into Yariel. To get him to let down his guard for once.

"I just want to give us a chance before Yari shuts it down."

Monserrat's voice was a lot gentler the next time she spoke. "I'm not gonna lie—you're really blowing my mind with how chill you are."

I could say I didn't get it either, but that wasn't true. I'd been waking up to my feelings for Yariel for years. "There's not much to get, Monsi. Yari and I hooked up. I'm fine that it happened and really wish it would again. But he's a stubborn asshole and has decided that he needs to protect my virtue."

She scoffed at that. "Maybe he's scared, Hatuey." I smiled at how she said my name. Ahh-too-ey. After almost three years of living in the States, I'd gotten used to hearing my name pronounced in a hundred ways, but hearing it now was grounding. Reminded me of who I was, and I needed that. Even as Monsi was naming the things I'd avoided thinking about for the last forty-eight hours. "He doesn't have the best track record with relationships, and he might be scared of starting something and messing up your friendship."

"He knows he could never lose my friendship. If it doesn't work, we'll get over it. We can go back to how things were before. " Even as I said it, I realized I sounded ridiculous. I wanted to believe we could overcome things not working out. But the newfound caveman in me, who only seemed to wake up whenever Yariel was in the picture, kept growling *mine, mine, mine*. No matter what I told myself or Monsi, I already knew that giving Yariel up would not allow for a neat and tidy ending.

Monsi's voice was as serious as I'd ever heard her when she spoke next. "There's no getting over you for Yariel. You know that."

I did know that. I knew it because I'd spent the last ten years actively avoiding what had been in front of my face. I'd had girlfriends I cared for, but always just right under surface had been the things I felt for Yariel and was never ready to look at too closely. The need I had for his time. The joy I got from his presence. For his body and warmth in my space. The purpose I felt, knowing he needed me. That other than his parents and his career, he valued my friendship more than anything else in his life. I was secure in that sacred corner of Yariel's heart where there was only space for a special few. I could admit, if only to myself, that in the past the fear of losing my place in his life had always kept me from reaching for more. But that was before I knew what it felt like to be his.

"If he's scared, he has to tell me. This is too big and too important to not at least talk about, and right now he's being a moody asshole."

"Because he's terrified," Monsi added, and then softened the blow. "And I know you are too."

I took stock of my body, what I was feeling, and noticed the rapid heartbeat, the jitters as we approached the part of the airport where we'd take the private jet to the DR. "To be honest, I'm more scared of not knowing than anything else. But I'm not the doom-and-gloom one in this equation, and I know we can be great together. I've always known that."

"He's been waiting for you for a long time, Haty. Don't forget that."

I sighed, feeling the weight of Monsi's words. Knowing what uncertainty did to Yariel. "I know."

I saw him before he noticed the car. Standing in his fancy baseball player travel clothes: custom slacks to fit that big body, leather ankle boots and the navy cashmere pea coat I'd helped him pick out. I was wearing a matching charcoal one he'd gotten me that day. His brown skin was flushed with red from the cold, and I was practically salivating watching him. His eyes were covered by a pair of aviators, but the hard line of his mouth told me I had my work cut out of for me for the next four days.

"I have to go, chula. Thanks for talking to me. I promise I won't do anything over the top. But I'm not letting him shut me out either. If I have to use a few tricks here and there, I will."

And because Monserrat loved us both but also lived for drama, she cackled. "So you're going to *seduce* him."

I thanked the driver as I stepped out of the car with my backpack slung over one shoulder, and my eyes trained in the direction of the man in question. I noticed the exact moment when he spotted me. His entire body went taut with alertness. A mirror to my reaction to him, and when he took off his sunglasses, those green-and-gray eyes burned.

When I finally responded to Monsi, he was making his way to me. His steps were quick, like he'd made himself wait but had given up resisting. Yariel could lie to me, he could even lie to himself, but his stare spoke loud and clear. He was in a bad way just as I was, and *I* was going to do something about it. "This trip has just officially become Operation Make Him Sweat."

I ended the call with Monserrat's throaty laugh in my ears and stayed put in my spot, waiting for my best friend come to me. No, I wasn't going to let him have his way.

When he finally got close enough to touch, I did. I pushed up and kissed him on the cheek. Ran my hand over his face, like I'd done thousands of times, but still it felt new, because all those other times I was not ready to claim him. I was ready now.

YARIEL

None of this was going according to plan. Hatuey's vibe had me all fucked up. He was supposed to be skittish, freaking out about having sex with me. But since we'd gotten on this damn plane, Hatuey'd been sending me looks like he wanted to swallow me whole.

"Fuck." I groaned as I shifted in the leather seat, hating myself for putting the words *Hatuey* and *swallow* together in my head.

"You look a little flushed, Yari." That smartass tone was not helping either.

I grunted in answer and turned to look at him, trying hard to assess if he was just messing with me. I glared in his direction, not dialing back my mood or my attitude at all. But he kept up that Mr. Chill thing that drove me up the wall sometimes, always sunny. Hell, most of the time seeing him all relaxed *did* go a long way to lighten my mood.

But I wasn't feeling friendly today. I felt reckless and turned on, and I'd be damned if I was going to let either of those get the better of me. He was on his phone now, but every few seconds would let his eyes wander my way, as if I'd vanish into thin air if he looked away for too long. If he was as pressed as I was, I couldn't see it. But I knew him as much as he knew me, and he had to be bugging too, even if just a little bit.

"Who are you texting?" I snapped, in a much sharper tone than warranted, and got an arched eyebrow.

"Just Monsi." He leaned back, brown eyes trained somewhere on my forehead. He licked his lips, and I swore I could feel the roughness of his tongue on my cock. I needed to look away, I really did, but it was like I was in trance and the pendulum was Hatuey's mouth. "You need anything?"

The question went straight to my dick, which was very eager to provide an answer. I shuddered out a breath and leaned in when he ran a hand over his chest. His finger just barely missing a nipple. The nipple I'd played with. Put my teeth on.

Shit. I wasn't going to survive this flight.

"Everything okay over here?" Thank god for flight crews. The flight attendant, who hopefully had not noticed my raging hard-on before I threw a blanket on my lap, stepped into the cabin. The interruption was the proverbial bucket of ice water I needed dumped on my fool head. But next to me, the demon I thought was my best friend just laughed at my highly flustered state.

I nodded while I glared at him, and pointed at the empty glass on the armrest tray. "I'll have another Zacapa on the rocks." I gestured to

Hatuey, who was grinning at me like a brown-eyed devil in jeans and cashmere.

"I'll have what he's having."

The flight attendant snapped her head in assent and quietly scurried away to get our drinks ready while I stared at him.

Had Hatuey's voice always sounded like sex? Or was that just my fucking psyche doing me dirty again? And because my dick was using about ninety-nine percent of the blood that was usually coursing through my brain, it took me a second to catch what he'd said.

And instead of just leaving it alone, I had to be a prick about it. "You drink rum now?" Why did I sound pissed about everything?

Hatuey remained unbothered, though. I could feel the tension in my neck and shoulders as he scrutinized me. That pink mouth of his in a lazy little smile, while his chocolate-brown gaze sharply assessed whatever he was seeing on my face. "I'm not afraid of trying new things."

Yeah, he wasn't letting this shit go. I gulped audibly as he took the glass from the attendant, who promptly excused herself and shut the door behind herself, leaving us alone in the private cabin.

I should've asked him why he was doing this. To stop acting like he could actually be my man. The idea of it, of having him in my bed forever, had been a fantasy I'd never been foolish enough to indulge in. I had him for everything else in my life, and I'd learned to let that be enough. I had too much as it was.

The professional baseball career; money to take care of my parents and my grandparents; good friends who loved me and supported me, and Hatuey—the one who kept me anchored. I wasn't greedy. I could've been fine like this. Maybe not satisfied, but content. Except now I knew how it felt to have his legs wrapped around my waist as I sank into him. To see him writhing in pleasure, needy for my mouth, for my cock. I knew it all, and I was starting to fear it would ruin me.

I chanced a look at him in the seat next to mine. He mirrored my fake relaxed pose, long limbs loose. "What's wrong?" Hatuey's worried voice snapped me out of my tortured sex thoughts. The flirtatious expression from before replaced by genuine concern.

"Nothing," I lied.

"Bullshit. Yari, we need to talk about what happened." I could hear the frustration edging into the worried tone in his voice. Hatuey was going to keep pushing, and I could not let him get to me.

I shook my head once and looked out the window, feeling like my chest was about to explode from the air caught in my lungs. But I was not turning around. If I looked at him, I'd give in.

I felt his hand on my arm and the warmth of his skin as he came closer. Still I didn't turn, because if I did, he'd see. He'd see that the madness of wanting him was overriding every decent instinct I had.

"I wanted you, Yariel." I stiffened at the hitch in his voice. "I'm not sure why it took me so long to figure this out, but—"

I spoke with my eyes still focused on the window, because I was a coward, "You didn't figure it out because you're straight, Hatuey. You were curious and now you know. Done."

He growled and my entire body went haywire. I knew better than to rile up his stubborn ass, but I was desperate. And if pissing him off was what needed to happen for him to get away from me, then that's what I would do. But I should've fucking known Hatuey Sanchez would have me by the balls no matter what I did.

"So you're going to use 1950s gay-slash-straight bullshit to talk me out of what I know I'm feeling? Is that what we're doing now?" The lecture would've been a lot less effective if he wasn't pressed up against me so his mouth was only inches from my ear and his hand was perilously close to my now extremely hard dick. I breathed through my mouth as my—until two days ago—straight best friend did his very best to turn my brain to mush. "You're telling me that the half dozen times I've gotten off thinking about you fucking me in the last two days is just curiosity?"

"Hatuey." My voice was nothing but need and desperation. I was cracking. "This shit isn't funny."

But he wasn't laughing, especially not when he ran a hand over my crotch and I pushed into it. Breath shuddering out of my lungs as that oh-so-fucking-good pressure promised the release I needed.

"Do I sound like I'm making jokes?" he growled into my ear as I held myself so tightly my teeth creaked in my mouth. He kept touching me over my slacks, and in the lust fog of my brain I had the fleeting thought that his long stroke was a fucking miracle.

"You know what I can't stop thinking about?" he asked as he pinched one of my balls and I practically came in my pants. I wanted to throw every bit of sense out the plane's window and let it tumble thirty thousand feet into the Atlantic Ocean.

"Fuck," I snapped out, as he did something particularly delicious to the tip of my dick and I felt the last of my restraint snap. "Why don't you tell me while you take my dick out, motherfucker? Are you trying to kill me?" I spat while I thrust into his hand.

That laugh, that fucking laugh…I would happily move mountains just to hear that wicked joy in Hatuey's voice. "Well, since you asked so nicely," he answered happily as he made quick work of pulling my throbbing dick out of my pants. "I can't stop thinking about giving you a blowjob. I found out two days ago that my addictive personality goes into overdrive when it comes to your cock."

I should've ended this right then. Told him he was going to regret this. That it was just the novelty of it. That he'd go back to the DR next week and see his family. Talk to his college professor/politician father and be mortified to remember he'd done this with me.

But I was weak and he was touching me like he'd been born to bring me off, so I undid my seatbelt, turned so I could get a good look at his face before I ruined both our lives, and I kissed him.

CHAPTER 4

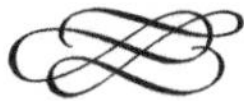

Hatuey

Airplane sex had not ever really been a bucket list item for me, but I was into it.

I was mentally doing fist pumps as Yariel dragged me unto his lap while he communicated in grunts. It might've been a good idea to think on why my best friend manhandling me on a plane was apparently all I wanted from life. But I was too busy climbing six-feet seven-inches of hot-as-fuck Dominican man. I pressed myself to him as he ran his big hands down my waist to my ass. Fingers digging in while I tried to get us close enough to smash our mouths together. We'd kissed when we hooked up. Not nearly as much as I'd liked, but enough to let me know pressing my lips to Yari's could very quickly become my favorite activity in life.

He was still not talking, but I was determined to bring out that filthy mouth. On our night together he'd given me a play-by-play commentary on all the ways he wanted to fuck me, and it had been hot enough to melt me into a puddle. But it was hard to multitask when I had Yariel pressing his mouth to mine.

"Is this what you want? Me crowding you, huh?" he demanded, as I held on to him. I could tell he was trying to shock me. Make me question what I was getting into. Step back, walk away. But I could see the lust in his eyes, the way his hands tightened on me as I pressed in closer. He wanted this as much as I did, so I asked for what we both needed.

"Besame, Yariel." I demanded with both hands pressed to the side of his neck, my skin tingling in anticipation.

He didn't answer, just licked into my mouth as his hands gripped my ass. I pushed into him as our tongues tangled, and I wondered how it was that I'd talked myself out of this for so long. This was clearly where I belonged. This was so obviously what I'd been missing. I just needed to convince the object of my desire that there was nothing fleeting about this. I wanted Yariel as my lover badly enough to disrupt everything.

I tuned back into the things we were doing together just in time to hear Yariel's filthy mouth joined the proceedings. "I can't stop thinking about your ass," he growled as he slipped a hand under the waistband of my jeans and slid two fingers down my cleft and right to my hole. "What I want is to bend you over that leather couch and eat your ass for hours, then make you choke on my cock."

I gasped, muscles clenching hard. Breath coming in spurts as he touched me exactly where he wanted to put his mouth.

"I want that." I begged as his hands played me like a well-used instrument. I'd used toys on myself plenty of times and knew for a fact my ass was extremely sensitive, but I never had anyone touch me there like this. Everything Yariel had made me feel so far was all-consuming. I pressed into his hand as his dry finger massaged the sensitive rim of my hole. "Push it in, harder," I pleaded, completely fucking thrown by the need in my voice. I loved sex, I did, and over the years had plenty of really great partners. But Yariel's hands were changing the course of my life with every touch.

"What if I told you I wanted to have you right here?" He sounded as winded as I was. He pressed his words on my skin, as I moaned, delirious from lust. "Strip you naked and splay you on that couch, make you scream my name so everyone on this plane knows I'm back here fucking you?"

I bucked as my dick pulsed against his. The images his words elicited were drowning out every ounce of sense I had.

"I'd love it. I'd let you have me here, I wouldn't care who hears me," I promised as I rocked hard into him, his own hips thrusting in unison with mine. Building and building a delicious pressure. I was so close to coming, I could taste it. "I only wish we could've been doing this sooner. That I would've acted differently on graduation night—"

I knew I'd said the wrong thing the moment it came out of my mouth, but it was already too late. Yariel's hands slid out of my pants like he'd been burned, and with the same ease that he'd plucked me out of my seat and settled me on his lap, he took me off. He wouldn't look at me and I knew enough not to ask what was wrong.

I *knew* what was wrong. I'd mentioned graduation night and almost talked about *the kiss.*

After getting my clothes back on properly, I turned to him. "You're not gonna talk to me?"

He was back to glaring at clouds, his jaw clenched so tightly I feared he'd chip his ten thousand dollar veneers. "There's nothing so say, Hatuey. We need to stop doing this. This isn't us. You're my best friend. We can't work like this."

I scoffed as I looked down at his still very obvious erection. His body language was off, his shoulders turned away from me, face like stone, but the evidence that he'd been right there with me just seconds ago was still on display.

"Why are you doing this, Yariel? If we can't 'work like this,'"—I made air-quotes to his turned back—"why did you just tell me you were going to fuck me blind on this plane? And what about me begging you to do it tell you that I'm not ready to see where things go with us?"

My chest was moving up and down like I'd been doing sprints. I wanted to put a hand on his shoulder and force him to look at me. The tension between us was a presence in the cabin, heavy and sickening. And I wasn't the only one reeling.

No matter how hard he tried to keep himself together, I didn't miss that when Yariel rubbed his hands over his face, there was a tremor there, the brown skin of his face ashen. And deep down I knew he was right to be scared. This was new territory for us, and now the person I usually went to when I couldn't figure things out was closed off to me.

"Yariel. Talk to me, please. I feel like I'm losing my mind with you. You tell me you want me, but then you push me away. This is us—we can talk about anything. Why can't we figure this out?"

He growled in frustration, head swiveling from side to side. "This is exactly why we need to stop this shit. We are going to ruin everything."

That hurt. Enough to knock the air out of my lungs. Maybe I was alone in this. Maybe it wasn't worth it to him to make all these changes. "You could just say this isn't worth it to you, Ya—"

He didn't let me finish, springing out of his seat like his ass was on fire. He sat across from me as I watched him in silent agony. "I need a little distance from you right now, Hatuey. Because I feel like I'm going to do something really fucking wild." He ran shaky fingers over his bottom lip as he found the right words. "This isn't about me wanting you. You *know* that. You fucking had to know all these years."

The sound that came out of his mouth was bitter and hollow, but I supposed he intended it to be a laugh. "You have to stop asking me, because I can't say no to you. And we just *can't.*"

I wanted to push him hard, prod with my mouth and tongue and dick until he broke, knowing already that those were the ways I could undo him. But that would only get me temporary satisfaction. He would let himself go until I did or said something that would get us back to another impasse.

Something was going on with Yariel. Something keeping him from coming to me. If I wanted to find out, I had to wait until his guard was lowered or he was too pissed to hold it in, and none of those things could happen on this plane.

So I conceded. "Okay. I'll stop asking." He gave me a narrow look, like he couldn't believe I was giving in so easily. I tried to smile as sweetly as I could. "We're fine," I reassured him, and made a show of grabbing my e-reader and picking up the drink that had been forgotten in the rush to get our dicks out.

Yariel watched me for a couple of beats and then hunched his big body to make his way to the tiny restroom. I pretended to contentedly read my book.

I'd let it go for now. If I wanted to win the long game, if I wanted to bring Yariel Cabral to his knees, it would not be on the offensive. I had to make him come to *me*. I had the next three days to do it.

Operation Make Him Sweat was still in full force—I just needed to change tactics.

CHAPTER 5

FRIDAY

Yariel

Contrary to what all Dominican mothers will tell you, one's dick cannot fall off from jerking it too much. In the twenty-four hours since I got on the plane to the DR with Hatuey, I'd gotten myself off so many times I was starting to worry about chafing. And apparently not even breakfast was safe. Because Hatuey had walked out of his bedroom in nothing but briefs and paraded his ass all over the kitchen until I had to get up in the middle of eating. Now he was out for a run and I was sweating already knowing he'd probably come back shirtless.

We'd gotten into Casa de Campo—the exclusive beach and golf resort where the team's fundraiser was happening—in the late afternoon and immediately had a dinner to attend, which at least gave me a reprieve from thirsting after Hatuey. Today's agenda for the fundraiser was not very demanding, so Hatuey had made plans for us since I only had to make an appearance at a black-tie gala that evening. The rest of the time was all for my best friend.

It was supposed to be a relaxing weekend at the beach, an excuse to come back home with my favorite person. A chance to get away from New York City winter for a few days. Instead, I was in a constant state of sexual frustration and really confusing feelings. From one moment to the next I'd go from wondering if it could really be true that Hatuey wanted this, to feeling resentful that I'd been robbed of years of having him. Resentful of the promise I'd made his father on the night of our high school graduation.

A promise I meant to keep, which was why none of this could work. I could never tell Hatuey his father had seen us kiss that night. That he'd told me I would ruin his son's life, his family's legacy if I went after him. That he knew I cared for Hatuey, and for that reason I could never let it happen again. And since then I'd kept my word. I'd told myself a thousand times that night was a fluke, a drunken mistake. That Hatuey didn't see me like I saw him. That he'd kissed me on graduation night because we were both terrified of what was coming.

I was leaving for college in New York and he was staying in the DR. That he'd been nervous about what that meant for our friendship, and he'd kissed me after too many shots of tequila. That story had kept me going for all this time, but now the floodgates were open and I was trapped by a promise I never should've been asked to keep.

If I gave in to what I wanted with Hatuey, I'd betray the trust of a man who, other than that night, had always been kind to me. Who had welcomed me into his home when I'd been homesick and lost. But it wasn't just that. If I broke my word, I'd have to tell Hatuey the truth. Hatuey worshipped his father. I'd do anything not to hurt my best friend like that, even if it meant denying myself what I'd yearned for most in life: Hatuey Sanchez in my bed forever.

Today was going to be hell if I didn't figure out how to keep it together. We'd be in each other pockets for the next twelve hours between our plans and the gala. Although it wasn't as bad as that, I *was* looking forward to some of it. We were going to see an arts and sports camp I was paying for but that he'd set up with the help of one of his college friends. I groaned at the idea of seeing Hatuey running around in a field, with a bright smile on his gorgeous face. But it would be nice to visit the kids.

My phone buzzed in my pocket and I quickly answered it, needing a distraction. I perked up when I saw it was my old hookup and now good friend, Juan Pablo Campos. Juanpa never lost an opportunity to bust my balls about my "hundred-year crush," but I was desperate to unload on someone and he would do.

"What's good, pa? You around this weekend?" That was code for *are you down to fuck later,* and I dearly wished I could at least muster up some interest. But my dick seemed dead set on ruining my life.

I shook my head as I looked at the door Hatuey would come through. "No, I'm in the island this weekend. And I thought you and Priscilla had patched things up."

"Nope, apparently I fucked up again, and now I'm single and available." If I didn't know him better I would've totally bought the unbothered tone in his voice. Among the other things that we had in common, Juan Pablo and I shared the shittastic luck of having fallen head over heels for people we couldn't have. So J was probably as pressed as I was at the moment, but that didn't stop him from getting up in my business. "You there by yourself?" he asked like the nosy asshole he was.

I made a sound that was more or less a no, and ran a hand over my face as I tried to figure out what to say about my current situation. "I'm here with Hatuey."

"Oh, El Hombre Perfecto's along for the trip. How bad are you pining right now?" Juan Pablo was a good friend, but could also be a real shit. Still, he was the one person who understood how complicated things were for me with Hatuey, him having his own struggles with the love of his life. With J and Priscilla it seemed like they could never manage to stay friends. For me it was that I could never leave the friend zone. Until this week.

I had to get this out of my system with someone. I hadn't felt like I could talk to our mutual friends. It would be too awkward, or worse, they'd try to make me talk to Hatuey about it. But I was going to lose my mind if I didn't get this off my chest. I needed some fucking advice, and ASAP.

I gripped the phone so hard it squeaked, and my mouth was dry as a fucking desert but somehow was able to get the words out. "We had sex."

"Uh, I know, that's why I was calling you." You'd think all this fucking baseball money I was making could buy me one decent friend.

"You're not funny. And I meant Hatuey, cabron."

Juan Pablo, who seemed permanently unbothered, actually sputtered when I shared the news. "Whaaaaaat? And you didn't say anything?"

"We haven't talked, genius. And besides, what was I going to say?" I asked, feeling a little put off by how unbelievable he seemed to find the whole thing.

"Uh, maybe that you finally got busy with the dude you've been obsessed with since high school."

"I wouldn't say obsessed," I protested.

"*I* would!" This was why my life was the way it was. I surrounded myself with pain-in-the-ass men. I didn't even respond, just gritted my teeth and waited for him to run his mouth again, because I was out of ideas for this fiasco and J was a jackass, but he was resourceful when it came to fuckboi tactics. "Yariel, even when we were hooking up on the regular—all we did was talk about Hatuey and Priscilla. I know you're in a bad way, because it takes one to know one, bruh."

I sighed, feeling some of the tension seeping out of me, hearing Juanpa's naked honesty. "It's just getting too messy, and I should've never gone along with it."

"What happened? Is he acting different? Are you having second thoughts?" he asked incredulously, probably because all I did was talk about how I'd give my left nut to be Hatuey's man and now that it was an actual possibility I was a full on mess.

I laughed, and it sounded as desperate as I felt. "Yeah, he's definitely different, except not how you'd think. He's gone from zero to sixty on me. I expected him to be all freaked out, but he's just fucking rolling with it."

"Wait, so the man you love and thought was straight is not so much, and now you have exactly what you've always wanted...but it's a problem?" He sounded legitimately confused and I could not blame him. "You're making my head hurt, man."

"I can't start hooking up with Hatuey. You *know* why." One particularly drunken night when Hatuey had cancelled on me to go see a girl he'd been talking to, I spilled my guts to Juan Pablo about the kiss and my pathetic decade-long crush.

J's scoff should've pissed me off, but instead I just felt grateful that I had someone to hear me out. "Right, your sacrificial lamb routine. The guy's dad told you when you were *eighteen* not to fuck his kid. What does that have to do with right now? You're both grown-ass adults. Who cares if his dad isn't into his son liking dick?"

"Those people were good to me, treated me like family when I was in the DR." I shook my head, nausea swirling in my belly just imagining their faces when Hatuey told him.

The teeth sucking from Juanpa did get me a little heated, because he was acting like he didn't know exactly what it could mean for a Dominican man to come out to his family.

"I get that you're a big-dicked All-Star athlete and shit, but you don't actually run the entire fucking world, Yariel. You got a man that you love..."

I made a noise that was something between and protest and a plea at the mention of the L word, but J kept talking. "No, you love him as a friend and more than that. And he's a good guy who loves you enough to be open to exploring a new path in your relationship, even when it was probably not how he envisioned things. And stop with this family bullshit. Hatuey is an adult—if he wants to be with you, he can tell his family *or not,* and however they choose to take it is their problem, not yours."

My heart lurched from J's words. The sick feeling of wanting something and hating myself for it at the same time felt like a storm raging inside me. I wished I could take everything he'd just said and run with it. To be selfish and snatch what I'd wanted for so long. But I couldn't risk believing I would get him and then have him walk away when the choice was his family or me.

"What if this is just him being curious, J? What if he ends up having a falling out with his family—or worse, losing them? He'll hate me." My tongue was dry and I had to press my heels into the cool marble floors just to keep from panicking again.

This time it seemed like I finally stumped J's positivity rant. He let out a long breath, and when he spoke his voice was soft. "I hear that, bruh. Losing him for good would be worse than never having him fully. Still, you have to let Hatuey decide that for himself. You need to talk to him. Tell him what's worrying you, because keeping him at arm's length might push him away too." It was easy for Juanpa to say; I knew from what he'd told me that Priscilla's family was as obsessed with them getting together as his family was. It simply wasn't the same for us. Just the thought of putting Hatuey in that position twisted me in knots.

And of course instead of accepting J's good advice, I lashed out. "Are you taking notes for yourself, Juan Pablo? Or are you just calling me to feel better about your own bullshit?" Redirecting was my friend, and maybe if I picked a fight with J I'd get my mind off the mess I'd made of my whole damn life.

His answer was not what I expected, though. "Yeah, actually I am. I started seeing a therapist a couple of weeks ago, because at least I'm smart enough to know there's shit *I* need to fix for Pris and me to be great. And if I ever get a chance with her again, I'm not going to waste it."

Those last few words clawed at me. I was wasting this chance. J was right, this was more than just the promise I'd made to Hatuey's dad—it was my fear that he wouldn't choose me. I hadn't let myself believe this thing with Hatuey was anything more than him being impulsive so I didn't have to find out. If I let myself go to a place where this was a real chance...no. I was not going there, I knew fucking better than to believe in fairytales.

Just as I was about to answer J, the door to the villa opened and an animated conversation between Hatuey and the housekeeper of the villa drifted in. My focus and my body automatically shifted in his direction. I could talk shit until I ran out of words, but my brain and my body still responded to him like he was the fucking sun.

"Yo quiero mango Banilejos, Yenni!" My heart pounded at the smile I heard in his voice when he asked for the Dominican mangos he always craved when we were in the States. A laugh from the housekeeper was the only response, and I wondered if she was already falling for him too. He walked in, and when he saw me an unguarded smile appeared on his face, for just a second, before wariness replaced it. "Yenny's going to try to find me some mangos." He bravely tried for a smile, but I could see that he was worried I was going to reject him again. I hated, fucking *hated* that I'd done that.

"J, I gotta go." I ended the call with Juanpa's final plea to "get my head out of my ass" in my ear as Hatuey gave my phone a very unfriendly look. He had his running shorts on, chest bare and slick with sweat. Everything I'd ever wanted standing in front of me, and I couldn't make myself take it. But the smile from a second ago had slid off his face and was replaced by an expression I couldn't quite identify. It was like he was trying to take my temperature from ten feet away.

He took me in, from my very unruly bedhead to the usual random team T-shirt and shorts combo I slept in to my bare feet. I was perched on one of the chairs in the kitchen overlooking the patio leading to a private pool, but Hatuey was not interested in scenic views. He looked like he wanted to murder my phone.

"What did Juan Pablo want?" His icy tone wasn't exactly surprising. Hatuey wasn't a fan of Juan Pablo. My best friend had always been pretty aloof when it came to the guys I'd dated, but with J he'd been as close to openly hostile as I'd ever seen him with anyone. Even after our short fling had long fizzled out.

"I thought he was done chasing after your dick." He practically spat the words as he came in closer, heated eyes roaming over me as if he was making sure his property was all still there.

Something twisted and feral crawled around my chest and my lungs filled with air at seeing him like this. Territorial and possessive. I wanted to show him where all my focus was. Pull him by the waistband—shove him up against the glass that looked over the Atlantic

Ocean—and fuck him until I'd slaked off this absurd fantasy that had wormed into my brain this week.

He was so close now that I could smell the sweat and salt from the beach on him. "Is the sand good for running?" I asked, knowing I'd get a rise out of him by ignoring his question.

Still he didn't move, and I knew he wouldn't until I gave him an answer. I had to bite down hard on the grin that was threatening to appear on my face, because even though I knew this was the road to perdition, I still reveled in seeing him jealous of Juan Pablo. "He just wanted to hang out. I told him we were away for the weekend."

"Right, like I don't know what *that* means." His jaw ticced, and again, every dirtbag instinct in me was pushing to the surface at once. It was ugly how happy seeing him practically snarling with jealousy made me.

"There's nothing happening with me and J." By now he was standing just inches from me. Towering over me for once, and he looked like my every fantasy. Beautiful, furious and ready to pounce.

"But there could be. You'll go back to New York on Sunday and pick up where you left off. Like nothing happened," he said, voice shaking. Fists opening and closing at his side, like he was keeping himself from grabbing me. "You'll act like everything's the same."

The need in my belly was burning my self-control down to ashes with every anguished word out of Hatuey's mouth. I wanted to howl in frustration at the guilt gnawing at me. I wanted to say, *Nothing is the same, and you know that night was everything to me.*

But when I opened my mouth, I made it worse. "I'll act like my best friend and I slipped up but don't want to risk things going badly."

Hatuey's fingers weren't what you'd expect. He was tall, and slim, with brown skin that looked like dark, flawless wood. He looked more like the image of a tortured poet than a politician, but his hands were rough. The pads of his fingers a little scratchy from all the years he played tennis and baseball. I braced for what I knew was coming when he reached me. Once he was close enough to touch, he ran his fingers over the side of my face, his expression intense and haunted.

"I hate that you won't let us have this. I hate that you don't believe in me." His voice was tight, needy. There was no mistaking the desire there. And maybe Juan Pablo was right—it wasn't up to me to decide for both of us.

"Of course I believe in you. But this is madness, Hatuey." I said weakly as I placed a hand on his flank, feeling the clamminess of his skin.

What if you change your mind? What if you stop wanting me?

It was on the tip of my tongue to ask it. To tear my chest open and let him see I was terrified, but his lips were so close and I'd held back for so long. He leaned into me, the T-shirt he'd been holding in one hand tumbling to the floor as his arms encircled around my neck. Our lips touched and I listed from the power of our mouths coming together. I imagined that we were inventing a whole new way to speak. Where words were superfluous and we communicated like this, mouth to mouth, tongue brushing against tongue.

"I can't get enough of your kisses." Hatuey had never been one to hold back, while I kept everything close to my chest; he pronounced his every desire for the world. "Your mouth." The two words were a full sentence. A statement of fact. "How did I never notice it's the most perfect thing in the world?"

"Stop saying shit like that, Hatuey." I mumbled as I pressed my mouth to his.

"It's true, it's perfect." He protested. "And now I can't stop wanting it."

I sucked in a breath, chest expanding with the air I was holding there while his mouth and tongue branded my skin. A nip on the blade of my collarbone, a gentle lick on the shell of my ear, soft lips on the tip of my nose. I should've stopped all of it, but my hands were on their own discovery expedition.

I slipped them into his shorts, my fingers grazing his cleft as he worked on sucking on my tongue. The memory of his heat, of how he felt, fueling my lust. I rubbed my thumb over his hole as he pressed his hard cock to my thigh.

"I want in again," I garbled out as I fingered him. "Hold you open while I fuck you with my tongue." I could've had him right there. He moaned, ass clenching on my finger.

"I can't stop thinking about what it felt like to have your tongue inside me." He gasped as I brushed his rim, my desire coiling tight with every sound he made.

"I can't think straight with the sounds you're making, Hatuey." He writhed, slippery like an eel as I touched him.

"Stay still," I growled—grabbing the back of his neck—while I took his balls in one hand and worked his hole with the other. "Stop fidgeting and work that ass, show me how you're going to take my cock."

"Ahh...god, why is that so hot?" Hatuey's eyes rolled back in his head, body soft and open to me. He was lost in what I was giving him, and I fully intended to take our friendship squarely down the path of destruction when the door to the villa crashed open, sending us flying apart.

"What the fuck?" I growled, as Hatuey tried and failed to hide his erection.

"Muchachos estan aqui?" Most of the blood that usually kept my mind functioning was in my dick, so I didn't place the voice until Hatuey cursed and made a mad grab for his shirt.

My heart literally lodged in my throat—and it was the only thing keeping me from throwing up all over the marble floor—when I realized the voice belonged to Hatuey's father. My best friend's eyes widened as he hurried to put on the now completely wrecked T-shirt from his run, while I dropped back into the chair, winded.

"I don't know what he's doing here," Hatuey whispered nervously as he walked to the foyer. I watched him go while I got my breathing back and let it sink in that my best friend's father almost walked in on us fucking. And when that fun fact finally hit, I really did almost puke.

Baseball players were a superstitious bunch. I usually wasn't one for giving credence to bad omens. But even I had to admit some things you ignored at your own peril. I was going to take this almost disaster as a clear sign that I needed to keep my hands off Hatuey for good.

CHAPTER 6

Hatuey

I loved my father, but his timing was shit.

I'd had him. I'd had Yariel right where I'd wanted him. Ready to finally admit—even if only while I distracted him with my tongue—that despite the headassery he'd been on for the last couple of days, he was as eager as I was to take things further.

But my father, bless him, had ruined all of it. Yariel looked like his entire soul had left his body when my father strolled into the villa unannounced. And now two hours later, we were still in a forced chaperone situation. Not that we could get up to much since we were also surrounded by about eighty teens who were doing their best to impress their idol, Brooklyn Bombers shortstop Yariel Cabral. And despite the few cringeworthy moments with my dad, the morning had been pretty amazing.

I stood back as I watched Yari stage an impromptu clinic with some of the kids who were at the camp today. He had them laughing and working hard, swinging bats and stealing bases, as he gave them pointers. He took the time to praise each one of them by name, and the kids beamed under his attention.

He looked so handsome and powerful. Moving that big, lithe body with confidence. He was comfortable in his own skin. The look of a man who knew the power he held and exactly how to use it. He'd come so far from the awkward teen he'd been when we first met. But that boy was still there in that open smile, and the way he lit up with a baseball bat in his hands. Yariel had always known where he belonged. I was the one who had never quite figured that out for myself.

And now here he was at twenty-six, a millionaire, a star athlete using his time and his money to give back to his people. Butterflies swirled in my stomach as I watched him, and I called myself ten kinds of stupid to not have noticed that this man was everything to me. That there was nothing in him I didn't want for myself. That I wouldn't worship if I was given the chance.

Mio. *Mi hombre.*

Nothing had ever felt that absolute, and I realized maybe I had known where I belonged all along too.

"Looks like the program is thriving. I like that you have STEM and arts too, not just the sports," my father said happily as he looked around. He'd been in a weird mood today, and I was worried that he'd had seen Yariel and me. Not because I was embarrassed, not really. But because I wanted him to find out differently. I looked at him now and he didn't seem upset—pensive, maybe, and genuinely pleased with what he was seeing. "You two always made a good team."

I blushed because today that felt real in more ways than one. "When money isn't an object, it makes things easier," I said, deflecting the praise.

My dad looked at me strangely, like he was trying to figure something out. But when he spoke his voice was tinted with real emotion. "He's a good man. Not everyone could shoulder the responsibility all that money and fame come with, but he carries it well. And I know you've helped him with that."

For as much as he never quite understood my friendship with Yari and at times seemed almost wary of how close we were, my father had always been good to him, and never missed a chance to tell him how proud he was of him. Yari's own parents were supportive but much older than my dad, and over the years he'd come to Papi to ask for advice about his career more than once.

My diaphragm contracted thinking of how he might react to hearing about what was happening between Yari and me. I wanted to be ready to tell him, but I could not ignore the real fear of what might happen when I did. My stomach roiled with doubt and I couldn't help looking at Yariel. I had to admit that as much as I hated that he was keeping me at arm's length, he was right. Taking this step was not going to be easy.

I shrugged, still working on an answer to my dad's comment, and kept my eyes on Yariel, who was now doing drills with the kids. I saw him call over a girl who'd been standing at the back, coaxing her until she walked toward him with her shoulders straight and head held high. He had that kind effect on people—when he called, they came.

I looked on proudly, watching the scene unfold. Yari made a point of waiting for her and I saw a smile appear on her face at whatever he told her as he handed her the bat. I knew what she was feeling, what she was responding to. From the moment I'd first felt it, I'd tried to be in the warmth of Yariel as much as I could. It was still my favorite place.

"Yariel is easy," I finally told my father. "He just wants to play baseball and give back as much as he can." My father's grunt told me he agreed, but his eyes were stormy as he looked at my friend.

Just at that moment, Yari straightened from demonstrating some moves with his bat and looked around the field. His hat covered his eyes, but my thumping heart knew who he was looking for. When he spotted me, the unguarded smile he sent in my direction turned my insides molten. He crooked a finger, not flirtatious or lascivious, but a sign of familiarity. A confident gesture of someone who knew he would get was he was asking for.

I looked at my dad, who waved in his direction. "Ve, te esta esperando." I nodded and almost started walking the distance to Yariel, but something about my dad's expression stopped me.

"Todo bien, Papi?" I asked, genuinely concerned at how serious he looked.

"You know I love you no matter what, right, mijo? Whatever makes you happy, I will learn to be happy with."

Was I that obvious? I turned my head to the side as my heart did its best to skitter out of my chest. I'd been wondering what this moment would feel like almost incessantly for the last few days; if I'd be able to handle it, if the possibility of my father looking at me differently was enough to make me want to hide what I felt for Yariel. I was relieved to find out that even though the panic was there, that I was worried, I still wanted to say it. That I would be ready once Yariel was.

I stepped up to him and patted him on the cheek, but he grabbed in a strong hug. I could barely get the words out once I'd caught my breath. "I know, Papi. Thank you."

I walked away with the February midday sun of the DR beating down on my shoulders, but the warmth in my belly was there for a completely different reason. Could I do what Yari did: risk his dreams to be open about who he was? Looking at him, I felt like I could. Like anything would be worth being able to go to him right now and kiss his mouth—tell him how proud of him I was.

Our eyes locked as I reached him, and for a second I saw in them the same yearning roiling in me. I could sense he was debating whether to reach for me or not, but at the last second he looked in the direction of my dad and it was back to business as usual. That stung, but I didn't want to ruin this day for him or for myself.

"Where do you need me?" I asked with a jumble of emotions still swirling in my chest, and he gestured toward the pitcher mound. I smiled at his suggestion that I get back in my old position. "Like the old days?"

"Like always." This time he was the one who smiled, and something about it made me hopeful that we could work this out after all.

Yariel

Today had been a lot, in both good and frustrating ways. Still, we'd managed to make the most of it. Seeing the kids in action at the camp had been great and I especially loved being able to see them playing and having fun, not just grinding in their practice. For so many Dominican boys baseball is not just something to do—it's a ticket out of poverty. A contract with major league baseball could mean a way to support their family, and as much as that can be a blessing, it's also very hard to enjoy something when the stakes are so high. It had been good to see the fruits of my own success give them a space to be kids too. And if I was being fully honest, it had been doubly special to have done it with Hatuey.

I sighed, remembering the few weird moments around his dad. It felt like everyone had their eyes on us, even if I knew they didn't. I hated that now I had to think about every little touch between us, when before it had been the most natural thing in the world to pull him in for a hug, to kiss the top of his head.

The image of Hatuey's father looking at us as we played in the field with the kids, the sadness in his eyes...that would keep me from slipping. I had to remember this wasn't just about what I wanted. It was about not letting down the people who had been good to me. And I knew Hatuey had been thinking things over too. He'd been quiet on the drive back to the villa, and once we got in he went up for a nap before getting ready for the dinner we were supposed to attend.

So there had been no talking about what happened this morning, and no more almost fucking encounters. Everything had been sedate, friendly and back to the normal I'd told him I wanted so many times. I fucking hated it.

Now I was standing in the big room overlooking the beach and waiting for him to come out. It was a black-tie affair, so I was done up in a full tuxedo, grateful for central AC and sipping some rum from a tumbler when he walked in. "I'm ready."

I had to bite my tongue to hold back the groan that almost escaped my lips when I saw him. Hatuey had always been beautiful to me. Not even teenage acne or the awkward braces years had been able to deter me. Hatuey had always been the embodiment of everything I wanted in a mate. And ten years of friendship had only made that more intense. The boy I'd loved had turned into a man I would've happily poured my life into.

I walked up to him without even telling my limbs to move, my body drifting over on its own volition. "I needed to get closer to admire the fit." We were such a contrast, him compact and slender, while I was just big.

"At least admit you wanted get a closer look at my ass," he said grudgingly while I rolled my eyes at his ridiculous and extremely accurate observation. He cut his eyes at me as he slid his hands in his trouser pockets and turned in a circle so I could admire him from all sides. He was wearing the Ralph Lauren tux I'd convinced him to let me buy for him, since more times than not he was my plus one for these types of events. I almost laughed at the fact that most of my teammates were convinced we were boyfriends. If they only knew.

"Looking sharp," I said, waving a finger at his forehead, where his hair was combed to the side, like one of those old Hollywood movie stars. "You going for the Cary Grant look?"

He shrugged, both hands smoothing over his lapels as he ran hungry eyes over my own custom Tom Ford ensemble. "I can pull off Cary Grant." He really could, down to the chin dimple and keen brown gaze. He grinned wickedly as he came close enough that he was eye to eye with my bow tie. "And you're putting out some serious 'M'baku goes to the gala' vibes right now." The next part came out in a husky whisper that went straight to my dick. "I'm into it."

I was too weak to resist touching him, but instead of palming the side of his face and bringing him in for a kiss like I wanted, I blindly placed the tumbler of rum on the sideboard beside us and straightened his tie. He wasn't a fan of bow ties, so I had an excuse to run my hand all the way down his chest. His nostrils flared and his breath hitched as I got to the spot right below his ribcage.

I stood there, swaying from the feel of him, letting myself have one more second of the fantasy in which there was no family to disappoint, no fallout from making him mine. He tipped his face up to me, asking. Offering his lips for the kiss I desperately wanted.

No, I could not forget the love with which his father looked at him today. I could not be responsible for taking that from him.

I stepped back and tipped my head, as if I to offer his outfit one last sign-off. "Ready?"

Hatuey gave me a long look. Like he wanted to crack my head open and look inside. But he didn't push, he didn't flirt. He just nodded and turned around, walking to the door as he answered, "Vamonos."

CHAPTER 7

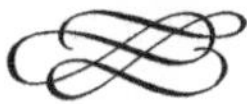

Hatuey

Once it finally sank in that I was in love with a headass stubborn fool, my plan really came together. Yariel wanted to act like a martyr and not touch me because "honoring my family." I was going to help him see how much he'd be willing to do to keep me once I started to slip out of his hands.

Some men you can reason with. And some men...you have to make insanely jealous in order to get them to pay attention. I was fine with this scenario. I may have never been Yariel's lover before this week, but I knew where every single one of his buttons was located. Tonight I was planning to push all of them until he broke.

"So there's a lot of hate-fuck energy happening here tonight. Is there something I need to know?" asked Chantal, one of my friends from college—and a PR executive for the company sponsoring this gala—as she sipped a flute of champagne, her eyes trained on the object of my irritation.

I took a sip of my own glass of bubbly and lifted my right shoulder in response. "Not much fucking to be had." I sounded a little bitter, but who could blame me? "But I *have* recently discovered that my favorite person on earth is also extremely good at fucking me."

I wasn't looking at Chantal but heard her struggle with not blowing champagne out her nose at my revelation. "Hatuey, for fuck's sake, warn a person," she wailed as I pulled a linen handkerchief out of my pocket and handed it to her. "You still carry those?" she asked, charmed, and even that hurt, because of course Yariel got me dozens of monogrammed linen handkerchiefs since I always kept one in my pocket, because he was fucking perfect.

"Thanks," she said as I indicated she could keep the soiled piece of linen she was attempting to hand me back. "How long has it been since you got your head out of your ass?"

I bypassed pretending to not understand the question since I needed all my mental energy focused on ruining my best friend. "Tuesday night," I muttered in frustration. "And since then he's been depriving us both of perfectly good sex because he's trying to 'save me from myself' by denying me access to his dick." I was going to grit my teeth down to dust if Yariel kept this shit up.

"Figures," she said, amused. "You're clueless, and him with his 'I am an island' thing."

I looked around before I moved close enough to whisper furiously in her ear, "Did everyone in the fucking world know that Yariel and I were soulmates except for me?"

She let out another throaty laugh and tipped her glass in Yariel's direction. "That man has always looked at you like you hung the moon. If you couldn't tell, you weren't looking very closely." Again, I was not going to argue, because it was more like I had been actively avoiding noticing. "He's always been pretty passive about it, though, like he was resigned." My stomach dropped hearing that. I'd been such a fucking dummy. "But tonight his vibe is pretty menacing. He's been sending people looks like he would tear up this whole fucking place if anyone dares to lay a finger of you."

At the moment he was being cornered by two older men who, given where we were, probably owned half of the island. But Yari wasn't even trying to pay attention to whatever they were saying—he was too busy glaring in our direction. His eyes seemed to be particularly focused on the sliver of space separating Chantal and me.

Jealous, baby? You better fucking be.

"Damn, that's hot. Even I'm getting hit with the pheromones, and dudes are not my jam." Chantal got even closer, and cupped her hand around her mouth for the next part. "FYI, Amir's here this weekend and he's throwing a party at his place. I'm going there after this. I've been kind of dating one of the news anchors on DRTV and she's going to be there. If you want to really make him sweat, there will be plenty of willing participants to help you get him there."

I laughed at the deviousness in her voice and turned to look at her. "So you're not even going to pretend to be surprised that Yariel and I hooked up?" I asked, with more disbelief than concern.

She shifted her gaze from the cluster of men surrounding my best friend to look at me. "Am I supposed to be? What's so monumental about two people with the connection you have getting together?"

I held Chantal's words for a second, took in the truth in them. The wonder that it was to hear them from a friend here in the DR, where for some reason I'd envisioned derision at every turn. In truth, I'd braced for it. Told myself I was okay with the outcome. That if I got to have Yariel, I'd deal.

But now I saw my friend standing solidly here. Living her life as a queer woman in the DR and telling me I didn't need to run away from who I was. It pried something open in me.

When I finally spoke my voice cracked just a tiny bit on the first words. "Nothing and everything," I said, with a flustered laugh, as I leaned in to give her a kiss on the cheek. "I just need to convince that big-ass stubborn mess, that we'll be fine if we do this."

Chantal stepped back from me, and the glint in her eyes told me something was happening, "You might get your first chance right now, because he's coming over here and he looks like he's about Hulk out on somebody."

I turned and immediately my breath started coming in short puffs as I watched him cross the large room with his eyes zeroed in on my face. His shoulders were back, chest out. That big body honed to perfection, making its way to me like I was True North.

But what had me sweating were his eyes. The fire there was familiar. It was a look I'd confused with concentration or focus in the past. And it *was* focus, but it was focus on me, *just* me. That was his "eso es mio" look. And if he was too stubborn to admit that's what he was thinking, I'd force it out of him. Even if I had to resort to desperate measures.

"Yari," I said as pleasantly as I could manage while he sent withering looks to the spot where Chantal had slid her arm around mine. "This is my friend, Chantal. Do you remember her?"

And because Chantal loved to start shit, she plastered herself against me before turning her face up to Yariel for a kiss hello. "Hatuey and I were just catching up—we used to be thick as thieves in college." She pouted adorably in her shimmery skin-tight dress that highlighted every one of her curves. "I miss him." She was a beautiful woman, and if she was not one-hundred percent Team Lady, I'd probably had tried with her. Of course, Yariel didn't seem to recall that fact and was flaring his nostrils like a pissed-off, six-foot-seven angry bull.

He practically smacked his face to hers and grunted out what I supposed was a hello, then immediately went back to trying to burn her arm out of its socket with his eyeballs.

"I lost you." Where was all this growling coming from? And why did he have to look this good even when he was telling a bald-faced lie?

"You seemed like you had your eye on him from over there," Chantal suggested sweetly, as she tightened her grip on my arm, eliciting a flutter in Yariel's jaw that was starting to worry and delight me.

"I was trying to find him so we could get going." He angled his chin in the direction of the triumvirate of older dudes he'd cut lose. "I was saying my goodbyes to Mr. Bermudez, but now that I've made my appearance we can head out." He looked at his Cartier watch and back at me. "It's almost ten and we have the tournament tomorrow.

I rolled my eyes at his grumpy ass. Like this was a real tournament and not just a chance for the Dominican one percent to play golf with celebrities. "It doesn't start until noon, Yariel," I countered, now for some reason determined to not come home. I loosened my grip on Chantal and slid my hands in my pockets, inching a bit closer to him.

"Chantal is going to a party at a friend's villa. It's close to ours, right?" I fluttered my eyelashes and looked up at him, as I waited for Chantal's answer, yep, he was sweating.

Chantal who, bless her, had seemingly been to this rodeo many a time, nodded and pointed in the direction of the golf carts, which were lined up to take guests back to their lodgings. "Yeah, you're in Las Brisas, and Amir's villa is like a five-minute walk from you. But he'll have carts there to take people home." She smiled wickedly then. "It should be a *very* fun time. He brought the DJ in from New York just for this party."

"What do you say? You up for some fun?" I wasn't being flirty exactly—I was just being me. The *me* I always was with *him* and I'd felt like I couldn't be for the past few days. But I wanted him to see that even if we became a different version of us, it would be a better one. The stuff that made us *us* would always be there.

"We can do some people-watching and then bed." That last part came out more suggestive than intended. He hesitated for a second, looking genuinely conflicted, but after a moment he dropped his shoulders and nodded.

"Fine, but just for a little bit." Those grunts were really going to fuck me up.

He stood to the side and waved an arm, indicating Chantal should lead the way. We started walking and she leaned in to whisper something in my ear as he followed us. I could almost feel the heat of his stare prickling the back of my neck. "I was serious before, if you really want to rile him up. You'll have plenty of chances there. Amir's parties are notorious."

"Oh." I looked over my shoulder to find him staring at us like he was already regretting the decision to go to the party. Lucky for me I was certain of one thing Yariel Cabral would never do: break a promise to me.

CHAPTER 8

Yariel

It's funny how I got paid millions to anticipate my competitor's next move, and yet my dumb ass kept getting played by my own dick.

I should've fucking known Hatuey was up to something, but when I saw him all cozy and shit with his friend, my whole brain reset. My entire mission in life had been to get two feet of space between them, permanently. Never mind that I'd met her before and should've remembered she was queer. But I'd turned into some kind of a Neanderthal from the moment I got a taste of Hatuey, so I'd let them talk me into coming to this little house party/orgy we were in right now. And this was not going to end well.

We'd been here for twenty minutes and already the host, his boyfriend and the DJ had hit on Hatuey. He was currently getting a drink at the pool bar while I stood by a palm tree like a tool in a five-thousand dollar suit. At least from here I had clear view of the bar, and had been watching as Hatuey dodged guy after guy. You'd think these assholes had never seen a man in designer clothes before, with the way they were pawing at him. Chantal, that traitor, had lost complete interest in my best friend the moment we walked in and bee-lined for a super tall woman who'd been holding court in a corner. They'd disappeared within seconds, so I assumed our time with Chantal had ended for the evening.

Not that I cared. My issue at the moment was that I could no longer even pretend Hatuey and I could go back to normal. So far in the past week, no matter how many times I told myself this was not a good idea, I kept trying to find a way around my hang-ups. And right now as I watched him get cruised by half of the gays on the East Coast of Dominican Republic, I wanted to walk up there and wild out on every guy who thought he had a chance with him.

And given how he was going for a gold star in "flirting with guys" at the moment, the lie I'd been feeding myself about him being confused was also not going hold much longer. I was ready to fight people, and even my stubborn ass knew that was no way to keep things platonic.

"Well, he's certainly being well received," Chantal chimed in, apparently no longer occupied with her hipster friend.

I grunted in answer and took a swig of my club soda, wishing I'd at least have the burn of a gulp of rum to distract me right now. Since I started playing professionally, I'd become a lightweight when it came to drinking. Which meant I got to watch the man I wanted for myself get pawed on by every guy in the vicinity while stone-cold sober. "Shouldn't you be talking to him? I thought you missed him so much you had to drag us to this party."

She snorted, a sound that didn't match the sleek dress, perfectly done hair and four-inch red-bottoms. "Hatuey's discovering things about himself and this is the perfect opportunity to explore some of them," she explained sarcastically as she gestured in his direction.

My back went ramrod straight and that fucking twitch in my left eye came back with a vengeance as I watched a twink lean in to sniff Hatuey's neck. "What the fuck?" I garbled out, practically choking on my own words.

I stepped forward, nostrils flaring, ready to go knock some heads at the bar. But at the last second, I resisted. If I let my emotions get the best of me, I was going to fuck this up. I recalled the feeling of seeing Hatuey's father looking at me with pride just this afternoon. Remembered how much it had meant to me over the years whenever he'd told me I'd done well. How much I respected the man. That would all go away if I pursued this with Hatuey. I'd seen friendships destroyed by blurring lines, by changing things, and I was not going to make that mistake with Hatuey.

"Yep, you seem like you're handling all this well." Figured that the one person I knew at this party would be another smartass.

I moved my shoulders up and down, trying to loosen the tension there. I felt like my head would pop right off my neck if I turned it.

"He loves you, Yariel. You know that."

I grunted. "And I love him. That has never been the issue."

"Then why are you hurting him and yourself?"

I knew Chantal wasn't trying to verbally shiv me, but the sound I made was that of a wounded animal being poked right where it hurt the most.

"I don't want him to have to hide who he is. I don't ever want him to experience what it's like for people to turn their back on you because of who you are." I angled my chin in his direction as he laughed at something the twink had said. The jealousy ate through me, and yet I couldn't get enough of seeing him looking free and comfortable in his own skin. "Look at him. He's like the sun, everyone orbiting around him. That's how it should always be."

These last few days had really done a number on me. I was spilling my guts to strangers at some dude's party. Or maybe I was just desperate for someone to talk me into going after what I wanted.

She snorted like I was an idiot. "It's funny, because that's exactly how he talks about you." I almost stumbled as her words sliced right through my heart. "You don't think he hasn't thought about that? That seeing how you had to fight to be open about who you are hasn't come up for him?"

"I just don't want to mess with what I do have. I don't want my selfishness to take his life from him."

I got teeth sucking in response, and I prepared for whatever Dominican woman talking-to I was about to receive.

"So according to you, Hatuey having a handsome man who's been his best friend since high school, who is devoted to him and also happens to be one of the most popular professional athletes in the world, is going to ruin his life?"

I kept my eyes on Hatuey as he threw his head back and laughed again at whatever the guy currently monopolizing his attention had said. In the major leagues my nickname was La Piedra because my batting face was so serious. Stony, stoic, unfeeling. If it was true, then I was starting to crack, because it was taking every ounce of energy I had to not do something that would probably put us on the morning news.

Chantal's voice brought me back from the precipice, but just barely. "He's not going to keep asking you. He's going to eventually stop and then you'll miss your chance."

And as if he'd heard her prediction and was determined to test her theory, Hatuey put down the drink he'd been holding and started walking in my direction, his eyes challenging. Like he could see the warring thoughts in my head.

I watched him coming toward me still feeling torn. Still not sure if I would ruin everything by giving into this, or if I was blowing my one real chance at happiness if I didn't. The truth was that for ten years I'd tried and failed to find someone who could make me forget my best friend. Who could fill the places only Hatuey seemed to be able to reach. And now he was coming to me, offering me everything I wanted.

And as it always was with fate and DJs, a song had to come on and ruin me. Like something out of a cheesy movie, the song that I'd secretly assigned to Hatuey all the way back in high school came on as I stood there drowning in indecision. This had to mean something, right? I listened to the words that for so long had been how I made sense of what I felt for Hatuey. A love that left me powerless, that I could not walk away from, unwilling to give up on. And now that it was within my reach, I refused to take it again and again.

I was a fool.

I took the first step toward him, but someone else got to him first. The man walked up to him without hesitation and asked him to dance as I watched from a distance. He was looking at the love of my life like he was ready and willing to do what I hadn't: claim him. And finally I was fucking done.

The realization hit me like a ton of bricks, like a truth that erased everything else that existed before it, and I saw it all clearly. If I'd give up everything for him, if I'd be willing to give up baseball, fame, fortune or whatever it cost me to have him, why couldn't I let him do the same for me? As I saw him dance the song I'd named ours with someone else, I finally decided whatever the cost that would get him in my arms forever, I was willing to pay it.

I turned to look at Chantal, who was still quietly observing the scene unfold. "I'm going to do it."

"Don't ask me for permission—I'm fully in support of this."

It only took like twenty steps to close the distance. Just as the song was about to end, I reached him, put a hand on his shoulder, and growled out something that sounded like, "Come with me."

The other man was about to protest, but Hatuey was already fully focused on me. "What's wrong?"

I took his hand and pulled him out of the dance floor and past the ring of people around it as fast as I could. For a fevered moment I thought it would be easier if I just picked him up and threw him over my shoulder, but suspected that would not go over well.

As we reached Chantal, I waved a hand at her and shook my head. "We have to go home," I said as I practically ran out of the house with him in tow.

"Go home for what?" he asked, still feigning an annoyance that was contradicted by the way his hand tightened in mine.

I didn't answer as I shouldered my way through the house and out the door. The air felt different outside, like oxygen could finally hit my lungs. My chest heaved up and down as we made our way down the path that would take us to our villa. But before we could make our full escape, Hatuey tugged on my hand and stopped.

"What's going on, Yariel?" He didn't seem angry, but he sounded like he was determined to get answers one way or the other.

"I'll tell you at home," I protested, wanting to move. Needing to get him where I could do and say all the things I wanted to. But Hatuey wasn't having it.

"No, I want you to tell me here," he insisted, pointing at the gravel path we were on, but I didn't miss that tiny glimmer of hope in his brown eyes.

"I can't talk right now, Hatuey," I explained, my throat prickling with everything that wanted to come out.

"Why?" His jaw had that stubborn set it got when he was about to get hella difficult, and he took his hand out of mine to cross his arms over his chest. "Tell me why you made me leave the party I was having a perfectly good time at."

Now it was my turn to get stubborn, so I planted my feet and met his eyes, which were daring me to fuck this up. To not give him what he'd been waiting for me to give him for days.

"Because I almost lost it seeing those guys flirting with you."

He raised his eyebrows at that, and the corners of his mouth lifted up a fraction of a centimeter.

"Because I was ready to wreck shop just from watching you dance our song with someone else too."

Now he looked genuinely confused, and opened his mouth to probably ask what the fuck I was talking about, but I kept going, needing to get it all out. "Because, I've been a fucking powder keg for the last four days and if I don't get you home so I can fuck you, I might die."

I sounded like I'd been running for miles by this point, and I felt it too. My eyes were blurry, and my heart hammered against my chest as Hatuey processed all the shit I'd dumped on him in the last thirty seconds. He opened his mouth, then closed it. Shifted from one foot to the other as he considered what to tackle first.

"Fuck, Hatuey, say something," I growled, like the demanding asshole I was.

He held up a finger, finally snapping out of whatever trance he was in, and stepped in closer. He looked furious and I wanted to wreck him. "First of all, hold your fucking horses. You've been tiptoeing around me for days now," he said in a huff. "Don't expect me to jump because you got all jealous and want to shove your dick in me to mark your territory or whatever."

Just the mention of my dick getting anywhere near him was enough to set off every nerve in my body simultaneously. But I was not longer driving this car.

"Second..." His voice was definitely on the sexier side of things now, and my cock was once again joining the proceedings. "It really pisses me off how hot I find this brooding asshole shit. I need to think about what's going on with me I really do."

With that he stalked off, in a break-neck power walk that had us at the door of our villa in a couple of minutes. We didn't talk as we made our way inside. I tapped in the code to the door noticing my hands shook as I punched in the numbers.

I reached for him once we were safely inside, but he moved back just beyond me. "Did you give us a fucking song and never bothered to tell me?" Now he was the one growling.

And I had to look away because my hands twitched and my heart was racing in that frantic way that only happened before I walked out in the field with only my bat in hand. That detached sensation of a moment being too big to take in all at once. I felt like I was floating as Hatuey scrutinized me. And I wanted to run, hide from what he was obviously seeing for the first time.

I'd been hiding from him. I'd been hiding all of it for so long. And now I was caught, without anywhere to run off to.

CHAPTER 9

Hatuey

If this were anyone else, I would've probably let my dick call the shots. But I knew the level of stubborn asshole I was dealing with. So I was going to keep my pants on until this man told me everything I'd been waiting to hear. What I now knew he probably kept bottled in for a decade.

"No, Yariel. I'm not going to give you a chance to get in your head this time. Once whatever is about to happen is done, I need you to be ready for the next thing, and the next thing won't work with you going all 'La Piedra' on me."

His eyes widened, the naked fear there making my heart ache. But I needed him to step up, come to the table and do this with me.

"I don't want to be the reason your family disowns you, Hatuey. *Never*."

I groaned in frustration because I knew Yariel would find something to martyr himself over. I also knew this wasn't an act or an excuse. He was in agony about this for good reasons, so I went with what I knew he couldn't deny.

"That is not up to you. And this is too big, Yari. Don't you feel it?" I asked, still blown away by the certainty I felt. That I wanted him not matter what it cost. Every single one of the questions about my life I never had the right answer for seemed clear now. And I needed to tell him so.

"Everything makes sense now. *Everything.* This is why nothing ever lasts with me," I said softly, needing him to calm down enough to really hear me. "Because you're mine. You've been mine since the moment I laid eyes on you, and I don't know how I've been so fucking stupid to not see what's been right in front of my face. Yari, don't *you* see?"

The agony on his face almost broke me. But if we didn't get all this out now, we'd be stuck on this loop of fucking—or almost fucking—and then Yariel freaking out forever. So I kept myself just out of his arm's reach, and spoke.

"I left this island going after you." I lifted a hand, pointing in the direction of the Atlantic Ocean, which was somewhere in the blackness beyond the window. "And you've been loving me this whole time. Whenever I cried over a breakup, whenever I said I'd never find anyone, you were there, loving me, letting me figure it out. Holding back. Not telling me it was you I needed." I spluttered as a watery laugh came out of my throat. "You're so much stronger than I am, because now that I've let myself see it, I can't imagine not having you completely."

He shook his head hard, his mouth twisted like he'd been mortally wounded. "Don't say stuff like that. You've been all I see for almost half my life, and if you decide later that you don't want me..." He gasped, like he was in pain, and I shook like a leaf in the wind from the need to reach for him. "If this is too complicated, I don't know what I'll do." He screwed his eyes shut then, hands in fists by his sides, as if the next part he had to say was coming from the deepest recesses of his soul. "But you've got to know there is nothing in me right now that wouldn't die for you."

There were a million things I could've said in that moment. That he didn't have to die for me, that we could and would be happy. That he was being dramatic, but I understood why he said it because I was right there with him. I loved him in every way I knew how to love. I was overwhelmed by how much. Every ounce of who I was boiled down to that, and it was terrifying.

"What's our song, Yariel?" My voice broke on his name, and that's when it finally happened.

Sometimes you read things in books like "I knew the exact moment I fell for him" or "I could see into his soul," and they sound farfetched, melodramatic. And I can't really say I can pinpoint the moment I fell for Yariel—it was probably the moment I met him. But I *can* say I knew the exact moment he finally believed I was his.

He closed the space between us until his heat seared my skin. And his eyes, they were burning. It was all there, I could see it. Fuck, I could *feel* it. Ten years of wanting and not taking. It had been days for me and I was practically coming out of my skin from needing more. To touch him as much as I wanted. To tell whoever I saw that he was mine.

I pushed up for a kiss, and he whispered it against my lips. "'Sin Voluntad.'"

Our song. Of course it would be "Sin Voluntad" by Gilberto Santa Rosa, my favorite.

I tightened my arms around his neck as he swayed us together, his raspy baritone in my ears singing about a love that makes you helpless. Love that calms and agitates. Love that changes everything. Love you're not willing to walk away from. We could've floated away, my feet lifted right off the ground as he sang all the things he hadn't been able to say for so long.

"Do you believe me now?" I asked as we moved, our bodies fitting perfectly together. I wanted to put my head on his shoulder and let him take me away, but I was waiting for him to answer, my face tipped up to look in his eyes.

I saw his throat work, his expression spooked but determined, and hope soared in my chest. "I want to." He said it strongly, as his hand slid from my waist to my ass and gripped me hard.

"I love you," I told him with my gaze still holding his. "And I want you more right now than I've ever wanted anything."

The rumble that came out of his chest was predatory, and made everything in me tighten with want. I could already feel his hands and mouth on me

"You know what I can't wait to feel again?" I asked as he swallowed hard, eyes like hot embers, practically glowing. "Your teeth grazing my back and neck. I get hard just from touching the bruise you left right here." I brought a finger to the spot he'd sucked on between my neck and shoulders.

His nostrils flared, body taut, ready to unleash all that power on me. I knew I had him, but I pushed a bit more just in case. "I jerked off thinking about you—"

"Hatuey." That was the last agonized word he uttered until he'd carried me to the master suite, his mouth hot on mine, tongue sliding in and shutting off all thinking and all conversation for the near future, and I was totally fine with that.

CHAPTER 10

Yariel

I tried to do the right thing, but I wasn't *really* made of fucking stone. Not with Hatuey telling me he wanted everything I'd craved. And now I had him in my bed, and my entire life was going to have to be rearranged. I would do whatever it took to keep him there forever.

"How do you want me?" he asked frantically as he worked on skinning out of every inch of clothing he was wearing while I tried to count backwards from twenty, just to keep from pawing at him like a fucking animal.

I gripped my hands together in front of my chest, still fully dressed as I watched him writhe and twist on my bed. "Slow down." Normal speech was beyond me now, and I thanked god Hatuey knew me like he did. With my size and the way I was feeling right now, I had to be scary. But it seemed Caveman Yariel was Hatuey's kink, because he was flushed red and panting, just from those two words. "Take your undershirt off…slowly."

"Bossy," he crowed obviously into it, hands pausing in the middle of pulling it off. Then—because he never fucking listened me—went for tight black briefs instead.

"You've been talking big all week," he teased, as his dick sprang out of its confinement and he took himself in hand. One long stroke and then another as he talked placidly while my back molars snapped together. "Let's see what you can do."

My mouth watered at the sight. He was circumcised, unlike me. The tight skin on the head glistened from the pre-come there. And fuck, I wanted all of it.

"Stop touching it, and come to the edge of the bed," I barked out, indicating the spot where I wanted him. "I'm going to suck your cock and play with your ass before I fuck you."

"God, I love your filthy mouth." He shuddered, and I've never seen a person move that fast. In less than a second was sitting at the edge of the mattress, legs splayed. "I'm not gonna last, Yari."

Hatuey gasped when I sank to my knees in front on him. "I'll take the edge off, so we can go slow," I explained as I ran a finger over his taint. "I want to see you." I explained placing my hands on his inner thighs, widening his legs more. That first night it had been dark and not nearly as slow as I would've liked. It was barely a taste when I'd wanted to feast on him. Answer every question I'd had over the years about what he liked, the touches that could make him melt under my hands. All the ways in which I could have him.

"Come on get me off, Yari." He coaxed, overeager and impulsive like he always was, but I was not rushing this.

"I've been waiting too long not to make this last," I warned him, before taking the head of his cock in my mouth. The moan that came out of him was sinful, and it would be my new mission in life to make that happen as often as possible. He protested when I released his dick, but I appeased him by lapping at his balls while my thumb pressed on his rim. I kept my eyes on him as I touched him, fascinated by how he responded to every caress. Eyes rolling in his head, teeth digging into his bottom lip. Lost in the pleasure I was giving him.

"Oh god, it feels so good. Don't stop doing that," he demanded as I used one hand to spread him open and flicked my tongue at his opening.

"Those sounds you make, baby," I said between licks, but he didn't answer, just pushed his ass out, silently begging for more. "I'm going to get you off and then we're going to work on answering some questions I've had for a while."

That seemed to finally cut through some of the fog. He lifted his head and looked at me, eyes curious. "What kind of questions?"

My heart beat a little faster as a wave of tenderness made my chest tighten. There had never been anyone in my life, before or after Hatuey, who cared about my wants and needs more than he did. And I should've reminded myself of that in the last few days. There had never been a question or a comment from me he didn't pause to consider. That he didn't give his full attention. He had always been my sun, but perhaps Chantal was right, and I'd been his too.

He angled his head, his cheeks flushed with want, and came close enough that he could touch my face. He ran the pads of his fingers along the edge of my fade. "It's so funny." His voice sounded meditative—mulling over this new thing between us. "There are so many places I've never touched you. So much I haven't explored."

A breath shuddered out of me as he pulled my head in for a kiss. The smell of cock and sweat and the rum I'd been drinking mingled with the taste of him. I was gone, as addicted as I knew I'd be.

When we pulled apart, he was winded and looked hungry. "What are these questions you need to answer?"

It took me a second to remember, but soon I was back in the game, ready to make him moan and scream for me. "I want to know what sound you would make if I licked you right here." I ran my thumbs at the juncture of this thighs, exploring the silky skin there, and leaned in to lick his taint.

"Ah." He moaned low and deep, eyes half lidded and heavy as I tasted him. My own eyes lifted to his, wanting to catch his reaction.

"My next question was," I said as I slid a finger to his hole, loving how his face went slack from pleasure, "what would you say if I asked who you belong to?"

I was impressed that my voice held as much as it did. I focused on loving him in this new way that involved touches and kisses, so many kisses. I saw the light go on behind his eyes when my words landed, and the smile he gave me was everything. "Tuyo, solo tuyo, Yariel."

Mine. Only *mine.*

I practically purred my approval and wordlessly took him in to the root as I worked the base of his cock with my hand.

"Oh, I'm not gonna last," His breath hitched on the down stroke, then I pressed my thumb to his hole and sucked hard again. He stiffened, and my name tumbled from his lips as I took everything he had. I tried to remember if anything had ever felt as consuming as having Hatuey like this. The hunger and the tenderness that seeing him spent with pleasure provoked inside me.

I pulled back after a few seconds, as he flopped on the mattress, eyes open but unfocused. "That was amazing," he said as I leaned over him.

"Are you tired?" I asked, totally fine with letting this be the end of the evening. I'd gotten so much already, but he was not having any of it. Hatuey sat up forcefully and went straight for my erection which was painfully hard at this point.

"No. I have plans for this," he growled as he tightened a hand on my dick. "You're not the only one who's been thinking about this nonstop."

I gasped as he stroked me over the fabric of my trousers, my eyes rolling in the back of my head as my gut turned liquid. "It's hard to put words together when you have your hands on me like that."

We were kneeling on the bed now, but I kept my eyes closed, needing a moment. It's a heady thing to have the desire of your heart come true. To have the one thing you'd yearned for finally within your grasp.

I felt him fumble with the fly of my trousers, which I had managed to keep on through all this. He lowered the zipper and tugged until he had my dick in his hands. He groaned, and I opened my eyes so I could see his face. I wanted to see him as he explored me. Find the same wonder on his face that I felt from getting to have him like this.

But when I looked I found no wonder, no surprise. All I saw was unbridled desire.

Hatuey licked his lips as he touched me, and I melted under his stare. With one hand still on my dick, he tugged on my shirt. "Get naked. I want to see you."

I made quick work of my shirt and helped him get me out of my clothes. In a matter of moments we were both naked and glomming each other at the foot of the king-sized bed.

"I love you." I said it because I could, and went in for a kiss. A hard open-mouthed kiss with teeth, and with every graze, every gasp we were inventing a new us.

I put my hands on him, slid them from his strong shoulders down to his ass and grabbed on as he bucked into me. "Yeah, touch me. I want you to fuck me so bad. Ride you, umm," He groaned like he was imagining something delicious. "Yeah, I want to climb on your lap and ride you."

"Are you trying to kill me?" I complained as a breath skittered out of me at the image. Of him astride my lap, taking his pleasure on me. I gasped, so turned on I was sure I'd come before we got anywhere near fucking. But without warning, he pulled back.

"But first I want you in my mouth." He shook his head and grinned at the expression on my face. "I need to finish what we started on that damn plane."

Before I could even come up with a coherent response he was pushing and tugging until I was flat on my back with my legs spread so he could kneel between them. He ran both hands over my thighs, a greediness in his eyes I'd never seen before. "I can't stop thinking of how it felt to have these slamming against me." His breath caught and I saw him harden from whatever was going through his head.

"You really want me like that?" It was a dumb question, insecure and stupid, because I could see he did. I could see it in the way his eyes couldn't stop roaming my chest. But still, the small part of me which couldn't quite believe this could be true had to know.

He didn't answer, just gave me a look that told me he was about to prove it to me. Once he'd positioned himself so he was face to face with my cock, he looked up, and the wickedness in those brown eyes had my stomach doing all kinds of backflips.

Once he had me panting, he finally talked. "Clearly telling you I want you isn't enough, so I'm going to have to show you. And I promise, once this is done, you're not going to have an ounce of doubt."

"Okay," I answered, dazed.

"When have I ever broken a promise I've made to you, Yariel?"

Never. Not once.

CHAPTER 11

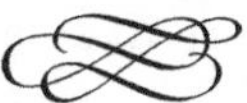

Hatuey

It's not like I didn't know Yariel was going to make me work for it. He was scared. I knew that. This was all exciting and new for me—for him it was the thing he'd told himself a million times he could never have. I knew that too.

Hell, that had always been us: me finding something I was into and wanting to dive in headfirst while dragging him reluctantly along. It only made sense *I'd* have to convince *him,* when he was the one who had been out for years. That's why all this mattered. He was the one who'd gotten there first. He'd been waiting, and I had to show him I wanted in. But mostly I just wanted to take care of him.

Our friendship had always been Yari coming to my rescue. Holding it down for both of us. I took a lot, I was greedy for the things I wanted and he always seemed happy to give me everything I needed. But now it had to be me who gave. Who took the time to address every whim and every want Yariel had.

"I love how you feel," I crowed as I ran a hand on the inside of his thighs. They were massive and sculpted from the grueling routines he did to make himself strong. No one worked as hard as this man did.

Yariel didn't believe in resting on his laurels—if he was passionate about something, he gave it his all. He'd always done so with me.

"I don't know where to touch first," I confessed as I cupped his balls and sucked on one, making his back arch off the bed. "You like that?"

He sucked his teeth, his jaw tight as I took him in my mouth, hands still busy playing with him. "Hatuey, fuck. I'm not gonna last." His voice shook and his thighs were like concrete under my hand as my head bobbed up and down, taking as much of him as I could manage.

"I want to make you feel good, Yariel. Tell me how to touch you, what you like," I demanded as I ran a thumb over his hole and stroked him, eliciting something as close to whimper as I'd ever heard from my best friend. "I can't wait to learn all the ways to please you."

I scattered kisses on the jut of his hip, his balls and even the tip of his cock, until he fisted the back of my head and guided my mouth to where he needed me.

"Stop playing and take it." I smiled around the mouthful cock, shivering from how hot it was to see him like this. I went to work on that big dick, and when I did, he sank back down, head on the pillow as he grunted his approval.

"Shit, that's good. Keep sucking on that. Use your tongue," he said, and it occurred to me that this was the kind of bossiness I could definitely get into. Every word out of his mouth made the temperature in my blood go up. "Mmm asi, cogelo todo."

Fuck, I was going to come just from hearing him.

"I'm gonna blow, baby. I want to be inside you when I do."

That got my attention. "It's hard to say no to a request like that," I gasped out after reluctantly taking my mouth off his dick, then made my way up his body. I pressed my mouth to his and asked for what I wanted between kisses. "Tell me how you'll do it?"

He ran the tip of his tongue along the shell of my ear as he grunted out a list of unspeakably filthy things. "I'm going to turn you around right now. Put you on your knees and then I'll get you ready. Work this ass like I've been wanting to."

I was sure my heart was going to burst out of my chest. "Ummm, how's it going to feel?"

He growled as he tightened a hand on the back of my neck and brought me in for a bruising kiss. By the time he released my mouth, I was lightheaded, and still I needed more. "Tell me."

"I'm going to be so deep inside. You're going to feel for days."

I had no idea where the sounds I was making were coming from, but Yariel's dirty promises were like a furnace in my gut. "God, that's what I want. Don't make me wait anymore."

And finally he didn't. In no time at all, Yariel had me on my knees, lubed fingers working inside.

"Tell me how bad you want this cock," he demanded as he pressed a finger to my gland, making me throb with pleasure.

"I want everything you give me. All of it." I pushed back into his fingers as he got me ready. I focused on the feeling of what he was doing to me. Those big hands gripping hard and gently touching me at the same time. The same hands that over the years had become as familiar as my own, and yet I never knew they could touch me like this. "I'm ready, please."

"Just a little more, baby." He worked what felt like two fingers in and out for a moment and then turned me around to face him. He was flushed, the light gray of his eyes swallowed up by the black of his pupils. His wide, generous mouth was pink and a little swollen from my kisses. I leaned in, wanting more. He grabbed my sides and pressed me tighter to him as our tongues slid together in a rhythm that was already as familiar and necessary as breathing. I ran my hands over arms, feeling the prickle of the hair on the palms of my hand while overwhelming possessiveness filled me. This man was mine.

"I love you." I said it right then because it felt as real as any truth I'd ever known about myself. "Te amo."

He made a tortured sound, like every word out of my mouth undid him little by little. He pressed his lips to mine, hard, and I let him look for whatever it was he needed to find with that kiss.

"I can't even remember a time when I didn't love you. You've been it for me since I laid eyes on the first day of class and you asked me if my Jordans were real."

I laughed at the memory, remembering the moment like it had happened yesterday. The way he looked, the way I felt.

"Did you really know?" I asked vaguely, knowing he would understand exactly what I was asking.

He nodded and kissed me again. "I knew you were the most beautiful boy I'd ever seen. I knew I must be gay because there was no confusing the things I wanted with you."

I could've drowned in conflicting feelings of lust and tenderness. "I get why you didn't, but I wish you could've told me then," I confessed as we continued to touch.

He shook his head, hands roaming back down my back and to my ass. He dipped a finger inside, making me gasp, and the consuming want came roaring back. "Everything would've been different if we'd done this back then."

Something about the way he said it made me think there was more I needed to know, but with his hands on me and in me. His teeth and tongue grazing the sensitive skin of my neck, my world whittled down to what Yariel was making me feel.

He handed me a condom that must have come from wherever he got the lube, and very carefully I rolled it on him while he gritted his teeth. He was big, and I knew from the first time those first moments were going to hurt, but I needed him inside.

He grabbed himself and asked very seriously, "Are you sure?"

I nodded, already making room for him. "Please, babe. I need you."

We breathed in unison as I moved so he was right at my hole. He stroked me with one hand as I took him in a little bit at time. The initial discomfort soon gave way to pleasure as Yariel worked on driving me crazy. He tweaked my nipples, stroked my cock, massaged around my rim until he was fully seated inside. He grunted as I moved, and the sound made me think of a rearing stallion ready to burst out of the gates.

"I feel you everywhere."

"I love being inside you," he said through gritted teeth as he pushed up a tiny bit and tilted me toward him, making something inside me go off.

"Ungh, do that again, harder." I didn't have to ask twice; soon he was fucking me with sharp jabs that were lighting up every nerve in my body. I twisted around to kiss him, and his tongue was hot and greedy, his moans of pleasure rumbling in my chest. "I love this. You feel so good, Yari."

"I knew it would be like this," he panted after a particularly delicious thrust. "I knew once I had you we'd both be ruined."

I shook my head and bit his bottom lip, then sucked on it. "I'm not ruined, I'm caught," I said, and went back for another kiss. And because he was a fucking showoff, Yariel tipped us down on the bed. Within seconds I was on my back with one leg over his shoulder while he fucked me in earnest.

"Mm, you were made for my cock." He growled as he pistoned his hips, turning my insides turn to molten lava.

I nodded, arms circled around his neck and holding on. Taking all the power that body was unleashing on me. "I was made for *you*."

His eyes widened, and it was like something snapped inside. He took my mouth hard as he redoubled his efforts, the angle hitting me exactly right with every thrust.

"I think I'm coming," I said between gasps. With another growl, he lifted my hips so he was fucking right into my gland, and soon I was screaming his name, muscles tightening from the waves of pleasure coursing through me. "Yari!"

I felt him stiffen above me, and I opened my eyes so I could see him. His lips pressed together as he emptied himself inside the condom.

"Dejame verte, mi amor?" I asked, wanting to see what was in his eyes, and when he opened them, I did.

There was no going back.

After a minute of lying there waiting our breath to return, Yariel carefully pulled out. Once he'd taken care of the condom, he came back to bed, and covered us with the blankets and slid behind me.

"How do you feel?" If I didn't know him like I did, I'd never be able to hear the worry in his voice.

I smiled as he ran his hands possessively over my arms. I pushed my ass back and put my hand on his thigh trying to reassure. "I'm a little sore and kind of tired, but I'm good. Really good." I almost left it there, but I knew what he wanted to hear. "I have no regrets. I love your kisses, your body, your mouth, your dick, and I am officially claiming them all."

"Good." That satisfied rumble in his chest was starting to become my favorite sound.

I turned around so we could be face to face for the last part of my speech. He looked so young like this, his hair a little mussed and his eyes soft. So much like the boy I'd met that school morning long ago. I reached out and ran a hand over his face, traced his lineup with the pad of my finger. "I know you're scared you'll lose me, baby. But you won't. This is just a new version of us." And because I wasn't anything if not extra…"One with lots more perks."

He still looked worried. "I can't lose you, Hatuey, but I also don't want to be the cause your fam—"

I kissed him to stop whatever was coming out and shook my head, brushing our lips together. "Nobody is losing anything. We're fine," I assured him as I shifted back into my little spoon position. "Let's sleep, baby. We'll make plans in the morning."

Within seconds I heard his breathing change as he fell asleep, and I stayed up a little longer, thinking about the future.

CHAPTER 12

SATURDAY

Yariel

"You know I'm going to want you in my bed every night, right?" I asked as I pushed the button that opened the blinds so we could see the sun come up. Most days I didn't have much use for the excessive amounts of money I made playing professional baseball. But being able to see the sunrise on the water with the love of my life in my arms was pretty fucking perfect.

"That's great, because I plan to be in your bed every night," he said smugly as he shifted trying to get closer. Hatuey had always been pretty touchy with me, but as a lover he was more of a lamprey. At the moment he was fully draped across my chest. The grin on his face so wide he looked like he was squinting. "I mean, I have to make up for lost time. And I'm hoping to be an expert on all things Yariel's privates by the end of the off-season. I'm counting on a lot of sleepovers. I'm already regretting the plan to go home for a couple of days—I wish you could come with me."

I stiffened at his words and then tried hard to relax my body, knowing he'd notice. "I can't. I have to report for all the pre-spring training stuff, and—"

He tipped his head up, and his smile had something in it that gave me pause. It was that smartass look he usually reserved for when he had something up his sleeve. "I talked to my dad yesterday."

This time there was no relaxing my body, because this was the conversation that could end everything.

"Oh?" That was all I could manage even though my head was swirling with questions.

"Yeah," he said, then pressed a kiss to my chest, which he was using as a pillow. When he looked back up, he had that impish smile again, and I was really close to throttling him, because love of my fucking life or not, Hatuey could be a real shit.

"Can you please tell me?" My voice shook, and that finally made him look a little less smug, but still he took his sweet fucking time.

"He just got this really weird look when he saw me watching you with the kids yesterday and then got all cryptic and asked me if I knew he loved me no matter what or something along those lines."

It took me a moment to process what he'd said, but when it finally landed the relief was almost debilitating. "He said that? I—"

I shook my head, not sure how to say the next part, but I knew that for this to really be real, I couldn't keep that secret. "Remember that night that we kissed?" That was a stupid question, but still I had to ask it.

"Yes. Of course I do," he said, eyes focused on me. Hatuey never shied from the hard conversations.

"He saw us. He was upset." I paused, not sure how to say the rest. Worried that he'd think I was accusing his dad when I understood why he'd done it. "I promised him—"

He angled his head to the side, his eyes worried but not surprised. "You promised him what?"

I closed my eyes, feeling the misery that had come back again and again since this week. "He thought you didn't know what you wanted. That you were worried about me leaving, so you kissed me because of that. He didn't want any opportunities for you to be impacted because of me."

I had my eyes closed still and my heart was beating so hard in my chest I could hear the blood rushing in my ears. But I felt his hands on me, warm and strong as he talked. "He probably had good reasons to worry back then, but I still hate he said that to you."

I opened my mouth to protest, scared I'd done what I feared and caused a potential rift between Hatuey and his father, but he kissed me again. And it was a firm, languid kiss. Like we had all the time in the world and absolutely nothing to worry about.

"I hate that you've been holding on to that for all this time." That was said with another brush of lips, this time on my neck, and the whisper of his warm breath on my over sensitive skin made a shiver run all the way through my body.

"Hatuey, this is serious," I protested weakly, as I gave him even more access to my neck.

I felt his hands come up to my face and his mouth making its way up too. "Open your eyes, Yari." I didn't want to, but he asked me, so I did. "My dad knows, okay? I told him and he's fine."

I stiffened. "No, Hatuey."

"Yes, Yariel," he countered. "When we got back from the camp yesterday and I went to my room, I called him. My life is my life, not my father's, he gets that." His eyes changed then, and for the first time I saw the same doubt there I'd been feeling for days. "Now if you have regrets, if you don't want this, then—"

That was not fucking coming out of his mouth. In two seconds flat I had him on his back, my entire body primed to show him just how wrong that train of thought was.

"I want all of it." I covered his mouth with mine, tongues sliding together, instant and complete connection. He jerked against me as I touched him, my hands rough as I grabbed and stroked all the parts that were now mine. "Mio."

I grunted as we moved together, already needing more, and my eyes on him. Always on him.

He held on to me and spoke around a smile so full of love it pierced my heart. "You're caught, Yariel Cabral. Forever."

I sealed his words with a kiss as the warmth of the morning sun promised that the first day of our future together was going to be a beautiful one.

BIOGRAPHY

Adriana was born and raised in the Caribbean, but for the last 15 years has let her job (and her spouse) take her all over the world. She loves writing stories about people who look and sound like her people, getting unapologetic happy endings.

When she's not dreaming up love stories, planning logistically complex vacations with her family or hunting for discount Broadway tickets, she's a trauma therapist in New York City, working with survivors of domestic and sexual violence.

Her Dreamers series, has been featured on Entertainment Weekly, The Washington Post, NPR, and was one of the TODAY Show on NBC's Hot Beach Reads picks. She's one of the co-creators of the Queer Romance PoC Collective. Visit her at: adrianaherreraromance.com

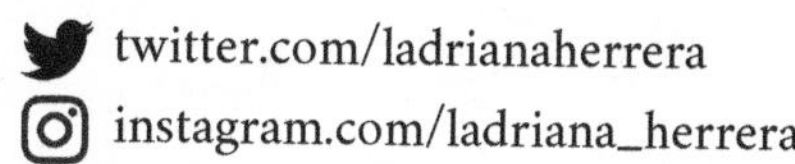

ALSO BY ADRIANA HERRERA

American Dreamer

American Fairytale

American Love Story

American Sweethearts

Mangos and Mistletoe

Finding Joy (June 2020)

Here to Stay (August 2020)

YES, AND...

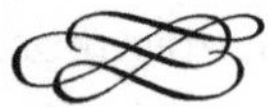

RUBY LANG

When rheumatologist Darren Zhang accidentally sits in on acting teacher Joan Lacy's improv class, he's unprepared for the attraction that hits him—and he's a man who likes to be prepared. Joan is caring for her ailing mother and barely has time to keep up her art, let alone date. But as the pair play out an unlikely relationship during stolen moments, they both find themselves wanting to say yes, and... possibly more.

* * *

Content Warnings: on-page sex, parental dementia, caregiver fatigue, adult ADHD, on page panic attack

CHAPTER 1

Week 1 - A Wednesday evening in February

ALL THINGS CONSIDERED, Darren Zhang, MD, thought he'd been doing well in this class, until the instructor clapped her hands and announced it was time to start their first improv exercise.

As far as he knew, there was not supposed to be improv in meditation. Because that's what he signed up for.

Meditation.

Breathe in. Breathe out. Think of nothing.

Acting out a scene was the opposite of nothing. It was a lot to think about, especially if it took place in front of the bright-eyed gaze of their sprightly instructor. It had been bad enough breathing loudly in front of her and doing weird—what did she call them?—vocalization exercises? He should have known he wasn't in the right place. She didn't seem like the type to teach meditation. Too energetic, not wearing any fringed clothing. She made big gestures with those white hands, and her skirt was a little too short for sitting cross-legged on the floor.

A dignified heterosexual man couldn't just get up in front of a pretty woman and do a *skit*.

Once again, he cursed Li-Wei, his friend and soon-to-be-fired primary care physician for suggesting—no, practically prescribing—a class.

"Next, you're doing to be telling me to do yoga and eat kale," Darren had almost yelled at his friend when Li-Wei brought it up during his exam. "Instead of coming to you, why don't I just log onto the internet?"

"Darren," Li-Wei had said drily. "It's your forty-second birthday and you're celebrating by having your annual checkup. Like you do every year. On your birthday."

"It's just a date. It's just a number."

"A higher number than last time. Like your blood pressure."

"What? What's the reading?"

High blood pressure. That was impossible. He worked out. Okay, so there was that pesky family history. And he drank too much coffee and didn't get enough sleep. But who did these days? The world was a mess, and Darren was one of the only things keeping it from falling into ruin.

"You're not in the danger zone, yet. But see this upward trend from the last five years?" Li-Wei asked.

Darren waved his hand for the chart. He read it. He went through it again. That was the problem with being a person of routine. He was consistent enough with his checkups that the numbers probably weren't lying. They were ticking subtly and inexorably higher. He wasn't in danger yet. But he was headed that way.

"I'm not going to suggest medications, but given your dad's high BP and your age, preventive measures should be fine for now. Try to cut down on the salt. And yeah, try a meditation class or yoga. I'd also suggest kale, like someone from the internet would tell you, but I suspect you already eat plenty of that."

Right.

So, meditation. That's why he was at this intro class which had… sketches? At the time, he'd hoped he could pop into the community center near the hospital, mouth breathe for 45 minutes, and cross "prevent impending death" off his list—all without major disruption to his usual routines.

Except now, as a couple of his classmates went to the front of the room, he realized with dawning horror that this was not the gentle, anonymous class he'd signed up for. It was definitely some kind of acting class. And the teacher, who'd seemed entirely too peppy and attractive to promote nice, even breathing in him, was an actor?

He hated rearranging his notions. So he pulled out his phone and surreptitiously checked his calendar to be sure. He was in the right room. This was the right time.

How, then?

He hit the link for the rec center that he'd copied in his calendar notes.

Dammit. He was in the wrong classroom. No. He was in the right room—but it was the wrong class. He'd entered the information a week ago, but there must have been a last-minute switch. He had to leave. But he'd already been in here for fifteen minutes, and exiting was going to be disruptive. The combination of wanting to be a good student *even if he wasn't taking this course* was at war with the desire to bolt and find the meditation room, where he'd already missed roll call and was thus probably labeled undependable.

Both ways led to utter and complete humiliation.

This could *not* be good for his blood pressure.

"I'd like to ask that we don't pull out our phones during class," the instructor said.

How had she done that? She wasn't even facing him.

His respect for her authority was increasing even as his embarrassment rose.

She turned around. "Darren."

She remembered his name.

"Why don't you come up and do this exercise with me?"

He found himself standing, smoothing his button-down like he always did, straightening his cuffs. Then he was at the front of the room, with five pairs of eyes on him. Thank God the class wasn't bigger.

"So we're doing to do an exercise called Fortunately, Unfortunately. Think of a situation, and another person shoots it down. The idea is to keep a story going. So, for example, I say, *Fortunately, I woke up early.* And you say, *Unfortunately, it was in a strange bed.*"

Darren couldn't help the choking sound that escaped his throat.

The instructor, Joan she'd said her name was, lifted one eyebrow but continued smoothly. "Usually, we'd try to have an uneven number of people doing this, so people don't always have to be in charge of one characteristic, but"—her voice faltered a little here—"we don't have as many students as anticipated, and I want this to be a lower-pressure exercise anyway, so we're just going to have you do one side this time."

She had freckles. And her reddish-brown hair was a brighter shade at the ends, as if she were growing it out, but not quite ready to let the old color go.

He wasn't sure if the pounding of his heart was due to stage fright, or because of an oncoming coronary event, or because he'd noticed so much about her.

Probably all three.

She began. "Fortunately, I found twenty dollars in my pocket this morning."

She motioned at him.

"Uh, unfortunately, it meant that I hadn't bothered to put my money away. In my wallet. Where it belongs. Otherwise how do you ever know how much cash you have?"

If he hadn't been standing so close, he would have never seen the slight trembling of her pink lips. Was she laughing at him? But wait, wasn't that... good? Had he made his improv teacher laugh with his first volley?

Her eyes glittered.

"Fortunately," she said, "I was able to buy a cup of hot coffee."

He missed coffee. "Unfortunately, I spilled it all over my clean white shirt."

"Fortunately, a handsome man helped me mop it up. And he said he had a detergent pen in his office."

He swallowed. *He* kept a detergent pen in his desk. It made sense. He also kept extra button-downs.

He looked at her swiftly. She was definitely amused.

He could feel the tips of his ears turning red—redder.

This was it. He was going to die up here.

* * *

"UNFORTUNATELY, the stain had really set in," the man in front of her, Darren, said.

Fortunately, that meant I had to take off my shirt—Joan Lacy did *not* reply.

This was going to be harder than she thought. Three-quarters of the way through her first class, and she was already raring to be inappropriate. It was improv—a certain amount of that was allowed—but she also needed to read the room. And this room—comprised of three senior ladies, two thirty-something women, and this man in front of her—was probably not in the mood for this turn in the exercise.

Besides, Joanie couldn't exactly flirt with a student on the very first day of the very first class she'd volunteered to teach at the community center. "Fortunately," she said, "I didn't care. Because at that moment I'd met the love of my life."

The rest of the class sighed. But Darren stiffened. She wasn't sure if his reaction was due to the love part, or the fact that the character they were playing didn't care for the stain still setting in her shirt.

Probably a little of both, judging by the looks of him. He was the outlier, not simply because he seemed to be a cis man in a room full of women, but also because he was the only one dressed like he was here for a business seminar.

Darren went back to his seat and, for a brief moment, seemed to slump in relief, before straightening to perfect posture once again. It was like watching a balloon inflate, except it wasn't mere air that filled him. He was lean and full of angles and sinew and—cheekbones. He one of those people who probably always looked good whether mussed up or pressed and dressed. But he was most assuredly pressed; his clothes retained paper-sharp creases along the shoulders and arms of the buttoned-up shirt, and down the long length of his trousers.

And... she was aware she shouldn't be thinking about his long lengths or his trousers.

Is that a detergent stick in your pocket, or are you happy to see me?

Oh, she could improvise with him all right. But this was class and not actual theater.

She put the poor guy out of her head for the next exercise. She had the group run through a couple more sketches with short breaks in between, told everyone what they should work on next week, and allowed herself to take a breath as everyone got slowly to their feet, the two younger women exiting first while Darren stopped to help Ms. Yvette, one of the seniors, get her walker.

"See you next class," Joanie called after them.

Darren shot her a guilty look, and Joanie realized two things right away:

1. This man would never lie to her.

2. He would not be coming back to her class.

Impulsively she set out after him. "Darren. You will be here next week, won't you?" She only sounded a little plaintive.

A pause. "Actually. Well, I was supposed to be in the meditation class but—"

"But they changed the room number because they had so many people sign up. Right."

She sighed. That goddamn meditation class. She was so over it. "I don't get it. Why is it so popular? Why that class?"

Why not my class?

But she knew the answer.

Improv. Acting. So frivolous. A class should be for learning useful things, like how to use power tools. She was useless in so many ways. A 35-year-old actress who'd tried to do experimental theater and of course couldn't make a living at it. She'd at least supported herself as a medical office manager for the past few years in Portland. But now she'd moved back home to Massachusetts to take care of her mother, and she didn't have a job or life outside of the house to prop her up.

She threw up her hands. "Can't people just get an app if they want to breathe loudly in a room?"

"I downloaded an app too, but I—it's just that meditation, well, especially now, could help me. Improv is more friv—I mean fun."

"More fun? You say that like it's a bad thing."

He shifted uncomfortably.

Despite feeling like an impostor, she made the same argument she'd made to the rec center manager. "I don't know about you, but I could use some fun in my life. One hour, one hour out of our lives where we can pretend to be other people, to go with the flow and see where an exchange takes us. Or to say out loud the things that pop into our heads, or to learn how to make a conversation tell a story, no matter how outrageous. Or just to learn to cooperate. Sometimes that's all it is. I volunteered to teach this class, but they're doing me a favor. I need this."

She put her hands to her temples. It wasn't his fault no one wanted to sign up for improv.

But of course he didn't have to know that. She straightened. "Well," she said briskly, "it's not your responsibility. Thanks for letting me know."

He lingered. "For what it's worth, I kind of had fun in your class. I mean, I was terrified, but you made it enjoyable. In a weird way."

"I was terrified, but you made it enjoyable in a weird way. You sound like everyone I've ever dated."

There was another pause.

Read the room, Joanie. Except maybe she'd read it too well, because the next words out of his mouth were. "Maybe I could buy you coffee? Since we've already gotten that out of the way? And to make up for me not being here next time?"

Yes! a part of her yelled. *Go out with a handsome man and fluster him for your paltry entertainment. God knows you don't get enough of that these days.* But the good, sensible part of her, which she was trying to listen to more these days, pointed out she didn't go out with people who didn't respect her. Actually, she didn't go out with anyone anymore. She couldn't.

She took a deep breath and mustered up some indignation. "You're hitting on me? After you've said you couldn't take my class?"

Surprise flashed across his face, followed by guilt, although the words that followed didn't seem to match the feelings she easily read on his face. "Technically, I wasn't signed up for your class. And it would be worse for you if we dated and you were my teacher."

"That may be the truth, but it's not exactly flattering."

That face again. But this time, his voice was full of the contrition she'd seen. "That didn't come out right. Never mind. I apologize. Never mind."

It was oddly bracing. Oh, she was attracted to him. She'd have to be dead inside to not notice his thick black hair, the smooth lips, the cheekbones, the firm rounds of muscle under his pressed clothing. But, she reminded herself sternly, a man who quit one's class and knocked one's calling as *frivo-no, fun,* was probably not someone she should go out with if she was a self-respecting, responsible person.

Or playing one. For now.

So she let him go, even as she admired his perfect posture and posterior, even as she gathered herself for an evening of going home and spending time—more time, there was always more time—with her mother.

CHAPTER 2

Week 2 – A Wednesday in February

DESPITE ARRIVING on time for the meditation class, it was already crowded enough that people were jockeying for prime spots on the floor. It seemed not only was he going to have to sit on the linoleum in his pressed trousers, he might even have to touch knees with another human being.

In sharp contrast, Joan's improv class, which he'd passed by a little earlier in order to get to this larger classroom, only had three students, and she herself was nowhere in sight.

Of course, it was early. Maybe she was somewhere else in the building, photocopying things, or preparing herself. Or maybe she'd breeze in at the last minute.

He probably wouldn't run into her. He half hoped he wouldn't. After all, he'd been so condescending, and she'd called him on it, which only increased his admiration of her.

The other half of that hope, the one where he could make it up to her, made him dress more carefully than usual that morning. And after work, he spent a lot of time figuring out what to do with his tie.

Leave it on? Take it off? But if he did, should he unbutton his shirt? Open? Closed? Collar popped up, hair slicked back, a song on his lips?

Right.

The meditation teacher only took attendance. She didn't ask where he'd been last week. It was all rather impersonal, which was what he'd wanted, wasn't it?

"Find a comfortable position," the instructor was saying as the stragglers filtered in.

Easier said than done in this class, he thought as he carefully angled himself away from the bodies of other students.

He was fine touching people to examine them, he was fine with handshakes and the occasional hug. This felt dangerously like fraternizing.

Besides it was difficult to keep his mind from Joan's class—from Joan. Especially because she was so nearby. All the expressions she'd sent his way when they were performing. *I didn't care. Because I knew I'd met the love of my life.*

He'd forgotten everything at that moment, forgotten he was in class, standing in front of a group of people. He'd neglected to breathe, forgotten he'd only just met her. Because he'd believed her.

That was *good* acting.

But that meant what she said hadn't been true. It was an illusion.

And then she'd looked disappointed when he told her he wouldn't be coming back. He'd seen many faces over the course of his work, but he'd never seen the joy slide off a face so completely. Her eyes dimmed. Her mouth went from being bright and upturned to a dull, sad sag.

He didn't know her. But for some reason, he hated that he'd done that to her.

So he'd gotten his work done that week. He saw his patients. Tested their joints and examined their skin, listened to whether they thought their medications were helping, sent samples to the lab. But in a part of his mind, he'd worried about her, cringed over his own actions, wished for a second chance—and he didn't know precisely why that was.

"Try to feel your bones sinking into the earth."

He wished he could feel exactly that. If only he could dissolve and forget himself, forget that he was always supposed to be upright and sturdy, that he had muscles and skin and bones and nerves.

He wished he wasn't a person who *remembered* everything, because that meant he replayed those awful awkward moments when he'd insulted her work. And then tried to ask her out.

Next to him, someone exhaled loudly. The teacher said, "Yes, breathe in, breathe out."

Another loud sound from his neighbor. *Show off*. By the end of class, he was sore from trying to hold his body in a relaxed position. He was doing it all wrong. It seemed to take him longer than these other loose-limbed students to unfold himself and get out of that classroom.

Then, there *she* was in the hallway locking the door.

Should he say hello, or did she even remember him?

"Darren," she said turning, solving the dilemma.

"Joan. Good class?"

He winced at his own tone. So hearty.

She smiled. "They're a great group." A pause. "And did you enjoy your meditation class?"

"No."

It came out more baldly than he'd intended, which was maybe why she paused before asking, "Then why take it?"

"I've been told I need to relax. My blood pressure's getting a little higher."

"Whose isn't these days?"

"That's what I said. Anyway, meditation was one of the suggestions."

"And you're trying all the recommendations your doctor gave you?"

"Of course, I am."

She smiled. "Of course, you are."

For a moment, he felt understood. He wasn't sure he liked it.

He said, "I wanted to apologize. For saying what you do isn't important."

"Well, you actually told me it was too fun and maybe frivolous, not that I thought about it all week or anything."

Was she joking with him? Had she thought about him all week? Although, it wasn't good if she'd been dwelling on his careless words.

"I was wrong. I mean, here you are volunteering at a community center, trying to help people."

"So it's because I'm donating my time that my vocation is worthy?"

"Well, yes?"

"But the class itself and my work aren't valuable?"

This was tricky. But he was starting to see her point. "It's a different kind of value from the kind I'm used to understanding, but I'm willing to go out and learn more."

She cocked her head at him. "Sounds like I wasn't the only person turning this over in their mind."

"More than I wanted to. All week really, I thought of it."

He couldn't lie to her. No, it was worse than that: he couldn't stop telling her exactly who he was and how he felt. It was terrifying. It was freeing.

She watched him for another moment. Carefully. Then, zipping up her jacket, she said, "Well then, come out with me. It sounds like you at least owe me a pity burger."

* * *

DARREN ORDERED the fish and a salad with dressing on the side. She shouldn't judge what other people ate, but she couldn't help herself. Maybe he had an allergy. Maybe he didn't want to attempt anything as messy as the onion double cheeseburger at Lucy's. Joan herself was a little daunted by the mountain of food in front of her, so she dipped a fry into the cheese oozing down the side of the patty before contemplating how to grasp the darn thing, let along take a bite out of it.

She didn't know exactly when she'd decided to ask him out. Maybe it was when he apologized the first time. She was always such a sucker for a handsome man who could make an abject apology. Maybe it was when he said he'd thought about it all week—about her, her feelings—in that deep voice of his.

Her own mother couldn't keep a memory for more than a half hour now, much less remember her only child.

It was nice to be *held* in someone's thoughts. Almost better than being physically touched, although she was sure he would do that too, if she let him.

She would probably let him.

Anyway, she'd never eaten Lucy's famous onion double cheeseburger before, and she owed it to herself to try.

"So tell me about yourself, Darren. What do you do when you're not taking classes at the community center?"

"I'm a physician. A rheumatologist. I work with patients who—"

A doctor. She started to laugh. It figured. She was fated to be surrounded by them. "I know what a rheumatologist does. You see patients with autoimmune conditions. Rheumatoid arthritis, osteoarthritis, SLE, Sjögren's."

He looked delighted with her, so she held up her hand. "Just because I know a few terms doesn't mean I can talk shop. I was a receptionist and office manager at a multispecialty practice. I'm not a health professional."

She took a tentative bite, and Darren, well, he watched her. Juice ran down her hands, her wrists. So much for looking sexy. Not that she was trying.

He picked up a bunch of napkins but didn't touch her until she gave him a nod.

He was gentle and thorough, and she didn't put down the burger the whole time. Instead, when he was done, she took another (neater) bite and closed her eyes, chewed, and swallowed.

"Thank you," she finally said. "Would you like a fry?"

"Are they salted?"

She put down the burger, wiped her hands again, and picked up one of the crispy pieces of potato. His eyes kept following her hands, her lips. Maybe he was thinking of the food.

She didn't think so.

"Not salted."

He nodded. "Thank you, I'll try one."

It was her turn to watch him.

He had very nice lips.

"So," he said, "you worked in a medical practice."

"Back in Portland, Oregon. I know all about doctors."

"That's a terrifying insight."

She had to laugh at his expression. "They were all right."

She hadn't minded her bosses. But there had been three of them, and they'd been friends for a long time, which left her outnumbered. Still, they'd been decent and concerned when she told them she was moving back east to take care of her ailing mother. They'd even given her work she could do remotely after hours. Although there wasn't really such a thing as after hours for Joan now.

"It was never supposed to be my forever job, anyway. I kept it while I ran a small theater company on a shoestring, getting grants and funding and sponsors—that kind of thing. Still, I would have been happy scrapping it out for the rest of my life."

But even that fight was on hold.

She took a big bite of her burger, getting a little bit of the stringy onion ring this time. She chewed slowly to savor it, but also to make sure she didn't talk and tell him any more than she wanted. For a while they were silent, listening to the noises of the bar, the clink of glasses, bursts of laughter from other tables, the thrum of music.

She appreciated that he didn't try to push her, try to ask her for something, try to distract her, that he was letting her just... eat. It felt like a long time since she'd been allowed to do that.

"Why did you call it a pity burger?" he asked suddenly.

"Because you're sort of dumping my class—or you did. It's a joke, though. I don't take your grand defection personally." She did. A little. Never mind that. "You should never take anyone for a fancy pity dinner. That just prolongs it. But you need to bulk up the person you're dumping with enough sass and energy so that they don't mind being let go by your fine self. So, a burger. Although it doesn't have to be a burger. A pity grilled cheese is also good, although the phrase doesn't have the same ring. But really, you're doing this so you don't have to feel guilty for getting my class canceled because of low interest."

"Is that going to happen? That's not why I'm taking you out."

"They're not ruthless at the community center—maybe they should be. But I probably won't be asked back."

Her phone flashed. It was her aunt, who was sitting with her mother tonight.

This probably wasn't good.

She was going to excuse herself to read it, but he gestured at her to take it at the table, then turned his head away tactfully to look at his own phone while she checked her message.

Your mom is all right, but I can't find her sleeping pills.

She'd have to call her aunt. "I'm sorry. I'm going to have to call back."

"Don't worry about it."

She got up and headed toward the bathrooms, which were a little quieter.

She was usually organized enough about the pills. But today she'd been in a rush, and maybe she hadn't put them in the container. Or maybe her mother had moved the box, even though they were hardly accessible. Or maybe—

In the back of her mind, she remembered all the times when she hadn't always been organized, all the times she hadn't been perfect in her attempts to care for her mother, which made her doubt herself even when she had done the right thing. She hadn't been around when her mom's dementia first started showing. Joan hadn't come back home until it was too late, and now she had to keep it together when it had already fallen apart. It was an effort to be this way, and it was wearing.

Her aunt wasn't picking up.

Had something happened? Had her aunt fallen? Had her mother done something to herself?

Maybe because Joanie hadn't put the pills in the right place, her mother had injured herself, and they had to go to the hospital. How could she make her aunt, her aunt who'd lost her husband not six months ago, sit with her mother while she, Joan, was out eating a burger and enjoying herself with a handsome man after teaching a class no one wanted or needed.

At least last week she'd gone straight home.

She should return now. She should just get back to that small, cramped house and take care of this, because she hadn't taken enough care before.

Dimly, she realized she was panicking as she gripped the wall. The already dark hallway was dimming around her, the light a far point away.

"Joan," someone was saying. "Joan, are you all right? Is everything okay?"

It was Darren. "I can't reach my aunt. I left her at home with my mom and I..."

She didn't know if he could understand her. The words came out of her chest in strangled gasps. What if he couldn't understand her?

"Come on. Sit down for a second."

She gave him her phone and let herself be gently guided out from the narrow, dark hallway and to a chair. He kept talking quietly as she put her head down between her knees. When she could breathe again, when she could be upright again, he handed her a cold glass.

She gripped it with both hands, afraid the condensation would cause it to slip out of her fingers, and the water would spill, and they would all surely drown.

She was glad he didn't tell her to drink. She nodded when he asked if he could check her pulse, and shook her head after her asked if she'd felt any pain or nausea.

She was aware that they were back in the main room. The sound of music and conversation was surprisingly comforting—the sound of people ignoring her.

When she finally felt able to lift her head again, she looked around the crowded bar, then back at Darren. How had he managed to create this small bubble? He was standing close, but not so close that her lungs would seize up again in panic. He was near enough that his neat, white shirt and strong, squared shoulders felt like shelter.

She sucked in another breath. "I have to go," she said abruptly. "My aunt."

"She texted a few minutes ago after you—"

After she'd panicked.

"I didn't look at the message, but her name flashed up on your screen."

She took the phone with still-trembling fingers. The message said, **Found them! They were where you said. Was distracted when looking.**

Joan let out a long, shuddering breath.

"Joan."

She held up her hand. She was forever holding her hand up to him, but this time it lacked the usual steadiness. "It's fine. My mom's fine. No crisis. But I should go." She added rather inadequately, "Thank you. I never thanked you for everything."

"Can I at least drive you home? I'm worried."

She could walk but… no, she had to get home. "That would be nice."

In a few minutes, he'd paid and had her burger packed up, and she was safe in his sensible car. She should be humiliated for falling apart so completely over some missing pills of her mother's. But somehow seeing his arms holding the steering wheel in the correct nine and three o'clock position, sensing his eyes sliding over to her when he thought she wasn't looking, she felt not humiliated, but relieved. Unburdened. If only for a few minutes.

He didn't ask her if it had ever happened before. He didn't *fret*, which was something she couldn't have dealt with.

Instead, when they arrived, he looked at her long and hard to make sure she was truly all right, then said, "Is there something you need that I can get?"

"No. I'm all right. You've done more than enough."

"OK. Remember to take your food. And blink the lights so I know you got in safe."

She almost cried right then. She wasn't in any shape to ask him in, although it would have been polite. She wasn't ready for anything. But with the gentle way he helped her, she understood right at this moment what it was to be cared for. It had been so long, she'd almost forgotten.

"I'm not usually like this."

Impulsively she reached past the steering wheel and closed her arms around him.

It was awkward, with their winter jackets, and his seatbelt, which he'd started to unbuckle because he was turning toward her.

And suddenly their chins were almost touching, and their warm breaths intermingled, invisible.

She closed her eyes and tucked her head into the crook of his neck. "Thank you," she said again and again and again.

Then she quickly untangled herself and slipped out of the car.

Up the steps she skipped, not looking back—there was no use in looking back.

But after she flashed the porch lights, once, twice, she did stay for a moment at the door, listening for his car to start, for him to drive away. Disappointed when he finally did.

CHAPTER 3

Week 3 - A Wednesday afternoon in February

"Eating another sad desk lunch, I see," Li-Wei said, breezing into Darren's office without knocking. "How's the blood pressure?"

"It was fine until you came in."

His health was holding steady, that was true. Darren had been monitoring himself in the mornings. Although sometimes, he did find it sad that it was one of the first thoughts he woke up to nowadays.

He didn't think of Joan first thing in the morning. That usually came later, when he sat in his car. The smell of her ridiculous burger had lingered overnight, just long enough for him to miss it when the usual scents of vehicle and exhaust returned. The fact he caught himself trying to find it in the air should have bothered him. It was her food—it wasn't *her*. If he were operating normally he should have been trying to spray his seats with something to make sure none of that beefy grease perfumed his clothing. But instead, the smell, and then the loss of it—it made him ache with something like loneliness.

That was silly though. He was attracted to her, and he felt bad because he'd quit her class—not that he'd been signed up for it to begin with and not that it was his fault. Anyway, they had too little in common. She obviously had her hands full, and wasn't quite coping, and he also was so terribly busy.

So busy.

By the time he'd argued with himself about the whole thing, he was usually already in the clinic parking lot, still sitting there as the car grew colder, lost in his thoughts about why he shouldn't check up on her. A couple of times, he'd almost been late.

He shook his head.

"Are you here to make a house call?" Darren asked his friend.

"No, I know you worry enough about it for the both of us. I'm here to take you to lunch."

"I'm eating, as you've already observed."

Li-Wei sat down and opened up a paper bag. He slapped a fruit salad down beside Darren's bowl of lettuce and legumes and unpacked an enormous sub for himself.

"Eat up, friend. I'm getting married."

"Again?"

"This is the second time. You only get to say, *Again?* in that tone of voice if I make a habit out of it, which would be at least three times."

"Congratulations! I wish you and Mona all the happiness."

He really did. Mona Shih was smart and determined and wonderful, and Li-Wei was a good guy. Darren shouldn't let his own cynicism about love and marriage infect his friend's happiness. Not that Li-Wei was letting it.

"You're coming to the banquet, of course."

"How big is this shindig going to be?"

"Tiny. Don't worry, you won't have to give a speech or throw a party like last time."

They both grimaced at the memory.

"This time you'll be less like a best man, more like a partygoer. You and Nasreen—you remember Nasreen?"

"This better not be a setup."

"Nasreen's married to another ob-gyn now. They set up a practice together."

"Oh."

"Nasreen's bringing her husband. The whole thing will be in Chinatown on a weeknight next month. One round table with a lazy Susan, twelve courses. That's it. You should bring a date because there'll be a lot of food."

He began his normal disclaimer that he didn't date, then paused.

Had last week been a date?

Did it count if it was your former teacher by mistake, and it had ended in a panic attack? Put it that way and it didn't sound... great.

But worry over Joan aside, he'd enjoyed himself, sitting knee-to-knee in a warm, crowded bar on a weeknight with a woman who had laughed at him and with him, whose hands cut gracefully through the air, who interrupted him when he was about to be his worst, most patronizing self, who'd smiled at him always like he was his best self.

It wasn't until later that he was surprised at how comfortable he'd been, even though he should have felt completely out of his element.

And best of all, he'd almost kissed her.

She would have let him too.

With a jolt, he realized he still hadn't answered Li-Wei. And Li-Wei had narrowed his eyes. "You went out with someone."

"I think I did. But I hardly know her. Not well enough to take to a wedding."

"The eating part only," Li-Wei held his thumb and index finger in a pincer. "The tiniest banquet. Miniscule. One, two speeches max. More like minor dinner theater."

"I would never take anyone to dinner theater."

But maybe Joan would enjoy that? She was a theater person.

Not that Li-Wei and Mona's wedding was a show. Not that Darren could take her to a wedding banquet—yet.

Wait. What was he thinking? He couldn't be thinking that way.

Yet.

"So how did you meet her? What's her name? Tell me everything."

Darren shook himself and gave his friend an abbreviated version of events. Li-Wei wasted no time in claiming credit. "I set you up!"

"Li-Wei, she may not want to see me again. I shouldn't see her. There's no future in it."

"But you want there to be. Because there's something between you."

"I don't even know her phone number."

But he knew where she lived, which sounded creepy. He hadn't driven by the house—hadn't been tempted. That was a line he would not cross until she invited him back. But he had a good memory, he always had, so he knew the number, knew the street, knew the number of streets—not many—separating his newer condo building from her staid and solid house on one of the older blocks. It wasn't the place he'd have imagined her living; he pictured something more vibrant for her. But it was the dead of winter in Cambridge, and even she couldn't make the bare branches bloom with her warmth, the way she'd heated his whole body in the car. He remembered sitting in the driveway with her, soft shadow across her cheek when she turned to him, the rustle of her down jacket and the puff of air releasing from it as she pressed herself into him, the cushion of resistance between both of them slowly leaking away.

He caught himself sighing again with longing, and Li-Wei, probably seeing something in his face, laughed.

His friend stood up and threw the balled up the wrapper from his sandwich into the wastebasket. Of course, it sank. "Thanks for agreeing to come. And Darren, if you don't know this woman's phone number, I suggest you find out tonight."

"YES, AND..." Joanie prompted Yvette, one of her senior students.

Ms. Yvette repeated it dutifully, but she looked stumped.

Joan repressed a sigh.

Class had felt off today. Like everyone was afraid. Or maybe it was Joan who was off, Joan who needed the little push, the small encouragement.

So instead she offered it to everyone else in her class.

She smiled at the hesitant Yvette and nodded to say she was doing well.

"The *yes, and...* keeps a story going," Joanie said. "Think of when you're in a conversation. You ask, *Do you like spring?* And the other person says, *No.* What does that do?"

"It makes the other person look like an ass."

"An ass who hates springtime."

"But at least it's honest."

"It might be," Joanie said. "But try this. Yvette, you ask me a question."

"Do you like... autumn?"

"Yes, and I like summer and spring too. Winter isn't my favorite season. Although I like feeling cozy in my jacket."

And she liked sitting with nice, handsome men in warm cars when it was cold outside.

"*No* stops the conversation. *No* changes the track, it focuses the story on the speaker instead of the collaboration. I know it seems like improv is supposed to be about fun and getting off good jokes, but it's also group work, and *No* throws off the dynamic. Even if you keep chattering away after saying *No,* it's there. You dropped it in and it sounds like you've started something new, even if you're continuing with the story. You can and should say *No* in life because you don't have to team up with everyone. In improv, it's different."

It was time to go. "Try saying, *Yes, and* in conversations this week," Joanie called. "Work on drawing it out."

The students filtered out slowly. Ms. Yvette's grandson, who was supposed to come and help her, hadn't yet gotten to the rec center, so Joanie helped her out the door and was going to walk her to the bench in the front hall of the rec center when Darren showed up.

She'd given up on him. Mostly. Rather, she'd been giving up on him slowly, piece by piece, all week. His arrival, however, gave her system a surge of pleasure. It was too much.

"Why weren't you in class?" Yvette interjected, clearly recognizing him.

Now it appeared the older woman had plenty of conversation to make where she'd been reticent before.

Darren blushed. Joan had never seen a man blush so much before.

"Oh, I was in the wrong classroom the first time. But I wanted—" He glanced at Joan, and for some reason, the sight of her made him stand up straighter. She had never inspired such good posture in anyone, let alone someone who was already plenty upright. "I wanted to see if you, Joan, were free after class."

Joan and Darren were helping Yvette down the hall. The older woman paused to glance at the two of them. "Are you asking Joan on a date?"

"I am."

"But we've—"

Joan was about to say they'd already been on a date, and it had ended with him having to support her while she had a panic attack about her mother, and that she really shouldn't be dating considering the circumstances. But Ms. Yvette was clinging avidly to their words, and Joan wanted to let him down gently after he'd been so gentle with her and because...

Because she wanted to go out with him, eat a proper dinner without feeling this hanging over her head. She *wanted* to be able to say *yes*, but—

Joan opened her mouth, and before she could demur, Yvette said encouragingly, "Yes, and..."

Dammit. She'd even gotten Joan's tone from class right.

But yes, and what? *Yes and kissing? Yes, and sex? Yes,* please*!*

Another chance. Another date, and this time there could be kissing and sex.

Darren helped Ms. Yvette sit down on a bench in the hallway and asked Joan, "Is your aunt with your mom again tonight?"

"Yes, and..." and her aunt had told her to stay out longer. She had things under control.

The pills were all in the right place. Joan had checked and rechecked. The emergency numbers were on the bulletin board and programmed in her aunt's phone. And her cousin, Gia, had even said she might stop by and check on the sisters.

Yvette smiled. "That's right. See, we all can practice continuing the conversation."

Ugh. What a time for Joan to find out her lessons were sinking in.

Ms. Yvette's grandson rushed inside, brushing snow off his shoulders, and Yvette rose to greet him. As she stepped out the rec center's doors and into the night, Darren and Joan waved and watched her small figure fold into the car.

They were outside now, their breaths showing under the lights. The weather was supposed to go below zero tonight. It was supposed to be the coldest day of the year.

"Here's the thing," Joan said, swallowing. "This is what I can give. One night a week. That's all. I'm taking care of my mother. She has early-onset dementia. We didn't always get along, she and I. When I was growing up, I was pretty rebellious. She always said I'd be the death of her."

"Joan."

"We don't have anyone else. Well, there's my aunt and cousin sometimes, but they have their own things to deal with right now. My dad left. And so there's no one else, you see?"

How could he see, though? He was so together, and self-possessed, and she was... not. Most of the time, even though she was in charge at the house, it was a role she hadn't wanted to take. It didn't sit right with her. He was groomed and organized, and he was a doctor. He'd probably never lost any pills. He probably had a plan for when he aged, for dealing with his parents, for anything life could throw at him. While she was in her mid-thirties and she had nothing of her own, except this class she was teaching, a class that would end in a handful of weeks.

"I don't have anything to give right now," she said again.

"I don't want to take from you, then,"

She closed her eyes. "Sure. OK. OK."

She started to step back, back into the rec center for a few minutes to catch her breath.

"No, I didn't say it clearly. What I mean is, I don't want you to give me anything. I want to take you to dinner. But only if you want."

"Just dinner?"

"Just dinner."

"That's all it can be, you know. I don't have time for anything else."

I don't have time for myself, she almost said. But it felt selfish to say it out loud. After all, she was here, teaching a class on improv. It wasn't even as useful as meditation, according to him. Except no, she was attributing it to him because sometimes she believed it herself.

But at least her volunteer shift was a justification to leave the house. Yes, she knew it wasn't healthy that she had to scrounge for reasons. It was enough to ask for time, to simply ask. But it was hard.

"Then, that's all it has to be," he said. "For me too."

* * *

THEY WERE SITTING in his car in the parking lot of Lucy's.

Normally, he would try to subtly hurry a date into the restaurant. It was cold and the longer they sat in the car, the more likely the windows would start to condense.

But they were both trying to prolong the evening. The longer they remained in the in-between space before eating dinner, the longer they'd have to just be.

Joan said, "Let's kiss first."

He didn't think he'd heard correctly.

"Kiss," she said again. "You know how to do that, don't you? You look like you'd be a good kisser. You have lips and a tongue."

She was trying to stir him up—it was how she was sometimes, he realized. He brought this out in her.

Well, it was working because he was stirred up. And he liked it.

He made his voice very even. "I don't know if I'm a good kisser. But we can practice."

She cocked her head as if he'd said something unexpected. He liked that, too. Maybe he had.

"You like practicing," she said, her voice husky.

He swallowed. "I like getting things right. And I don't mind working for it."

She turned carefully toward him, the quiet click of her lips parting in a tiny sigh. But in the silence of the car, in the dark night with snow falling softly outside, he felt its ripples; the sound resonated deep inside him, a penny dropped into a deep well, a wish.

He unbuckled his seat belt and put his hand on the clasp of hers, waiting for her yes. She nodded and he unfastened that too, with steady hands, releasing it so the metal tab wouldn't hit her.

She hid a smile he could see even in the darkness of the car. "What is it?" he asked.

"Nothing," she said. "This."

He moved her hand to the back of his head, pulling him toward her, and kissed him.

Their lips glided over each other, gently for a time. The warmth was good. Then she opened her mouth and he felt himself surging forward, his arms pulling her toward him, his own shoulders digging hard into the seat in his eagerness. Her tongue stroked his, and the scent of coffee and lip gloss and the velvety hot pull of her mouth filled him. He scrabbled to unzip her jacket, breathing heavily, then his fingers stole deep into the damp warmth underneath, down to soft, warm skin. She gasped a little then, to feel the strokes of his fingers on her, and he swallowed her gasp, took her surprise deep within him, greedily, and let it warm him as he pulled her closer still.

She was murmuring now, a slow stream that started in her throat, every small vibration of speech making him lose himself more and more until finally, he told himself he had to stop.

Her eyes were still closed, her mouth still moving. "Please," she whispered.

He panted. He wouldn't be able to withstand another *please*. But her eyes opened slowly and she smiled a small smile. "We should go inside," she said, every word dragging out reluctantly.

He swallowed. He stroked her skin again and took a deep calming breath, just like the ones he'd been learning earlier tonight, and willed his excitement down. He noticed they had indeed fogged up the windows. That it was getting cold. He'd promised her food.

He helped her zip up her jacket, and they climbed out into the chilly night together.

Inside, she bantered with the waitress and ordered the cheeseburger again, a determined light in her eyes. He found himself bracing pleasurably for better.

"So, Darren," she began, "how old are you? Have you ever been married before? Any kids?"

"I'm 43. Divorced more than ten years. No kids."

"Divorced?"

She sat back as if he'd managed to surprise her, although he doubted very much he had.

"What was your wife like?"

"She's a physician, like me. We met in med school. She's out in California now."

"Did she break your heart?"

She'd leaned in, like an interviewer. Another mannerism. She was playing with him, and he loved it. "Is that why you're all buttoned up? Because all that secret heartache could come bursting out at any moment?"

She was trying to get a rise out of him, because maybe he'd gotten one out of her. But he was good at this, being steadfast in chaos. That's where his strength lay. "No, I've always been like this."

"Even as a child."

"My school had a uniform. I loved it."

"And now you have a white shirt and pressed trousers. You probably wear a white coat in your office too."

"Sometimes."

"No heartbreak, then?"

"My ex and I did hurt each other, but splitting was for the best. But it was my father, who was like me, not an easygoing man, who probably really shattered me. Shortly after the divorce, my father died of a stroke."

"Oh." She put her hand to her lips. "I'm sorry," she murmured.

He leaned forward and touched her arm. "It's okay. I've had time to sit with it even though I haven't talked to anyone about it for years."

She held his gaze.

"You'll really tell me anything, won't you?"

"I will."

A pause.

He said, "It's hard to separate these two events in my head, even though the only way they're connected is by time. It isn't logical—all my mixed emotions about being abandoned by people who should have loved me enough to stay. Then I used to feel guilty for having that reaction. I was thinking like a child. So I tried to put that whole knot of feelings away. Except when I couldn't."

He took a sip of water. "The best solution seemed for me to keep doing what I was doing. Although maybe now, I realize I feel different. Right at this moment with you, it doesn't feel bad to talk about it. I'm more at ease than I've been in years."

He couldn't help glancing up for her reaction. She took his hand, and for a while, they stared at the other patrons and listened to the *thump-thump* of music.

"I get the guilt," she said, after a while.

"We don't have to talk about it if you don't want to."

"Oh no, no. You see, now the floodgates are open. Everything you said, it *is* a knot of feelings. My mom isn't going to get better. This is the new normal for us, but I still can't wrap my head around it. And the funny thing is, she's nicer now to me, but somehow that makes it worse. I'm not allowed to be angry with her. I'm not allowed to resent her, because now she's so docile and helpless.

"My aunt comes over twice a week. And we have a home health-care worker a couple of times to help bathe her and things, and so I can have some time to myself. But I want more, and I can't ask my aunt. Her husband died recently. She has her own things to worry about. It's just—I love my mother in a complicated way, but I don't like taking care of her, and that makes me feel like the terrible daughter she always told me I was."

"You aren't terrible. All of this you're telling me says that's not true."

"That doesn't stop me from feeling it. Especially because I've lived with it for so long. When I was an artist—I'm still one, although I don't feel like much of one these days—but when I was more of a practicing artist, all this stuff about not being a good daughter, that was all material. We could improvise all the angry conversations we had in our heads, refine them, perform them, put them outside of ourselves, make other people sad or happy to watch. It became something else. Now I don't do that as much anymore. And it's like you said, I don't know what to do with all of those emotions. Luckily, half the time I'm too tired to feel too much."

It was his turn to squeeze her hand, to look at their fingers intertwined, yet another knot of complicated feelings.

A curl of excitement—or was it hope?—came up from his stomach. "Fortunately," he said as lightly as he could, "our food is here."

She raised her eyebrows, catching on as the waiter set down their plates.

"Unfortunately, yours looks bland."

"Fortunately, I'll be able to steal one of your fries."

"Unfortunately, you'll have to let go of my fingers to do it."

"That is unfortunate," he said.

What was this feeling? Grief? Release? Giddiness? Maybe that was it. He nabbed a fry with his free hand and was rewarded by her surprised laugh.

Then she swiped the beer he'd surprised himself by ordering, took a long swallow, set it down, and wiped her mouth, her eyes never leaving his. "You're grinning like a little boy," she said after a moment. "I knew you had it in you."

"Know what? I sure didn't."

CHAPTER 4

Week 7 - A Wednesday in March

"You should stay out longer," Aunt Sylvia said.

As if *that* didn't throw Joan into a small panic. She ended up dropping her keys with a clatter and spent another minute sweating and searching for them in the dim hallway.

Her aunt continued calmly, not caring Joan was going to be late getting to the community center. "I'm prepared to take over for an entire night. Have been for a couple of weeks ever since you started seeing your friend. I could have Gia stay over, too. It'd be like a sleepover."

It would be nothing like a sleepover, but her aunt was kind. Even so, the fact that Sylvia had figured out Joan was seeing someone, combined with the fact that Sylvia had just endorsed a full night out with a boyfriend *while they were standing in front of Joan's mother...* Well, that brought out more guilt than Joan could deal with, especially right now.

Then Joan's mother chimed in and giggled, "Sylvia, you know we can't stay out all night long."

But she addressed herself to Joan, even though Joan didn't look *that* much like her aunt when she was younger.

"Joanie's a grown woman," Sylvia said firmly.

"My little Joanie?"

The laughter fell away in an instant, and her face, always so fine-boned, was clouded with confusion. Joan's heart gave a painful twist. For one instant, her mother had known who she was. Too bad neither Joan nor Sylvia agreed with her.

"Go," Aunt Sylvia told Joan calmly. "And think about what I said."

"I will," Joan muttered, running out the door.

But she knew she shouldn't.

She lived by routine now. Groceries during Monday and Thursday home visits. Friday doctor appointments, occupational therapy appointments, sometimes a whole day of them. Occasionally, they took a walk around the block in the mornings, if the weather was nice. It hadn't been good this winter. Remote freelance work putting together newsletters in the evenings, when her mother was supposed to be in bed. Her mother's illness often disturbed her sleep, even though the pills were supposed to help. That meant Joan couldn't always sleep either. She needed a haircut. She needed a long, hot bath instead of a rushed shower. On Saturdays and Sundays she felt like climbing the walls, maybe because there was no hope of someone relieving her, no hope of going out. But for several Wednesdays, she had her class. And afterward, she had Darren, Darren's kisses, his voice, his calm.

He'd asked her once or twice if she might want to come to his condo. He'd cook for her. He offered to come visit her on weekends. He was probably very good with sick people, and her mother would be charmed. But Joan kept him at arm's length. She wasn't ready, and he hadn't pushed. He hadn't tried to make her feel guilty, hadn't tried to make her take more time than she felt comfortable taking.

It must have been frustrating making out with her in the car in the parking lot of the restaurant, stealing kisses over dinner, enduring her bolder and bolder caresses in the driveway of her mother's house. It was frustrating for her. She was impatient with herself, but that wasn't exactly anything new, was it?

She didn't want to see his condo. It would probably be perfect, neat and organized. He likely never had to look for his keys. Anything he cooked would probably be delicious and nutritionally balanced. She didn't want to have sex with him because she was sure it would be good, and then she'd want sex with him all week and would have no way of relieving herself of her want.

When she got to class, right on time, luckily, she noticed Yvette was missing. "She's got the flu," Yvette's friend Nancy said. "She's in the hospital. She's not doing too well."

The remaining students struggled through the exercises... But the class had gotten into the rhythm of having Ms. Yvette there. Too bad Joan noticed how well they had all worked together only after the chemistry was gone.

But the evening got worse.

At the end of class, the person waiting for her wasn't Darren. It was Apoorva, the community center director. "Can we talk?"

"I know what this is about."

Why was Joan shaken over the end of a volunteer position? Especially since she'd known—she'd told Darren, she'd told herself over and over—the class would be canceled.

Apoorva shook her head but didn't deny it. "I'm afraid for our evening classes we just need something that brings more bodies in."

"Like meditation."

"Yes. But I was thinking, if you wanted, we could schedule you for daytime summer classes. You'd probably have some teens interested—we'd like to increase our numbers in that group."

"I can't teach day classes."

"Think about it," Apoorva said.

She put her hand on Joanie's arm and left.

Joan didn't know how long she stood in the middle of the classroom with the lights still bright on her, the chairs unstacked.

"I'm sorry I'm late," Darren said rushing in. "I—"

He stopped. "Joan, are you all right?"

She breathed in and out. She could do that, take deep breaths, feel them flow to her fingertips. "It's been a bad evening. Ms. Yvette's in the hospital. Do you think you could take me to visit her there?"

It turned out they couldn't. Even with Darren flashing his ID, they wanted to keep visitors to a minimum, which was understandable in these times. The more Darren talked and talked with the nurses, the more Joan felt her frustration mounting.

Finally, she put her hand on his arm. "It's okay," she said. "Everyone's doing their best."

Besides, from the sounds of it, Yvette would probably be out by next week, but she likely wouldn't make the very last class.

Joan's last class.

Breathe, Joan.

Darren said, "The good news is she's recovering, but it's after visiting hours and we're not her relatives. I could push it more—"

He would try too. He'd do this for her.

"I'd like you to take me home," she said, seizing her last bit of control of the situation.

"Of course. Aren't you hungry, though? We could grab something on the way. Maybe get a treat for your aunt and mother?"

"I mean to your home."

He stopped abruptly.

"Are you sure?"

His voice was low but full and urgent. She felt a surge of something like power for the first time all evening. She could have this one good thing in her life that she wanted *right now*. Just once. She could seize this moment, this single night, before she had to be realistic, before she had to face herself and her failings, before life closed up around her.

Couldn't she?

"I need this. I need you."

Darren took her elbows and towed her slowly to him. He looked into her eyes. Whatever he saw there satisfied him. With one hand on her back, he led her gently out of the hospital and to his car.

Snow was falling again, and Darren seemed to drive especially carefully as if to give her time, as if to give himself time. She took out her phone and texted her aunt. **Would you be able to stay over tonight while I'm out?**

The text came back right away. **Of course! She's having a good evening. Don't worry.**

She looked at the text until her screen faded to darkness.

When she glanced up, she found Darren observing her.

She didn't know how he did it, how he managed to make his gaze both concerned and intense and... loving. How did that come across in his face? Was it the way he held his lips, his eyes that could convey all of that to her in semidarkness? If she were still acting she'd learn from him, scrutinize every shadow across his forehead, the light across his severe cheekbones, observe the way his mouth was both soft and strong. But after next week she wouldn't be teaching or acting anymore, would she? There was no point in studying—she should simply *feel*.

She moved swiftly to kiss him, to reach her hand inside his coat, over the crisp, white shirt to where his heart lay beating fast and solid. And she kissed him until a van behind them honked.

While he drove on, she threw her whole body into letting him know this was what she needed. By the time they pulled up to his condo, he took his hands off of her deliberately and pushed his hair back until it stood up. "I don't want you to get cold out here," he said. "But I'm going to need a few minutes before I can get out of the car."

"Give me the keys," she said. "I'll be waiting."

She felt reckless. She could be wild for the first time in a long time. She had nothing to lose. Throwing open the door to his house, she breathed in and out in the silence, feeling her lungs expand powerfully. She should be feeling terrible. Her student was in the hospital, the term was near the end, and her delusions of being some sort of artist were too.

But tonight, it didn't matter. She took off her shoes and jacket and started prowling through his house, still in the dark, touching everything, trying to memorize through feel, trailing her fingers along the wall, fanning herself with the mail stacked nearly on a table. She stepped into the living room area and stood in the middle, curling her toes into the soft rug.

She hadn't expected him to have a rug so impractical, something that probably had to be cleaned often. Then she leaned over a table and switched on a single lamp, and the warmth of its glow made the room beautiful.

The door opened and she glanced over to Darren, who was staring at her. He was taking off his shoes. His coat was open, then off, his shirt unbuttoned the way she'd left him.

She pulled off her sweater.

In a breath, he was on her, his hands on her back, on her waist, over her breast, his body warm and strong, lifting her, then pushing her down into the warm embrace of his couch.

She ran her fingertips lightly over his brows, over the sharp lines of his cheekbones, his features clear and stark and angled, written boldly and beautifully. No wonder his face was so legible to her. Then he turned and kissed her palm, wet and lush, and she felt an answering warmth flood her.

He'd pulled her clothing off, piece by piece, her bra the last piece to go. But she remained warm and languorous, writhing under his fingers and mouth. He slid down farther, farther until he was between her legs.

He knelt, his face intent. Then he looked into her eyes once, swiftly, and she caught her breath. No one had ever looked at her this way before, nakedly desirous, rising between her knees even as he remained fully clothed, his shirt and collar still pristine and white.

He bent and eased his thumb along the inside of her trembling leg, pressing hard along the muscle there. He brushed his cheeks along that place, a soft stroke before he turned and closed his teeth gently on the spot inside her thigh, and she gasped again. Desire gushed out now, and he slicked his fingers through her.

In a moment, he had his mouth on her and she cried out, twisting as he teased her with the softness, the wetness of his touch. She reached down to him, to his hair, to brush the stiff collar of his shirt. She wanted to grab it, twist her fingers in it, to pull him up and tell him something important about what this night was to her, but he was doing something with his hand and his tongue, and she couldn't think except to try and hold onto the moment before it burst. Then she gasped again as he pulled her knees over his shoulders, sliding her down further, and he applied himself to her, bearing down on that spot between her legs until she fell back, unable to hold her head up any longer, unable to do anything except cry out raggedly as the orgasm took over.

They were both panting, his cheek heavy on one of her thighs.

She was staring at the ceiling. Maybe, if she asked nicely, he'd let her stay here like this forever, naked, legs open, dazed and warm.

In a moment, he'd risen and was standing over her, staring down.

"Let's go upstairs," he said decisively.

She nodded or at least wobbled her head. It was too much effort to move.

A smile touched his lips, so rare and beautiful she didn't want him to look away. But he crouched again, and scooped her up against him and started walking slowly toward what she hoped was his bedroom.

She pulled herself back a little too study him. His face was once again set in determined lines, and she shivered a little even as she smiled.

"Are you cold?" he asked.

She shook her head still smiling, and of course, he had to kiss her there, pressing her back against the frigid wall of the stair landing, and between his kisses she squealed, "Just get me to your room."

"I'm trying, but you keep looking at me like that."

He lipped her neck and carried her the rest of the way, before letting her spill gently onto the bed. She hadn't expected the mattress to be so soft. She started to laugh again.

He paused while unbuttoning his cuffs. "What is it?"

She flung her arms wide, and of course, his eyes followed the movement of her breasts. "This. This is so luxurious."

"Did you expect me to sleep on a wooden board?"

"No, but you're a sensualist at heart."

The half-smile lit his face again, and she watched as he unbuttoned. Suddenly, she couldn't stop staring at him, at the firm chest beginning to appear in glimpses as the shirt came undone. Her eyes traced the curves of muscles hugging his lean torso, and when she glanced back up their gazes clashed again.

"When you look at me like that," he said, his voice quiet and fierce, "I want to fall on you and ravage you. But that's not what I do, is it?"

She scrambled up and licked her lips. Her voice came out hoarse. "You could give it a try."

His smile widened, but still, he continued methodically.

The shirt came off. He turned to drape it on the chair behind him, and she watched the shadows play across the muscles of his back before he turned to face her again. He unbuckled his belt and drew it smoothly through the loops, then let it slip through his fingers to the floor.

Her breath was loud in the quiet room. Her hands slid down her sides and she started rubbing herself as he slowly eased the zipper over the ridge in his pants. It was his turn to laugh, a short, sharp sound as he finally managed to free himself from his trousers, then pull his boxer briefs down.

"I want to touch you," she whispered.

"Be careful," he said.

She got on her knees. Her fingers were still slick from her excitement, and when her fingers closed around him, a strangled sound came out of his throat, even though his face was still harsh with concentration. She slid up and down, then bent to lick him, and he said, "Joan,"— just like that, one word and then they fell on each other. He was scrambling for a condom as she whimpered, and waited until he pushed his way inside her.

And she was full of him, so full, his skin felt hot against hers, rippling with energy she wanted to grasp. She scrabbled her fingers over his back, trying to hold on as he pumped into her. How could she have thought he could be contained in all the straight lines of his face and body? He was chaos and desire, and he was surging into her, his hands and tongue and lips touching every part of her, his biceps and back and thighs tight and neck straining as he reached himself down, deep into her once again. And his voice, she was surrounded by his sounds, his groans, the suck of his mouth, the breath of him.

She kissed him frantically, even as their bodies, sweating and straining, slammed against each other. He pulled his lips away with a gasp, and she cried out. She was close, so close, and the closer she felt, the farther away it seemed. He pushed her down, pulling her arms overhead, and her back arched as she screamed again.

Then he was bearing down into her, a final rush of warmth flooding their bodies. In the darkness of the night, they were quiet again except for their harsh, shuddering breaths.

* * *

DARREN HAD his blood pressure monitor strapped to his arm when Joan awoke. She blinked at him confused, so he kissed her carefully. "Good morning."

She grunted and closed her eyes again, but she didn't look displeased to see him. Not a morning person, he guessed and added it to the file of facts he did know about her. He knew the bigger things, at least he thought he did. But the smaller habits he hadn't learned seemed more pleasurably daunting this morning. For instance, he had no idea what Joan liked for breakfast. It was something he should have asked her.

But he was determined not to be anxious about it even if he only had—he thought about the contents of his fridge—a loaf of sodium-free bread, natural peanut butter, bananas (they'd already eaten some peanut butter and banana sandwiches late last night), some greens, and protein powder for smoothies.

He'd find out what kinds of things she liked. He'd order the groceries she liked. Cheeseburgers. He could find a way of getting Lucy's delivered. Of course, takeout fries were never as good, but they weren't the main attraction anyway. He and Joan would have to figure out their respective schedules. Already his head hummed pleasurably at the idea of incorporating her into his life. They wouldn't have that much time together because his practice was busy and she was taking care of her mother, but maybe once a week she could spend the night after her class.

His armband beeped.

"What are you doing?" she mumbled.

"Checking my blood pressure."

"How is it?"

"It's fine."

He felt good. He felt great. If they had time, maybe they could repeat some of the highlights of last night before he went to the office.

"Is the meditation class still working for you?"

"Actually, I stopped going."

She laughed softly without opening her eyes and moved, her body making the sheet rustle softly. He loved the intimacy of the sound. "You? Dropped a class? This is unexpected. I'm glad I'm not the only one who lost students, though."

He groaned. "The class was stressing me out. All those people and all that sweat. So I looked inward and I... decided to quit."

Eyes still closed, she smiled. "You've grown as a person."

"I think I have. I mean, if the whole idea behind it was to make me less anxious and prolong my life, well, I'd rather actually enjoy my life."

"My God, what is happening to you?"

"You're happening to me," he said seriously. "And it's not like I'm pooh-poohing the idea of meditation either. I've got apps, and I think I'll take another course. Just maybe in a different venue. Something more formal. But I can still pick you up on Wednesdays after your class."

Her body suddenly went still.

"I don't—I don't know if I can do that."

"Well, we don't have to figure it all out now."

"You're very confident. About the future."

Her eyes were open now, and she was staring at the ceiling.

"I don't mean to be presumptuous. I really hope this means we can keep seeing each other? I like you. A lot."

He was not good at talking about his feelings. He was probably messing something up.

"Did you ever think," she said, still not looking at him, "you were with me because I'm safe?"

"Safe? What does that mean? You're the most exciting person I know."

"I'm safe because this has to be temporary. It would never work out between us. You knew that. You knew that, didn't you?"

"Why? I didn't know that. We said Wednesdays only, but didn't last night change things? Was it not...? Do you regret this?"

His heart flipped slowly and sickeningly.

She let out a breath, then turned out and put her face in the pillow. Her voice was muffled. "It was everything. I loved it."

"Okay."

Damn, he hated the uncertainty in his voice. It made him cut off his own words.

"But I don't have enough reason to be able to do it again. I'm already spending too little time at home as it is. I'm constantly falling behind."

"You spend all your time at home. And you're doing great."

She was alive and marvelous, and he didn't know how to tell her—no, to convince her.

"You don't know. You don't know anything."

"Joanie, please look at me," he begged.

She turned over slowly. She looked as miserable as he felt.

"Can I fix this? If you'd let me—"

She sat up. "What? Take over? Organize everything? Pay with your money? Have us all wearing crisp white shirts by the end of day two?"

They both took in a sharp breath of air.

"That was unfair," she muttered. "I'm sorry."

She got up and started searching for something to wear. And being the poor pathetic man he was, his heart broke a little more at the sight of her shivering and determined and angry at him.

"Everything is downstairs," she muttered, stalking out.

He got up too and pulled some clothing out of his closet, pausing before grabbing a *blue* button-down today.

That'd show her.

He found her in the living room where she was putting her bra back on. His body gave a futile throb of longing.

But she wasn't looking at him. Next were her leggings, which she pulled on in short, jerky motions. "Why do you think this works? Why do you like me? Why do you want to spend time with me?"

He considered this carefully. What was she asking for when she looked at him this way, obviously in pain?

"I like you because you're funny, and I love how bright your eyes are and how they stare at me and challenge me. I like the short skirts you wear, even when it's bitter cold out. The first day, I saw it and wondered how you were going to sit on the floor and meditate with us, and I like the fact you're itching to tell me I'm a pervert for thinking about it."

She gave a watery laugh.

"I like the fact you're playful, and you actually believe I can play back—you expect that from me. I don't think people see this in me. I like that you wanted to go see Yvette last night, that you care about your students."

She was smiling a little bit, and he let out a quiet breath of relief. He buttoned his top button and said, "I like kissing you, I like how you kiss me back, how warm you are, how your fingers feel on my skin. Everything about you is thrilling and exciting and sexy. But it comes down to one thing: You make me happy."

He paused.

So did she.

She blinked. "I make you happy?"

"And... I make you happy, too?"

She finished putting on her clothing. "What happens when I'm not fun and sexy anymore? Because I have to tell you, I don't feel fun most of the time. Every day, every night, I'm taking care of my mom. When I'm not watching her, I'm cleaning up after her. When I'm not cleaning, I'm cooking for her. She wanders. She has insomnia and drugs I have to keep track of for that insomnia. This was the best night's sleep I've had in years, even though we didn't sleep much at all—"

She blushed a little at that. She went on hurriedly. "Sometimes my mom eats her lunch, and she forgets and tells me to make her something to eat, and when I don't she gets mad. Or she cries. Or once when I was doing laundry downstairs, she ate and ate until she was sick.

"What I'm saying is I can't be your fun. I can't be your happiness, because I can't be fun or happy. I should have tried to do this. I should never have taught the class. It's over. I keep thinking like I'm an artist who's just put her dream on hold, just for now. But this isn't a pause. It's over. I need to let it go."

"Joan. You're a wonderful teacher and actor. You don't have to let anything go."

"You don't understand. How would you know anything? You quit my class after one day. And I heard last night, I won't be renewed because of low enrollment. I couldn't keep it up. This was my last chance. I'm too tired too and heartbroken to try again."

"You can find another class."

"I'm a volunteer! They don't even want someone who's working for free!"

"There are other volunteer positions. Joan, I've been in a classroom with you. You're wonderful. I don't understand how you can argue that people need art and beauty so passionately, but you don't believe you deserve it for yourself. That's the problem, isn't it? You don't think you're allowed."

She started to get her shoes and coat. After a frozen moment, Darren followed.

"Darren, I like you. I could even love you. Despite all the shitty things I said to you this morning, I think you're fun and kind and honest and sexy. But I... I don't know if I'm the person you think you know. I hardly love myself right now. I made a decision last night that I'm not going to try to be an artist anymore. It's not sustainable. So I don't know if we should be together even if... I want to."

He wanted to gather her into his arms. She wasn't crying. She was just so blank. But when he reached out, she flinched.

"Joan, we can talk about this. This is something we can do together. You can teach other classes, or not. I'll still like you if you do other things."

"How can you know that? We've only known each other for a handful of hours spread over a handful of weeks. I don't have time to figure this out. I have to get home to my mother."

"I'd like us to still talk about this."

"I can't. Not right now."

She avoided his eyes.

"At least let me drive you home."

"It's not far. I know where we are."

"It's cold though. Or I can walk you."

"No."

"Joan."

"Don't. Don't follow me. Don't walk me. I need this time. Give me this."

He didn't want to, but the way she had to plead made something hard and painful lodge in his throat.

She opened the door and stepped carefully out into the dark, cold morning.

"What about you, Joan? Don't you deserve something for yourself? I'm not saying it has to be me. I'm not fun, or anything. But something else. You need something."

He called out after her departing figure. But she didn't turn, and he wasn't sure she'd heard him.

CHAPTER 5

Week 8 – A Wednesday in March

JOAN'S MOTHER was crying again. They'd both been doing a lot of that all week.

Today the thing setting her mother off was seeing Joan in a dress.

"It's my last day of class, Ma. I'm going to be late."

"My baby's grown up. She's leaving the house."

Joan held back a sigh. "I'm coming back. I'm always going to come back."

"You look so beautiful."

"Thanks, Ma."

She kissed her mother on the cheek, which made Ma cry more. "Why are you so nice to me?"

"I'm not as good as you think."

"Leave her. She'll be fine," Aunt Sylvia said, pushing Joan toward the door.

"I know, I know, I'm going."

She grabbed the brownies she'd baked for her students and a pile of mail to read during the break. Maybe it would take her mind off the fact she wouldn't see Darren after class. He'd texted her a couple of times, and she'd listened to his voicemails too. But for some reason, she felt too heavy, too sad to respond. Even now, she felt the weight right on her lungs, over her heart.

Focus. Breathe.

The brisk walk to the rec center helped. And so did the faces of her students, minus Ms. Yvette. Somehow, she got through the first part with a headache of held-back tears building behind her eyes. And when her students went out to get water and broke off into small groups to talk about the next scenes they'd be working on, she spent one minute thinking about how she was really, really going start sobbing, until she remembered she had a pile of mail.

Most of it was straightforward: bills, ads, an energy company urging her to switch utilities, a flyer from a local theater group. The last letter was from the local hospital. She put off opening it while tearing the plastic out of the windowed envelopes, before putting the rest in the recycling bin.

It was all mixed up—her fatigue, the feelings about giving up acting, Darren. She couldn't separate the strands if she tried. When she was younger, when she wasn't caring for her mother, she could put in a full day at the clinic and then go and perform plays, or hustle for grants, or produce shows that only her fellow actors and their loved ones came to. She didn't feel hopeless. But now, what was she? She took care of her mother. Her friends and colleagues were back in Oregon. She didn't even have a class to teach anymore. What could she possibly bring to any relationship that wasn't loneliness and loss? He was—he was so much. And she felt like so little at this moment.

Stop.

Breathe.

With shaking fingers, she forced herself to open the last envelope. She scanned it. Then tried to slow her thoughts and go through it again.

"Joan? Are you all right?"

It was Nancy, Yvette's friend.

"I'm confused. I don't know if I'm reading this right."

"I don't mean to pry—well, I do, actually."

"It's a recruitment letter for a place in a research study about caregivers of seniors with dementia?"

Her voice rose uncertainly, even though she'd mostly trained herself not to do that. She tried again. "It offers care for my mother twice a week for a few hours, and counseling for me. I'd have to keep a journal, which I already do. Is this real?"

She put the paper down. "I didn't apply for this. There must be some mistake."

"Oh, the research hospitals around here always got stuff like this going on. I'm in a sleep study."

She peered over Joanie's shoulder.

"Maybe your doctor recommended you."

"They're not affiliated with this hospital. The only one who I know is..."

Darren.

But that couldn't be.

Her phone beeped. The break was over. She wiped her eyes and squared her shoulders. There wasn't much left time left and she had to try and enjoy this last class. "Let's have group one come up," she said, injecting a note of briskness that she didn't feel into her voice.

At least she'd have those skills forever.

They went through the exercises, everyone laughed and shared, and gave pointers and interrupted. They ate brownies, and her students asked Joan if she'd be teaching again next semester. And she shook her head. Although, in the back of her mind, she realized if she did this study, she might be able to teach the daytime summer classes.

The big surprise, though, was at the end, when Ms. Yvette wheeled into the classroom, with a big, handsome grandson to watch over her, and everyone clustered around to hug her and tell her she shouldn't be out and about.

"I'm fine! I'm just in here for a minute. And I heard there were brownies."

"Ms. Yvette, please take some. And your grandson, you should have some too."

"Joan, I just wanted to stop by and tell you I absolutely loved improv. It was scary sometimes, but I've never laughed so much in my life. I'll take any class you teach. I wrote to the director to tell her."

"Same here!" Nancy said.

"I'm going to do that when I go home," another student chimed in.

The class broke up in a flurry of good wishes and promises to keep in touch—it was all Joan had ever wanted from teaching. Once again, Joan found herself walking Yvette out to wait while her grandson brought the car around.

"It was wonderful of you to come while you're recovering."

"I don't know if you realize how important your class has been these two months."

"Oh, it was... fun. That's all."

"It made me feel more confident. It made me think of how I interact with other people. I still laugh about the silly things we said. That's more than enough. And now, I hope you go out and celebrate with that doctor of yours."

"Oh, we... I broke up with him last week."

"Why? He seemed to adore you, and he treats people well. Plus, a handsome doctor like that."

"Without getting into it, I don't have time. And I don't feel like myself lately. I don't think I have anything to offer anyone."

Ms. Yvette didn't say anything. She only cocked her head.

"What?" Joan asked.

"What, what? You think because I'm an old lady, and I almost died last week I'm going to give you some words of wisdom about what you should do?"

Well. Yes, Joan had sort of hoped for that.

"Joan, I got nothing original for you. If he treats you bad, then leave. But other than that, I'm the one who needs a little push here more than you. Could you—?"

She gestured at her chair.

"Oh. Of course."

Joan wheeled Yvette down the ramp and watched Ms. Yvette's grandson as he lifted his grandmother tenderly into the SUV and folded the chair away. She waved at Yvette until she couldn't see her anymore.

It wasn't snowing today. It felt almost mild. Spring was here—reluctantly, but still, it was in the air.

She should go home.

Instead, she started walking, then running.

She didn't stop running until she got to Darren's door.

He was leaving when she arrived on the sidewalk in front of his house. She was panting and gasping. She hadn't run like that in years. And now she was breathless, and he was... immaculate.

He wasn't wearing a coat. Instead, he had on a gray three-piece suit that, instead of pulling him together, seemed held together by him—his beauty, his lean strength, his elegance, his upright and perfect posture.

But his shirt, Joan noticed through her sweaty haze, was unbuttoned, and a tie swung loosely around his neck.

And while his face hardly moved, he'd seen her, and he was coming across his lawn, ignoring the mud and snow that was surely clinging to his perfect shoes, to come to her. To come to a stop, in front of her.

He put his hand up as if to touch her, and then he pulled away quickly, as if he'd learned not to be burned by the likes of her. Her already overtaxed heart gave a guilty throb. She'd done that.

His face, though, seeing his face etched with concern would break her. "Joan? Are you all right?"

"I'm fine. I'm okay. I just had to see you."

"Wasn't today your last class?"

He remembered.

"It's done. It was beautiful. Yvette came for the last couple of minutes."

She dug through her purse for the letter. "I got this."

And she burst into tears.

* * *

HIS BODY HAD MISSED HER. That was the first thing he noticed when she flung herself at him. The second was that she was softer, more difficult to hold than he remembered, even though his memory was only a week old. Her tears were warm, and they were making his shirt wet. Soon, if she kept crying, they'd track in thin streaks down to his cracked, parched heart.

He wanted to say something, but his throat was dry too. So he held her until her sobs subsided, and then they were simply quiet, standing on the sidewalk in front of his house.

"I'm sorry," Joan said.

"No, don't be sorry. I don't even know what you have to be sorry for. *I* should apologize. I was the one who pushed you too far, too fast last week. I made all these assumptions. I know you feel overwhelmed."

"I am," she admitted, her face still hidden in his shirt.

They kept standing there, unmoving. Darren didn't know how long. He didn't care. He didn't want to let her go. But after a while, she spoke again. "You, on the other hand, seem calm—"

"I'm told this is my thing."

She laughed. "Let me finish. You seem calm, but your heart is beating so fast."

She looked up finally. Her eyes were red-rimmed, and her hair tousled. The muscle in his chest gave another painful thump.

"Thank you. For thinking of me."

She held the letter up and let him skim it. "This was you, wasn't it?"

"All I did was suggest you as a potential candidate. I don't have anything to do with the study, really." He hesitated. "The thing about this one, though, is that it includes a counseling component."

"I liked that part best of all."

"I'm glad."

"Are you saying this as a doctor?"

"I'm saying this as someone who cares for you."

Her arms tightened around him.

"I don't have anything to give you back."

"You don't have to give me anything. You and your mom both meet the criteria. I didn't think you'd figure out it was me. It's not an obligation. I just wanted you to—to have this. You can take it, or leave it if you think the requirements are too intrusive. But if you do end up in it, I hope you take the time they offer you and do something fun sometimes. I hope you take care of yourself. Because that's important."

"What if I said I want to teach at the rec center this summer? I might be able to do a class for teens."

"I think you should. And maybe sometimes, we could go out to lunch afterward."

"I'd like that, but a long lunch in the middle of the day? What will your patients think?"

"I don't know about my patients, but my office manager will probably be happy I won't be working straight through."

A neighbor who Darren knew slightly walked by with her dog. She stared at the two of them, hugging on the sidewalk. He waved at her over Joan's shoulder.

The woman put her head down and hurried off.

Joan rested her cheek on the damp spot of his shirt. "Darren?" she asked hesitantly. "You're all dressed up. Do you have somewhere you need to be?"

"I'm supposed to be at my best friend's wedding banquet soon."

She made a choking sound and tried to escape, but his arms tightened around her.

"Darren, I'm making you late. You must hate that."

"I don't. Not at all," he said truthfully.

He didn't feel a single twinge. He'd rather this moment didn't end.

"But I've messed up your shirt and I—" she lifted her head briefly to peek over his shoulder. "I think I knocked your tie into the mud."

"I don't care."

She gazed up at him again, soberly. He'd never been able to lie to her. He wasn't lying now.

And as he looked at her, he realized that all along, he could tell when she'd been playing too. "I'll be honest," she said. "I don't know if I really can be an actor anymore. It still hurts to think about it.

Although maybe I can be a teacher. All of this, not just the last sad week of being without you—but over the last year of caring for my mom, I've slowly realized I need to change who I think I am. I'm not the person you met two months ago."

"Well, I'm not the person you met two months ago either."

She blinked. "That's true."

They leaned together again. Joan whispered, "This whole time, I've been afraid of what might happen if I let go of who I think I am."

"That's my line."

She started giggling, and the feeling of her laughter as he held her was the best feeling in the world. "How do you live like this?"

"The answer is that I couldn't. But when I walked into your classroom, I was ready. You believed I could be playful, and I sort of became someone who is sometimes. I'm still having trouble with the concept of letting go of some of the things I've held so tightly for so long, but that playing goes a long way. We can try these new roles together. I can't think of who else I'd rather figure all of this out with than you."

"Same," she whispered.

She reached up and kissed him, and it was soft and sweet.

He rested his cheek in her hair.

She said after a while, "I want to stay here, but I'm going to be the responsible one again and ask if you should get to the banquet."

"Come with me."

This time, she pulled away. "Darren. I can't. It's a *wedding*."

He had to chuckle at that. "A small casual one. It's on a Wednesday night for a start. They wanted me to bring a date. And you're wearing a dress."

She started to laugh even as she shook her head. Her eyes were smiling, though, and he knew she was thinking about it.

"Please come. Li-Wei and Mona will be delighted. We'll eat some delicious food, and Li-Wei will try to explain the symbolism of the dragon and the phoenix, and I'll tell him he's full of it, and we'll spend the rest of the evening arguing until Li-Wei's new wife rolls her eyes."

"You make it sound great, but do you really think it'll be all right?"

"I think it will. It's a couple of hours for one night. And then some other evening, maybe we'll go out, or I'll come over and meet your mom. And another time we can do something else. I'm going to try not to ask you for everything at once. I'm going to ask you one question at a time. And maybe you'll give me one yes, and... maybe another later, and maybe another after that. That's all. We only have to think of the yes in front of us. So, how about it? Come with me? One yes now?"

Her eyes were bright with tears and something that glimmered like hope.

"Okay."

ACKNOWLEDGMENTS

Readers, thank you so much for all your support over the years. It was such a delight to come back to the Practice Perfect universe and learn more about Joan, who always seemed (to me) a little left out of the circle of friendship that forms that series.

Many thanks to Olivia Dade who asked me to be a part of this amazing collection of writers. She is an inspiration, a cheerleader, a damn good writer, and an exceptional friend.

Thanks also to the wise and lovely Emma Barry, who cast a careful and compassionate eye over this manuscript, and to Adriana Herrera and Cat Sebastian whose energy and humor are unmatched. I am lucky to know them.

Thanks so much to Isabel Ngo and Tessera Editorial for checking over this story so carefully.

To my husband, the most solid and unflappable person I know, thank you for being you.

BIOGRAPHY

Ruby Lang is the pen name of nonfiction writer Mindy Hung. Her essays and articles have appeared in *The New York Times, The Toast,* and *Salon,* among others. She enjoys running (slowly), reading (quickly), and eating ice cream (at any speed). She lives in New York with a small child and a medium-sized husband. Find Ruby at RubyLangWrites.com and on Twitter, Instagram, or Facebook.

facebook.com/RubyLangWrites
twitter.com/RubeLang
instagram.com/ruby.lang

ALSO BY RUBY LANG

Thank you so much for reading "Yes, And…" It was a delight to return to the universe of the Practice Perfect series, and if you enjoyed this story, you might also like *Acute Reactions, Hard Knocks,* and *Clean Breaks*. (Joan is a minor character in all three.)

TOMMY CABOT WAS HERE

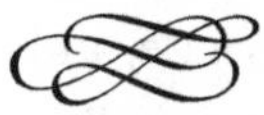

CAT SEBASTIAN

This story is for the people of fanfic Twitter, Sirius Black, my mom, and James Buchanan Barnes.

Massachusetts, 1959: Some people might accuse mathematician Everett Sloane of being stuffy, but really he just prefers things a certain way: predictable, quiet, and far away from Tommy Cabot--his former best friend, chaos incarnate, and the man who broke his heart. The youngest son of a prominent political family, Tommy threw away his future by coming out to his powerful brothers. When he runs into Everett, who fifteen years ago walked away from Tommy without an explanation or a backward glance, his old friend's chilliness is just another reminder of how bad a mess Tommy has made of his life. When Everett realizes that his polite formality is hurting Tommy, he needs to decide whether he can unbend enough to let Tommy get close but without letting himself get hurt the way he was all those years ago.

* * *

Content warnings: on-page sex; references to homophobia and sex between underage characters

CHAPTER 1

MASSACHUSETTS, 1959

Surely by now, after a full month at Greenfield, Everett ought to have gotten over the dizzying sense of unreality he experienced whenever he remembered that he wasn't one of the uniform-clad students. Here it was, already October, the leaves red and orange with the passing of time, not a trace of summer left in the air, and he still couldn't shake the idea that the past twenty years amounted to nothing more than a daydream, and that the next time he walked into his classroom he would need to sit at one of the desks rather than stand before the chalkboard.

The great lawn was filled with parents who had come for the annual exercise in staged reassurance known as Visiting Sunday, during which they could see for themselves that their sons hadn't wasted away or returned to a state of nature after a month out of their care. Everett half expected to look up and see his own parents in their shabby old-fashioned clothes, instead of these strangers—some of whom, astonishingly, were younger than himself. The children had been combed and scrubbed and stuffed into their Sunday clothes by housemistresses, faculty wives, and in the case of one exceptionally bedraggled young man, Everett himself. That too—the taming of the cowlick, the unpicking of shoelaces, the last-minute sewing on of mismatched buttons—had sent Everett's mind careening wildly backward to a time when he had performed the same tasks for his classmates.

He shook hands with a few of his students' parents, made the appropriate remarks, and had a cigarette halfway to his lips when he saw—well, he was ashamed to admit, even to himself, that his first thought was that he was seeing a ghost. But ghosts surely did not take surreptitious bites of chocolate bars, nor could they possibly have leaves clinging to the backs of their trousers from illicit leaps into the gardeners' neatly raked leaf piles. But if not a ghost, then who was this child with his black hair and blue eyes, that unmistakable Cabot nose, and that even more unmistakable Cabot air of pedigreed good humor?

Well, Greenfield had to be crawling with Cabots, surely. It stood to reason that the Cabot family would as a matter of course send its sons to the school that had educated its fathers and grandfathers and which boasted not only the Cabot Library but also the Cabot Gymnasium and Cabot Tennis Courts. This child, who had just shoved the entire chocolate bar into his mouth and stuck the wrapper up his sleeve before turning to the headmaster with the insouciance of a born sinner, could be any one of a number of Cabot progeny.

As Everett watched, a man approached the child, casually passed him a handkerchief, and stuck out his hand to greet the approaching headmaster. With a shaky hand, Everett managed to light his cigarette. He inhaled and did the math: Tommy's son was born in '47 and would now be twelve, so just the right age for first form. Everett let his gaze slide up the man who stood beside the child, up the legs of a suit that probably cost more than Everett's car, up the lean body he had spent fifteen years trying not to think about, and finally to the face of the man who had been his ruin.

He puffed out a surprised gust of smoke. If not for the child and the math, he might not have recognized Tommy. The man was in desperate need of a haircut, and whatever efforts he had made with a razor must have happened in a dark room with a dull blade. Around his eyes were lines that hadn't been visible in the society photographs

Everett's mother still insisted on clipping out and sending to him. There was something in the way he held himself, a rigidity and tension, that was new and unsettling, and would have been disconcerting to see on any Cabot, but most of all Tommy.

Before Everett could quite make sense of the fact that Tommy Cabot was suddenly a few feet away, Tommy was turning toward him. Everett froze. He didn't do terribly well when things didn't go according to plan, and he certainly hadn't planned on suddenly coming face to face with Tommy. If he had been prepared, he would have come up with something to say, something safe and polite. But now he was faced with the decision of whether to seek cover in a nearby cluster of faculty or walk toward Tommy and the headmaster and probably make a mess of things. He stepped forward. No matter what had happened, he wasn't hiding from Tommy. He owed them both more than that.

"Mr. Clayton," Everett said to the headmaster, and then turned to Tommy, his hand outstretched in the best approximation of a polite greeting that he could manage.

Tommy's face split into a smile that made Everett's stomach drop. "Hell and—language, damn it, sorry about that Daniel," he said, ruffling the child's hair, "damnation, is that you, Ev? Of course it is, come here." And then his arms were around Everett, who was left holding the cigarette in one hand, and with the other hand patting stupidly at Tommy's back. He smelled the same, damn him, like the sort of aftershave you could only buy at a department store. And if he was broader and had lost all the angularity of youth, his body still felt recognizable, mapping onto Everett's body in the same way they always had. Everett extricated himself as soon Tommy loosened his hold.

"Of course," Mr. Clayton said. "You were in the same graduating class."

"Class of 1941. We were roommates," Tommy supplied.

"In that case, I'll leave you to catching up," the headmaster said, and proceeded across the lawn to shake hands with more parents.

Everett wanted to call him back. Or follow him. Or possibly sink into the earth.

"What are you doing here?" Tommy asked. He was still smiling, as if this was excellent, such a happy coincidence, what a delightful reunion. "Last I heard you were in England."

"I only came back a few months ago." Everett's voice sounded rusty and strange, as if he hadn't used it in the years since last seeing Tommy. He was afraid that if he spoke, all that would come out would be a confession, fifteen years' worth of *I miss you*. Instead he took a drag from his cigarette and tried to school his expression into professional nonchalance.

"This is Daniel's first year," Tommy said, gesturing at the spot where his son had stood a minute earlier. "What year is your son in?"

Everett gritted his teeth at the reminder that of course Tommy would assume that Everett had made the same choices Tommy had, that after all these years Tommy still didn't realize that not everybody sailed through life without consequence. "I don't—I'm not," he stammered. "I'm teaching here."

"You aren't one of Daniel's teachers, are you?"

"I only teach sixth and seventh years," Everett said. "I haven't seen Patricia." That was the ticket, remind himself—remind *both* of them—that Tommy was married. He pointedly gazed around the lawn for a bright blond head.

"Oh," Tommy said after a moment. "She isn't here. She's in California."

Everett frowned. California was about as far as a person could get from a husband whose life was divided between Boston and Washington. "Well," he said tightly. "Give her my best." He had liked Patricia. Hell and damn, he had been there on their wedding day. He had danced with her while she kept up a steady stream of chatter that even at the age of twenty-three Everett understood to be the sort of kindness meant to save him from having to make conversation. Now he wondered if she had known, if she had suspected the special kind of hell it was for him to be Tommy's best man.

Tommy pressed his lips together. "I'll be sure to do that," he said.

He had gray at his temples. His shirt was badly ironed and his tie had only a perfunctory knot. That last detail was horribly familiar—God only knew how many times Everett had tugged Tommy behind the chapel or into a stairwell and insisted on making sense of his tie. Now he was old enough to understand that Cabots could get away with sloppiness. He also understood that letting Everett fuss over him had been part of Tommy's game. He had let Everett have those proprietary touches, had let Everett believe that whatever existed between them actually mattered. Tommy was a Cabot, born with a silver spoon and the unchallenged conviction that he could have whatever he wanted; back then, he had wanted Everett, and hadn't ever stopped to consider what harm he might be doing.

"I see a parent I ought to speak to," Everett lied, and left Tommy standing alone.

* * *

Tommy needed a drink. He also needed a nap, and possibly to lie down on that hideous carpet in his living room and stare at the ceiling and cry. Nobody had told him how much of his late thirties would involve lying on floors and crying.

He watched Everett stalk across the lawn. The man looked exactly the same as he had the last time they had seen one another. His battered wire-framed glasses had been swapped out for a heavy black pair, but they sat crookedly on his nose the way they always had. His pale brown hair had been combed into submission and neatly parted on the side, but Tommy knew that all it would take was a stiff wind to reveal its curls. Everett still had the same air of brittle rigidity, as if his collar had been starched three times over. But now it was as if that starch had been baked into his bones. Tommy had used to love coaxing Everett out of his stuffier moods, teasing and cajoling until Everett finally gave in and laughed. The man he saw now looked like he hadn't smiled, let alone laughed, in years.

But Everett still had the same smattering of freckles on his nose, and that too made Tommy want to cry. To be fair, everything made him want to cry these days. That, he supposed, was what came of resolutely refusing to experience human emotions for the better part of a decade. They wound up making a huge mess when they finally did come out, like a suppressed sneeze.

Tommy still found it hard to accept how thoroughly Everett had walked away from him fifteen years ago. It had taken five unanswered letters for Tommy to get the picture that Everett didn't want to hear from him. He had even asked a mutual friend whether there was something wrong with postal service in Oxford, and in response got a peculiar look and the intelligence that Everett was writing to people, just not, it would seem, to Tommy. It made no sense at the time. Everett had been his best man, much to the confusion of his brothers. Everett had been rock-solid during the ceremony, remembering everything from the rings to all the names of Tommy's aunts. And then he and Pat came back from their honeymoon and discovered that Everett had put an ocean between them, without so much as a word.

That had been his first real loss. He had lost friends in the war, but that was the first time he had wanted to draw the curtains and grieve. He had asked Pat—not once, not twice, but almost daily for months—if he had done or said something unforgivable the day of the wedding. But then his oldest brother had won a seat in Congress, and Daniel had been born, and suddenly his days were busy, if not exactly complete. He had thought that would be enough, and for a while it almost was.

Seeing Everett today was just another reminder of how far Tommy had fallen, of how little was left of the man he had wanted to be. Fifteen years ago, Tommy had a bright future and a loving family; now he was alone and unmoored.

He crossed the lawn to say goodbye to Daniel, who was with a few of the younger children, all of whom looked like they were about twenty minutes away from becoming feral. He went to shake Daniel's hand, but Daniel pulled him into a hug. "It'll be all right, Dad," he whispered. Tommy managed something about seeing him the following weekend and congratulated himself on not weeping all over his son's shoulder in front of the kid's classmates.

As he made his way toward the road that led into town, he saw Everett clustered with a group of parents. His back was straight; his hair still hadn't gotten mussed. Fifteen years was a long time, and maybe there wasn't much left of the Everett he had loved. Maybe that had all been in Tommy's head in the first place. Mere boyish antics. Experimentation, as his psychoanalyst had suggested. Maybe Tommy had driven Everett away by being too—too bent, too effusive, too selfish, too much.

He shoved his hands in his pockets, which would probably ruin his suit, but it wasn't like he had much use for hand-sewn suits anymore. He made his way down the road, and when he finally looked over his shoulder, the peaks and towers of Greenfield had disappeared into the autumn foliage.

CHAPTER 2

The rest of October was an exercise in patience. Whenever Everett stepped outside, Tommy Cabot was there. He arrived at the school every Friday afternoon to pick up his son, sometimes wearing an alarming pair of denim trousers. Once he made an appearance at the high table during dinner, evidently as the guest of the provost. At that point, Everett decided to become intensely interested in a conversation about the World Series that was happening among some children who had evidently smuggled in a wireless. By the end of the meal, he had accidentally invited the children to his office to listen to the game without the burden of rule breaking, so for six evenings he had a crowd of children packed into his office. He didn't even like baseball. Nor, he was becoming increasingly convinced, children.

Worst of all were the football games. Tommy was at every home game, a flesh and blood ghost haunting the bleachers. Everett liked football, damn it. He had missed it in England. All he wanted was to sit in the stands, a muffler wrapped around his neck, a copy of The Economist open in his lap to peruse during the lulls in the game. Instead he hardly noticed what was happening on the field. He saw Tommy, still so handsome despite his careworn air, sitting next to his son. He saw Tommy exchange cordial greetings with parents and faculty, flashing the smile that won the Cabots Senate seats and judgeships. He saw Tommy and every time he was struck by the utter wrongness of Tommy being over there and Everett being anywhere else in the world but by his side. For years they had sat in these stands together, two halves of a whole, and now this distance felt unnatural.

But Everett had put distance between them for a reason. Staying in Boston would have meant getting his heart broken every time Tommy showed up and slung his arm around Everett's shoulders, every time Tommy acted like a kiss or a grope or even more didn't mean anything. He put himself out of Tommy's range, and after the initial misery of separation, he learned to live outside the context of his friendship with Tommy. He wasn't the same person he had been all those years ago; he had made a life for himself, something safe and sane and quiet. Something with no room for Tommy Cabot. What Everett felt when he looked at Tommy was only nostalgia, that was all.

Well, he was going to have to get over it and his current strategy of staying away from Tommy wasn't working. It was only tricking him into thinking he missed things he certainly was better off without. At halftime, he made his way to the empty seat beside Tommy.

"May I?" he asked, hearing the stiffness in his own voice.

Tommy looked up at him with wide, startled eyes. "Please do," he said.

"Hello, Daniel," Everett said. "Are you enjoying the game?"

The child hesitated. "Well, I'm enjoying the chocolate," he said diplomatically, gesturing at the thermos in his hand.

"I'm afraid young Daniel doesn't appreciate the finer things in life," Tommy said with a sideways smile at his son that hinted at a longstanding joke between the two of them, and Everett was forcibly reminded that he had been out of Tommy's life for longer than Daniel's entire existence.

The game started up again, and for the following quarter they sat shoulder to shoulder, only occasionally murmuring such boring commonplaces as "that was a bad hit," and so forth. The strain between them was so palpable that Everett started to think other people could see it.

Everett tried to tell himself that he didn't mind, that it was for the best, but this ranked among the more miserable moments of his life, outmatched by a handful of funerals and Tommy's wedding. He was settling in for some good old-fashioned wallowing and self-reproach when Tommy let out a low and exasperated chuckle. "This is horse shit," he said, low enough and close enough that only Everett would hear. "Whatever the hell happened to make it so that we can't even talk, can we just be done with it? Every time I see you, I feel so ashamed of whatever it was that I did."

Everett didn't know what disconcerted him more, this tactless honesty or the idea of Tommy Cabot being ashamed of anything. He cleared his throat and tried to sound normal. "You didn't do anything wrong," he said, irritation bleeding into his voice at being asked for sincerity on a topic he'd rather never acknowledge.

Tommy fell silent for long enough for St. Matthews to score a touchdown. When he finally spoke, his voice was even softer than it had been before. "You know, I told Daniel that he'd make friends for life at Greenfield. I told him that I had made the best friend I ever had." He took a shaky breath. "And that holds true, what I told him. Other than my brothers, I've never—fuck." He cast a frantic glance at his son, and Everett wasn't sure if Tommy was more concerned about the profanity or the suddenly misty quality of his voice. Tommy passed a hand over his eyes and sat up straight, as if trying to get control of himself. Everett earnestly wished him success, because he did not know what to do in this situation.

Then Tommy glanced a hand across Everett's knee. And, God, that was what had started it all in the first place, Tommy Cabot's inability to keep his hands to himself. Affectionate by nature, he was always reaching out for whoever was near: an arm around the shoulder, a pat on the back. Everett, the only child of distant parents, soaked up Tommy's attention and had fallen in love with him long before those easy touches became something different. Hands on one another in the showers. Mouths, but only if they were drunk. Kissing, eventually, but they never talked about it. They never talked about any of it. What was there to say? *So, Cabot, are we in love or just regular old friends with a habit of getting one another off?* His face heated just thinking about it.

Everett made a snap decision. "Come on, Daniel. I see some other boys in your year over there by a plate of franks. Let's see if I can't pull rank and get you to the front of the line."

He led the boy to his friends, resisting the urge to look over his shoulder at Tommy.

* * *

TOMMY HAD BEEN TRYING to keep his distance from Everett, both because Everett clearly didn't want anything to do with him, and also because Tommy wanted to curl up and die whenever he thought of Everett not wanting anything to do with him. He'd never forget how stiff and uncomfortable Everett had been when Tommy, motivated by bad judgment, wishful thinking, and about three fingers of scotch, had attempted to embrace Everett on Visiting Sunday, as if the past decade or so hadn't happened, as if they were friends.

He hadn't expected Everett to come sit by him, and still couldn't figure out why he had, if all he wanted to do was sit there and radiate starchy discomfort. The contrast between Everett's stiffness and the three students in the row in front of them, who were unsubtly passing a flask back and forth while whispering things that made one another dissolve into shaking laughter, was too much for Tommy. He remembered when he and Everett had been the ones laughing and earning reprimanding looks from nearby adults. He remembered all the times he and Everett had slipped off at halftime to make use of their empty bedroom. If anyone had told him then that fifteen years would pass during which he and Everett wouldn't exchange a single word, he wouldn't have believed it. And what was more, he didn't think Everett would have believed it either. It was just another thing that Tommy had failed at, and it seemed grossly unfair that this failure from the past was being thrown in his face right at the moment when he had to try to piece together a future.

Now Everett was coming up the steps, sitting back down. Tommy hadn't expected that either. He had rather assumed that Everett would deposit Daniel in a place mercifully far from his father's emotions, and then make himself scarce.

"That was kind of you," Tommy said. He couldn't be sure, but he thought Everett was watching him out of the corner of his eye.

"Nothing of the sort." The syllables jammed together into one formulaic nonsense word, nothingofthesort, its only purpose to dismiss Tommy's feelings. Tommy dug his fingers into the fabric of his trousers, into the meat of his thighs.

"It was kind of you," Tommy repeated. "I'm trying to spare Daniel the worst of things." *Ask me what I mean,* he wanted to shout. A simple "how so" would do the trick. *Make a conversation with me. Meet me half-way. Pretend we knew one another once.*

One of Everett's fingers slid beneath the edge of his cardigan—the man was wearing a cardigan for God's sake, he wasn't even forty and he was wearing an argyle cardigan with scratchy-looking plaid woolen trousers. One of his long fingers insinuated itself into the cuff and Tommy guessed he was fiddling with the stem of his watch. As far as Tommy knew, that was Everett's only nervous tell.

And then—Jesus Christ, ghosts were so thick on the ground in this place he could hardly fucking breathe—he remembered Everett spending the entirety of fourth period Latin fiddling with that watch stem. Before class, Tommy had said something filthy to him, some effortless and eager promise he fully intended to deliver on, but not before he spent an hour watching Everett slowly lose his mind instead of doing his declensions. But that tinkering with the watch stem had been the only outward sign that Everett had been distracted; the bastard had even primly raised his hand a couple of times. After class Tommy had dragged Everett into a broom closet as if it were the most normal thing in the world.

"Tommy. What the—" Everett had started, but Tommy was already groping at his zipper.

"Tell me to stop if you don't want it," Tommy had mumbled into the wool of Everett's school sweater.

"I'm not going to tell you anything of the sort, you moron." And then he had dragged Tommy even closer by the tie, pushed him against the wall, kissed him stupid. Stupider, rather. He had been operating at a baseline level of moderate stupidity since the first time Everett had caught him looking and then looked back in return. But this, daytime kissing, Everett's mouth taking him from frantic lust to something gentler, that had been new. "I'm not going to tell you to stop," Everett had repeated. "But I am going to tell you to wait until we can do this properly."

"Do tell me how to properly jerk you off, Ev," Tommy laughed.

"We'll have the room to ourselves this afternoon while Bond and McNamara are at football practice."

"That's hours from now. You want me to have a hard on for *three hours?*" And then, in the dark of the broom closet, he realized that this was exactly what Everett wanted. "What is the matter with you?" he asked, but it came out all breathy and wanting.

"You are, you miserable bastard." And, Jesus, hearing Ev swear had gone straight to his dick.

They had managed to wait until they were back in their room, even though Everett had made a big show of needing to put his books on his desk and hang up his jacket and then take out his pen and make a note to himself.

"If that note doesn't say 'let Cabot play with my dick,' I'm never speaking to you again." Everett had giggled, actually giggled, and let Tommy push him onto the bed, let Tommy strip him with deliberate care, kissing every slice of skin he exposed.

That, Tommy realized later, much later, when it was far too late for epiphanies to count for anything, was the day he had—he desperately wanted to say something maudlin and dopey like *lost his virginity,* even though he had technically accomplished that task the following summer with one of the girls his brothers brought to the summer house. It was the first time that they had taken their time with it, the first time they actually planned the thing in advance instead of acting like it was a matter of happenstance when they found themselves jerking one another off.

Now Tommy drew in a breath of cool fall air and dragged his gaze away from Everett's wrist. "It was kind of you," he repeated. "Thank you for that." And then, because maybe he was a bit of an asshole, and maybe he just didn't want to leave until he had some sign that Everett was really still there underneath all the starch and stiffness, "I know strong emotion is difficult for you." It was true, though. Everett had always blushed and turned his head away when Tommy got sappy on him.

"What the—"

"Thanks, Ev," he said, cutting the other man off. He rose to his feet and made his way down to where Daniel was watching the game with a few of his friends. "I'll see you Friday," he said, leaning in. Daniel waved his goodbye, and Tommy walked home.

CHAPTER 3

"Dr. Sloane?" asked a tentative voice from across the dining table. "Dr. Sloane?"

Everett looked up to find ten pairs of eyes fixed on him, and gathered that the children had been trying to get his attention for some time. "I apologize," he said, putting down his empty fork. "Woolgathering, I'm afraid. How can I help you—" he struggled to remember the name of the red headed sophomore who had spoken "—Mr. Maclean?"

"Well, you know how you have that transistor radio," Maclean said. "And it was awful nice of you to let us listen to the World Series in your office."

"Even though Rourke drank all your root beer," said a freshman, earning himself what sounded very much like a kick under the table.

"It's just that some of us were wondering if you might like to listen to football, too—"

"The Giants are on a tear—"

"And we'd hate to break the rules by using Rourke's radio."

"We love following rules," said the freshman.

"Rules are our favorite."

Everett tried to look suitably unamused by all of this. The fact was that he had every intention of listening to the game anyway. He just had no interest in sitting in his tiny office with ten loud and sweaty adolescents. The World Series had been bad enough. When he had agreed to take this position at Greenfield, his only thought had been getting a job that paid decently and was within driving distance of his mother. He had received the expected offers from a handful of universities, but the prospect of having to adapt to a new set of department quarrels and academic rivalries left him cold. He had had never minded instructing undergraduates and thought that maybe he could try his hand at teaching slightly younger students. On a whim, he wrote to Greenfield. His single stipulation had been that he would teach only sixth and seventh years; this, he thought, would prevent him from having to interact with actual children. He had no nieces or nephews. None of his friends in Oxford had been parents. He was fairly certain he had never talked to a child since he had been one.

What he had forgotten was Greenfield's tradition of assigning dinner tables at the beginning of the year: each table sat ten students of various ages and one faculty member. Attendance was expected each weeknight. Everett had gotten used to the routine by now. The students mostly preferred to ignore him and carry on their own conversations. From where Everett sat, he could see the Latin teacher with a book open in front of him, and two of the younger teachers carrying on a conversation with one another from their separate tables. Everett's only recollection of these meals during his time as a Greenfield student was bolting his food as quickly as possible in order to get back to more interesting things.

"I did plan to listen to the game this Sunday," he said. "But don't you think you'd be more comfortable listening in the lounge of your dormitories? I know radios are allowed there. At least they were twenty years ago."

The table erupted in a chorus of protests. From what Everett could gather, one housemaster insisted on rooting for the Patriots, another housemaster required quiet in the lounge, and yet another had an infant daughter who cried when the cheering got too loud.

Everett very nearly suggested that they take their contraband radio and listen behind the boathouse or under the bleachers or in one of the perpetually empty study carrels on the top floor of the library, which surely was what half their peers did if they wanted a bit of time to themselves. But the red headed sophomore—Maclean, he remembered—did not look like the type to willingly violate rules. Having to hide behind the boat shed would completely ruin the fun for him. Everett had been much the same way before Tommy had gotten his hands on him.

"You could come to my rooms," he said. Teachers had dinners and coffees and card parties in their rooms, he knew. Listening to a football game wasn't so different. "I'll get root beer and..." he struggled to think of what children ate. "Candy. I'll get candy. You'll need to clean up after yourselves and all your homework needs to be done before the game," he added, feeling like he ought to at least extract some minor concessions for his largesse.

After the children left the table, Everett realized he would need to go into town and get root beer and candy. He had three days before the game, but at this time of year snow could start at any time, and he figured he ought to make the trip while the weather held up. It was already dark, the autumn sun having set over an hour ago. But he had a flashlight in the pocket of his coat, and he knew the grocery store didn't close until eight. He supposed he could have driven, but it seemed a hassle to get the car started for such a short trip.

Half an hour later he stepped into the A&P, his glasses fogged and his fingers tingling with the returning blood flow. He didn't bother taking a cart, instead looping a wire basket over his arm. When he found the candy aisle, he realized the US candy industry had been busy while he was overseas. He recognized M&Ms and put some in his basket. He could not remember having ever seen Peanut M&Ms, but the concept seemed both straightforward and praiseworthy, so they went into the basket as well. A few Hershey's bars. Perhaps some licorice. There. Now all that was left was to find root beer.

"Oh." It was more a puff of air than an actual sound, and Everett knew before turning that it had come from the mouth of Tommy Cabot.

"Tommy," he said.

"You know, you're the only one who calls me that," Tommy said. "Other than my brothers, and they aren't—anyway. Good Christ." He raised an eyebrow at Everett's basket. "What are you planning to do with that all that? Your teeth will rot."

"Students," he said shortly. Tommy's own cart was filled with actual food. Macaroni, some parcels wrapped in butchers' paper, a cabbage, a loaf of bread. There was dish soap in there, and what looked like clothespins. Surely Tommy had a housekeeper to buy—and cook—his macaroni. Moreover, what was Tommy doing buying groceries here at all? Everett had assumed Tommy drove from Boston to pick Daniel up every weekend; it hadn't occurred to him that Tommy might actually live in town.

"I have to get root beer," Everett said instead of coming up with anything more intelligent.

"This is extremely competent bribery, if that's what you're doing," Tommy said, like he thought the awkwardness in the air might dissipate if he just ignored it hard enough. "Soda pop is two aisles over." He followed Everett, as if it were perfectly normal for them to go look at root beer together.

"It's not bribery." Everett placed twelve bottles of what seemed to be the most popular brand in his cart, then turned toward the cash register, hoping that Tommy would say goodbye and finish his shopping. Instead Tommy followed him.

"If it isn't bribery, what is it? I don't recall teachers giving us root beer. Daniel certainly hasn't mentioned it." He peered into Everett's basket. "And you got the good brand!"

"If you want a bottle, Cabot, all you have to do is ask." It came out of his mouth before he even knew what he was doing, that old easy teasing tone that he wouldn't have been able to summon up if he had tried. But standing in a mostly empty A&P, its night-dark windows reflecting their images back at themselves, Everett forgot all the very good reasons he couldn't let his defenses down around this man.

Tommy let out a surprised laugh, as if the last thing he had expected had been a halfway friendly comment. A bit of tension seeped out of his posture. Jesus Christ, what kind of asshole was Everett being, when Tommy—*Tommy*—was braced for impact whenever Everett opened his mouth. Everett had tried to achieve some level of professional cordiality by sitting next to Tommy at last week's football game. But he should have known that cordiality would never be enough between them. Compared to what had come before, tepid warmth was an arctic blast.

He paid for his groceries haltingly, American currency still foreign and unwieldy in his hands. Then, the paper grocery sack balanced on his hip, he waited for Tommy to pay. He didn't pretend he was doing anything other than waiting, and saw Tommy glancing at him out of the corner of his eye, as if expecting Everett to bolt. Everett's face heated with shame.

When they stepped outside, the sky was black, clouds covering the moon and stars.

"It's going to snow," Tommy said. He was right, of course. They both had spent enough winters in western Massachusetts to know what this heaviness in the air meant. "You'd better hurry. Where's your car?"

"I walked."

Tommy raised an eyebrow. "Then you'd really better hurry." He walked in the same direction as Everett. Evidently thinking this required some explanation, he cleared his throat. "My house is a few blocks from here. Right off Maple Street."

That didn't make sense. Everett had just walked the entire length off Maple Street from Greenfield and there weren't any houses. There never had been. Unless—

"I bought the old Franklin place," said Tommy, and Everett didn't need to see his face to know the exact sheepish expression it held.

Everett laughed. He couldn't help it. That house had been a shambles twenty years ago, the sort of place Greenfield students dared one another to approach on moonless nights.

"It's not that bad!" Tommy protested. "I've nearly got all the mice out. And it's the closest I could get to Greenfield without living in a camper on school grounds and mortifying my only child."

"Why, though? I mean, if you wanted to be near Daniel, there are boarding schools in Boston and in Washington. Come to that, there are day schools in Boston and Washington." Tommy didn't say anything, and the silence stretched long enough for Everett to glance over at him. The other man's jaw was set. All right then, so that was a sore spot. Everett shifted his grocery sack from one arm to the other, and stuck his newly empty hand into his pocket for warmth.

"You ought to leave your groceries with me," Tommy said abruptly. It'll snow any minute now, and your bag will get wet and fall apart. You'll never get all those sweets back to school."

"I really shouldn't—"

"It hardly even rates as a favor. Come back tomorrow. If I go out, I'll leave the bag on the porch."

He was right, damn it. Everett followed Tommy up the long gravel driveway toward the house. It was too dark to get a good look at the place beyond a sense of hulking dilapidation.

"You could come in for a drink," Tommy said as he climbed the porch steps and took a key from his pocket. His breath was a pale, translucent cloud against the dark of the night. "Warm up before you head back out."

"No," Everett said too quickly. "I can't—I ought to hurry back before it snows." He put his bag beside Tommy's. "Thank you. Good night." He shoved his hands in his pockets and walked away as quickly as he could.

* * *

"DARLING, you do realize it's past two in the morning," Pat said, her voice tinny and distant.

"I keep getting all your time zones mixed up," Tommy protested. "I never know whether to add or subtract."

"Is anything wrong with Daniel?"

"No, nothing like that. I'm sorry. I'll call you tomorrow."

"Don't bother. Actually we're just getting in. Harry, say hello to

Thomas." In the background, Tommy heard a shouted greeting. "Now, what's the matter?" Pat asked.

"Why does there need to be a problem? Maybe I just want to hear your voice. Maybe I want to spend all my money on transatlantic telephone calls." He heard her sigh, and didn't bother arguing anymore. "I saw him again."

"Harry, darling, make yourself useful in a different room for a few minutes." Then, a moment later, "Was he chilly and rude?"

"Not as bad as before."

He heard the familiar sound of Pat lighting a cigarette. "Is that a good thing or a bad thing?"

"I don't know. It was a mistake to come here, wasn't it?"

"So what if it was? Would it be the first mistake you've ever made? No, and God willing it won't be your last. Have it out with him, Thomas. I might have my own theories about why he stopped talking to you after we got married, but I don't want to put words in his mouth."

"Patricia," he pleaded. He had told her the whole tale after he realized that he was—bent, gay, whatever. She had lit a cigarette and stuck it in his mouth, then lit one for herself, poured them both stiff drinks, and announced that she wanted a divorce. Tommy hadn't been expecting that. They were Catholic, at least in a Sunday mass and paternoster sort of way. But as soon as she said the word, he knew she was right. It was easy enough to get a divorce in Massachusetts, and Pat wanted a chance to fall in love without being branded an adulterous jezebel. He was hardly going to deny that to her.

"I'm serious," she said. "He's already being a misery. You have nothing to lose. Tell him what you think. Tell him how you felt when he stopped answering your letters. Tell him how you felt before that, when you were at school."

"Since when do you make so much sense?"

"Probably since I started spending hundreds of dollars on psychoanalysis, darling. I'm for bed. Tell Daniel I adore him, that he should keep an eye out for a care package filled with macarons, and that I'll see him on Thanksgiving."

He hung up the phone, feeling like there was only one flaw in Pat's reasoning: he did have something to lose, even though it was the tiniest and puniest scrap of a thing. He had barely been able to endure chilliness from Everett; he didn't think he could take outright hostility. Not after his brothers and mother had sent him packing. Not with Pat on the other side of the world. He felt fragile, a blown and painted eggshell, something that would crumple at the slightest mistreatment. And he didn't think he could stand it if Everett were the one to crush him.

CHAPTER 4

Everett got halfway to the old Franklin place—he couldn't quite think of it as Tommy's house—before realizing he ought to have brought something. He was visiting a person's new home, a person who had done him a favor no less. And here he was, arriving empty handed.

The previous night's flurry had only amounted to few inches of snow, most of which had already melted from the street, but it crunched under Everett's feet as he walked up the gravel driveway. The path leading up to the porch, though, had been shoveled, and the porch itself was swept clean of snow. There was no sign of his grocery bag by the door, which meant that Everett would have to knock. He did so, his heart pounding relentlessly against his ribs.

He was about to raise his fist and knock again when he heard the doorknob rattle and the creak of an ancient hinge as the door swung open. Tommy wore a fuzzy sweater and those alarming denim trousers. His hair was rumpled, as if he had just woken from a nap, despite it being seven in the evening. He looked, in other words, heartbreakingly familiar. Lit only by a dim lamp behind him, he could have been the boy Everett had loved.

Everett's gaze skittered away, landing on the contents of the house.

He got a glimpse of a ladder, a couple of buckets, and some furniture covered in sheets.

"Painting," Tommy said. "Come in and I'll give you the cook's tour."

Everett wanted to protest that there was no need, that he'd take his groceries and be on his way. But he remembered that he was trying to make an effort to be less standoffish, to make it so Tommy didn't flinch every time he opened his mouth. "Sure," he said, trying to sound like he meant it at least slightly. "I'd love to see the place."

Tommy flashed him a smile Everett hadn't seen in over a decade, crooked and unguarded and nothing like the smile Cabots pasted on for voters and cameras. Everett felt like he had done something very clever.

The house was—well, frankly it was a disaster. Everett would be the first to acknowledge that he knew little about what houses looked like when they were in the process of being taken apart, or put back together, or whatever was happening here. The entire field of home renovation was a closed book to him. The one thing of which he was certain was that no Cabot, past or present, had ever lived in a place that was missing an entire wall, pipes and wires exposed for all the world to see.

"Plumbing," Tommy explained, leading the way between the beams that now supported the ceiling and through a rabbit warren of crates and boxes. "And wiring. And I didn't like that wall anyway. Here, this is Daniel's room." He pushed open a door. The walls—all thankfully intact—were freshly painted blue, and the bed was covered in a neat plaid bedspread. A dresser held a model airplane and a photograph of Patricia. "And this is mine." He gestured across the hall, to a room that was the mirror image of Daniel's room, but with a large, unmade bed. Everett looked away, feeling vaguely that he had seen too much—not only Tommy's bed, but the entire domestic fact of this house. Tommy Cabot was a father, and not only that, but one who chose bright blue paint and cheerful curtains for his son's bedroom. "Upstairs is more of the same, and the less said about the cellar, the better."

Everett tried to come up with something complimentary to say. "It looks like you've been doing a lot of work," he finally settled on, carefully stepping over a bucket of something mysterious and opaque.

Tommy snorted. "I know it looks bad, but it's very much in a darkest-before-the-dawn state at the moment. I was able to buy the place outright and still have enough left over to eat, without needing to worry about getting another job right away."

That made Everett look at him sharply. As far as he knew, the Cabots were as rich as they had ever been. If they sold even one of their homes on Cape Cod, they could probably buy an entire township's worth of houses nicer than this one. But Tommy was here, not working for his brother's Senate office or any of his other brothers' campaigns. He wasn't working for Patricia's father's law firm. He was tearing walls out of a run-down old farmhouse that was located near nothing except his son.

"Did something happen to Frank?" Everett asked. "Last I heard—not that I make it a point to follow—oh damn it." His face heated, so he polished his glasses on his handkerchief just for the excuse to look away. "I thought you were his chief of staff. And, I mean, you'd have to live under a rock not to know that he has his sights set on the White House next year." He shoved his glasses back onto his face and straightened his tie. "Why are you here, and not in Washington?"

It was none of his business; it was a personal question, the sort of vulgar conversational overreach he had been raised to scorn. But Tommy was tossing out these clues, this trail of breadcrumbs that made it seem like he wanted Everett to ask.

Tommy let out something that might have been a laugh when it grew up. "My services are no longer required. It seems I'm the black sheep of the family."

"What?" Everett said, genuinely shocked. "You?" Tommy had always done everything his family wanted. He had gone to Harvard and then law school instead of joining the army like Everett and most of their Greenfield classmates. Not only did he marry the daughter of one of Boston's wealthiest families, but he married *at all*. "If I had to bet on the Cabots having a black sheep, I'd have put all my money on Frank."

That must have been the right thing to say, because Tommy laughed in earnest now. "I know. But it turns out the Cabots aren't interested in sullying their reputation by associating with queers who have estranged wives."

Everett flinched as if he had been hit. It wasn't that word—well, it was partly the word, and it was partly that it came from Tommy's mouth, but it was mostly that Tommy had applied that word to himself.

"Shit, I'm sorry," Tommy said, and Everett had no idea what he was apologizing for. "This conversation needs wine."

Everett wanted to decline—it would better to keep his wits about him, his defenses intact. But Tommy was right: this conversation needed wine, at the minimum.

"That is," Tommy went on before Everett could continue, "if you want to hear about it. I'd understand if you needed to leave. It's getting late."

"No," Everett said promptly, with a weak attempt at a smile, and watched the tension leach from Tommy's shoulders. He hated that new tension, hated everything that had happened to put it there. "Wine would be lovely."

He watched as Tommy dug through a crate, eventually coming up with two goblets that he polished on the hem of his shirt. Also in the crate was a bottle of wine. "That's Pat. She's a planner. As a matter of fact—" he rifled through the crate some more, and came up with a packet of cigarettes, which he tossed to Everett. "I knew there had to be some in the house."

"I don't really smoke," Everett said, catching the packet.

"You had a cigarette in your mouth when I saw you on Visiting Sunday."

"Nerves," Everett admitted, and Tommy gave him a long and inscrutable look. Maybe he hadn't expected Everett to admit to a weakness.

Tommy took the sheet off what turned out to be a serviceable looking sofa and sat at one end, an ankle balanced on the opposite knee. Everett duly sat at the other end, grateful that the glass of wine at least gave him something to do with his hands.

"So," Tommy started, dry as dust. "You may have noticed during our time at Greenfield, that I like messing around with other men."

Everett knew his face was beet red. He ran two fingers under a collar that now seemed uncomfortably tight, and then downed half his glass of wine. "That did not escape my attention," he said to his glass.

"I may have overstated the fact—it was only you. But the principle holds." Tommy gave a shaky laugh. "You may also have noticed that I was never terribly interested in girls. Amazingly, that is not something that changes even when you marry a beautiful and brilliant woman."

"How did they find out? Your family, I mean." Blackmail, Everett figured. That was always the nightmare scenario: a night with the wrong person, a too-observant neighbor, a bitter ex-lover. He had spent half his life worried about that himself.

"I told them."

Everett stared. "Why on earth would you have done that?"

Tommy's jaw was set again. "Funnily enough, that's exactly what my mother and Frank wanted to know. In any event, it doesn't matter. It's water under the bridge." Everett had the sense that if he had responded differently, Tommy wouldn't look so strained now. He finished his glass of wine, and before he could search for a place to set it down, Tommy leaned over and filled it up again.

"Won't you tell me the truth?" Tommy asked, his voice barely audible. "Unless telling me will only make it worse."

"Tell you what?" Everett asked, his mouth dry.

"What I did that was so unforgivable. I know you said I didn't do anything, but I don't believe that you would do that to a friend—that you would walk away without a word—if they hadn't done something awful."

Everett wanted one of those cigarettes but he knew that if he tried his hands would shake too hard to light it. He looked hard at Tommy, at the tension around his eyes and the tight line of his mouth.

Surely Everett could give him an answer. It was one sentence. He could say one sentence. "I couldn't let myself..." No that was the wrong sentence, damn it. "Every time I saw you, I broke my heart."

He almost spelled it out further, almost said it plain as day: *I loved you, I couldn't have you, and I had to stop torturing myself. I deserved more. I deserved a life.* But he couldn't make his mouth shape the words, and it shouldn't matter anyway—their shadow was right there in the words he had spoken.

TOMMY LOOKED at the man sitting on the other end of the sofa. Everett's gaze was fixed directly ahead of him, and at no point in his matter of fact statement had he even flicked a glance in Tommy's direction. *Every time I saw you, I broke my heart.* There were only so many ways Tommy could interpret that. He supposed it was possible that Everett had been heartbroken by Tommy's inadequacy or some other failure on Tommy's part and couldn't bear to look upon such a flawed and fallen creature—but those were Tommy's present-day fears. The Tommy of 1945 had been clean and golden. He drew his knees up to his chest, not caring that he was getting plaster dust and God knew what else all over the sofa.

No, Everett had to be referring to the regular kind of heartbreak. And, God, it shouldn't be such a relief to know he hadn't been the only one. "I didn't know," Tommy said, which at least made Everett look at him.

"You weren't meant to," Everett answered.

Tommy downed the rest of his wine and hugged his knees closer to his body. "Here's a funny story," he said, looking at the wall in front of him. "I didn't figure it out until, what, last year? My sister Agnes's husband had an affair, and when Agnes sat in our living room crying her heart out, I thought to myself: that's how it was when Ev left. That's how it is when you're in love with someone, only to discover they don't love you back."

Everett said nothing. His eyes were wide, and it looked like he might have fallen over if he didn't have supernatural powers of self-control and about a pound of starch ironed into his shirt. He cleared his throat, he fiddled with his watch stem. "I didn't know," he said finally. "You said things, but you were like that with everyone."

Tommy gave a slightly hysterical laugh, but he knew what Everett meant. *Smith, you damned magician, pour me another one of those drinks. Calloway, I'll adore you forever if you score a touchdown against St. Paul's.* He had been young and unguarded, and he had learned that he could say exactly what was on his mind if he paired it with a charming smile. Nobody would take him seriously if they didn't want to; they would remember the warmth, not the content. And perhaps he hadn't taken himself quite seriously either.

"My point is that *I* didn't know either. I knew I loved you, but I loved a lot of people back then, so I told myself it didn't matter, that what I felt about you wasn't any different. And I knew I didn't ever want to stop touching you. But I didn't let myself figure out what that *meant*. You were my best friend and I loved you," Tommy said, mostly because he needed to say it out loud in order to remind himself it was true. "And I also liked fooling around—oh, to hell with euphemisms. I liked having sex with you. It's just that I didn't add all of that up in my mind and come up with Tommy Cabot is Gay until long after you were done with me."

"Done with you," Everett echoed faintly, shaking his head.

"I'm being an asshole, I apologize. You were protecting yourself, I know."

"I just wanted a chance—"

"Stop." He held up his hand. He didn't want to hear Everett say all the things that Pat had told him—*I just want a chance to love someone and be loved back.* He couldn't stand that two people he cared about had needed to run away from him in order to be happy. "You deserved that. You deserved a chance at whatever you wanted. Did you get it?"

Everett swallowed, and Tommy watched his throat work beneath his starched collar. "A couple times I got close, I thought. It never worked out, but—" He stopped abruptly and reached for the bottle, dividing the last few inches of wine between their glasses. "I don't want to talk about this with you." His voice was taut.

"Right. Of course not." Tommy wrapped his arms tighter around his knees. "I'm sorry that I made you think you didn't mean anything to me—"

"No," Everett said, and his tone was gentle, gentler than Tommy had heard it in fifteen years. "I never said that. I knew we were friends. But I thought the rest of it was just a convenient arrangement for you. Schoolboy silliness that lasted too long. It wasn't a wild surmise on my part. You got married, Tommy. What was I supposed to think?"

Tommy swallowed. "I wanted it to be one of those arrangements. I told myself it was." His eyes were wet, and, just, fuck this. He scrubbed his sleeve across his eyes and hoped Everett didn't notice.

"Use this." Everett handed him a crisply folded linen handkerchief.

Tommy mopped at his face. "Thanks." He took a deep breath and let it out. "I really thought I could have you and Pat both—or rather everything Pat meant," he said glumly, directing his words at the empty fireplace in front of him rather than look at Everett.

"You weren't used to things not going your way," Everett said, and it might have been an insult but for how gently he spoke the words.

Tommy groaned, remembering himself at fifteen, even at twenty-five. He had been brash and overconfident, with the casual selfishness of someone who never doubted that his desires aligned with those of everyone else. "I must have been insufferable."

"You were wonderful," Everett said immediately, and with a fondness that made Tommy turn his head. Everett looked away and began winding his watch. "Can we agree that we were both idiots—"

"Yes."

"—And just let bygones be bygones."

Tommy hated that phrase. He wished he could let one single solitary stupid thing actually be a bygone. Instead he was dredging up every one of his ancient misdeeds and spending days turning it over and looking at it from every angle like a jeweler examining a gemstone. But he nodded anyway.

Everett looked at his empty glass. "It's late. I ought to be going."

"Right. Of course." They rose and stood awkwardly in front of the sofa, neither of them moving. "Can I—oh, fuck it. Can I hug you? You can say no. I'm just drunk and maudlin and in a house with an ancient furnace and—"

"It's okay." Everett turned, one arm slightly raised, as if he had read about hugs in books but hadn't ever thought to try it out himself. Tommy stepped forward and leaned in, closing the gap, his arms around Everett's neck.

Tommy had wanted this contact, needed it, in order to cancel out the memory of that horrible Visiting Day embrace. This was better. Everett's hands were on his back, his chin on Tommy's shoulder. Tommy buried his face in Everett's neck, his cheek pressed against the fuzzy wool of Everett's sweater, to see if they still fit together as well as they used to. He waited to see if Everett went cold.

But that didn't happen. Instead Everett stroked a hand up his back and softly whispered "shhh," as if he were soothing a baby. And that—Jesus Christ—he needed that. He needed to be soothed. For his whole life there had always been someone there to put an arm around him, to bump shoulders while they walked down a hall. Nieces and nephews to hold, women to dance with—and now it was all gone.

"I'm crying into your collar," he mumbled.

"That's okay too." Knowing Everett—if he really still did know Everett, which he supposed was an open question—it probably wasn't okay at all that Tommy was soaking his shirt in tears and worse, but it was nice of him to say it was. It was even nicer that he kept murmuring comforting nonsense, kept his arms tight around him. Nicest still was the idea that even after making a royal mess of everything, somebody might still want to hold him and make him feel better.

CHAPTER 5

"Did you send me a plant?"

Everett's hands stilled on his coat buttons. The previous night he had left Tommy's house in a fluster of awkwardness and mutual reassurances, and without the goddamn root beer. At that moment he was preparing to make the trip back to Tommy's house. But now Tommy stood in the door to his office, Everett's sack of groceries on his hip.

"I'm here to take Daniel home for the weekend, and I thought I'd bring your things." Tommy put the paper bag on Everett's desk. "One of the kids told me where your office was. I shouldn't have—sorry to intrude."

"No," Everett said, realizing he had to say something or Tommy was going to retreat in confusion and embarrassment. That too was new—Everett hadn't thought any of the Cabots were capable of this strange self-effacement that kept creeping over Tommy. He had always been bold as brass, charming as the devil himself, and Everett hated everyone who had made this man doubt himself, while also suspecting that he had done some of the damage himself. "I was just startled. Thank you. I wasn't relishing the prospect of trudging through yet more snow." They had gotten another two inches during the day.

"So," Tommy said, still smiling. "Did you send me a plant?"

"I, well, yes. Did the florist not include a card?" He had called the florist first thing in the morning.

"If they did, it must have blown away before the plant made it to my door."

"Then how did you know it was from me?"

"Because there are three people in the world who know where I am. One is Pat, and ficuses really aren't her style. Five dozen hot house roses, maybe, but not a ficus. Another is Danny, and I don't think twelve-year-old boys go in much for potted plants as gifts. And the third is you."

Everett blinked. The rift between Tommy and his family must have been deeper than Everett had imagined if Tommy's brothers and mother didn't even have his address. That was almost unimaginable—the Cabot boys were always in one another's pockets, from childhood to Greenfield to Senate campaigns. As for Patricia, surely estranged spouses didn't send plants or flowers or anything at all to one another.

But now that he thought about it, Everett wasn't sure how things stood between Tommy and his wife. It was hard to imagine any Cabot getting divorced, so likely this would be a temporary separation before they figured out a way to reconcile. Perhaps they, like Everett's parents, would maintain separate bedrooms in the same house for forty years, only speaking to one another at mealtimes, and always in tones of icy cordiality. Perhaps they would have an arrangement that would allow Tommy to pursue casual encounters. An arrangement that would allow for—for Everett to get his heart broken again.

Last night it had felt good and right and achingly familiar to have Tommy in his arms, to give Tommy whatever comfort he could. Their bodies still slotted against one another effortlessly. Everett knew himself well enough to know that if Tommy had kissed him, he'd have gone along with it, and was simultaneously disappointed and relieved that he hadn't had a chance.

"Thank you for the ficus," Tommy said solemnly, the corner of his mouth barely twitching up in a smile. "But what did I do to deserve the honor? Slobber all over your sweater?"

"It was supposed to be a housewarming present," Everett said, his face heating. He couldn't think about Tommy crying—actually in tears! Tommy Cabot!—without blushing. He had never seen Tommy cry. Everett didn't really care for displays of emotion, either in himself or in other people, but there was something terribly touching about the fact that Tommy could do that now. It made Everett feel protective, which was not something he had ever expected to feel about Tommy.

"Ah. I wasn't sure if it had something to do with the language of flowers or whatever it was my grandmother used to talk about. But that was all about bouquets, and I don't think potted ficuses entered into it. I'm afraid I let my imagination run wild about what a ficus might mean." He cocked an eyebrow.

"Thomas," he scolded, cheered by the familiarity of half-heartedly clinging to stodginess while Tommy wheedled and teased.

"I thought it might mean 'congratulations on your new home, hope you remembered to wrap the pipes before they freeze.' I did wrap the pipes, and I'm prouder than you can imagine for having remembered that was something that needed to be done."

Everett shook his head. "You are ridiculous." They smiled stupidly at one another for a moment before Everett cleared his throat and looked away. "Thank you for bringing my groceries. I hate to think what would happen if Sunday arrived and I didn't have food during the football game."

"Ev, are you letting students listen to the football game in your rooms? Everett Sloane," he said, a wicked smile spreading across his face, "are you the fun teacher?"

Everett felt his face heat. "I am nothing of the sort." He adjusted the lapels of his coat. "I couldn't keep cramming them into this office. You see the size of it."

"You *are* the fun teacher. You bought them candy and root beer. I bet you're going to make popcorn."

He was not going to make popcorn, mainly because he had forgotten it existed during his time in England, damn it. "You see, the housemaster is a Patriots fan," he started, trying to keep his face straight, and then failing miserably when Tommy laughed, a delighted cackle Everett thought he'd never hear again. "And if I don't invite them, they huddle around a contraband radio."

"Because schoolboys hate breaking rules."

"*I* did!" Everett protested. "Well, until I was swayed by your bad influence," he added, attempting to sound severe. Tommy, confident that any scrapes that he got into could be smoothed over with a smile and the mere fact of his last name, flouted the rules with a carelessness that drove Everett half crazy. Everett's parents had lost most of their money in the stock market crash; he had gone to Greenfield on a scholarship, always afraid that one false step would get him kicked out. Tommy had the cheerful certainty that everything would be fine, because for him it almost always was: whatever happened, his family would be there for him.

And now he had lost that. Everett felt a pang of grief for the boy Tommy had been and the loss he had suffered. But at the same time, he could meet the man before him with something like equality.

"God, I was an asshole to you," Tommy said, his thoughts evidently proceeding along the same lines as Everett's. "When I think of the number of times I coaxed you out onto the roof to smoke."

"That was nothing. I thought I'd have to murder you after the bonfire incident."

"Or the time I convinced you to skip class and go out in the row boat."

Everett was smiling broadly now. "I went willingly, every time. Those are some of my happiest memories."

Tommy looked alarmed. "Please never tell Daniel half the things we got up to."

"Never," Everett promised. He tried to imagine Tommy's son sneaking out of class to steal a rowboat, and failed utterly. "It seems impossible that we were ever so young."

The smile dropped from Tommy's face and Everett wanted to kick himself. "Whenever I look at Daniel, I think the same thing. When you're that young you don't realize you're young. You think you're a man of the world. You don't realize what's in store for you."

That turn of phrase brought Everett up short. He knew what Tommy meant when he thought about what had been in store for a younger version of himself. But what had been in store for a younger Everett? He glanced around his office, at the neatly arrayed books on his shelves, his cardigan draped over the back of his chair, and four blank walls. It was peaceful. Orderly. Those were good things. He tried not to think about what his fifteen-year-old self would have made of it; that person wasn't here anymore.

"You have plenty of good things in store for you yet," Everett said, because he couldn't believe anything else. "We both do." At the sight of Tommy's smile, Everett's heart gave an agonized little thud.

From downstairs came the sound of doors opening and adolescents tramping through the halls. "That's the end of the day, then," Tommy said, not moving. "I'd better go get Daniel."

"Thank you again for the, er, root beer delivery."

"Thanks for the ficus. And thank you for—for everything last night."

"No," Everett said, his cheeks heating. "That's not something you need to thank me for."

Tommy regarded at him for a moment. "See you around, Ev."

When he was once again alone in his office, Everett put a hand over his heart as if that would settle it down. It didn't. He hung up his coat, straightened his tie, and sat down to grade some exams.

* * *

WHILE WAITING downstairs for Daniel to get his overnight bag from his dormitory, Tommy let himself take a good look at the place. The oak floors were maybe a little more scuffed than they had been twenty years ago, and the furniture in the lounge had long since been replaced by sofas and chairs that already looked well-used, but he would have known the place anywhere. He walked over to a window seat, got down on his knees, and squinted.

When he and Ev were seventh years, Greenfield was hit by a snowstorm bad enough to keep everybody indoors for a couple of days.

Restless, and more than a little fortified by contraband gin, Tommy had taken his pocket knife and gouged his name into the wood paneling beneath one of the windows. "What are you doing?" Everett had hissed when he realized what Tommy was up to. "Might as well put a signed confession on the headmaster's desk."

"Too late, it's already done," Tommy had said.

"Well, it's stupid. Now your name is on the wall. What good does that do you? It doesn't even make any sense."

Tommy had been about to protest that vandalism didn't need to make sense, but Everett took the knife from his hands and crouched down beside him. Everett, Tommy realized, was well on his way to being quite drunk.

"There," Everett announced a moment later. "Now it's a complete sentence. Subject and predicate," he said grandly.

"Your objection was on grammatical grounds?" Tommy marveled, peering at Everett's contribution. Beneath Tommy's name, Ev had neatly added the words "was here." "You should have added your own name."

"Redundant, Mr. Cabot!" Everett announced, evidently channeling their rhetoric teacher. "Obviously, if you were here, then it stands to reason that I was as well. QED."

"QED, eh?" Tommy asked, raising an eyebrow. He took the knife from Everett's hands. Everett probably shouldn't have anything sharp until tomorrow morning. Then he leaned in and added a heart around both their contributions.

"What's that supposed to mean?" Everett sniffed. "Also, it's lopsided."

"I drew a heart around Tommy Cabot and the implied Everett Sloane." He waited for the penny to drop, and saw Everett's cheeks flush red. "QED," he said, folding the knife up and sliding it into his pocket.

Now, in 1959, it was still there. The carved lines had been covered by layers of varnish, but when Tommy ran his finger over the surface, he could feel the letters, could feel the lopsided heart. *Tommy Cabot was here.* He tried to imagine having half the confidence that he had twenty years ago, tried to remember what it felt like to have the world laid out at his feet. That boy had no idea how fragile he really was. But that confidence had come at a price—he had needed to keep secrets even from himself. And it turned out the world hadn't been at his feet after all. But he was still here anyway, and there were things that couldn't be taken away from him.

CHAPTER 6

After depositing Daniel at his residence hall on Sunday afternoon, Tommy took a stroll around the Greenfield grounds until he saw someone he recognized as one of the English teachers. "Hello," he said affably, shamelessly deploying the Cabot smile.

After five minutes of conversation, he had precise directions to Everett's rooms. He had always been good at this. Christ, on a larger scale, this had been his job: glad handing, diplomatic evasions, gentle persuasion.

For the first time in the past few months, he wondered what Frank was doing without him. No, that wasn't right—he wondered whether Frank was capable of being Senator Francis Cabot without Tommy there to grease the wheels. Some bitter and venal part of him hoped that his brothers all regretted disposing of him like so much garbage, that they never met with any kind of success ever again. But that, too, was a loss. He had spent his entire career working for his brothers, and in his heart of hearts he believed that they were on the right side of history and doing important work. They had taken that away from him too. And yet—other people were doing important work. Other people could use someone to grease the wheels.

The game was over, and Tommy expected to find Everett alone—possibly surrounded by empty bottles of root beer and candy wrappers, but definitely alone. Instead, a teenager opened the door, took one look at Tommy, and shouted, "Dr. Sloane, there's an adult at your door."

"Let him in, Rogers, for heaven's—oh, hello Tommy." He had on a shirt and tie and his argyle cardigan. Tommy was starting to harbor impure thoughts about that sweater.

"Came to see if you needed help drinking root beer, but I think you have all the help you need." There were twenty children in Everett's not particularly large living room. "You're the fun teacher," he said under his breath.

Everett glared at him, but without any heat. Then he cleared his throat. "All of you, if you want to come back next week, have exactly thirty seconds to get out. Jenkins, take that blasted Monopoly game away with you. Rogers, we'll pretend I don't see that deck of cards or the fact that you have money on the table. Twenty seconds!"

The room cleared with ten seconds to spare. Tommy let out an impressed whistle and Everett rolled his eyes. "Are you here to drop Daniel off?" Everett asked, picking up empty bottles.

"I came to say hello and see if you wanted to go for a walk after being cooped up all day. There's still an hour or so left of daylight."

Everett's brow furrowed in what Tommy recognized as a sign he was looking for an excuse to say no, but then he appeared to come to some kind of decision. "Sure." He took his coat and hat off pegs by the door. "Let's."

Tommy hadn't expected it to be so easy, and realized he had no idea where they might go on this walk. For all he knew, the paths had changed in the past twenty years, and even if they hadn't, he might not remember his way.

"Tommy?" Everett looked concerned.

"Ah, sorry." He smiled brightly, which for some reason only made Everett look even more worried. "Let's get to it then."

Outside, they meandered silently in the direction of the lake.

There was an old path that traced its circumference, ground in by generations of students burning up their adolescent energy, or seeking a private place to drink or—he glanced at Everett—finding other ways to amuse themselves. Tommy halted in front of the chapel. He hadn't approached it from this angle during any of his trips to campus that fall, and now he noticed that in the open space before the steps stood a bronze statue. When he got closer he saw that it was a memorial to the Greenfield alumni who died in the last war. He ought to have known there would be something like this; in front of the dining hall there was a similar memorial to the alumni who had died in the previous war. He had been at its dedication, too young to attend Greenfield himself but mightily pleased that he got to go along with Frank, Louis, and Robert, who all looked splendid in their uniforms. Mother had shown him the name of some Cabot uncle or cousin engraved on a plaque. And now this new memorial held the names of people he had known, his own generation's dead and lost.

"From our year it's Bond, McNamara, both the Calloways, and Ted Armitage," Everett said.

Tommy knew they had died, of course—he kept in touch with half the graduating class. Or, rather, he had until this past summer. He supposed letters were accumulating in the post office box Pat set up for him. These men died fifteen years ago; it was hardly news. But something about knowing that their names were here for future generations of Greenfield students to see, and knowing that there would be more memorials, more children who sneaked past the shadow of an earlier generations' dead in order to skip class and play pranks and make love, only to years later have their names etched on a plaque—it made Tommy's stomach lurch.

"Hey, now." Everett's hand was on his arm.

"It's nothing," Tommy said thickly. "Don't mind me. Nothing to worry about." Still, Everett squeezed his arm before letting go, and Tommy wondered if maybe Everett was getting used to Tommy's odd bursts of emotion. When Tommy looked over at him, he thought the other man's expression was, if anything, fond.

The weekend had been warm enough for the snow to melt and their boots made squelching sounds in the mud. "Do you remember how cross I was when you enlisted?" Tommy asked.

"How could I forget?" Everett asked dryly.

"I couldn't understand why you wanted to—" he gestured backwards in the direction of the memorial. "We had both been accepted to Harvard." For a moment the only sounds were their footsteps and the wind blowing through what leaves remained on the trees. "Did you do it to get away from me?" At the time, that possibility hadn't occurred to him, but after their discussion a few nights earlier, Tommy had to ask.

To his surprise, Everett smiled. It was his old lopsided grin—starting on one side, as if he couldn't fully commit to expressing happiness, before dragging the other side up with it. "Honestly, when we were eighteen, enlisting seemed easier than having a conversation about my feelings."

Tommy smiled back helplessly. "Because now you love having conversations about your feelings?"

"I'm doing it now, aren't I?" Everett huffed out a laugh. "It seems to be the cost of doing business with you." He bumped his shoulder into Tommy's, as if to let him know that he didn't mind, that it was a price he gladly paid.

Tommy's eyes were starting to water—of course they were, it was a day ending with y—and Everett was looking at him, so there was no hope of going about this discreetly. He dug through his pockets, looking for a handkerchief, but only came up with his house keys and a fistful of receipts.

"Here." Everett stopped walking and held out his own crisply folded linen handkerchief. But before Tommy could use it to wipe his eyes, Everett lifted his hand and used his thumb to brush a tear off Tommy's cheekbone.

"It's all right," Tommy said. "I'm not sad, not really. Sometimes I cry when I'm happy, or Daniel gets a good grade, or I can't pry the lid off the paint can. Honestly, I blame Frank," he added nonsensically, making an effort at a watery smile.

"Fair. What makes it better?"

"Better?"

"What makes you feel better?"

Tommy's breath caught on a sniffle. He wasn't used to thinking about what he needed to feel good. He wasn't sure it was possible. He wasn't sure he deserved it, and the idea that Everett might want to give that to him made him flush, from his cheeks all the way down his neck.

"What I mean," Everett went on, "is that the other night you wanted a hug. Is that—does that help?"

Tommy blinked as he slowly understood that Everett was offering a hug. "Yes," he said.

Everett glanced around, as if he were about to rob a bank rather than hug a friend, but they had wandered off the path and were concealed by a stand of pine trees. Nobody would see.

Tommy stepped close. "I'll probably make a mess of your coat."

"Go ahead," Everett said, closing the distance. Everett stroked his hand up and down Tommy's back, through layers of cable knit sweater and wool coat, and Tommy settled heavily against his chest.

* * *

If Everett had any sense of self-preservation at all, he would have kept Tommy at arm's length. But that had always been the problem: Everett's total lack of self-preservation where Tommy Cabot was concerned. They were the same height, but he felt like he was surrounding Tommy, like Tommy was melting against him, his face buried in Everett's neck, his weight against Everett's chest. He continued to smooth his hand across Tommy's back, but Tommy seemed like he needed more comfort than whatever could be had through so much fabric. Everett slid his hand under Tommy's coat and felt the other man sigh.

He wasn't surprised when Tommy pulled back just enough to look at him, a question in his eyes. And then a glance that flickered between the eyes and the lips, a raised eyebrow—it was as if they had done this only yesterday. Except instead of leaning in, Tommy huffed out a laugh and looked at the ground, his cheeks pink from more than just the cold. Tommy was hesitant, embarrassed even, and Everett didn't quite know what to do with that, so he removed his hand from Tommy's back and used it to tilt Tommy's chin up.

"You all right?" Everett murmured.

"Yes. I just—it's been a while."

It took a moment for Everett to understand that Tommy wasn't talking about the last time they had kissed, but rather the last time he had kissed anyone at all. Everett felt like his heart might break, right then and there. "Well," he said, "would it be all right if I kissed you now?"

Tommy's eyes opened wide, as if he hadn't been expecting the question, as if he could never have expected any such question. And that only made Everett want to give him every kind of tenderness and consideration he could think of. "Yeah," Tommy said, and it came out as a puff of air.

Everett traced Tommy's lower lip, running the pad of his thumb along its soft curve, before he leaned in and replaced his thumb with his own lips. He kept the kiss light, skimming his mouth over Everett's, bringing his hand to cup the back of Tommy's head. He wanted Tommy to know that he deserved to be touched like this, deserved to be treated like something fragile and precious.

Twenty years ago they would already be on the ground or up against a tree, clothing unzipped and shoved aside, hands in one another's trousers. Twenty years ago neither of them could have known that they both might, in different ways, spend the rest of their lives in the shadow of those rushed, laughing kisses. He wasn't even sure either of them had known how sweet those frantic couplings had been, how precious their clumsy teenage fumblings would later seem. This, today, wasn't rushed and it was bittersweet at best. It felt like coming home to a building he hadn't known was still standing.

He pulled back, still making soft circles on Tommy's back, still carding his fingers through Tommy's hair. This was the wrong way to end a kiss if you didn't want to pick it back up later on. Maybe love was like one of those plants that lay dormant in the desert for years, only to be revived at the first sprinkling of rain. He ought to be angry with himself for letting it happen, for once again taking his heart out and thrusting it at Tommy Cabot. But this time Tommy knew.

He smiled against Tommy's cheek.

CHAPTER 7

"Which do you want first? Good news or bad?" Pat asked, her voice tinny over the phone.

"I don't think I'm in any shape for any kind of news," Tommy said.

"I'm not getting there until late Thursday. Because of the snow, we can't get a flight from Idlewild to Logan, not for love or money. And Harry's quite adamant that we not attempt to drive until the storm has passed."

"I suppose the good news is that I get Daniel for Thanksgiving." That really was good news—he hadn't been relishing the prospect of spending a holiday alone.

"You'll get me too, as soon as I can get a flight."

"Good God, Pat, I'm not running a hotel. I'm barely even running a house. And—wait—what on earth am I going to feed Daniel for Thanksgiving dinner? Macaroni?"

"Call a caterer, darling."

Tommy wanted to tell her his days of calling the caterer were long past. He had needed to count his pennies in order to pay the man who installed sheetrock in the living room that morning. "You'll have to sleep in the bathtub, and Harry on the floor beside you."

"Very bohemian." Or at least that was what Tommy thought she said.

"The line is breaking up, Pat."

"It's the storm. See—" The line went dead.

Well, whatever happened, he wasn't feeding his son macaroni for Thanksgiving. After hanging up the phone, he flicked on the kitchen light and took his copy of *The Joy of Cooking* off the shelf by the sink. Eating nothing but scrambled eggs and tinned soup had only made his situation seem even more hopeless, so he tried a new recipe almost every day. The results had been mixed. Fettuccine Alfredo and pineapple upside down cake were unqualified successes. Split pea soup, on the other hand, had been every bit as dismaying as he remembered it being in his childhood. And he thought it highly unlikely that he'd ever make use of the pages devoted to skinning squirrels or cooking muskrats. Cooking, even the failures, at least gave him something to do, a way to fill his newly empty days. So did tearing the house apart and putting it back together again. Nailing in moldings and ripping out mildewed paneling, baking a cake and roasting a chicken—these all gave him immediate, visible, results. He was feeding and sheltering himself, and that had to count for something.

He flipped through the index of the cookbook, trying to remember what foods typically appeared on his mother's Thanksgiving table, and then was hit with the fresh realization that all his brothers and their families would be together in Marblehead, just a few hours away. Nobody had explicitly told him not to attend, just as nobody had specifically told him to resign his post. They had just made it clear that his continued connection with the family—as if he were some kind of hanger-on, and not their brother and son—was no longer desirable. So maybe he didn't want to replicate whatever was on his mother's holiday table, after all.

He put on his boots and heaviest coat and made his way to the grocery store, figuring he could persuade somebody there to tell him what they made for their own family Thanksgivings. As he walked, he could see his breath in the air before him and the air had that heavy stillness that presaged a coming storm. He was glad Pat wasn't going to try to drive in it.

An hour later he had purchased a turkey, a can of something that called itself cranberry jelly, potatoes, more butter than he had ever seen at once, flour, apples, several tiny jars of spices that the store manager assured him were indispensable to any well run Thanksgiving supper, and his usual weekly groceries. He was about to arrange for delivery when he saw Everett get out of a Packard that was parked in front of the store. He hadn't even realized Everett had a car.

Everett saw him, saw his eight sacks of groceries, and raised his eyebrows. "Put them in the back seat," he said. "I need the trunk for my newest bad idea."

A man came out of the electronics store across the street carrying a large box with RCA printed boldly on the side. Tommy grinned. "I knew you were the fun teacher. Listening to the game wasn't good enough for your precious—"

Everett elbowed him in the ribs, and Tommy thought he hadn't been so happy in years. They hadn't seen one another since their walk in the woods two days earlier, but Tommy had been trying to gin up an excuse to stop by Greenfield, and also trying to figure out whether he even needed an excuse in the first place. The way Everett had immediately offered him the use of his car made him think he might not. He climbed into the passenger seat feeling mightily pleased with himself.

"Are you expecting to be snowed in?" Everett asked when he slid behind the steering wheel, gesturing at the mountain of groceries that occupied his back seat.

"No," Tommy said, "but I probably should have thought of that. It's Thanksgiving dinner. Daniel was supposed to go visit his grandparents with Pat, but the airports are all in a state because of the storm. How many children do you expect to have this Sunday to watch the football game on your fancy new television?"

"None, because they'll mostly be home with their families. I, on the other hand, will be watching the game in blissful solitude." He took a hand off the wheel and straightened his tie. "Or, with any adults who might be interested."

"Is that an invitation? I'll bring you all my delicious leftovers. Wait, Ev, what are you doing on Thanksgiving?" He decided not to give Everett time to come up with an excuse. "You'll come have supper with Daniel and me, unless you're too much of a coward to eat my cooking."

The corner of Everett's mouth twitched in the beginnings of a smile. "I was going to visit my mother, but it's been a long time since I drove in a snowstorm."

"Then you're definitely eating with us."

Neither of them said anything while Everett turned onto the street that led up the hill toward Greenfield and Tommy's house. Tommy watched Everett's hands, his long fingers wrapped around the steering wheel.

"Won't Daniel think it's odd that I'm there?" Everett asked.

"I've already told him that he'll make friends for life at Greenfield," Tommy said, trying for an easy tone. "He'll think nothing of it."

It bothered him, though, that they couldn't just eat a (probably badly cooked) turkey together without always having at the backs of their minds the fear of people whispering. He wondered what it would be like to just stop worrying. He didn't think he wanted to be completely out, but he also didn't want to pretend to be straight anymore. What if he stopped trying to hide it, stopped trying to erase his truth and make himself fit for public consumption? He could cope with whispers; he had dealt with worse.

Everett pulled into Tommy's driveway and slid out of the car before Tommy could insist on taking in his own groceries. It still took three trips between the two of them. "What in hell did you buy?" Everett asked when he hefted the bag containing the turkey.

"I bought what the lady told me to!"

They loaded the bags onto the kitchen table. A previous owner had, at least, fitted the kitchen with a decent gas stove, a huge sink, and an ice box that somehow was still working after at least twenty years of neglect.

"I can't believe you're actually going to cook all this," Everett said as he hefted a bag onto the table.

"Ye of little faith."

Everett peered under the brown paper that wrapped the turkey and recoiled. "It's not going to win any beauty contests."

"It's raw. You have to cook it. You apply heat and it becomes edible. Look!" He pulled the cookbook off the shelf above the sink and flipped to the T's in the index. "Turkey, roast. It's…okay, I guess I'm waking up early on Thursday."

Everett snorted and looked at the book over Tommy's shoulder, resting his hand on Tommy's back. "Serves 12?" He lifted the brown paper again. "I don't know about that."

This was an old game, and Tommy was nearly giddy to realize he still knew its rules: Everett acted prickly and impossible, and Tommy teased him out of it. "Turkeys come in different sizes, Ev. Don't insult him. Besides, I have a meat thermometer."

"What should I bring?"

"So you'll come?" He grinned broadly. Everett was still touching him and this was just going very well indeed.

"Yes, I'll come."

Tommy put the cookbook on the counter and turned to face Everett fully. "Good." He leaned forward, brushing his lips over Everett's. It was a kiss without much heat, soft and lazy. There was something about the gentleness of Everett's kisses that scrambled Tommy's mind—his fingertips on Everett's jaw, Everett's hand firm on Tommy's hip, a soft exhale, a barely whispered name. He had never expected to receive such careful touches. It was, he thought wildly, rather like how he had touched Pat years and years ago, when they were newlyweds, and that idea ought to put him off but it didn't. He liked it, even though it made him blush with a mixture of embarrassment and pleasure.

"Where did you go?" Everett asked, pulling back enough to look at Tommy.

Tommy shook his head, hoping his flushed cheeks spoke for themselves. Everett drew him in closer again, this time just for a hug.

"Did your house grow a new wall?" Everett asked after a moment. He was still holding Tommy against his chest, so the words were spoken into Tommy's hair.

It took Tommy a moment to realize that Everett was looking over his shoulder into the living room. "What—no, the handyman installed it yesterday. Sheetrock is one of those things I haven't figured out how to do on my own." He nuzzled into the crook of Everett's neck, shamelessly seeking out more contact. "How long before you have to be back at school?"

"I have a class in half an hour." Which meant he probably ought to have started back already, so Tommy planted one more kiss on his cheek and stepped reluctantly out of his embrace.

As he watched Everett's car back out of the driveway, Tommy wondered if he ought to have told him about the divorce. But even now, months after Pat had first said the word, it felt impossible—not unwanted, just unlikely. The Cabots were Catholic, famously so; they were also profoundly wrapped up in their public appeal, even more famously so. No Cabot had ever been divorced. But this had to be Pat's choice—she'd be living with the stigma of divorce much more than he would.

Everett knew that Tommy and Pat were separated, of course, but Tommy still wanted to reassure him that whatever was happening between them wasn't an affair, that there wasn't anything seedy about it. He wanted to tell Everett that he'd be free—but that would be a lie. As a Cabot, he'd always have the public eye on him. Tommy might decide that he could tolerate whispers and speculation about his personal life, but that didn't mean Everett would want any part of it.

There had been a time when being known as a friend of Tommy Cabot would have been a good thing for anyone; now, it was a liability. *He* was a liability. He was also a mess: he had no plans for the future, no prospects, no family but one son and an estranged wife. He was washed up.

But Everett knew all that, and he still had carried in Tommy's groceries and then kissed him in the kitchen.

CHAPTER 8

"Everything is delicious," Everett said for perhaps the fifth time.

"Stop sounding so shocked." Tommy slid the remaining pie toward Everett.

Daniel had long since left the table, opting instead to sit on the floor and tinker with the antennae on the television set that Everett brought over.

"I'm not shocked or even surprised. You always were good at everything you set your mind to." Everett, who two minutes earlier would have insisted he could not manage another bite, took a small slice of apple pie anyway. Tommy refilled their empty wine glasses. They were sitting in what a week before had been a dusty shambles, but was now identifiably a dining room, with pale green walls and matching curtains.

"You're just trying to sweet talk me," Tommy said over the edge of his wine glass.

"So what if I am?" Everett grinned. He felt loose and happy, an order of magnitude more relaxed than he had thought himself capable of. And it wasn't just the wine or the good meal. When he first saw Tommy the previous month, Everett had thought him only the shadow of the pampered young aristocrat Everett had fallen in love with all those years ago. But Everett was realizing that he liked this man more. He liked the gray at Tommy's temples and the lines around his eyes, liked the way Tommy doted on his son, and if he hated that life had robbed Tommy of some of his old easy confidence, he loved the courage and vulnerability that stood in its place.

Everett ate the last bite of his pie and got to his feet. "Go watch television with Daniel and let me wash the dishes."

"He's only gotten static. I think I want to watch you wash the dishes." Tommy eyed him with a frankly tipsy admiration, his chin resting in his hand.

"Well, fine. Feast your eyes." Everett knew he was blushing but after three glasses of wine, didn't much care. After carrying the dishes into the kitchen, he made more of a show than necessary of taking off his cardigan and rolling up his sleeves. As he plugged the drain and filled the sink with water, he felt Tommy's hands settle onto his hips. When he poured dish soap onto a cloth, he felt hot breath on the side of his neck, followed by the scratch of Tommy's stubbly jaw.

"You know," Everett said several minutes later, "the dishes might get washed a lot faster if you kept your hands to yourself." It took an effort to make himself sound stern when Tommy was busily applying his mouth to that spot at the back of Everett's jaw that made him want to moan.

"Come here," Tommy said, "I want to show you something."

"I bet you do." Everett dried his hands on his trousers and followed Tommy through a door and down a rickety flight of wooden stairs. The cellar was dark except for whatever moonlight filtered through a narrow window near the ceiling, but he let himself be led by the hand to wherever Tommy wanted to take him.

"Danny won't come down here because he thinks there are spiders. Or ghosts. Or both," Tommy said, his voice pitched low.

"He's probably right," Everett said, letting Tommy back him against a wall. "But I don't care. Let them watch."

Tommy laughed, and Everett caught his smiling mouth with his own. The cellar was cold and the wall at his back was hard and damp, but Tommy was so warm, and everywhere their bodies met was a fire about to blaze. Tommy must have felt it too, because he gasped when Everett pushed against him. Then Tommy's fingers were at his neck, loosening his tie and unbuttoning the top button, spreading the collar wide enough for him to kiss the notch between his collarbones.

"Tommy," Everett said, breathy and needful, a finger curled around the other man's belt loop, keeping him close. Tommy kissed his way up to Everett's jaw.

"Mmm?" Tommy steered Everett toward what turned out to be the furnace, backing him up against a wall that was surprisingly warm.

"Can I?" Everett brushed the backs of his knuckles across Tommy's zipper and got a gasping sound in response.

"Yeah," Tommy breathed.

Everett kissed him hard. He cupped Tommy's face in his hands and tried to make the kiss say everything words were too awkward for. Then he dropped to his knees. "Let me take care of you, all right?"

"I swear to God if you make me cry when you're sucking me off I'll never forgive you—" Tommy broke off when Everett mouthed gently at the fabric of his trousers. After Everett undid Tommy's belt and eased the trousers just low enough to give him access, he kissed Tommy again through the thin cotton of his shorts.

The last time they had done this was etched into Everett's memory. It had been a swelteringly hot summer day, when even the Sloanes' gloomy house was sticky with heat. Everett had only been out of the army for a few weeks. In Europe he had convinced himself that he had gotten Tommy out of his system. Then Tommy came to meet his ship, and he had known he was wrong, that he might always be wrong, that there was no life for him anywhere near Tommy Cabot. Tommy visited Everett's parents' house, all smiles and charm, and asked whether Everett had been avoiding him. He had made it a joke, but Everett had seen the hurt in his friend's face, and felt like the world's biggest heel. So he had lied and said that of course he hadn't been avoiding Tommy, and within the hour they were behind the gazebo, Everett's trousers around his ankles, Tommy's mouth wrapped around him. Everett had let himself believe that maybe they were in this together, that maybe they had been all along.

"I thought you'd die," Tommy had said, afterward. "Don't go off to any more wars, okay? I worried myself sick." And a moment later he had told Everett that he was going to ask Patricia Mulligan to marry him. That night Everett wrote to his old mathematics teacher at Greenfield, asking for help in applying to a university in the UK.

Everett didn't want to run away again. But he had a suspicion that staying would involve a level of honesty that he didn't think he was equal to, a degree of candor that would only make everything so much worse when this came to an end.

"Listen," he said now, as he eased Tommy's shorts down, kissing each inch of skin he exposed. "I need you to know that I'm glad we're doing this." That was the most he could manage at the moment, and he hoped it was enough. He kissed the soft skin where leg met torso and looked up to where Tommy's eyes glinted in the darkness. "I'm just really glad that we're both here."

He ought to say more, ought to admit that he was pretty sure he hadn't ever stopped loving Tommy, that he had never even understood what love meant until he had known Tommy. He could have said that he had grown up in the coldest and most silent of families and falling into Tommy's orbit was probably the best thing that could have happened to him. He could have admitted that he tried not to skim American newspapers for any mention of the Cabot name, but failed, always failed, and probably hadn't even tried that hard in the first place.

Instead he attempted to show Tommy all those things, as if somehow a blow job were a secret language capable of communicating decades of emotion. He really was an idiot, but he was an idiot for Tommy Cabot, and maybe that wasn't such a bad thing.

He felt Tommy come apart under his hands and mouth, dissolving into breathy moans and Everett's name. He remembered what Tommy liked—how could he forget?—and gave it all back to him with fifteen years of interest. Tommy's hands fell to Everett's head, one combing through his hair and tugging ever so slightly, the other caressing the shell of his ear. When finally Tommy went rigid and spilled into Everett's mouth, Everett was painfully hard in his own trousers.

"Come up here," Tommy said. "Come *here*." He tugged Everett up, kissed him hard and slow on the mouth, and then slid his hand into Everett's unfastened trousers. "Is this all from sucking me?" he asked, and somehow made it sound more like genuine bewilderment than an attempt at seduction.

Everett shoved his pants down and let his kisses devolve into bites and frantic mouthing as Tommy stroked him, Everett's fist over Tommy's fingers. When he came it was with his teeth against Tommy's shoulder, his one hand clinging to Tommy's shirt.

They got themselves cleaned up and went back to the kitchen, where they took turns washing and drying the dishes. Then Tommy pried Daniel away from the television for a game of rummy.

Shortly after Daniel called rummy for the third time, they heard tires crunching on the snow outside. "Who can that be?" Tommy asked, going to the window. "There's four inches of snow and more on the way."

"Dad, that looks like—"

"Goddamn it, it is."

Father and son were out the door before Everett could ask who it was or what was happening. He stood in the open doorway as a woman in a fur coat and matching hat hugged Daniel. When the moonlight caught her face, he knew it was Patricia. But now Tommy was hugging her—not only hugging her but spinning her around in the falling snow, telling her he was thrilled to see her, while also yelling at her about snow chains.

"One of Harry's friends flew us into Westover," Patricia said when Tommy put her down. "Tell me you have macaroni. I'm starved."

"Not so much as a single noodle, but about half your weight in turkey and stuffing, not to mention pie. There you are, Harry," he said, turning to a person Everett hadn't even noticed. "I don't know whether to thank you for delivering Pat or sue you for reckless endangerment. Do they not have snow chains in England? Or common sense?"

"Hullo, Thomas," said the person who must be Harry, emerging from the shadows. She—yes, safe money was on *she*, despite the trousers and the mannish glasses—shook Tommy's hand and let Daniel take the suitcase she carried.

"Everett!" Tommy called. "You remember Patricia."

And then Everett was hugging Patricia too, or rather being hugged by her. "You, darling, look marvelous," she said.

Everett, blushing, let himself be swept into the house, where he shook hands with Harry, who turned out to be a Miss Harriet Gladstone, "but do call me Harry unless you mean to wound me to the quick."

Dazed, Everett opened a bottle of champagne that seemed to have emerged from Patricia's handbag and poured its contents into five glasses, because even Daniel was to celebrate his mother's return. And the mood truly was celebratory; there was no mistaking Patricia and Tommy's delight in this family reunion. None of this made sense: Tommy and Pat seemed happier to see one another than most happily married couples did, at least in Everett's experience.

"We got here just in time," Harry said, pulling back the curtains. "I swear there's another inch since we came inside."

Alarmed, Everett came up beside her and peered out the window. "I'd better be going." He reached for his coat but Tommy checked him with a hand to his shoulder.

"Greenfield is on the top of a hill, and you don't have snow chains any more than these idiots do," Tommy said.

"You have a fixation on snow chains," called Patricia from the kitchen, where she was fixing plates for Harry and herself. "Really, Thomas, I ought to have guessed you'd have learned your way around the kitchen," she went on. "Three months ago you probably couldn't have made a grilled cheese sandwich but now you've gone and done this. By the time I see you on Christmas, you'll have taught yourself Russian and built a rocket ship. I'm so depressed that I'm not a genius too," she said emerging from the kitchen to beam wildly at her husband, who returned the smile. Harry rolled her eyes at Everett, as if he too were in on the secret.

What struck Everett most was that just a few hours ago he had said almost the same thing to Tommy about how quickly he picked up skills. Patricia knew Tommy better than Everett did, now, because she had been there after Everett ran away.

"So will you stay?" Tommy asked him. "There are a couple of spare rooms upstairs. You won't have to sleep in the bathtub, which is what I threatened Pat with."

Everett didn't want to stay, an outsider in this family he didn't understand. Just being here made him feel jealous—not of Pat, but of their easy affection and the fact that he'd never have Tommy this openly and honestly. And seeing Tommy with Pat made it impossible to forget that he was *Tommy Cabot,* a man with connections and a future. He needed to remember that Tommy had a life, and that it was wildly unlikely that his future would include Everett.

"If Patricia got up the hill this far without snow chains, I can get up to Greenfield. I have brand new snow tires," Everett added. Tommy walked him out to the car. Before sliding behind the wheel, Everett looked at Tommy. He rested his arms on the top of his door, keeping the metal and glass safely between them. He wanted to ask for reassurances that Tommy wasn't going to go back to Boston and resume something that looked like his old life. He wanted to know that whatever they were doing together wasn't just a diversion while Tommy figured out how to get back on his feet. But he also knew that anything said in response to that sort of question wasn't going to be worth much.

So instead he tried for honesty, but maybe the sort of honesty that let him rebuild some of the defenses he had let down over the past few days. "I want you to know that whatever happens I'll be glad we had this time together."

"What does that mean?" Tommy asked, frowning.

"Honestly, Tommy, don't you think that you'll eventually be done with this? Refinishing moldings and cooking suppers? At some point you'll decide to use your mind—and, frankly, your name—for other things." He didn't say *and then you'll leave me behind,* because he was trying very hard here not to be pitiful. "You're Tommy Cabot. You aren't going to spend the rest of your life pottering around the house."

"Of course," Tommy said, looking stricken in a way Everett

thought vastly out of proportion to anything he had said. "I wish I could offer you what you deserve. But, yes, I'm a Cabot, and there's no undoing that."

Everett gripped the cold metal of his car door. He hadn't expected Tommy to just agree like that. He got into the car. "Thank you for a lovely dinner," he said, and shut the door, trying not to notice that Tommy's face fell.

* * *

AFTER DANNY WENT TO SLEEP, Tommy went out to the living room to sit with Pat and Harry. Pat wore a flannel dressing gown, and Harry wore a pair of old fashioned pajamas and what appeared to be a smoking jacket. They were sprawled out in opposite directions along the sofa, Pat's toes tucked under Harry's backside. Tommy lowered himself into the arm chair, the hours of cooking finally catching up with him.

"My lawyer filed the paperwork yesterday," Pat said.

Tommy's heart pounded in his chest. It was stupid to be afraid now, of all times, months after they had come to this decision. His family had already washed their hands of him; news of the divorce would hardly make things worse.

"You doing all right?" he asked.

"I'll feel better after the news breaks," Pat said. "It's rather like waiting for a bomb to go off." Harry absently patted Pat's knee.

"Courts will be closed until Monday, so the papers shouldn't get hold of the news until Tuesday," Tommy said. "Unless they already know, and haven't published because Thanksgiving is a useless day to break news."

"I suppose we'll find out." Pat lit a pair of cigarettes and offered him one. "I like Everett. Always have," she said. "On our wedding day he looked like he wanted to throw himself off a bridge. I thought you were oblivious."

Tommy flicked a pointed glance at Harry, not liking that Pat was speaking so freely about Everett in front of someone else.

"Harry's okay," Pat said.

"What she means is that I'm as queer as a clockwork orange," Harry said, reaching out to steal a drag from Pat's cigarette. Pat blushed.

"I *was* oblivious. Despite the fact that we were very literally having sex and I routinely told him I loved him." He raked a hand through his hair. "How could I have been so stupid?"

"Because you had so much at stake, darling. For you to acknowledge that what you and Everett did wasn't just youthful hijinks, you had to let go of so much of what the world expected of you. It's a horrible thing, choosing between loving yourself and letting yourself be loved by the world, and even worse to have to make that choice when you're young and desperate for approval."

God, it had only been in the last few years that he finally admitted to himself that he was living—a lie, he supposed. He hated that phrase, living a lie—he couldn't look at Daniel or even at Pat, at the family they had made and the time they had spent together as a lie. He hadn't been lying to himself when he asked Pat to marry him, and he hadn't been lying to her—but he also hadn't been capable of seeing the truth for what it was. And now that he could, now that he knew who he was and what he wanted, he still didn't know if he'd get a chance to live that truth.

Tommy didn't realize his eyes were tearing until Pat handed him one of her lace-trimmed handkerchiefs.

"Is it even fair," he asked, "for me to start something with him, knowing that at any moment my family or the newspapers might get a hold of it?"

"He knows who your family is," Pat said. "Just because they're terrible doesn't mean you need to spend the rest of your life alone." She reached out and squeezed his hand. He squeezed back, grateful that despite everything she was still his friend. "Listen to me. Try to believe that you deserve to be loved. Not because of your family, not because of your looks or your charm. Just *because*. Can you do that?"

"I mean, not really, Pat," Tommy said. "Be serious."

She waved a dismissive hand. "Do I need to remind you that you aren't the only Cabot who has a private life they'd rather not see used against them? Think of all Robert's affairs. I don't think his pants have been zipped for five consecutive minutes since 1942. And how many times has Frank's oldest gotten into scrapes? They ought to be simply terrified of you, and I'm embarrassed for them that they aren't."

"Patricia," he said. "This is Machiavellian."

She took a long puff from her cigarette and grinned at him. "If you think I spent fifteen years as a Cabot and came away without learning anything about politics, you can guess again. Sweetie, you're going to be fine, I'm going to be fine, Daniel's going to be fine. As for Frank, he can choose whether he wants to be fine or…not fine." She gave a one shouldered shrug that was slightly terrifying. "What are you going to do with yourself after the dust settles?"

He frowned. "Everett asked the same thing. He seems to think that at any moment I'm going to pop off and run for attorney general or something."

"And are you?"

"I couldn't."

"Why not? Your brother doesn't own the family name. You're still a Cabot, and that Senate seat will still come open next year, if that's what you want. Or if you prefer to stay behind the scenes, you could see if some other politician needs a legislative director or chief of staff. You realize that there are dozens of people who would hire you for no reason other than that you've had a falling out with Frank."

"I—I hadn't thought of it that way," he stammered.

She gave him an indulgent look. "On second thought, maybe stay away from politics. Go write a book or raise show dogs or something. But first, maybe reassure your friend that whatever it is you do, there's room in your life for him if he wants it."

"Everett knows…" He broke off, remembering Everett's parting words. "I'll tell him tomorrow, but I wouldn't blame him if he thought I was a bad bet."

"Are you certain I can't have my cousins break one of Frank's kneecaps? Just a little bit?" Pat asked sweetly. Beside her, Harry choked on her cigarette smoke. Pat got to her feet and kissed Tommy's forehead. "Now do you feel better?"

The truth was that he really didn't, but Pat had given him a good reminder that his life hadn't ended when his family decided they were finished with him. He hoped that whatever lay ahead of him included Everett, but even if things didn't work out, that didn't mean he was doomed to a life of uselessness and sorrow. He still had value—as a person, a parent, a friend, even as a Cabot.

CHAPTER 9

Greenfield was dark and quiet when Everett returned. Most students and faculty had gone home for the holiday, lending the school an abandoned quality that was only exaggerated by the snowy hush that had fallen over the campus. He made his way through empty corridors and silent stairwells before letting himself into his rooms. One by one, he flicked on all the lights in the place and cranked on the radiator, trying to dispel the gloom. Tommy's house had been pleasant and noisy, but that atmosphere of good cheer hadn't belonged to him. These two rooms were Everett's home, at least for now, and he would do well to remember it. He brushed his teeth, put on his pajamas, and slid between the cold sheets of his empty bed, all the while trying not to think of how he could have been doing all those things by Tommy's side.

When he woke, the light shining through the cracks in the curtains was unnaturally bright, and Everett knew that when he looked outside he'd see a world blanketed in white. He stepped into his slippers and made his way to the window. The snow had stopped falling at some point during the night, and the landscape that greeted Everett was serene and still, the snow unmarred by a single footstep.

When he turned to face his bedroom, it seemed equally serene: his spare blanket neatly folded at the foot of the bed, his wardrobe containing neatly pressed shirts and trousers, a small stack of unopened mail on the dresser. He liked things to be orderly, neat, predictable. But at some point he had crossed from order into sterility by refusing to let anything messy or complicated into his life. He had stopped letting anything into his life, period. And that was fine if he wanted to live out the rest of his years in a too-neat bedroom, more concerned with staying safe and protected than with living a life. He thought of all the things he could have told Tommy the previous day, all the opportunities he had to admit what he felt, what he hoped, what he wanted in return. And instead he had very deliberately pushed Tommy away in order to preserve his own—his own what? His dignity? His safety?

The landscape had changed by the time he stepped outside. A handful of students were engaged in a snowball match on the great lawn, and the groundskeeper had already shoveled the walk. In the dining hall, there was nothing but cold cereal and toast to be had, and the usual arrangement of assigned dining tables appeared to have been forsaken in favor of the few remaining students congregating at a single table. When Everett approached, he saw one of his senior calculus students reading a copy of that day's Boston Globe. When the boy shifted back in his seat, Everett caught a glimpse of the front page and felt the breath go out of him.

"Mr. O'Connor, may I see the first section of the paper when you're done with it?"

Maybe O'Connor was feeling generous, or maybe something like panic had leaked into Everett's voice, because the boy handed him the entire paper without hesitation. The headline—large type, just below the fold—read "Youngest Cabot in Divorce Scandal." He read the entire article, then read it again from the start.

In addition to reporting the news that Patricia Mulligan Cabot's lawyer had filed divorce papers on Wednesday, the article quoted a Cabot family insider that "it's extremely unfortunate that some members of the family are behaving so unreasonably about what ought to have been a private matter." The article went on to insinuate that Senator Cabot's office had been in a state of confusion since Tommy's departure during summer recess, and then ended by hinting that the voters of Massachusetts had been done a disservice if Senator Cabot dismissed his chief of staff over a matter that had nothing to do with his abilities. A source "close to Mrs. Cabot" stated that the divorce was amicable and that the couple waited for their only child to be adjusted to life in boarding school before breaking up their household.

"I feel bad for the kid," O'Connor said. "It's not fun to have your parents dragged through the news."

Everett imagined it was not fun at all, and also that it wasn't terribly fun for either Tommy or Patricia. He wanted to go to Tommy, to see if he was holding up all right. But none of this was really his business—it was a family matter and he was an outsider.

Except—he could still stop by. He could still be a friend, and if Tommy didn't want him there he could leave. It felt much safer to stay away, to not risk the possibility that Tommy wouldn't want to see him, but Everett was starting to grasp that not a lot in life was compatible with perfect safety.

He thanked O'Connor for letting him read the paper, and made his way out to the parking lot. The Packard was covered in snow. It was temperamental enough in cold weather to make shoveling it out a waste of time, when instead Everett could just walk to Tommy's house. His boots were sturdy, his coat was warm, and even after years away, he knew this part of the country as well as the back of his hand.

He expected to find Tommy alone, assuming that Daniel and Patricia and her friend would have left for Boston as soon as the roads were plowed. But when he stepped into the driveway, he saw Daniel building a snowman with Harry, while Tommy leaned out an upper story window and pelted them with snowballs he collected from a slope in the roof. Everett again was overcome by that sense of intruding into Tommy's real life. But then Tommy caught sight of him and his face split into a grin, and Everett found himself hastily ducking a snowball.

A minute later Tommy was at the front door, smiling and out of breath, his nose red with cold. "I knew you couldn't keep away."

"Have you read the paper?" Everett asked. "The Globe?"

"It's very good, isn't it?" Patricia asked, coming up behind Tommy. "Harry is the source close to Mrs. Cabot. I, of course, am the source close to the Cabot family. Reporters are such darlings." She kissed Everett on the cheek and went outside, the door swinging shut behind her.

"I just wanted to tell you that everything I said last night was stupid," Everett blurted out. "And that I'd like a chance to fix it, if you'll let me."

Tommy's eyebrows shot up, but he gestured for Everett to follow him into the kitchen, then closed the door.

"Last night, I thought that you might just get into the car with Pat and go back to your old life. So I tried to push you away and that was wrong. I meant what I said, about being happy for you, whatever you chose." Everett swallowed, fighting the urge to clam up and let things stand the way they were. "But what I should have said was that I hoped whatever you chose would have room for me."

Tommy closed the gap between them, his hands on Everett's waist. "There's room. I would have made room no matter what. If that's what you wanted."

"That's all I want," Everett said. "For us to make room for one another."

* * *

BY THE AFTERNOON, Pat and Harry had left to bring Daniel to Boston for the weekend.

"Will you stay?" Tommy asked when he and Everett were alone in the newly quiet house. "Or are you expected back at school?" He turned to the stove so he wouldn't have to look at Everett. "I mean," he said, pouring the remaining cocoa into two mugs, "would you please stay?"

"Most of the faculty won't be back until Sunday, so nobody will miss me."

"Good," Tommy said, and handed Everett his cocoa. "Great." He wasn't sure why he was nervous now that they were alone, but he was.

Everett put his own cup down on the counter and then gently took Tommy's and put it down too. His arms came around Tommy's middle, pulling him close. "What is it?"

"I don't know what I'm doing here," Tommy said into the wool of Everett's sweater. "I don't know how to be with someone."

"Is this about sex?" Everett asked slowly.

Tommy made a frustrated noise. "Partly. I hate being bad at things."

"You aren't—" Everett broke off. "All right. Did you enjoy what we did in the cellar yesterday?"

"Yes, but you did all the work."

"I enjoyed it too. You were lovely," Everett said softly, his lips brushing Tommy's ear.

Tommy shivered and felt his face heat and he didn't know why—embarrassment at the compliment? Embarrassment at needing this kind of reassurance in the first place? "If you say so," he mumbled.

"And we can figure out other things we like, if you want to."

"I want to." After years of denial, just being able to want something and admit it to himself felt important. "I want to do this so badly. I mean, with you in particular, but also in general." He took a deep breath and pulled back far enough so he could look Everett in the eye. "I told myself that it didn't matter if I never was with anyone that way again, but it does."

"Yes," Everett said, his grip tightening and his eyes flickering darkly. "What's the other thing that's bothering you?"

"I don't know how to be together. I don't know how to be in love, when it's something that we're doing together." Tommy broke off when he realized that he had just assumed a hell of a lot.

"I want to love you like this," Everett said, brushing his lips across Tommy's, so soft and slow that Tommy almost moaned. "And I want to love you by helping you with that mountain of dishes in your sink.

And I want to love you by waking up next to you tomorrow. I want to love you by being there when you do whatever you decide to do next month, or next year. I want to love you any way you need to be loved."

"Everett," Tommy said, almost breathless.

"I don't know what I'm doing either. But I want to love you when we make mistakes, and I want to love you when we don't know what to do. Is that okay?"

"Everett," Tommy repeated, and kissed him. When they parted, Everett pulled off his sweater, rolled up his sleeves, and made good on his offer to wash the dishes. By the time they had dried the dishes, put them away, and then heated up some turkey for supper, Tommy's nervousness had dissipated. Everett would occasionally put a hand on Tommy's hip or the small of his back as they passed in the kitchen, and he would let it linger there, just a little. They were the smallest touches, just enough to tell Tommy that they were in this together.

They drank their cocoa in the kitchen because it was only the two of them, and it was the warmest room in the house, warm enough that Everett loosened his tie. There was something so characteristic about the way he paused before undoing his top button, as if he hated to see it go, that it sent Tommy's mind reeling backwards to all the other times he had watched Everett undress—out of the corner of his eye, plausible deniability strictly guarded, even if two minutes later they'd have their hands down one another's pants.

But now he could let himself look, he could sit with the knowledge that he liked the look of Everett's forearms, wiry and dusted with dark hair. He could admit to himself that he wanted to press his mouth to the notch between Everett's collarbones, and that in all probability he was going to do exactly that in just a little while. He wanted this, and that wanting was a part of who he was.

"You all right?" Everett asked, fiddling with the stem of his watch.

Tommy caught the gesture and signed in relief. "Thank God. You're nervous too. After that speech you gave me I was beginning to think you were suave or something, that you had…I don't know, *moves*."

"I have moves!" Everett protested. "I was about to suggest that we play Yahtzee."

Tommy laughed, weightless with happiness and Everett smiled back at him. "I love you," Tommy said, because it was the truth and his heart felt full with it.

Everett reached across the table and took Tommy's hand. "I love you too."

And then, God fucking damn it, Tommy's eyes started to water. "Sorry," he said.

"There's nothing to apologize for." With his thumb, Everett swept a tear off Tommy's cheekbone. "I think it's sweet."

Tommy wrinkled his nose. "Fuck you."

"I think *you're* sweet." Everett got to his feet. "You're adorable."

"Oh my God." Tommy tried to cover his face with the hand Everett wasn't holding, but Everett grabbed that wrist too and used it to haul Tommy to his feet.

"When did you get so cute? I could eat you up."

"I'm going to sink into the earth," Tommy lamented, but he was pressed against Everett's chest, nothing but a few layers of fabric between them, so he had things to distract him from his mortification.

"I just like you so much, Tommy Cabot." He put a knuckle under Tommy's chin, tilting his face up. For some reason the gesture made Tommy's knees go weak, as did the heat and tenderness in Everett's eyes. "I'm really smitten with the person you turned into, even with the crying and the blushing."

"I'm blushing too? Oh, fuck me."

"I mean, I could. I would. I think I'd do whatever you wanted at this point."

Tommy groaned and his hips bucked helplessly against Everett's. "Wait until you see me sobbing over old picture albums. You'll be overcome with lust."

Everett was shaking against him, and it took Tommy a moment to realize that he was laughing. "How the hell am I so hard while I'm laughing?" Everett gasped. "What the fuck."

In an attempt to remind Everett that this was a seduction, not comedy hour, not the Jack Benny show for God's sake, Tommy slid his thigh in between Everett's legs and pressed their bodies together.

Now Everett groaned and Tommy rejoiced in having regained the upper hand. He took both sides of Everett's shirt in his hands and pulled him in for a kiss. Everett's mouth opened for him and Tommy kissed him urgently.

"Bedroom," Tommy said.

In a fit of inspiration, earlier that day Tommy lit the kerosene heater in the bedroom, so it was actually warm enough for them to take their clothes off. Tommy pulled his sweater over his head, and then Everett's hands were on Tommy's shirt buttons. God, it was a relief to have Everett's hands moving over him like this, doing something as intimate as undressing him. He took Everett's shirt and undershirt off and then they were skin to skin. He could feel Everett's heartbeat, could feel Everett's chest rise and fall with every breath. Everett's hands were on Tommy's bare shoulders, then at the small of his back, touching and exploring and just reminding Tommy that he was there, that they were together, that this was happening.

Tommy steered them both toward the bed, pushing Everett back and climbing on top of him. "This all right?" he asked.

Everett unbuckled Tommy's belt. "It's all right," he said, grinning crookedly. Tommy returned the favor, then slid Everett's trousers and shorts down along narrow hips and long legs. He took a moment to gaze up the length of him. He had known this body: where to touch Everett to make him beg for more, the shape of the birthmark on his arm, the texture of hair on Everett's chest, the precise location of the scar from when Everett had his appendix out. And he'd get to know it again, he'd get to look and touch, he'd learn it by heart.

"Don't I get to leer?" Everett asked.

Tommy stood up long enough to remove the rest of his clothes, then made to get back onto the bed.

"Wait," Everett said. "Let me look at you."

Tommy knew he was blushing. Not out of embarrassment—well, not entirely out of embarrassment. He knew his body wasn't the same as it had been at twenty but he also knew that Everett liked whatever he saw—the man's eyes were wide and hungry and he wasn't making any attempt to conceal it. It was being wanted so openly that made Tommy's face heat. He supposed that at some point he'd get used to it, this shared wanting, and it would become obvious, second nature, something to take for granted. But now it felt almost precious to have Everett's eyes on him like this. He was half hard and gave himself a stroke, watching Everett's gaze travel downward as he did so.

It really didn't matter how out of practice he was, or how nervous. Everett's arms were open for him when he got back into bed, Everett's hands stroking and soothing as Tommy explored his body, remembering old ways to please him and discovering new ways.

"Can I suck you?" Tommy asked. He spoke the words into the tense muscles of Everett's stomach, grateful for the darkness.

"Yes, God, of course."

"Tell me if there's something you need." Oh God, that sounded terrible, as if he were a hotel maid asking if Ev wanted a fresh towel. He ducked his head and gingerly sucked the head of Everett's cock. Just the taste of him, the feel of him hardening even more on Tommy's tongue, had Tommy wanting to rut against the mattress. Instead he sucked again.

"Tommy," Everett gritted out. "Can I put the light on? I want to watch."

Tommy couldn't imagine that there was much to look at, unless Everett enjoyed watching men confuse themselves on his dick, but if that's what Everett wanted, so be it. He lifted his head. "Sure."

He heard Everett pull the lamp chain and then the room was lit up, somehow overbright even though the day before that lamp had seemed so dim he wondered if there was something wrong with it. Everett propped himself up on an elbow and—oh God help him—spread his legs wide, knees bent.

Tommy bent his head for another tentative suck, this time keeping his eyes on Everett, who looked to be in the grips of some kind of sex hypnosis. Tommy thought this was probably a good sign. Everett stroked a thumb down Tommy's cheek, and, Jesus Christ, he was feeling himself inside Tommy's mouth, and nobody could blame Tommy for the noise he made.

This wasn't as difficult as he remembered. He didn't try to get the whole thing in his mouth, didn't worry he looked like an idiot when he accidentally went too far and his eyes watered and he gagged a bit. Because he sort of liked it, and Everett sure didn't seem to mind, if the state of his hard on and the quality of his profanity were any indication.

"My God, look at you," Everett said, cupping Tommy's jaw. He was braced on an elbow, stomach muscles clenched, and when Tommy glanced up at him he saw wild eyes and reddened cheeks. His body was taut with the effort of keeping still, his jaw clenched to stay quiet. This was something, seeing Everett, usually so reserved and staid, just completely lose it.

This, Tommy realized, was what he had been nervous about—not just his ability to please Everett, but the half-formed idea that owning up to how he felt, how he wanted, how he wanted to *be* wanted, would lead to something irrevocable. And so it had. For months he had known that the old Tommy Cabot was gone, and he had feared that left him without an identity, without a future. But he had both a future and an identity, and they were tied up together in this—being queer, being in love, being someone who had been lost and then found.

"Tommy, now," Everett warned, and Tommy pulled off, replacing his mouth with his hand. He wanted to watch, wanted to see Everett come, and know he had made it happen. Everett's entire body went tense and still, then he made a sound of strangled relief and—there, watching Ev come all over himself, watching Ev watch himself do so, moreover, had been every bit as good as he had hoped. He knelt, taking himself in hand, fully aware of Everett's eyes boring into him, and brought himself off.

It was quiet, no sound but their ragged breathing and the hum of the kerosene heater.

"I think it's safe to say you aren't terrible at sex," Everett said after they had cleaned themselves off and returned to bed, the quilt pulled up around their chins to ward off the chill of the night.

"I may need to spend the rest of the weekend persuading myself of that," Tommy said, his head pillowed on Everett's shoulder.

"Am I supposed to object?"

"Might take longer than the weekend. Might take years."

Everett snorted and kissed the top of Tommy's head. "I'll be happy to do my part." Outside, the wind picked up, and when Tommy turned to the window he saw fat snowflakes starting to accumulate along the mullions.

"Plenty of firewood," he murmured into Everett's skin. "Even if the furnace goes out."

And then, warm and safe, he let sleep overtake him.

CHAPTER 10

"So," Everett said one Sunday morning in December. They had the house to themselves, Daniel having decided to spend the weekend at school studying for his final exams. "Christmas."

Tommy put his newspaper down. In the weeks since Thanksgiving, newspapers had started to appear at Tommy's house—not just the Boston Herald, but the papers from all over the state as well as the larger national newspapers. This, Everett realized, was Tommy plotting out his next steps, and it made him almost giddy with anticipation. "Hmm?"

"If you wanted, we could drive Daniel to Boston ourselves. Spare Patricia the trip." Everett knew Daniel was spending most of the Christmas vacation with his mother and her family, and didn't like the idea of Tommy being alone for any of it. "I wanted to see my mother on Christmas Eve, but then after that we could drive back. If you wanted to, you could come with me. My mother always liked you."

"Sure," Tommy said, pouring them both some orange juice. "But why do you look like you're asking me to do something truly untoward?"

"My mother knows about me. That I'm gay, I mean. She doesn't know about us, but—God, you've met her. She'd know. Not that she'd tell anyone. Having a bent son would never do." Everett knew he was rambling and tried to rein it in. "She's mentioned an interest in meeting any of my special friends."

"Everett," Tommy said, his hand over his heart. "Are you saying that we're special friends?"

"Oh God," Everett groaned.

"Are we going steady?"

Everett threw a piece of bacon at him. "I should damned well hope so. You've led me astray if we aren't."

"I wouldn't have guessed that Anthea Peabody Sloane would be so open minded."

"She isn't...warm," Everett said, deciding this was the fairest way to describe his mother. "But she's loyal."

Tommy reached out and squeezed his hand. "I would love to see your mother. As it happens, I have my own bit of family diplomacy to conduct. Frank's eldest, Peter, has written to me. Actually he wrote to Danny and asked him to pass on the message, which I suppose is the only way any of my family has of getting in touch with me, not that the rest of them have made the attempt. In any event, my nephew asked if he might meet with me, and he's coming this afternoon."

"Do you want me out of here?"

"No," Tommy said. "But you may not wish to be here, if he's inclined to draw conclusions from the fact that we're having a cozy Sunday together."

"I'll stay," Everett replied immediately. Every day he cared less and less what conclusions strangers drew about him. That might make it difficult to keep a job at Greenfield, but there were plenty of colleges in Massachusetts. Plenty of colleges and plenty of politicians. He and Tommy would be fine.

They cleared the breakfast dishes and spent the rest of the morning reading the newspaper in companionable silence on the sofa. When the knock came, Tommy swung his legs off Everett's lap and answered the door.

The boy—the young man, really—who walked into Tommy's living room had the Cabot nose and general air of well-fed confidence that mostly came, Everett suspected, from some combination of privilege and good tailoring. He had his father's linebacker build, but there wasn't a trace of Frank's smugness about him. In fact, he had the air of having arrived hat in hand.

"Come in," Tommy said, and introduced Peter Cabot to Everett with no explanation for Everett's presence other than describing him as a friend.

"Thank you for meeting with me, sir," Peter said. "First, I ought to say that I haven't come from my father, and that he doesn't know I'm here."

"I wouldn't have thought you were in league with him, Pete. Take a seat." Tommy sat beside Everett on the sofa.

"Thank you," Peter said, sitting in the arm chair. "I overheard my parents talking, and they said that—" He broke off, shaking his head. "No, I should start by saying I'm queer. That's what Walsh said to do. That way you know I'm not trying to make trouble. Anyway, my father said you and Aunt Patty were splitting up because you're gay—that's not the word he used—" Peter hesitated again, clearly flustered.

"You don't need to repeat the word he used," Tommy said gently.

"Right. So I just wanted to tell you that I think it was—honestly really shitty—sorry sir—for them to treat you the way they did. And I don't know if they found out and took you to task or if you told them. Or if maybe I have the facts all mixed up and you and Aunt Patty split because of some other reason, in which case I'm really sorry for coming here and—"

"Yes, I'm gay. And yes, I told them," Tommy said.

"That took a lot of guts, sir. Anyway, that's what I came to say."

"You drove four hours from Cambridge to tell me you think I have a lot of guts."

"Walsh says we have to stick together."

Everett was rapidly forming the opinion that this Walsh, whoever he might be, was the brains of the operation. "I quite agree with your Mr. Walsh," Everett said.

"Oh! I also wanted to tell you that Aunt Patty called on my mother when I was home a few days ago, and told her—very politely, you understand. She brought a fruitcake and a poinsettia. She told her that it would be a real shame if anybody found out about the girl my brother Lawrence got pregnant or any of the girls Uncle Bobby got pregnant or the car Lawrence crashed. And that, um, they probably all ought to work very hard not to make her mad because when she gets mad she talks to too many reporters."

Tommy looked like he didn't know whether to laugh or cry, so Everett—hell, in for a penny—put his arm around him. Then he slipped off to reheat the casserole Tommy had made the previous night. From the kitchen, he heard Tommy and his nephew talking about Harvard and football. "If your dad does find out and he cuts up rough," Everett heard Tommy say, "you know where I am. Here, you should take my phone number. And Aunt Patty's too, come to think."

When the kid had eaten two-thirds of the casserole and left, Everett sat back down on the sofa, pulling Tommy against him. "You did good," he murmured. "And your nephew is right that you're brave as hell, in case I haven't told you that recently." He pulled Tommy onto his lap and kissed him, slow and lazy, relishing the weight of the other man pressing into him, the feel of cold fingertips against his face, the smell of paint and sawdust that he was beginning to think of as home.

At some point when they were curled up on the sofa, snow began to fall again. On the way to bed, Everett looked out the window and saw the full moon reflecting off a universe of fresh snow. He couldn't see the rust on his Packard or the half-chopped wood Tommy had forgotten to put into the shed. There was no mud, no mistakes, just a landscape saved and transformed by something as ordinary as cold and water. And here they were inside, flawed and messy, safe and warm, loved and loving. He let Tommy take him by the hand and pull him into the bedroom.

The End

ACKNOWLEDGMENTS

Many thanks to Melinda Utendorf for editing, Margrethe Martin for making sense of this story when it was in its larval stage, all the other authors in this anthology for giving helpful feedback and reassurance, and especially Olivia Dade for putting this all together.

BIOGRAPHY

For more info about the author, visit

Cat's Website: http://catsebastian.com

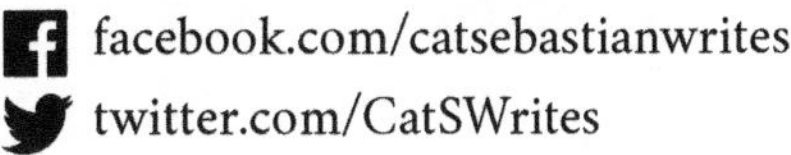

Cover design by Zoe York.

Book formatting by BBForever.

CPSIA information can be obtained
at www.ICGtesting.com
Printed in the USA
LVHW091120120520
655425LV00002B/491

9 781945 836114